D1083957

Witch Angel

Witch Angel

Trana Mae Simmons

Five Star • Waterville, Maine

First Edition
First Printing: June 2005

Published in 2005 in conjunction with Tekno Books and Ed Gorman.

Set in 11 pt. Plantin by Ramona Watson.

Printed in the United States on permanent paper.

Library of Congress Cataloging-in-Publication Data

Simmons, Trana Mae.
    Witch angel / by Trana Mae Simmons.—1st ed.
        p. cm.
    ISBN 1-59414-325-0 (hc : alk. paper)
    1. Inheritance and succession—Fiction.   2. Guardian angels—Fiction.   3. Plantation life—Fiction.   4. Time travel—Fiction.   5. Louisiana—Fiction.   I. Title.
    PS3619.I5615W58 2005
    813'.54—dc22   2005004990

Dedication

To Shari and Ocie

Sammi, David, Cody and Tara

Chapter 1

"You've just gotta listen to me, Francesca."

Shreds of mist scattered around the hem of her red dashiki as Sylvia traipsed back and forth through the fluffy clouds in front of Francesca's desk. One of the beaded, cornrow braids that Violet, a fellow guardian angel, wove in Sylvia's hair fell over an eye, and the angel brushed it back impatiently. Face set in resolve, she stared past the computer at her superior.

"I need a vacation," Sylvia insisted. "I love being a guardian angel, but I've been taking care of Jacki for over fifteen years—ever since I joined your band of angels. That lady gets into more trouble than a six-week-old kitten exploring its new home!"

Francesca steadily returned Sylvia's gaze. "I've never had one of my guardian angels ask for a vacation in all my millennia. What makes you think that after just fifteen years—not even a blink in time—you can turn your assignment over to someone else?"

"Not even a blink in time?" The errant braid bobbed free again and Sylvia shoved it behind her ear. She clasped her fingers behind her neck as though massaging an ache, but Francesca had never known one of her angels to have an ache anywhere.

"Give me a break," Sylvia said. "Your idea of time doesn't fit here, because things aren't like they were the last time you looked down at Earth in the Fifties. Darn it, the stress in a living woman's life today is a thousand times greater than it was years ago."

"Surely, Sylvia . . ." Francesca began.

Suddenly Sylvia stared down through the clouds bunched around her feet and her eyes widened. With a gasp of dismay, she waved an apologetic hand at Francesca and disappeared.

Francesca shook her head and pushed the Enter button on her keyboard. The screen leapt to life, and she typed a number to key it into the little black angel's status. Immediately, the screen filled with a picture of Sylvia zipping to the front of a white Jeep traveling down a highway at a speed a fraction below dangerous. The instant Sylvia reached the driver's side fender, the tire blew with a horrible bang. The Jeep swerved and the woman behind the steering wheel frantically fought for control.

Sylvia grabbed the fender and skidded along beside the Jeep, her bare feet dragging on the pavement. She steadied the rocking vehicle and shoved her shoulder against it, returning it to its own traffic lane a split second before an oncoming eighteen-wheeler barreled over a hill. After she guided the Jeep onto the berm of the road, Sylvia fluttered a few feet above it and glared through the windshield at the woman, who gripped the steering wheel with white-knuckled fingers.

"When are you going to learn that a car's got more speeds than just 'stop' and 'pedal to the floor,' Jacki?" Sylvia demanded, though the woman, of course, heard nothing. "Don't you know even new tires can have defects?" Sylvia lifted her red dashiki skirt and raised one leg to swipe at the dirt on her foot. "I suppose you think it was your first-rate driving that kept you from hitting that darned semi!"

"Whew," Jacki breathed. "I'm sure glad my guardian angel was on the job today."

Francesca giggled, and Sylvia threw a furious glare overhead. "I heard that! You think it's funny, but on top of everything else I have to deal with in this assignment, Jacki acts like having a guardian angel's her right. That she can take stupid chances because I'm always gonna be sitting there on her shoulder—protecting her!"

The Jeep door opened, and Sylvia glanced down at Jacki, evidently assuring herself that her assignment's body hadn't suffered any physical damage. Other than a paler-than-normal face and the slight tremble when Jacki lifted her hand to push back a tress of brown hair, she appeared unscathed. Thankfully, Sylvia's assignment knew the value of seatbelts.

Sylvia returned her attention to her superior angel. "This one's a heck of a responsibility, Francesca! And you'd know how much of a strain it is, if *you* were emotionally involved in this business! But, nooo! You just sit there behind that darned unemotional computer and push buttons to run your unemotional program!"

A flicker of hurt stabbed Francesca, and she pushed another keyboard button, blanking out the screen. Elbows on the shining desk surface, she steepled her fingers and pressed them against her mouth while she contemplated Sylvia's tirade. Could the other angel have something there? Was she too out of touch?

She enjoyed her job. She felt needed and wanted—proud of the fact that not one of the humans she had paired up with anyone in her band of guardian angels had ever met a premature death. Why, look what happened to Abbott, who headed up another group of guardian angels. He'd assigned an angel who had only recently transferred into his band of experienced guardians to that politician on earth one time, and an assassin had slipped through the angel's vigilance.

Sylvia had been dependable from the first day she arrived, fresh from spending an eon helping newly-arrived, bewildered human spirits adjust to their new state of being. That duty had at least brought her into daily contact with humans and life on Planet Earth. Francesca had thought Sylvia an exceptionally fine addition to her own guardian angel band. But after only fifteen years—the short span of time in which Jacki, her widowed assignment, had been struggling to raise her two children alone—Sylvia wanted, of all things, a vacation!

"Aw, Frannie," Sylvia said as she reappeared in front of the desk. "I'm sorry. I didn't mean to yell at you. You know I love you, and I've always been able to come to you and talk when I wasn't sure about something. But can't you see the reason I blew up was because I need a break?"

Francesca gripped the edge of her desk and pushed her chair back an inch or two as she studied Sylvia. Though she treated all her angels with an even hand, this one had found a special place in her heart. Her independent streak stirred admiration, and even this partial apology was an element of Sylvia's nature—a plea for forgiveness, yet a justification of her actions.

"I'd be willing to discuss it with you further," Francesca said. "But a decision like you're asking me to make can't be undertaken lightly. I'll need to know more about your reasons for such a request—why you think life on Earth has become so complicated that it's affected your ability to deal with protecting your assignment."

"Then listen, Frannie," Sylvia said eagerly. "These days there's lots of single-parent families, most of them from divorce and headed by women—black women, white women, and every other color sister. And these women are making decent lives for their families, instead of sitting around hankering after the men who walked out on them. They've opened things up—gotten help they didn't used to have by building it up for themselves. But then they've gotta juggle the stress of jobs, kids, and housework."

"What's happened to their dating lives?" Francesca asked worriedly. "Women weren't meant to go through life alone."

"I could point out plenty of women who wouldn't agree with that—who'd tell you they're doing fine and dandy without a man messing up their lives, thank you kindly, ma'am."

Francesca opened her mouth to speak, but silenced herself at Sylvia's negligent wave.

"All right. All right," Sylvia admitted. "Most women still hope they'll find a decent man to fall in love with. But that's just more stress, especially when a woman already has kids, like Jacki has. Jacki has to look for a man who'll not only make her a good husband, but be a good daddy, too. Did I tell you about that one man my Jacki met who . . . ?"

"Sylvia, I've told you that your human assignment has to make her own decisions." Francesca crossed her arms and buried her hands inside the long sleeves of her white robe. "You have no business intruding in that side of your assignment's life. You've got a measure of latitude in dealing with your guardianship, but you can't interfere in emotional decisions—you're just there to keep her body safe until it's time for her to join us."

Sylvia blew out an exasperated breath, as though trying to release some tension with the air. She leaned on the desk, and her determined countenance forced Francesca another inch back into her padded chair.

"You're not listening to me," Sylvia protested, shaking a finger for emphasis. "What I'm trying to tell you is that Jacki's not just an *assignment*. I can't help becoming involved with her. Frannie, two hundred years ago, life was real hard on both men and women, because they had to work their fannies off to even put a meal on the table. Maybe they didn't have time to worry as much back then—I don't know. These days they buy their food at a grocery store, but the emotional stress human women like Jacki have to deal with is just as wearing. I care about her—and it's stressing me out. That's why I need a break!"

"Sylvia, you're not human. You've never been human. How can you experience stress?"

"I've been dealing with humans day-in and night-out for a millennium!" Sylvia threw her hands in the air and her wings fluttered in agitation, sending ripples from the neck of her red dashiki all the way to the hem. "You don't seem to realize how stressful that can be. All you do is sit there every day in your nice, soft chair and keep track of everyone from a distance. If you see one of us getting in over our heads when an *assignment* runs into more danger than usual, you push a computer button."

"Well there," Francesca said around a smug look. "That shows you I'm not behind the times."

Sylvia's face creased in puzzlement and she spread her hands palms up, shrugging her shoulders. "How does that show me anything?"

"My computer . . . which, I might add, I've been using very adequately for quite some time now. Why, I even sat in when that computer programmer who joined us years ago wrote the program for me. I explained my job to him, so the software would suit my needs, and it's the very latest technology. It even has some commands that won't be invented on Earth for decades yet."

Sylvia groaned under her breath, but Francesca continued, "And look at you. Your hair and dashiki are perfect examples of how progressive our band of angels has become under my leadership. I paid attention when all of you told me that you'd like to set your own hair styles and decide on wearing apparel yourselves. Some of the other angels . . ." Francesca lowered her voice, ". . . even wear their robes fashioned like those culotte things—almost like pants."

"You're missing my point, Frannie. I'm not complaining about things up here—it's things down there!"

"Sounded to me like you didn't think I was paying attention to what my angels need," Francesca grumbled. "Questioning whether I really care about all of you."

"Frannie, your computer's been great for you, not that you really need it . . ."

"I don't," Francesca put in. "But it's sort of fun working with it."

"Yes, but it's given you a . . . well, a sort of separation. I'm involved directly—close to the emotions of what's happening to my assignment, as well as the people living around her and the lifestyle on Earth. It's stressful, Frannie."

Muted thunder rumbled from a storm cloud in the atmosphere below them, and a bolt of lightning flashed. Sylvia blinked and slipped a contrite glance from beneath a pair of long eyelashes. "I didn't mean it to sound like you don't care about us, Frannie. Really, I didn't." She dropped her head even lower and nervously fingered her red skirt. "Uh . . . I should probably check on Jacki—make sure she's not getting wet. She had that bout with bronchitis last winter. And I forgot to check and see if she has her cell phone with her. She has a tendency to forget it now and then."

"She's fine," Francesca replied. "Here. See for your-self." Francesca turned the computer on again and swiveled the screen base so Sylvia could see.

Sylvia grinned delightedly as she watched a handsome, mid-thirties man emerge from the semi pulled up behind the disabled Jeep, jump lithely to the ground, and stride to-ward Jacki's window. Jacki cracked the window and he said, "Please don't be frightened, ma'am. The name's Peter McNeely, but I answer to Mac. Saw you pullin' off the road with that flat tire when I went by, so I turned in at the first spot I could find big enough to jack my rig around in. If you don't have a cell phone, I can call someone for you on my radio. Or . . . I could change the tire for you."

Jacki bit her bottom lip for a moment, then asked, "Aren't you one of the referees at the football games in town?"

He nodded. "Yep. I take short hauls these days, so I can be home weekends for the games."

Spirits lifting, Sylvia scooted onto the desk, her eyes never leaving the computer screen as Jacki rolled her window down. "Boy, ain't he a hunk, Frannie?"

"A hunk of what?" Francesca asked curiously.

"A hunk of man," Sylvia replied. "Look at the buns in those tight jeans. I've always admired a cute bottom on a man."

Francesca felt her cheeks pinken, but she continued gazing at the screen, where Mac was lifting a tire jack and spare tire out through the Jeep's hatchback. A few spatters of rain hit the ground as the thunderstorm moved down through the atmosphere. Mac turned up his shirt collar, then rolled the tire to the front fender, and bent down to position the jack.

By the time Mac had the tire changed, his sodden shirt

clung to his shoulders and rain streamed down his face. He carried the tire jack to the rear of the Jeep and secured it again in its holder. Wiping his face on a soaked shirt sleeve, he returned for the ruined tire and rolled it along the muddy road berm.

"I'm afraid you're going to have to clean out your spare tire well," he called toward the driver's seat as he hoisted the mud-globbed tire over the bumper. "But you'll need this rim when you buy a new tire."

"Please don't worry about it," Jacki replied. "I really appreciate your help, and I'm sorry you got wet."

"Ah, what's a few drops of rain?" he said with a laugh as he started to close the hatch.

"Wait," Jacki called. "How much do I owe you?"

The upraised hatch protected him somewhat from the falling rain and Mac hesitated. Sylvia and Francesca stared back and forth between Jacki's heart-shaped face peering around the front bucket seat and Mac, whose face mirrored irritation. Jacki's wispy fringe of brown bangs ended just above her sea-green eyes, which were shadowed with concern as she fingered an overstuffed purse on the console. For a split second, Mac acted like her offer of money pricked his masculine ego, but Jacki responded to his frown of annoyance by tilting a delicate chin up a prideful notch.

Mac's irritation vanished, replaced by a look of dawning realization. Perhaps he admired her desire to pay her own way. Or maybe he just wanted to prolong this meeting for another moment or two before she drove out of his life. Francesca sighed and murmured, "I sure can see the emotions between those two. It's cozy under that hatch, isolated from the pouring rain in a protected area. Can't you see how he's attracted to Jacki?"

Sylvia nodded agreement as Mac's full lips formed a

slow smile and a teasing glint highlighted his eyes. He asked, "How much do you think it's worth?"

"I hope not more than twenty dollars," Jacki said with a relieved laugh. "That's all the cash I have. I don't suppose you take credit cards?"

"Nope," he replied. "But I'll tell you what. Bein' a bachelor truck driver, I usually settle for the special at whatever truck stop I'm near when it's time to eat. I . . . uh . . . didn't notice you wearin' a wedding ring, so I *would* accept dinner instead of money. A home-cooked meal might be nice, but dinner out with a pretty companion would work, too. 'Course I'd like to know your name first."

"Oh. I—I—" Jacki ducked her head for a second, then looked back at him. "It's Jacki. Jacqueline Benjamin. And I might be able to manage the dinner out. Stoves and I aren't exactly good friends. Microwaves—"

"Yuck," Mac interrupted. "Warmed up, already-cooked food isn't my bag." He picked up a boy's tennis shoe lying in the rear of the Jeep and held it high enough above the back seat for Jacki to see. "Guess you'd have to arrange for a babysitter, huh, Jacki?"

Her husky-soft laughter blended with the sound of the rain pelting the Jeep's roof, and Jacki shook her head, sending silky hair swirling around her face.

"Don't mention that word in front of my son," she said. "Or my daughter, either. They both made sure I knew they'd outgrown having a sitter two years ago. If my son had been with me instead of at football practice just now, he could have changed my tire, too."

"I'm sure as hell glad he had football practice," Mac murmured under his breath.

Sylvia and Francesca continued watching while Jacki suggested a restaurant and they arranged a time to meet.

Mac finally closed the hatch and stood with his hands jammed into his jeans pockets as the Jeep drove away. After it disappeared, he raised his head and shouted into the pouring rain, "Ain't it a hell of a beautiful day, world?"

"Hummm," Francesca mused. "Looks like your assignment's going to have someone else helping take care of her for a while. Maybe a less-experienced guardian angel might be able to manage for the time being."

"Does that mean I can have my vacation?" Sylvia asked hopefully.

"No," Francesca said. "It means that as soon as I call Violet in to replace me, *we'll* have that vacation. Or, we should probably more properly call it a sabbatical for both of us."

"You're going with me, Frannie? Great! Vacations are always more fun when you have a girlfriend to share them with. Where can we go?"

"You said you needed to get away from the stress of modern-day life, my dear. With that in mind, we'll choose a less stressful place, where you can relax and we can continue our discussion."

Chapter 2

"Alaynia Cecile Mirabeau, where the heck did you go wrong this time?" Alaynia Cecile Mirabeau muttered to herself.

Loathe to admit she was lost—and reluctant to stop and ask directions in a strange place—Alaynia glanced quickly at the notes in her hand. The car wandered across the middle stripe in the two-lane country road, and an angry horn jerked her attention back to her driving. A dirt driveway up ahead came into view, and she flipped her blinker on and braked.

She must have missed a turn somewhere. In Boston, she could have pulled over and studied the street map she kept in the dash—after making sure her doors were securely locked. Here in the Louisiana back country, some of the roads weren't even on the map she'd picked up at the rental car company. And evidently the directions she had written down when she talked to the Baton Rouge attorney were about as useful as her Boston street map would have been in a Southern city.

Alaynia pulled into the driveway and eased to a stop. A ramshackle structure lay at the end of the rutted path, and a tattered window curtain moved slightly. But before she could distinguish the features on the face behind the cracked window pane, a mangy hound scrambled from beneath a sagging porch. Snarling and snapping its teeth, it raced toward her car.

She hastily shifted into reverse and backed from the driveway. Retracing her previous path, she drove toward a crossroad she'd passed a few minutes ago, where she'd noticed a sign advertising Bar-B-Q painted on a right-pointing arrow. Surely a place that wanted customers wouldn't have a vicious animal waiting to attack.

Aware of her penchant for getting lost when her thoughts wandered while she drove, she'd left the Baton Rouge hotel that morning with what she considered ample time to spare before her meeting with the attorney. St. Francisville, the lawyer had assured her when she called his office yesterday afternoon, was only a half-hour drive north of Baton Rouge. He would wait for her at the plantation manor house, five miles northeast of town. All she had to do was take a right on the first county road she came to after she passed through town, then bear left at each intersection until she came to a sign he would nail to a tree at the entrance to the plantation's driveway. But, damn it, had he said the driveway where he would leave the sign was on the right or on the left? He'd given her his car phone number, but she wasn't quite ready yet to call him and admit she couldn't follow what he had assured her were explicit, uncomplicated directions to Chenaie Plantation.

Besides—she glanced down at her cell phone, which protruded from her open purse—talking on the phone while she drove could be just as distracting as rambling thoughts. If she couldn't find out at the Bar-B-Q stand where she'd taken a wrong turn, she could call from the parking lot before she drove back onto the highway. She pushed the air-conditioning control up another notch, and cool air gushed from the air-conditioning vents.

July is not the month to visit Louisiana, the attorney had said when he first contacted her in Boston three weeks ago. *Why don't you wait until October or so? Your inheritance isn't going anywhere.*

Shimmering heat waves on the road ahead emphasized the attorney's warning. Alaynia lightened up on the gas pedal and squinted at the mirage as the road appeared to undulate and disappear. But where at first the heat waves had looked like gently rolling breakers on an incoming tide, they suddenly wavered higher, towering halfway up the trunks of the huge jack pines along the highway.

She flicked a glance in her rearview mirror. No other vehicle in sight. When she looked back at the road ahead, she gasped at the closeness of the mirage after her split-second of inattention—and how high the heat waves now towered. They oscillated in a rippling barrier a hundred feet wide, so tall they even covered the tops of the pines. Her heart pounded in terror and she jammed her foot on the brake pedal. The car screeched down the highway amidst two black streaks of smoking rubber.

The heat waves shimmered over her. She twisted the steering wheel to aim the car into the ditch, but it slid inexorably through the shining barrier before it came to a halt with a jerk that snapped Alaynia's neck and released the airbag.

July 1875

Anger rankling, Shain St. Clair pulled his ebony stallion to a halt just beyond the boundaries of his plantation. "Whoa, Black," he muttered.

The buggy carrying that damned carpetbagger, Fitzroy,

disappeared down the road to St. Francisville, a trail of dust in its wake. He hadn't really thought Fitzroy would turn back for another try at changing his mind, but he'd followed the Yankee at a distance anyway—ready to make his point in a less polite manner if the need arose. Back at the manor house, he'd been all too aware of his little sister, Jeannie, hovering within hearing distance.

One of these days, that bastard was going to go too far. Fitzroy had sent one of the stable boys out to call Shain away from his inspection of the fields, as though he had a right to interrupt the plantation's daily business, and Shain arrived back at Chenaie's manor house in an already testy mood. The sight of the portly Yankee on the front veranda—feet propped on the railing as he sat in a rocking chair sipping a cool mint julep—sent Shain's rage boiling as hot as the Southern day.

Worse than that, he'd had to keep a cap on his fury and decline once again Fitzroy's so-called business proposition. Now there would be another confrontation with his neighbors, who desperately needed the Yankee money the company Fitzroy represented would bring them.

His stallion pricked its ears, and Shain studied the underbrush beside the road. "Come on out, Cole," he called.

Rifle negligently held in one hand, Cole Dubose stepped out onto the dirt roadway. Shain studied Cole as the other man walked toward him. More than once in their younger years, he and Cole had been mistaken for brothers. Cole's hair still shone with raven highlights, but it hung well past his shoulders, even longer than Shain's, which he'd been trying to find time to get cut. His friend's clothing was clean, but ragged, and Shain would have bet there wasn't more than a pound or two variation in their weights—or a half-inch difference in the breadth of their shoulders.

Despite his annoyance over his disrupted morning, Shain's gaze softened as Cole approached. Cole's lips quirked into a half-grin in the several days' growth of beard, but the shadowy depths of his brown eyes didn't lighten.

"Good thing Black's got sharper ears than yours," Cole said as he laid a hand on the stallion's neck. "Been a Yankee patrol, you'd be on your way to prison camp now."

"Wouldn't be the first time," Shain drawled. "And reckon I could find me some disreputable swamp rat to help me escape again."

Shain reached down and shook Cole's hand. "Hello, friend," he said sincerely. "How've you been?"

"Tolerable," Cole replied. He nodded his head in the direction the buggy had taken. "You consortin' with Yankees these days?"

"Hell, half of Louisiana is Yankee now. And they're pretty easy to pick out—guess you recognized where Fitzroy had come from, even without hearing his Northern twang."

Cole chuckled and brushed a lank of black hair away from his face. "Yeah, they're the ones with meat on their bones. It's gonna take the South longer than ten years to grow enough food to put back on all the weight its people lost during the war."

"Look, Cole," Shain said. "When are you gonna give up your no-account lifestyle and settle down? I tried to find you a couple months ago, after I fired my overseer, but even Tana didn't know where you were. That damned overseer worked my field crew so hard that two of my men passed out from the heat. I'm keeping a close watch on Carrington, the new man, but he seems all right so far. He better be, for what I have to pay him. I sure as hell could use you, though."

As Shain anticipated, Cole shook his head. "No offense,

friend," he said in a bitter voice, "but if I ever get the urge to baby a bunch of cotton or cane plants along again, I'd prefer doing it in my own fields. And I've got about as much chance of that as we do of fightin' the war over again and winnin'."

"If you ever change your mind . . ."

"I won't," Cole said flatly.

"Well, I've got to get back to Chenaie. Get your horse and come on. Jeannie will be glad to see you, and we can send word to Tana that you're here."

"I'm not in a socializing mood today. But I guess I better ride by and say hello to Tana and Little Jim before I leave. Knowin' Tana, she's probably already heard I'm around, and she'll cast a spell on me if don't stop in."

"Tana hears you talking like that, adding fuel to the rumors she's a voodoo practitioner instead of a healer, she'll make you wish all she did was cast a spell on you. You recall that willow switch when she caught us spying on the girls at the swimming hole?"

"Ouch." Cole grimaced. "Do I ever."

"How's Little Jim?" Shain asked. "Tana hasn't brought him around in a while."

"He's the same," Cole said with a shrug. "His body's twenty, but his mind's still five. He's happy out there in the woods back of Chenaie—Tana doesn't want him exposed to the nasty remarks he hears when she brings him into contact with what we call polite society. Little Jim doesn't understand when people laugh at him, and Tana's too proud to put up with them treatin' her son like that."

"She knows I'll fire anyone at Chenaie I hear making fun of Little Jim," Shain growled. "Hell, after the Yanks destroyed your place and murdered your folks, Tana could've gone anywhere. Instead, she came to Chenaie and took care of Jeannie when she heard my father's sister was dying of yellow fever. I'll never be able to repay her for that."

"You've given her a place to stay, and a cabin of her own to care for Little Jim. But look, you said you needed to get back to Chenaie. I just came by to ask if you knew that a timber crew was markin' trees on Chenaie land. You figurin' on sellin' off some timber? If you are, I think you ought to ride out and look at what that company's doin' to the forests they're workin' on now."

"That son of a bitch!" Shain snarled. Startled at the angry voice, Shain's stallion half-reared, then skittered sideways. Shain quickly brought him under control. "The man you just saw leaving was Fitzroy, and he works for that damned Great Lakes Timber Company that's moved in down here in the South. I told him again today that I wasn't interested in selling off Chenaie's timber rights!"

"Looked to me like they were layin' out a new roadway," Cole said. "From where they're cuttin' now, they could save a full day haulin' their logs to the river if they came across Chenaie land. Float the logs down to the sawmills in Baton Rouge faster and get the money in their pockets sooner."

"They start clearing that roadway, you let me know," Shain said in a deadly voice. "That was Fitzroy's alternate proposition this time—if I didn't want to sell the timber, he wanted to buy a right-of-way. I told him the same thing I did the last time he offered me one of his deals—not only no, but hell, no."

"I'll keep an eye on them," Cole agreed. "Give Jeannie my regards, and I'll see you another time—when I can stay longer."

Cole disappeared silently into the underbrush, but instead of immediately heading back to his fields, Shain sat motionless on Black for a while longer. The timber company must have been pretty damned sure he would agree to a right-of-way if they'd already begun marking the land they wanted. Maybe some of the recent problems he'd been having on Chenaie weren't accidents. Carrington, his new overseer, had been mentioning his own concerns lately.

Muted hoofbeats sounded as Cole rode away, back to the drifting lifestyle he'd taken up after he came home and found not only his home destroyed and parents dead, but the land seized by the bank for unpaid taxes. He could only imagine his friend's heartbreak—the same misery he would feel if he lost Chenaie.

Black snorted and lifted his head. Suddenly a hell of a noise split the air—something between a puma's shriek and a woman's scream. Black danced wildly, ignoring Shain's grip on the reins.

A brilliant flash of light rent the air, and Black neighed in frenzy, reared, and pawed in terror. Cursing the stallion under his breath, Shain clenched his thighs and wrapped the reins a turn around his hands. He shifted his weight forward and pulled the stallion's head against its chest, bringing its front hooves back to the ground. The horse attempted one more plunge, but finally stood trembling beneath him.

With Black under control, Shain glared around him as he reached behind him for the pistol in one of his saddlebags. His arm froze in mid-swing. "Holy shit! What the hell's that?"

Shain stared at the colossal, white—whatever it was—in the ditch across the road. Maintaining his firm hold on the reins, he closed his eyelids briefly, then slit them a hair's breadth. The white—whatever it was—still sat there.

A cloud of smoke drifted across the road from beneath

the black wheels, carrying a strange odor, which stank like burning kerosene when a lamp wick needed trimming. The thing crouched there growling—well, more like a grown barn cat's gravelly purr—but nevertheless, warning Shain to keep his distance.

"Damn it, St. Clair," Shain muttered. "You're sitting here acting like that thing's alive, when it's probably just one of those machines that Crazy Jake's always working on."

But this machine looked a cut above most of the inventions Jake called Shain over to view. The glossy white paint gleamed, and whatever powered it made the engine run a lot smoother than anything Jake had come up with so far. But he damned sure didn't have time to mess with one of Jake's inventions right now.

A shadow flickered against the smoky window pane in the machine's side, and Shain squinted as he tried to see through the reflected sun glare. It looked like there was a white air bladder inside it—but one a thousand times larger than the small airbags he cleaned from the insides of catfish. Catching a glimpse of a feminine face, he bit off a gasp and sprang from his stallion. That damned sure wasn't Jake inside there!

Released from Shain's hold, Black whirled and bolted down the dirt road. Shain took a hesitant step forward before he stopped in stunned amazement when the machine's side split wide open and a pair of slender, feminine legs appeared.

Those damned sure didn't belong to Jake—or Zeke, the elderly former slave who lived with Jake and made sure the inventor ate a meal now and then. Eyes narrowed in contemplation, Shain stepped back deeper into the shadows beneath the live oak's branches.

Chapter 3

Alaynia shoved the collapsed airbag aside and slid out of her seat. The blast of heat outside the air-conditioned car hit her full force, and the ache in her neck and shoulders reminded her just how badly she could have been injured if it hadn't been for the airbag and seatbelt.

She shrugged in irritation as she glanced at her wristwatch, then at the front of the car, trying to determine what she'd hit to trigger the airbag. The hood appeared undamaged, but since the car had landed nose-down in the ditch, she couldn't really tell if maybe the bumper plowed over a piece of guard rail. She brushed at a trickle of sweat streaking her water-based makeup and started around the car door. Stopped when her heels sank in dirt.

"Damned if I'm going to ruin a pair of hundred-and-fifty-dollar shoes," she muttered. "I'll call someone to come pull me out."

But the darned phone was on the passenger floorboard with the scattered contents of her purse! She propped her hands on her hips and studied the situation.

Only Shain's eyes moved as he tore his gaze away from the bare legs standing in those shoes with the ridiculously high heels and upward. The satiny material of the blue skirt ended an inch or two beneath gently rounded hips, outlining them perfectly. Her hands splayed on the swell beneath her trim waist. He couldn't see her fingers, but a brilliant red color tipped her thumbs. The white blouse hung more loosely than the skirt, but her back tapered nicely—what he could see of it beneath a riot of silky brown curls cascading past her shoulders.

She appeared at ease with the machine and reached back inside to twist something. The purring growl died, and then she reached farther in. The skirt slipped up farther with her movements and exposed more lush thigh. Way before Shain decided he'd had enough, she straightened, with a small black object in her hand. She pushed something on it, held it to her ear, then pulled it away to peer at it. Then she tossed it inside the machine and turned around. This time she held what looked like a key ring, some sort of leather case also dangling from it.

"Oh!" Alaynia raised a hand to shade her eyes against the brilliant sun. "I didn't see you at first," she called toward the man standing across the road under a tree draped with Spanish moss. "Say, do you happen to have a phone I could use?"

When the man only stared at her, Alaynia cautiously unsnapped the leather case over the can of mace on her key chain. Darn it, she knew better than to immediately strike up a conversation with a stranger. A woman alone could never tell what might happen. She shifted the mace to her left hand and grabbed the car door with her right. If he ran toward her, she could be back in the car with the door closed and locked in a split second.

He took a few steps away from the tree, but still didn't say anything. Alaynia shook her head as she studied him more closely. Definitely masculine. Probably at least six-one, and she'd always had a weakness for males with slightly long, black hair. His eyes appeared brown from this distance, but the shadowing tree limbs made an accurate determination of color impractical—even with him staring at her with that wide-eyed, astounded gaze.

And, good lord, where had he bought that clothing? It looked new, but the style seemed too outdated for even one of the dowdier Boston thrift shops to carry. His white shirt with semi-flowing sleeves should be cool in this heat and humidity, though, so maybe Southern men tailored their styles to suit the weather they had to endure, and the heck with fashion.

The fawn trousers fit his lower body like a layer of paint, and Alaynia's cheeks flushed as the thought crossed her mind that he must only have a pair of skimpy briefs beneath that tightness. Or—maybe even just a jockstrap.

"Uh . . ." she began.

The man finally spoke in a slow, Southern drawl, which matched his hesitant steps as he walked another few feet toward her. "Are you all right, ma'am?"

The concern in his tone and his politeness alleviated her anxiety a little. "I appear to be," she replied as she glanced down, then back at him. "But I need to call a garage to get my car out of the ditch."

"Car," he repeated. "Is that what you call that white machine there?"

Alaynia's fingers tightened on both the car door and her mace. "Uh . . . maybe you could just go call someone for me, and I'll wait here until they come."

"And what name would I call someone at a *garage*, who I wanted to come pull a *car* out of the ditch?" he asked in a curious voice and with a lift of one raven eyebrow.

Alaynia caught the teasing note, but it was way too darned hot to enjoy a flirtation, even with a man this good-looking. "Whatever the hell the mechanic's or the wrecker driver's name is," she said impatiently. "Mack, Eddie, Billie Bob."

"Not Jake, huh?"

"If Jake's his name, call him that for heaven's sake," Alaynia replied. "Who do you use for your car?"

"I don't own a car," he admitted as he took another step, eyes flickering from Alaynia to her car. "In fact, I've never seen a car before in my life. But I wouldn't be adverse to you or Jake showing me how it works, since it looks like a hell of an interesting concept. What powers it—steam, like most of Jake's other machines?"

That did it. Alaynia jumped back into the car and closed the door. She jammed her finger on the lock button, breathing out a relieved sigh at the reassuring click of the locks engaging. She shoved aside the deflated airbag and threw a quick glance at the man, who thankfully hadn't moved any closer, then leaned over to dig through her purse contents on the passenger floorboard until she found her metal nail file, which she gripped along with her mace.

The interior of the car sweltered without the air-conditioning, and perspiration plastered her silk blouse against the leather seat. Another glance told her the man had his hands on his hips, head cocked to one side. She started to feel rather foolish—and awfully damned hot.

Still . . . a woman couldn't be too cautious. Alaynia picked up the phone again, turned it on, and pressed it to her ear. Only static, even when she flicked the button off, then on again. Still no dial tone. She pushed nine-one-one anyway. The static continued. Damn.

She aimed a red-tipped finger at the push buttons again, but suddenly her hand froze. A dawning realization of something out-of-kilter filtered into her senses, and she slowly raised her head and looked out through the windshield.

The road—it couldn't be. She'd been traveling on an asphalt road, and now a dirt road ran beside her car. Could she have somehow slid onto a side road when she skidded down the highway? She twisted around, but no matter how hard she strained, she couldn't see an intersecting asphalt road back that way. Neither did she see any sign of the shimmering mirage she had skidded into.

She slid the key into the ignition switch again, turned it forward, but none of the accessory lights came on. She tried to open the window a crack, but when she pushed the power button, the pane only groaned faintly, not moving. To top everything else off, her battery must be going dead.

A drop of sweat dripped from her nose, and Alaynia swiped the back of her hand across her upper lip and frowned in disgust when she looked down. Antique beige powder smeared her hand above a streak of summer bronze lipstick. She twisted the key again. She desperately needed air-conditioning. Not even a faint click sounded, let alone the reassuring purr of an engine leaping to life. She patted her foot on the gas feed. Nothing. Keys dangling in the switch, she shook her head in disgust and leaned back against the seat.

Now what was she going to do? With the phone on the blink, she couldn't call for help, or even contact the attorney to get corrected directions to the stately Southern mansion she had inherited—even if she could get the car started again. And the devilishly-handsome man across the road evidently had a screw loose somewhere. Too bad. Wonder if he would turn out to be a neighbor to Chenaie?

At the rapping noise in her ear, Alaynia turned her head straight into the concerned gaze of the man her thoughts had wandered to.

"Look, my name's Shain St. Clair, and I own a plantation not too far from here," he called through the glass. "I'll take you there, if you'll come on out here before you pass out from the heat."

Alaynia smirked distrustfully at him, and he spoke again in a reassuring tone. "I'm perfectly respectable and my sister lives with me, so there'll be a woman there with us."

Alaynia closed her eyes in dismissal. The temperature continued to climb inside the car—she swore she could feel each new degree—and more rivulets of perspiration crept down her face.

Shain stepped back and eyed the white machine she called a car while he tried to decide what the hell to do next. The woman evidently was in control right now, keeping the door she'd stepped out of earlier firmly closed between them despite what had to be sweltering heat in the interior. Maybe taking this woman into his home for even a brief time wasn't such a good idea—could she be touched in the head?

She was only half-dressed, and she babbled nonsense about things called garages and phones. He moved around to look through the front window pane on the machine, which was clear instead of covered with a smoky tint, as the side panes were.

The woman had to be at least twenty-five, but she wore her hair loose instead of tethered back in a fitting style for a woman her age—a style that wouldn't tempt a man's touch. Sunlight streamed through the front window, shooting golden highlights from the shiny mass, which would slither through a man's hands nicely despite the curls and waves.

Gorgeous blue eyes peered out at him through the glass for just a second, but her skin had to be why he didn't notice a wedding ring on her left hand—the one she had draped on the wheel in front of her. Blotchy, it spoiled her entire appearance. And the sweat running down her cheeks carried streaks of the black kohl she used around her eyes, further blemishing her face in stripes.

He had enough on his mind right now—trying to get the plantation back on its feet and keep tabs on his baby sister, along with wondering what crooked trick Fitzroy would come up with next. Hell, he didn't need a beautiful woman complicating matters.

Suddenly the woman slumped over the wheel in front of her. Good God, she'd passed out. Shain leaped back to the car door.

He pounded on the side window, but the woman didn't budge. Neither did the glass pane. It appeared stronger than normal glass, which he could have shattered with one thrust of his fist. Glancing down, he saw a metal hinge on the side of the machine. He grabbed it and lifted, then hastily drew his hand back and sucked on his burned fingers.

The sun beat down on him, and sweat pooled in his armpits and slid down his ribs. It was hot enough to almost make him promise to live a sin-free life, rather than risk the even more blistering blazes in Hell. And it had to be at least twenty or more degrees hotter inside that damned machine.

The woman slipped sideways and fell across the seat, her mouth partly open in a pant.

"Goddamn it, she's gonna die in there," Shain muttered. He raced back across the road and grabbed a dead limb from under the live oak. When he got back to the machine, he swung the limb over his shoulder, prepared to shatter the window pane. But the woman had regained consciousness and now sat back up in her seat, swaying unsteadily. Shain rapped on the window again, and she turned her head weakly toward the noise.

"Damn it!" Shain yelled. "You're going to die in that heat in there! You better get the hell back out here before you faint again!"

She stared at his face for a second, then at the limb propped on his shoulder. Understanding her concern, he threw the limb across the dirt road. She drew in a tortured breath, probably filled more with heat than the air her lungs demanded, and jabbed at something below the window. Her other hand fingered the ring of keys hanging from the column attached to the wheel in front of her.

She started to slump forward again, then jerked her head back up in response when Shain pounded on the machine's door. Her lips moved in what could have been a moan of misery, and she clutched at her stomach and gazed at him through the window. Licking her lips and frowning in confusion, she squinted as Shain shouted loud enough for his voice to pierce the glass pane between them, "You've got to get the hell out of there! Come on! Open this thing up!"

"Open?" her lips imitated in response.

She steadied herself with one arm on the wheel and glanced down at something on the inside of the door. Blinked her eyes once, then closed them, her eyelashes remaining glued to her cheeks.

"Goddamn it!" He thudded his fist on the window in an accompaniment to the curse, and her head jerked up from her chest, her lids slowly lifting. "Open this thing, or I'm going to kick that damned window in!"

"I'm trying," she appeared to whimper.

He bent his head close to the window and could see her red-tipped fingers weakly pressing various buttons on a panel inside the door. Nothing happened when she pushed one after the other of the four buttons grouped together. Finally her index finger touched a lone button an inch or so behind the others. She shoved at it, and Shain gratefully heard the faint, answering click of locks disengaging.

The door opened and she slid out and tried to stand. Her legs crumpled under her, and Shain caught her as she fell.

Chapter 4

Shain hefted Alaynia against his chest. Her inert body sagged in his grasp, head falling back and arms and legs dangling limply. She didn't look that heavy, but her lax muscles made holding her difficult. With a grunt, he shifted his hold and tried to ignore the feel of her long, bare legs in one hand, the breast beneath the hold of his other hand. Staggering across the road, away from the white machine, he laid her down in the shade beneath the live oak.

She was going to get dirty, but he couldn't help that. His spooked stallion had carried off the only available blanket beneath its saddle.

Shain stood and, fingers to his mouth, whistled shrilly. That damned stallion better not have gone far, or there would be hell to pay when Shain finally got back to the stable. The bushes lining the road a hundred feet or so away rustled, and the stallion stuck its head out, ears flickering and eyes rolling in wariness.

"Blast you, Black! Get over here!"

The horse tossed its head and took a tentative step onto the roadway. When Shain whistled again, it walked hesitantly toward him, but stopped a dozen feet away. Nostrils wide, it eyed the machine across the road and refused to move any closer.

Shain glanced at the beautiful woman sprawled at his feet and his lips thinned in worry. He had to get her cooled off—and fast—or she would indeed die. He strode forward and picked up the stallion's trailing reins, but when he tried to lead Black forward, the horse shied and tossed its head. Shain tugged again, and Black planted his feet, refusing to move.

Afraid of injuring his favorite animal's sensitive mouth, Shain tied the reins to a sapling beside the road. He grabbed the canteen from his saddlebag, hurried back to the woman, and knelt beside her. Uncapping the canteen, he pulled his handkerchief from his back pocket and saturated it with water.

The cloth bag around the container had helped keep the water cool, and Shain wiped the wet handkerchief over the woman's face. He snorted in astonishment when a layer of tan color stained the cloth and the blotches on her face disappeared. Evidently she used some sort of powder on her face, similar to what his sister, Jeannie, used when she could get away with it. Once clean, her skin glowed a healthy, peach color.

Unconsciously glowering at women's foolishness in covering up flawless skin, Shain moistened the handkerchief again and sponged the remainder of her face clean. The black streaks beneath her eyes proved harder to remove, and he gave up on them. It was more important right now to cool her body.

He tilted the canteen, dribbling water across her neck, down her blouse. The woman never stirred. Reluctantly, Shain unbuttoned the top two buttons on her bodice. After saturating the handkerchief again, he reached inside the blouse for the ribbons on her chemise, preparing to untie them in order to lay the wet handkerchief directly on her chest.

Instead of a chemise, Shain touched bare skin. He shoved the blouse open further. The firm mounds of her breasts were supported not by a corset, but a fragile, skimpy piece of rose-colored lace. He scowled as he recalled the feel of her corset-less body in his arms. Damn, everything about this strange package of womanhood puzzled him.

The barely perceptible rise and fall of the woman's breasts finally penetrated Shain's thoughts, which were veering away from methods of treating heat faintness toward another way a person's body could get overheated. He hurriedly hid the breasts with his soaking handkerchief and slid one arm beneath the woman's shoulders to lift her against his chest.

"Come on, honey," he murmured as he tipped the canteen toward her mouth. "Let's try to get some of this water inside you, instead of just on the outside."

Sylvia lay down on her stomach and propped her chin on her palms as she peered over the edge of the cloud. Though she and Francesca had both been a little worried at first that Alaynia's fear of Shain might cause irreparable harm to her health, it appeared she would recover. Already Alaynia's eyelids were fluttering in response to Shain's ministrations. She glanced at Francesca, who still stood upright beside her. Instead of watching the scene beneath the live oak, Francesca scanned the surrounding sky.

"Hey, Frannie." Sylvia kicked her legs up and down and her dashiki hem slid up her brown legs; feathers of cloud mist scattered around Francesca's feet. "I unlocked the door, and he has her out of the car now. Take a load off and lie down here with me for a while. This cloud's as comfortable as one of those featherbeds I've read about from back in olden times."

Francesca gazed disdainfully down her slender nose. "Angels have no need to rest, Sylvia. It's not as if we have a physical body that has to recoup itself."

"Who said anything about *needing* to rest? Vacations are for doing what you want to do, not what you have to do."

"We aren't on vacation yet, Sylvia. We have to take care of this little matter first. And we both ought to be honored that we were chosen for this assignment, since it's a step above what a guardian angel usually has to handle. Our getting the summons shows that someone has noticed our effectiveness and has confidence in us—trust in our abilities."

"Trust—schmust," Sylvia grumbled. "Or maybe it's just that we were available at the right time. I mean, Violet had already taken over for you and picked out someone else to watch over Jacki. One more minute and we would've been gone to . . . we never did decide where we were going on our vacation, Frannie. And now it's been delayed again."

"Hush your griping. We've got to talk to Basil."

Sylvia rolled over and rose to her feet. "Well, where is this Basil guy?"

"Over there." Francesca nodded toward what looked like just another cloud in the clear, azure sky. The angels' eyes could discern what human eyes would miss—a recognizable shape to the irregular white mass. As they watched, it faded and disappeared.

"When are you going to tell me what this is all about, Frannie?" Sylvia asked in exasperation. "My idea of a stressless vacation is definitely not visiting a time period where black people are fresh from being kept as slaves—and still treated like second-class citizens. I've used this corporeal body ever since I saw that horrible slavery thing happening while what they called the South in the United States was being settled."

"It was definitely not a time in history humans should be proud of," Francesca agreed. "All of the cultures that have practiced that barbaric custom over the years should be ashamed of themselves."

"You got that right. And the magnitude of it in the South made it a particularly grim time." Sylvia suppressed a shiver, but her wing feathers fluttered. "The sooner we get out of here, the better—at least in my mind."

"Oh, this shouldn't take long, my dear," Francesca replied with a negligent wave of her hand. "We just have to talk some sense into Basil and have him return Alaynia to her own time."

"You better be right about it not taking long. I want my vacation."

"Hush and quit acting so churlish, Sylvia. Some things are more important than what you want."

"Churlish? Now, you listen here, Frannie. You granted me this vacation. I think I have a right to be *churlish,* whatever that means, about it being delayed!"

"Churlish means . . . well, it means 'difficult,'" Francesca explained. "It really pains me at times to realize how much flavor some of us have lost from the language these days. I think 'churlish' is a much more appropriate word to describe your behavior."

"That does it!" Sylvia traipsed across the cloud with her hands propped on her hips and brown eyes glittering in indignation. "I thought it would be fun to have someone along to share my vacation. But if all you're gonna do is find fault with me, I'd be better off alone. Talk about stress! Your picking at me over the way I behave is—"

"WHAT ARE YOU DOING IN MY SPACE? GET OUT OF HERE!"

Braids bouncing, Sylvia whirled toward the thunderous voice. Shock clogged her indignant reply in her throat, and she protectively lifted her hands. With a millennium of existence behind her, she hadn't thought anything would ever scare her again, but the ugly, ferocious countenance hovering a bare dozen feet from her froze her scream somewhere down there with her words. Wings fluttering, her feet backpedaled without conscious direction from her mind. A second later, she peered over Francesca's shoulder.

"You're the senior angel here," she whispered with a mixture of fright, along with anger and embarrassment over her fear. "Who—or what—is that thing? An *evil* spirit?"

"No. A spirit, but not an evil one, Sylvia." Francesca spoke to the apparition. "Tsk, tsk, Basil. You're scaring the bejeebers out of Sylvia here. Take on your normal form immediately."

"Says who?" the apparition snarled. Instead of obeying, it screwed up its muzzle and drew back its upper lip to bare a pair of sharp fangs. Smoke issued from two large, green, pointed ears on its head, and it hissed out a mixture of steam and flames.

Sylvia stared at the apparition in fascination, less fearful now that Francesca hovered between her and it. When the smoke covered its face for a second, she glanced over the rest of its body—then broke into unrestrained laughter.

"Oh, Frannie," she said around her laughter, "look at him. He's making himself a monster on top, but he can't change his lower body! But where are his wings?"

"Basil's a human spirit—a ghost, not an angel," Francesca explained. "Ghosts don't have wings."

"Well, none of the human spirits I ever worked with ever looked like that. But then, I've never run into an earthbound human spirit before—a ghost. Say." Sylvia studied the ghost in an appraising manner. "That lower part of him's pretty cute."

"Like one of those hunks?" Francesca asked.

"Could be," Sylvia mused in reply. "Let's get a closer look."

Basil snorted in anger and disappeared in a cloud of mist. A split-second later, he reappeared, this time in the form of a man somewhat resembling an older version of Shain, who was still nursing Alaynia down below the three hovering figures.

"Stay away from me!" Basil demanded. "How dare you attempt to examine me like I was some blooded stallion up for auction! And I've already ordered you out of my space!"

"Basil, Basil," Francesca said with a shake of her blond head. "You didn't used to be like this. What in the world's come over you?"

"You just said it," Basil growled in a low voice. "The world's come over me, along with what they call *progress*. You can both just heist your tails back to wherever you came from, because . . ."

"Tails?" Fists clenched, Sylvia flew at Basil. "Why, you male chauvinist pig. Women don't have to put up with being called names like that!"

Before Sylvia reached him, Basil disappeared again, reappearing after she whooshed by in the same place he had occupied. "Girl, I've been practicing my craft for almost two hundred years, and if I don't want you to touch me, you won't."

"Don't you dare call me a girl, you . . . you *ghost!*" Sylvia sputtered as her anger heightened. "You listen here, buster . . ."

"Calm down, Sylvia," Frannie said.

"Then do something," Sylvia demanded. "Or let me. Our powers have to be stronger than his. We're lots older!"

"It doesn't work that way, Sylvia," Francesca informed her companion with a sigh of annoyance. "I'll explain later.

For now, I can do without your remarks about our age. But since you brought it up, please behave yourself and try to act like you have a little maturity to go with your years of existence."

Francesca crossed her arms and turned a stern look on the ghost. "We've been sent here to tell you that you need to send Alaynia back to her own time immediately, Basil."

"Hah," Basil sneered. "I might not have been around quite as long as you, Francesca, but I know that I've still got a measure of free will here, just like I had when I was alive. I've got no intention of sending that little chit back there, so she can destroy the peace of my plantation."

"Basil . . ." Francesca began, but the ghost wasn't there. Without apparent effort on his part, he had disappeared, leaving behind empty air where he had hovered.

Beneath the live oak tree, Shain heaved a relieved sigh as Alaynia opened her eyes fully, blinked, and screwed up her face in a frown as she tried to focus. He set the canteen down beside him and barely managed to tighten his grasp on her when she lunged away with a gasp of fear.

"Hey, easy," he murmured, as though soothing a still-unbroken colt. "You'll feel better in a minute."

"I'm fine now," Alaynia said in a flat voice. "Get your damned hands off me."

"Well, if you aren't the ungrateful female," Shain muttered. "Maybe I should just throw you back inside that machine and see how long you last."

"That would be preferable to lying here while you undress me further." Alaynia glanced down at the handkerchief over her breasts with a meaningful look. "Let me up."

Shain released her and rose, eyes narrowing in resentment at her implication. "You don't even have enough clothing on to notice if you lost a piece. When we get to the plantation, you'll have to wait somewhere until I bring you out one of Jeannie's dresses. My household staff will think someone attacked you, if they see how you're dressed now. And if my field crew notices you, they'll think I made a morning call at Polly's Place and brought one of her girls back with me."

Sputtering in indignation, Alaynia scrambled to her feet. She swayed and grasped for support. The nearest stability available was Shain's chest, and she leaned against him, fingers curling into his white shirt. Her forehead fell on his shoulder, and he chuckled wryly and wrapped his arms around her.

An unfamiliar scent rose from her hair, and Shain tried to place it while she clung to him. Not honeysuckle alone—more like a mixture of that and wisteria. Whatever the blend, he couldn't imagine one of Polly's girls using anything so faintly enticing. They usually slathered on a perfume strong enough to withstand their evening's exertions.

"I . . ." Alaynia pushed against him and leaned back in his arms. "Look, I apologize. I know you were only trying to cool me off. But I don't appreciate one bit your insinuation that I look like a prostitute!"

Shain trailed his gaze downward. The handkerchief had fluttered to the ground when she jumped to her feet, and her blouse still gaped open. He had to admit that the scrap of rose lace probably had an easy job maintaining those breasts at a proper pout. Still, he'd turn Jeannie over his knee if she ever even thought about going out without a corset on her newly-blooming figure.

Alaynia gasped and reached to button her blouse. As soon as she had it closed securely, she twisted from his grasp. Her quick movement evidently brought on lightheadedness, and she grabbed the arm Shain held out.

She took two deep breaths and appeared less woozy. Still holding his arm, she bent down and removed her shoes. Dangling them in her fingers, she took a step back, steadier now without her heels sinking into the dirt.

"I've got some mineral water in my cooler," she told Shain. "I'll probably be all right as soon as I get some liquid in my system."

Shain sauntered along behind her as she walked toward the car. Lord, did that man ever move more decisively than a languid walk? She stepped more firmly in counteraction to his lazy stride and grimaced when her bare feet kicked up swirls of dust.

"You're not going to jump back in there and lock yourself inside, are you?" Shain asked as she reached for the back door handle.

Alaynia threw an irritated glance over her shoulder. "I think I've got a little more sense than that." In deference to the heated door handle, she gingerly pulled the door open and ducked in to reach for the cooler in the middle of the seat, along with one of the Styrofoam cups in the open plastic bag. She should have remembered she had those drinks with her earlier, but she excused her lack of memory. She'd had other things on her mind . . . especially after she noticed the man now standing too close.

And she heard that man whistle under his breath as her skirt rode up until it barely covered her hips. When she backed out of the car, her rear hit him right where she could feel the start of his arousal—and a second later, she whirled and hit him with the cooler just below his belt buckle with a satisfying thud.

Hands clasped protectively over his privates and a look

of stunned betrayal on his face, he landed spread-legged on his ass. Alaynia smirked in satisfaction as she swung the back door closed and stepped over his outstretched legs. She set the cooler down and reached inside the still-open driver's door to grab her key ring from the ignition switch.

"This stuff's pretty wicked," she warned Shain as she turned around, the mace firmly in her grasp. "It's not that pepper stuff. It's what the cops use. And I've practiced with it until I'm a pretty good shot." Keeping both the mace and her eyes trained on Shain, she reached down and fumbled the cooler lid open.

Shain glared at the leather-covered cylinder in her hand. "Goddamn it," he snarled as he rose to his feet. "You knew I was behind you, and you backed into me! It was an accident."

"Yeah, and that thing was just accidentally growing between your legs!" Unable to remove the screw cap from the mineral water while she held the mace in her other hand, Alaynia placed the Styrofoam cup over the bottle's stem and settled for running the bottle around her neck. Cool water dripped down her chest, pooling between her breasts. She sighed in pleasure.

Shain shook his head. "Let me tell you something, lady."

"Alaynia," Alaynia interrupted, wondering at the same instant why on earth it mattered to her if this man knew her name. "Uh . . . I seem to remember you yelling your name through the window. Shain, was it?"

A derisive sneer on his lips, Shain bowed. "Shain Christopher St. Clair of Chenaie Plantation, at your service, Alaynia whoever the hell you are!"

The mace started to slide from her suddenly numb fingers, and Alaynia reflexively tightened her grasp. "You . . . you can't be! He said Chenaie had been empty for five years."

46

"*He* obviously misinformed you. Chenaie hasn't been empty for even five days since my grandfather built it seventy years ago."

"Then there must be two plantations with the same name around here," Alaynia said in protest. "My Chenaie's almost two hundred years old, not just seventy. Maybe you know it as Oak Grove, the English translation for Chenaie?"

"Nope," Shain denied. "I know every plantation in this end of Louisiana—even the new names for those the damned Yankee carpetbaggers picked up when the rightful owners couldn't pay those hellacious taxes on them. There's not a two-hundred-year-old manor house in the bunch of them. Chenaie's one of the oldest in this end of the state. You'd have to go to New Orleans to find anything older."

"Your grandfather can't own *my* Chenaie," Alaynia insisted. "I've got a deed to it in my briefcase."

"My grandfather's been dead for over twenty-five years," Shain informed her. "I own Chenaie now, and I don't care what kind of a case you're carrying your deed around in; it's fake. Probably came from some damned carpetbagger, who also lied to you about the age of the manor house." He eyed her suspiciously. "I suggest you find who sold you that bogus document and try to get your money back, whatever good that'll do you. He's probably hightailed it into Yankee-land by now, where he's drooling over your money and laughing up his sleeve."

"I didn't buy it—I inherited it!" Alaynia insisted. A bead of sweat rolled down her forehead, into the corner of her eye, and the saltiness stung. She backhanded the pain and inadvertently pressed the release button on the mace. A stream of liquid hissed out and spattered against the Styrofoam cup capping the bottle of mineral water, which she now held near her waist.

Horrified, Alaynia shut her eyes and threw the bottle and mace away. She stumbled backward, came up against the open driver's door, then lurched sideways. Her foot hit the cooler, and bottles and cans clinked as it tipped over. She lost her balance completely and landed with a thud. A stabbing pain shot through her hip, which had ended up on the edge of the cooler lid. Eyes firmly closed, she rolled over twice, away from the car.

When she finally dared open her eyes, she saw that Shain had ducked to the back of the car when she tossed the mace away. His gaze followed the cloud of mist, which trailed from the car's door to the middle of the road, and then his eyes centered on the Styrofoam cup, now curling in partial disintegration.

Obviously seething with fury, he glared at her sprawled figure. "Damn you! What the hell were you trying to do?"

Alaynia scrambled to her feet and held out her hands. "Don't get in that mist," she pleaded, though the cloud was quickly dissipating. "It'll burn your eyes terribly."

"As if you give a damn," Shain snarled. "You've been threatening me with that stuff for the last five minutes! What the hell's in that container—some type of acid? You almost sprayed it in my face!"

Aware of her defenselessness against his enraged anger, Alaynia cautiously glanced around for her mace. It lay a fair distance from Shain's boot. As soon as her eyes fell on it, he took a few steps forward and bent down, tanned fingers closing around the leather case. He straightened and studied the cylinder, apparently discerning that it was safe enough to handle as long as he kept his finger away from the release button on its top. He damned sure wasn't going to give it back to her, though. With a flick of his wrist, he sailed the key ring across the road, where it disappeared in the underbrush.

"Damn it," Alaynia shouted, "I didn't mean to fire it—it was an accident. And my car keys are on that ring!"

The trail of mist had disappeared by now, and Shain shrugged. "You're real familiar with accidents, aren't you? You've accidentally wrecked one of Jake's machines, and accidentally scared my horse half to death. Tell me, where did you accidentally lose the rest of your clothes?"

Alaynia scurried behind the feeble protection of the driver's door, but Shain only reached down to grab one of the bottles of mineral water. When he glanced at her wary face, he smiled grimly.

"I've got to tell Jake to make me one of those things," he said in a nonchalant voice, his anger evidently appeased somewhat in face of her apprehension. He nodded his head at the ground, where quickly-melting ice cubes lay scattered among the cans and bottles, and lifted an inquiring brow. "How long's it keep that ice frozen?"

"All day," Alaynia replied in a grudging voice. Without her mace, she didn't feel nearly as confident, especially with his taller height towering over her on the other side of the door.

Shain lifted the mineral water higher. "Too bad I don't have an opener with me. This sure would taste good."

"It twists off." Her voice came out still less than friendly, still cautious.

"Oh." Shain closed his fingers around the cap and turned it. Tossing the cap aside, he extended the bottle to Alaynia. "Here. You didn't get to drink the other bottle you picked up."

She licked her dry lips and cautiously stretched her arm over the car window to accept the bottle. Jerked her hand back as soon as her fingers closed, and moved a couple steps backward before she tilted the bottle to her lips.

Shain shrugged and picked up another bottle. While he unscrewed the cap, he sauntered toward the horse Alaynia had noticed tied down the road.

"Uh . . ." She took a step or two after him. "Uh . . . where are you going? I want to ask you some more questions about Chenaie."

Shain ignored her until after he untied the reins and swung into the saddle and turned the horse around. Then he took a deep swallow from the bottle.

"Good," he said in a somewhat surprised voice. "You ever get by *my* Chenaie, maybe you'll give your recipe to Jeannie, to pass on to our cook."

"Mr. St. Clair. Shain . . ."

"Don't worry," Shain said. He drank another swallow, then reined the horse back down the road. "I'll ride over to Crazy Jake's and have him come get you. But that's all I'm going to do for you. Your next accident's liable to prove even more hazardous to my health!"

Alaynia stared open-mouthed after him until he disappeared in a bend in the road. Then she stomped over to the driver's door and slid into the seat. Yelping, she jumped back outside, bumping her head on the door frame in her haste to escape the hot seat leather against her bare legs.

"Damn!" she muttered. "Damn, damn, damn, damn, damn! Damn it to Hell!"

Suddenly she gawked down the road. He was sending who after her? Jake? *Crazy* Jake? Shain himself was definitely a touch light in the head, insisting that he owned a plantation the attorney had assured Alaynia had stood empty ever since her elderly great-aunt, Miss Tilda, entered a nursing home.

She hadn't had much of a chance to try to make sense of his strange behavior so far. Instead, she'd been too busy trying to overcome her bout with heatstroke and keeping out of Shain's reach. He didn't own a car? Had never heard of a garage or phone?

If Shain was an example of a sane man in Louisiana, what sort of man would he send back here—a man Shain himself called crazy. Crazy Jake.

The heck with trying to figure out how Shain could claim ownership in a plantation with the same name as hers. She had to get out of here before Crazy Jake arrived.

She couldn't get to the gym bag in the trunk, which contained her running shoes. She'd locked the glove box over her rental papers after she picked up the car, and the trunk release button was inside it. The keys were lost somewhere across the road in dense underbrush it would be fruitless to search. Besides, she'd read that Louisiana snakes were poisonous. And what good would the keys do her if the car still wouldn't start, although at least she'd have the mace again. She grabbed the expensive heels again and slipped them on with a grimace at her dirty feet.

Crazy Jake. Yep, Shain had definitely said *Crazy* Jake.

"Get the hell out of there, snakes!" Alaynia yelled as she stomped her feet heavily while she trudged across the dirt road.

Chapter 5

Twenty minutes later, Shain rode down the rutted lane leading to Jake's ramshackle cabin. The smell of meat cooking over an outdoor fire drifted in the air, and his stomach reminded him that he'd promised Jeannie to return in time for the noon meal. Well, it wouldn't be the first time an unforeseen problem had kept him from keeping a promise to his sister.

Is that what Alaynia is—a problem? The thought flashed through Shain's mind, and he immediately contradicted it. *Nope, not my problem. If anything, she's Jake's—or . . .*

Could she have some connection to Fitzroy? Was it only coincidence that both the carpetbagger and Alaynia had designs on Chenaie? *His* Chenaie.

"But where the hell did Fitzroy find someone like that?" he muttered aloud. "Still, she seems more like Jake's type, what with that machine and those other strange things she's got—and talks about." Black's ears swiveled at his voice, and the horse shook its head, blowing through its nostrils.

"Yeah, boy," Shain said. "My feelings exactly. She sure is a riddle. But guess only someone as crazy as Jake would ride around in a darned machine like the ones he's always working on. Even Zeke won't have anything to do with them."

Shain rounded a bend in the shaded lane and emerged into a clearing, where Zeke tended a smoking fire beneath a large haunch of meat spitted over an outdoor pit. The huge barn off to one side overrode the tiny cabin, and the barn was in much better repair. A fresh coat of whitewash covered its walls, while the cabin walls were a washed-out gray. Cracks ran across both window panes in the front of the cabin, and the open door swung on one hinge.

Shain made a mental note to send his carpenter over with new window panes to replace the broken ones, as well as tools to repair the door. Jake kept his barn in meticulous shape, and even slept in it most nights. Zeke didn't know a hammer from a nail, but he could cook up a meal rivaling the spread Shain's cook turned out for the rare entertaining they could afford. And Zeke had served the St. Clair family from birth until his freedom after the war, when for some reason he'd taken a shine to Crazy Jake and decided the man needed a caretaker.

Yet as Shain rode toward the elderly black man crouched by the fire, he recalled the hours on end he'd spent with Zeke while he grew up—the tales the old ex-slave had spun to amuse a small boy—the treats Zeke had smuggled up to his room when Shain was once again being punished for defying another of the multitude of rules of conduct for a young gentleman his father demanded he abide by. Zeke deserved a decent place to live and sleep.

Black snorted again, and the elderly figure rose to his feet.

"Massa Shain," he called, swiping his hands down the front of the stained apron covering his bare chest, then waving one hand to urge Shain forward. "Just in time to eat. Come sit a spell."

Shain dismounted and led Black toward the fire. "Zeke, the war's been over for ten years," he repeated for the hundredth time. "When are you gonna learn that you don't have to call me 'Master' these days?"

Zeke chuckled and wiped a bare forearm across his sweat-beaded brow. "You always been Massa, even when I changed your nappies the times that there nurse a' yours would sneak off to spark with that there field hand."

"But you're working for Jake now, Zeke."

"Don't know's I'd call it workin' for him. More like he needs me to take care of him and make sure none of them there 'vention things he's always workin' on turns on him and eats him up. Me, I gets a place to live and only has to do what I feels like doin'. Ain't no money changes hands."

"Just so you remember there's always a place for you at Chenaie, Zeke."

"Knows that. And 'preciates it, I sure do. But I ain't ready to just lay back and wait for death to pick me off. Rather be takin' care of my own self for a while yet."

Shain shook his head and gave in. He didn't have any idea of Zeke's true age—the dark-brown, wrinkled face beneath the white shock of tight curls had been one of his first memories. And Zeke had served both Shain's grandfather and father. Indeed, some of the tales Shain had begged the old slave to relate had been about his grandfather, Basil St. Clair.

"Whew," Shain said. "It's too blasted hot here by the fire, Zeke. I need a drink from your well, and Black probably could do with a bucket of water." He led Black away from the pit. Though still a blazing hot day, the slight drop in temperature was a welcome relief.

Hell, he hoped that Alaynia woman had sense enough to stay in the shade and not take shelter in that oven-hot machine again.

"Where's your canteen?" Zeke asked as he followed Shain over to the well. "Done told you over and over not to ride out summertime without water."

"That's part of what I've come here to see Jake about," Shain explained as he dropped the bucket down the well shaft. "I had a canteen, but I forgot it in all the commotion of meeting Jake's new partner."

"New partner?"

As Shain turned the wooden crank to retrieve the bucket, he peered down the dark shaft. "Yeah. Alaynia, she said her name was. Zeke, you're gonna have your hands full here with those two. She's just as crazy as Jake—crazy as one of those hoot owls Jake keeps for pets in that barn."

Shain grabbed the wooden bucket and poured the water into another pail beside the well. Carrying the second bucket over to Black, he stroked the stallion's sweat-wet neck as the horse lowered its head. When he turned back toward the well, Zeke's face was screwed up into a frown that wrinkled it even deeper than usual.

"What's wrong, Zeke?" he asked. "You scared of this Alaynia? Wouldn't blame you if you were. She's one mighty dangerous woman—I found that out for myself."

"Not scared," Zeke denied. "Just wonderin' who she be. Don't know no lady named 'Laynia."

A small, wiry man wandered out of the barn just then, diverting Shain's attention from Zeke. Jake had long ago removed the barn doors, and even most of the front wall. The empty space surrounding him dwarfed his five-foot-four figure, and his nondescript clothing hung on his small frame, blending in with the shadowed recesses behind him. He pulled a once-white handkerchief from his shirt pocket and wiped his face, then ran a hand through the shaggy, gray hair frizzed around his head.

"Zeke!" the man called. "That meat ready yet? I swear you cook that stuff close to the barn just so the smell won't leave me alone. Gives my stomach the grumblies and I can't concentrate on my work."

Shain ambled toward the approaching figure and extended his hand. "Howdy, Jake. Got a few minutes to talk before you eat?"

Jake squinted his eyes. "Shain?" He pulled a pair of half-moon glasses from his other shirt pocket and perched them on his nose, winding the wire arms behind his ears. Belatedly, he reached for Shain's hand. "Shain St. Clair. You haven't been around in a while. What can I do for you, neighbor?"

"All I want is a drink of water for my horse and me," Shain replied. "And to let you know where your latest invention's at, over on the road leading to Chenaie. Black would appreciate your getting it back over here to your place before I have to ride into town again. He refuses to pass it, and—"

"What the heck are you talking about, Shain?" Jake interrupted. "What I'm working on is setting over there in my own barn."

"Then what the hell's that white machine in the ditch over on Chenaie Road?" Shain asked. "And who's the woman driving it around?"

"Woman?" Jake's pale eyes sparkled with indignation behind his glasses. "Some woman's competing with me around here—trying to beat me to my next patent? We'll just see about that. Zeke! Zeke, hitch up the wagon while I fetch my tool box!" Bandy legs pummeling, Jake headed toward the barn again.

"But Mister Jake!" Zeke called after him. "The food be ready now. It's gonna get dried out."

"Tough tittie," Jake yelled back. "Get that blasted mule between the traces, or I'll do it myself!"

Laughter rumbled in Zeke's broad chest and he shot Shain an amused look. "I'd like to see Mister Jake try that again. Last time he did, old Stubborn knocked him for a loop and it was half a hour a'fore he woke up. He laid up two days after that a'fore he could get outta bed."

"Then I'd be obliged if you'd hitch up Stubborn yourself this time," Shain replied. "I'm mighty interested in seeing Jake's reaction when he gets an eyeful of this machine, and we need to keep him conscious for that. Think I'll just follow along and show Jake exactly where it's at."

"Let me get that there meat off a the fire first," Zeke said with a sigh.

"I'll do that. You go catch Stubborn."

Shain rode beside the wagon Zeke drove and explained the circumstances surrounding Alaynia's appearance out of nowhere to Jake. Jake continued to assure him that he had no connection with the strange woman—or her machine. At one point, Jake glanced over at Shain, an astonished look creasing his face.

"She said what?" Jake asked.

"That she has a deed to Chenaie," Shain repeated. "I tell you, Jake, she's as crazy as . . . uh . . ." Shain's words trailed off as a flush covered his face.

"Don't worry, neighbor," Jake said with a chuckle. "I'm well aware that folks around here call me Crazy Jake. They can call me anything they want, long's they leave me alone to work on my inventions. Shoot, Shain, what do people think I live on, if not the money I've already made from selling patents on my inventions?"

"Guess I never thought about it, Jake. Been too busy trying to keep Chenaie afloat."

"You know, Shain," Jake mused. "I'm always looking for

investments—diversifying my money, the banker calls it. All I need's enough to buy parts for whatever I'm working on. You ever need a loan . . ."

"I'm fine, Jake," Shain reassured him, though his thoughts continued around a mental shake of his head. *Sure Jake could loan him money*—the old man had definitely gone around the bend into loony land now, thinking himself rich. Shain had never seen him in anything other than those shabby clothes, which not even the men on his field crew would deign to work in. And the only time any repairs got done on Jake's rundown cabin, Shain had to instruct Chenaie's carpenter to do them. Once in a while, Jeannie returned from one of her frequent visits to Jake and Zeke with a piece of metal for their blacksmith to shape, though, and Jeannie always had a coin or two from Jake to pay the man.

"Lordy God A'mighty!"

Zeke jerked back on the reins, and Stubborn responded with an outraged bray. The mule abruptly sat down in the road, tipping the wagon forward when the traces bent with its body, and hee-hawed its displeasure. Jake and Zeke grabbed the front of the wagon, barely keeping themselves from tumbling straight onto Stubborn's back.

"Zeke!" Jake demanded as he scrambled from the wagon. "The next piece of meat I want to see roasting over your pit is a haunch from that lop-eared son of a bitch's tail end!"

Stubborn swung his head around, and Jake jumped back a foot. The mule's teeth snapped shut a scant inch from Jake's shoulder. Jake danced out of range of Stubborn's reach. "Try to bite me, will you?"

Shain just sat on Black, chuckling under his breath, his gaze traveling back and forth from Zeke's stunned, open-mouthed face to the sight down the road that had triggered the black man's amazement.

Two bare, tanned legs and a shapely rear poked out from beneath the upraised front of the white machine. The rest of the feminine body was ensconced in the compartment holding the engine, which powered the machine. Shain leaned on Black's neck, dangling his reins in his fingers as he waited to see what would happen next.

Appearing only slightly less amazed than Zeke, Jake maintained a good distance between himself and Stubborn as he walked around the animal. Scratching at his frizzy hair, he pursed his lips in thought and studied the scene a hundred yards or so away.

Alaynia wiggled backwards and glared at the car engine. She'd poked. She'd prodded. She'd wiggled those two clamps on the battery, as she'd learned to do in the ladies' mechanic class she once took. She'd even unscrewed that wing-nut thing and looked down inside the air filter thing-a-ma-bob. Nothing worked.

Frustrated, she walked around to the driver's door again and reached inside. Steeling herself to touch the key she'd retrieved from the underbrush, a key which had grown almost too hot to handle from the sun beating through the windshield, she twisted it once again.

Nothing.

"Damn!"

Alaynia straightened and stared down the road, where Shain had disappeared almost an hour ago. This time she saw something other than a lonely dirt trail.

Shain. She recognized him and that horse. Some elderly black guy sat on the seat of a decrepit wagon, which had a dappled mule sitting in front of it. Yes, sitting, not standing. Alaynia shook her head and stared at the other figure.

A few feet in front of the mule stood a short man with Albert Einstein hair. She'd bet her bottom dollar that was Crazy Jake. She started to reach inside for the key ring holding her mace, then withdrew her arm.

The hell with it. She was hot—tired—sweaty—filthy. She'd missed her appointment with the attorney. To top it off, the ice had all melted because she'd neglected to close the cooler lid. Her mineral water and diet drinks were now lukewarm bottles and cans. And she'd broken a fingernail on the can of diet soda she'd opened a minute ago.

She propped her hands on her hips, fists clenched in anger. "Hey!" she yelled toward the group down the road. "Are you going to sit there and amuse yourselves watching me make a fool of myself? Or does one of you big, strong, masculine men have an idea how to get this damned thing running again that my poor little female mind hasn't thought of?"

Shain threw back his head and laughed, then urged Black forward when Jake started walking toward Alaynia. The closer he got, the more he could see of the damage the past hour had done to her. Dust covered her legs, and here and there he noticed scratches. She must have gone chasing after those keys in that short skirt.

His amusement gave way to a sense of guilt. He shouldn't have left her. He could almost hear his dead father's biting voice, chastising him for leaving a lady alone in distress. But his father had probably never in his life run across a woman like this, who could swing whatever weapon she had handy with a deadly aim at incapacitating a man.

Or a woman as immodest, who apparently didn't give a

damn that she was showing more bare skin than was proper anywhere except between a set of silk sheets.

Wrinkles patterned her blue skirt, and she'd pulled her blouse free from the waistband and tied it beneath her breasts. She'd even unbuttoned the top two blouse buttons again. An irrational desire to untie that blouse and jerk the tails down to cover her flat, tanned stomach stole over Shain—along with the urge to shake her silly for having the audacity to denude that much of her body where other male eyes could study it.

Other male eyes? He sure wasn't turning his gaze away from all that feminine flesh. Why the heck should he care if his companions didn't? But a glance back at Zeke showed him ignoring Alaynia and, instead, patting Stubborn. Ahead of Shain's stallion, Jake eagerly scrutinized the machine, paying no attention to the scantily-clad driver.

Alaynia's full breasts heaved in indignation as Shain and Jake approached, and grease smears streaked her face. Her eyes were the only cool thing about her. They glared at Shain, spitting icy chips of fury.

Shain pulled Black to a stop. "You go ahead, Jake. I've already seen that machine."

Jake shrugged and continued on his way. He headed for the front of the machine first, and stuck his head beneath the hood. Turning her back toward Shain with an impudent swing, Alaynia joined the wizened figure.

"You must be Jake," Alaynia said. "I hope you can get this thing started. All I want to do is get back to my hotel room."

Jake whistled under his breath. "Good grief, woman. You didn't put this thing together all by yourself, did you?"

Alaynia closed her eyes briefly in frustration and

clenched her teeth. "Detroit put this *thing*—this *car*, together," she gritted. "I rented this *car* in Baton Rouge. What the heck's wrong with all you men out here in the boondocks? You act like you've never seen a car before."

"Haven't," Jake admitted as he withdrew his head from the engine compartment. "Seen some pictures of horseless carriages the inventors are also calling automobiles. They say they'll carry people around, like Shain said this one did you."

"Car's another name for automobile."

"Duryea sent me a drawing of the one he's working on in a letter a while back," Jake went on as though she hadn't interrupted. "Said he's patterning it after that Benz machine in Germany. But since somebody's already come up with something this refined, I guess the rest of them might's well retire for good. Where'd you say you got this one?"

"Baton Rouge!" Alaynia repeated. The man wasn't only crazy, he was senile—evidently living out his second childhood more than a hundred years in the past. Maybe she ought to feel a little sympathy for him, but right now sarcasm seemed to be the only emotion she had the energy to dredge up.

"You do know there's a city named Baton Rouge south of us, don't you?" she snarled. "Even if you've never been out of the county, surely you've seen it on TV."

"Parish," Jake corrected her. "In Louisiana, they're called parishes, not counties. This is West Feliciana Parish. And don't know as I'd call Baton Rouge a city, even though the townspeople aspire to that some day. Say, what powers this car thing?"

"Oh, for pity sakes." Alaynia shoved a gnarled tendril of hair back from her forehead. "Gasoline. You know, gas, G-A-S. That stuff that comes out of the end of the nozzle when you stop at a service station to fill up?"

"Never heard of that, either," Jake mused. "And what's a TV?"

Alaynia rolled her eyes skyward and breathed out an infuriated breath. Though massive trees shaded each side of the dirt road, the sun beat down mercilessly on the opening where she stood. She glanced over at Shain, who sat a dozen feet away on his huge, black horse. His hair hadn't frazzled in the heat. Indeed, she didn't even see one bead of sweat on his face.

He raised his eyebrows inquiringly, firing her anger further, and Alaynia clamped her teeth shut before she could childishly stick out her tongue at him. Realizing Jake had moved, she turned to see him poking his head inside the driver's door.

"Look," she said to Jake's bent back, deciding to ignore his idiotic question about a television. "Will you please just take me to the nearest phone so I can call Triple-A? My cell phone's on the blink, too."

"Which thing's that?" Jake asked over his shoulder.

"That black receiver on the seat!" Alaynia almost screamed.

Jake backed out of the car with her phone in his hand. "This?"

At Alaynia's nod, he turned the phone over and over, then pushed a couple of the buttons. She snatched it away from him and held it up to his ear.

"See?" she said. "There's just static."

"Sorry," Jake said with a shake of his head. "Unless my ears are getting bad, like my eyes, I don't hear a thing."

Alaynia pressed the phone to her ear. Dead silence. She lowered it, pushed the On button, and tried again. Silence.

Tossing the phone past Jake, onto the seat, she said,

"Figures. Do you have a telephone at your place I can use?" When Jake stared at her with a contemplative look, she softened her tone. "Please?"

"Miss . . . Alaynia, did Shain say your name was?"

"Alaynia Mirabeau, and I apologize for acting like such a bitch," she replied, noticing Jake's frown of disapproval the instant she uttered her last word. "What's wrong now?"

"Well, you have to admit, Miss Mirabeau, that your language is rather . . . ah . . . colorful for a lady."

"I'm hot and tired, damn it! All I want right now is to get back to my hotel and soak in the bathtub. Forget this day ever happened and start all over again tomorrow."

"Have to go to Chenaie if you want a tub bath," Jake told her, a speculative gleam in his eyes. "Zeke and I make do with a wooden wash barrel. And you're not going to like me saying this, but I've got no idea where the closest telephone is. Where in the world did you come from, Miss Mirabeau?"

"Boston," Alaynia said with a tired sigh. "And I wish I'd never left."

"What year?" Jake asked.

"What . . . what year? Why on earth do you want to know that?"

"What year?" Jake repeated patiently.

Alaynia bit her bottom lip worriedly and backed away a step. Crazy. Crazy Jake, and he was just as crazy as the man sitting behind her on that huge horse, wearing outdated clothing.

"Miss Mirabeau," Jake said soothingly. "There are no telephones right now—just telegraphs. And no horseless carriages like your car here. I'm working on a steam-powered harvest machine to use in the hay fields, but it'll be a while before I'm ready to apply for a patent on it. Miss

Mirabeau, the year right now is 1875."

"No," Alaynia breathed, shaking her head and holding her hands out in denial. Good God, he sounded serious. "It's 2005. I've got proof. I'll show you!"

She shoved past Jake and bent inside the car to grab her briefcase, then ducked back out of the car in time to see Jake gesture to Shain. Shain dismounted and, after tying the horse's reins around a nearby bush, sauntered up to the car. She swung the door shut and laid the briefcase on the car roof.

"Here." Alaynia turned with the sheaf of papers in her hands, shaking them under Jake's nose. "Here's the deed to Chenaie that Miss Tilda's lawyer sent me." She shuffled through the papers to the last page and held it out. "See? Right there, the date. It says June 29, 2005. It's signed by her lawyer as personal representative of Miss Tilda's estate. He recorded it and sent me a copy."

Shain stared over Jake's shoulder. "That's what it says, Jake. What do you make of it?"

"I'm no lawyer," Jake replied, "but a 2005 deed doesn't seem to me to be worth the paper it's written on in 1875."

"Damn it, it's 2005!" Alaynia said with a stamp of her foot. She turned her glare on Shain, but he shook his head in both rejection of her assertion and confirmation of Jake's contention.

"Miss Mirabeau, have you been assisting someone who's working on a time travel machine?" Jake asked. "If so, I'd be mighty interested in spending a while with you before you return to wherever you came from."

For a brief second, Alaynia closed her eyes. The combination of the heat, her dead car, and the frustration of having to deal with two males obviously trying to delude her drained her stamina totally. What on earth could they be getting out of trying to scare her like that? They had their act down so pat, she'd even felt a tinge of belief for a second.

Opening her eyes, she said stubbornly, "It's 2005. You two can cut the crap now. One of you go call a mechanic for me, or else get the hell out of my way so I can go myself."

Jake stepped in front of her in a movement Alaynia took as threatening rather than protective. She gasped in fear, stared past the smaller man at the larger barrier Shain's muscular body made to any escape attempt she might make, and fell back against the car door. She covered her face with trembling hands, but despite her attempt to trap it in her throat, a sob escaped. Another one followed, and she clenched her fingers tighter, tears continuing to trickle past her hold.

"Damn it, don't." Shain moved around Jake and pulled Alaynia into his arms. She buried her head against his chest, shoulders heaving and sobs escalating, and he glanced help-lessly at Jake as he patted her on the back.

Jake's explanation made about as much sense as any-thing he'd heard so far. She *had* appeared out of thin air— amid a screech and cacophony of sound and smell that de-fied any other rationalization. She hadn't passed Fitzroy on her journey—the carpetbagger's horse would have bolted back toward Chenaie, if it had encountered her car.

He didn't believe some of the rumors circulating about Chenaie, but Jake seemed definite about the possibility of this time travel concept. The things she had with her—how could they be explained otherwise? Her clothing—or rather lack of it. His palm brushed the bare skin on her back, the jolt of sensation triggering his groin's tightening and the swelling against his trouser front once again. Damn, did all women where she came from exude the type of sexuality that could bring a man to readiness so quickly—or was there something special flowing between the two of them?

He groaned under his breath and, after a glance at the thing on the ground she'd called a cooler, shifted his leg around to position it between her thighs as he continued to hold her. She snuggled even closer, and the hot streak of desire spread from his groin through the rest of his body. Only Jake's presence kept him from making a total fool of himself as a vision of her spread out on the back seat of that car with her bare legs wrapped around his waist flashed through his mind.

With a supreme effort, he dredged up some semblance of control. "She's had too much to handle today," he told Jake in a quiet voice. "I'd better take her to Chenaie. Do you really think she got here through a time machine?"

Alaynia pushed back in Shain's arms and pounded on his chest. "I. Flew. Here. On. A. Plane!" She punctuated each word with a thump, swiped the heels of her hands beneath her streaming eyes, and continued, "I stayed at a hotel in Baton Rouge last night and rented a car this morning from Hertz! I was supposed to meet Miss Tilda's lawyer at ten o'clock, but I got lost! I . . . I . . ."

Suddenly Alaynia's mouth dropped open and her tear-misted blue eyes stared up at Shain, filled with deepening alarm. "The mirage. It . . . it couldn't have been. Could it?"

"What mirage?" Shain asked.

After a calming breath, Alaynia appeared to get a slight measure of control over her emotions again. Instead of replying to Shain, she looked down the road at the wagon. The dappled mule was on its feet, and the elderly black man stroked its neck.

She turned toward Crazy Jake, who met her gaze without

evasion, paying close attention to every word she spoke. That left Shain, and he stood patiently as she cautiously removed his arms from her waist and stepped back to study him.

Then she pinched her wrist severely.

"Don't do that!" Shain grabbed her hand and held it. "You've already got enough scratches and bruises on yourself." He tenderly traced a darkening spot on her arm. "What happened there?"

"I hit it on the cooler when I fell," she answered distractedly.

Shain placed a finger under her chin and gently drew her gaze to his. "You've had a rough day, Alaynia," he said quietly. "I'll take you to Chenaie, and you can rest. Get a bath and something to eat. But I'm afraid you're still going to have to wait out of sight until I can get you something decent to wear from my sister, Jeannie."

And as soon as he got her off his hands at the manor house, he was going to turn right back around and have a nice, long, private talk with Jake. Either the inventor had gone completely bonkers, or maybe, just maybe, Jake was right. After all, Jake had come up with his explanation without even seeing Alaynia's arrival himself, though he had informed the inventor of the aspects of it.

Alaynia's mind whirled. *Better to just go along with them. Find some way to get back to Baton Rouge and sanity. Maybe that old black man will take me in his wagon.*

Shain's clothing reminded her of what those almost-too-handsome-to-be-real men wore on the covers of the historical romance novels she loved to read. The first thing she had thought of when she received the letter notifying her that she was the sole surviving heir of Miss Tilda's estate had been how exciting it would be to actually live in one of those old Southern mansions.

But not in the actual year of one of the time periods she enjoyed reading about!

This had to be some sort of farce. She was probably still lying over there in her car—knocked unconscious despite the airbag.

She hesitantly looked over at the car seat, almost expecting to see a twin to her own body slumped over the wheel. Empty. Well, shoot, yes, the seat was empty. She'd been in and out of it a dozen times today. That didn't mean anything, though. She never saw herself in her dreams—she only experienced the sensations in the nighttime delusions.

Mentally exhausted with trying to battle her confusion and ever-increasing fear, she had no choice but to go along with the charade the men were obviously acting out—at least until she could get back to . . .

Back to where? her mind asked. Surely she wasn't starting to believe that crazy inventor. Somewhere there had to be a sane person in all this madness.

"What—?" Alaynia cleared her dry throat. "What sort of clothing does your sister wear?"

"Like I said, something decent," Shain replied. "Something that covers her up ten times more than what you're wearing."

Alaynia stiffly brushed his hands aside and walked over to the car. She reached inside for her key ring and carried it with her to the trunk, where she inserted it in the lock and twisted it. The trunk lid lifted to expose a clutter of garment bags, suitcases, and boxes. She pulled her large suitcase toward her and unsnapped the clasps.

"I had Patti, a seamstress friend of mine, make these for me before I left Boston," she said. "I had some stupid idea that I'd feel more at home in Miss Tilda's house dressed like a simpering Southern belle."

She removed a light, cotton, floor-length gown covered in tiny, pink rosebuds and shook it out before she held it up in front of her. "Will this do?" she asked Shain.

"Do you have some petticoats and proper underthings?"

"I am not going to swelter myself in this heat," Alaynia said with a determined tilt of her chin. "And, before you ask, I did *not* bring a corset with me. Patti also makes costumes for some of the playhouse wardrobe mistresses, and I tried one of those damn things on once. You can forget that! No wonder Southern women were always swooning. I've even read that corsets were the reason so many women died in childbirth. The blasted things were laced so tight they sometimes broke women's ribs and they healed crooked. Broke again in childbirth."

"Can you maybe tone down your language a little?" Shain asked in an amused voice. "*Southern* women don't curse."

"I'll try," Alaynia promised as she looked around for a place to change clothes. "Think you guys could turn your backs?"

"I'm glad to see modesty has still survived in the future," Shain said with a chuckle as he complied.

Glancing around the trunk lid, Alaynia saw that Jake had returned to his eager examination of the engine compartment and had his head buried inside it again. Still, she kept the trunk lid raised while she slipped off her soiled clothing and shimmied into the gown. One thing she had insisted that Patti change from actual adherence to earlier fashion was zippers instead of buttons up the backs of the gowns. She managed to slide the gown closed on her own, then lifted the hem to stare at her shoes.

She had two pair of flimsy slippers in the bag, which she had bought after studying some old *Godey's Lady's Books*, *Peterson's*, and *Graham's* that Patti loaned her from the theater's research material—and a pair of riding boots to match the habit Patti had made for her. The long gown would cover her footwear, though. After glancing at Shain's back, she dug in another bag for her running shoes and replaced her heels with them. Smoothing the dress skirt, she called around the trunk lid, "I'm ready. Will you at least take my bags with you?"

"Maybe you'd better just put what you think you'll need in that one large case there," Shain replied. "We'll have Jake drop that one off at Chenaie, and take the rest of your things over to his place."

"Why?" Alaynia demanded. "I'll need my clothing, and it's scattered through all my bags."

"You better just pick out the clothing you say you had your friend make and whatever's suitable for our servants to see. They're in and out of the bedrooms cleaning."

Alaynia muttered her dislike of his mandate, but bent back into the trunk and spent a few minutes transferring articles into the large suitcase. When she finally snapped it shut, she inserted her luggage key and locked the case. Swiping backhanded at the beads of sweat covering her forehead, she lifted the heavy suitcase to the ground and slammed the trunk shut.

"Miss Mirabeau?" Jake walked up to them, seeming unaware of her change in attire. "I'd be glad to borrow another mule from Shain and tow your machine to my place. Keep it for you until you're ready to use it again."

"It's not going to do me any good like that," Alaynia said. "Go ahead. But I want all my things kept safe."

"I'll take care of them." Jake rubbed his hands together,

probably in anticipation of having privacy to study the machine he for some reason thought came from the future. "And you can come over anytime you want to see your . . . uh . . . car."

"I'll do that," Alaynia promised in a stern voice. "So don't you dare remove anything from it—or take anything apart. Somehow, that thing's got to get me out of here, after I figure out how it brought me here. Unless," she added in a voice lacking conviction, "you two are willing to admit you've been making a fool of me about what year it is and help me get back to Baton Rouge."

"I'm sorry, but it really is 1875," Jake told her solemnly, though he couldn't quite hide the excitement in his bright eyes. "But I promise that I'll take very, very good care of your car."

"Please do," Alaynia breathed in tired resignation.

Jake turned away and motioned to Shain. "Let me show you the engine in this thing," he said. "Then we can load her things in the wagon."

As soon as the men both bent their heads beneath the hood, Alaynia took a deep breath, hiked up her skirts, and ran.

Chapter 6

It had to be here somewhere. Alaynia kept running, eyes searching ahead of her for the mirage. Not that she really believed those demented men who thought she'd traveled through time, but the mirage had to be connected somehow to the confusing events of the past hours. It was the last thing she'd seen on the asphalt road, which just had to be here somewhere, too. Surely the paved highway would lead her back to sane civilization.

After several hundred yards, a stitch jabbed in her side. Darn it, her three-times-weekly jogs around the inside track at the air-conditioned health club hadn't prepared her for the exertion of running through this heat. She jammed a hand against the pain in her side and kept going.

Her mind told her there was no way the asphalt road could be this far away—even traveling at highway speed, her car couldn't have slid this distance. Sweat poured down her face and her chest heaved, her breasts straining against the tight dress bodice. Still the dirt road stretched ahead of her, and she passed no opening that could have been a driveway leading to a house somewhere.

Bright dots danced in front of her eyes, and Alaynia stumbled to a stop.

"Stupid," she murmured around her gasps for breath. "You just suffered one bout in this heat, Mirabeau. Next thing you know, you'll end up in a hospital."

Even her head was pounding. Swaying unsteadily, she

reached around and lifted her hair from the back of her neck to let the perspiration evaporate. The pounding grew louder, and she groaned under her breath as she recognized hoofbeats. As surely as though she had eyes in the back of her head, she knew what the noise meant. Turning, she faced the rider on the black horse defiantly.

Shain pulled the horse to a halt. He dangled the canteen he'd had when she woke up in his arms by the strap. Temptingly, he swung it back and forth.

"It's five miles from where you took off running into St. Francisville, the closest town," he drawled in that lazy voice. "You want to borrow this for the trip?"

Mouth thinned in anger, Alaynia stomped forward and swiped the canteen from his grasp. She twisted the top free and took a greedy swallow, then poured some water into her cupped hand and splashed it around her neck. Replacing the lid, she swung the strap over her shoulder and began walking down the road at a slower pace.

"Thanks," she called back. "I'll ask someone to return the canteen to you later."

After a second, she heard the horse's hooves again. Instead of receding, the sound kept pace with her. She stiffened her shoulders and refused to glance behind her, kept walking, staying in the shade along the tree-lined roadway. For what she judged to be about an eighth of a mile—once around the health club track—her irritation continued to mount. The horse plodded along in her wake at the same, steady pace, never narrowing the gap nor attempting to pass her. And never stopping.

She paused to take another swallow from the canteen and the hoofbeats paused. When she resumed her forward march, the plop of hooves continued. Gritting her teeth, she kept her eyes resolutely ahead of her, ears hopefully straining for the sound of a car engine coming down the road.

Instead, she heard only birds in the overhead branches. Once a blue jay streaked across the road, its shrieks of annoyance at her intrusion mirroring her own growing vexation. The same tangled underbrush she'd had to wade through in search of her keys grew beneath the huge trees, negating any thought of moving off the roadway. The horse's hooves plopped.

Soon she realized one of the sounds she'd thought was a bird also kept pace with her. The whistle rose and fell in the cadence of a tune, which imitated the beat of a Sousa march. As soon as she realized her steps were matching the beat, she clenched her fists and whirled.

The horse tossed its head at her unexpected movement, but Shain tightened the reins and casually leaned his arm on the stallion's neck. "Had enough walking?" he asked.

"Damn it! Go away, will you? I can take care of myself!"

"Sure you can," he said agreeably. "You've been doing real good so far."

"Look, you just go on back there with your friend Jake and make sure my car's there for me when I get back from St. Francisville with a mechanic. I'll handle things on this end."

"Only mechanic I know in this entire parish is Jake," Shain said with a slow grin. "Closest thing you'll find in St. Francisville is a blacksmith. You bring him out here to look at that car machine, he'll probably go back and send the parish sheriff out to pick you up—ship you down to New Orleans to an asylum."

"I am *not* crazy," Alaynia gritted. "You and Jake are the ones who're out of your minds—trying to convince me that it's 1875."

Shain shook his head sadly. "The only reason I'm not carting you into town myself and shipping you off is because I saw you appear. And I've spent enough time with Jake to know there's changes coming up. Who's to say that one of them isn't a time machine, which could've brought you back here from the future?"

"My car is not a time machine!"

"Well, the year sure as hell isn't 2005," Shain said with a shrug. "And you're sure as hell real, so there's got to be some explanation. But if you go running around in St. Francisville, spouting off about it being 2005 to people who didn't see you appear out of thin air like I did, you can bet that cute bottom of yours that you'll end up in a nuthouse. You better come on back to Chenaie with me."

"And just how will you explain me to the rest of the people you say live at Chenaie?" Alaynia demanded with a toss of her head. "Since you seem to have it fixed in your mind that I've appeared out of nowhere?"

"Been thinking about it while I followed you," Shain mused. "Figured we'd say you were Jake's niece. You came out here to surprise him—found out he didn't really have an appropriate place for you to live while you visited him. I'm doing the neighborly thing and letting you stay at Chenaie."

"That's mighty obliging of you, since Chenaie belongs to me."

"That's another thing you're gonna have to keep quiet about. Look, they used to burn witches at the stake up North. And there's enough voodoo practitioners left among the Negroes to get people spooked, if you go on insisting that you're from over a hundred years in the future. It could be mighty dangerous for you around here, Alaynia, unless you listen to me."

Alaynia swallowed a new stab of fear. This couldn't be

happening. The mirage couldn't have been a time warp. Things like that only happened in people's imaginations.

"Take me into St. Francisville," she pleaded. "I'll decide what to do from there."

"Don't be stupid," Shain said, evidently losing his patience. "I've got a plantation to run, and I don't have time to waste protecting you in town. Besides, you probably don't have a dime of spendable money to use to get a place to stay. Jake's your only hope of figuring out how to get back to wherever you came from—and I'm the only one who can protect you while he works on that."

Alaynia twisted around to stare down the road. It stretched endlessly ahead of her. If Shain was telling the truth, it would still be another four-and-a-half-mile walk into town—four and a half miles of suffering in this humid heat. Besides, Chenaie was where she'd been heading anyway. Maybe at her planned destination, she could reason out this mess.

"I still don't believe you," she said as she faced Shain again. "It's going to take more than just your saying so to prove to me that I've traveled back in time."

"Suit yourself." Shain turned his horse around and started back down the road. "When you come to your senses, anyone can tell you where Chenaie is."

"Wait!" Overlooking her long skirts, Alaynia took a stumbling step after him. Her hem ripped and she jerked her skirt higher. When she glanced up, she saw Shain turn the horse sideways and extend a hand to her.

"I . . ." Shrugging her shoulders in defeat, Alaynia trudged toward him. "I guess maybe I'll go have a look at Chenaie."

Shain withdrew his hand when she reached for it. "First you have to promise you'll go along with the story I made up. Hopefully, Jake will get your machine hidden in his barn before anyone sees it. He values his privacy, so his place is back where no one bothers him, but I want your word that you'll keep quiet about the rest of this."

"I don't have much choice at this point," Alaynia spat. She swept a sweat-matted curl from her cheek. "Otherwise, you'll leave me standing here in this heat to die."

Shain chuckled under his breath and held out his hand again, removing his booted foot from the stirrup at the same time. "Suppose that will have to do," he said as she placed her hand in his. "Always did admire a plucky woman. I think you and Jeannie are gonna get along fine."

Alaynia swung up behind the saddle. Squirming, she adjusted her skirts, then grabbed his waist as the horse started off. Almost immediately, she adjusted to the horse's smooth gait and dropped her hold to the saddle cantle, unconsciously flexing her fingers at the lingering feel of the firmness of Shain's muscles.

Shain glanced over his shoulder. "Appears you've been on a horse before."

"I've ridden, yes," Alaynia replied shortly.

"Southern women usually ride sidesaddle."

"Women in 2005 ride astride," Alaynia countered. "It's a heck of a lot safer."

"That's what Jeannie keeps trying to tell me," Shain admitted before turning his concentration back to the road ahead of them. "Why don't you tell me a little about yourself while we travel?" he asked. "Where'd you learn to ride?"

"At the orphanage," Alaynia replied bluntly. When Shain shifted around with a sympathetic look on his face, she stared steadily back at him. "I didn't even know I had a Great-Aunt Tilda until a couple months ago. In fact, I didn't know I had any relatives at all."

"And since your great-aunt passed on," Shain said, "I guess that leaves you alone again."

"I'm used to it," Alaynia said with a shrug. "I've been alone for a long time."

Black tossed his head up and whinnied loudly, side-stepping across the roadway, and Alaynia threw her arms around Shain. She held on even after he steadied the horse and pulled it to a halt. Beneath her tightly clenched legs, she could feel the stallion trembling.

"Snake slithered across the road," Shain said quietly. "Black hates them. Sit still for a second, until Black realizes the thing's gone."

Alaynia clenched her arms tighter, burying her face on his broad back. Not only the horse hated snakes. Despite the muscled barrier of Shain's back, she could feel her skin crawl as she thought of how frightened she'd been digging through the underbrush after her keys—the keys this man had tossed into that dangerous territory.

Gritting her teeth, Alaynia pushed herself upright again. "You didn't worry about snakes when you made sure I had to go after my keys."

"I didn't think you'd be foolish enough to pull a stunt like that. I told you I'd be back with Jake."

"Crazy Jake!" Alaynia said with a huff. "And you were acting just as crazy as you said Jake was. What did you expect me to do—wait there for you to bring back another demented person for me to deal with?"

Shain nudged a willing Black forward once more, shaking his head as he rode. "Looking back on it, I can see how I probably scared you," he half-apologized in a grudging voice. "But I'm afraid our code of manners in the South doesn't contain any rules for dealing with strangely-clad women from the future, who appear bent on emasculating us."

Alaynia drew in an indignant breath, but Shain continued, "What do you do for a living? You must be . . . what . . . twenty-five? Been out of the orphanage for a while, I guess."

"I'm a historical interior designer," Alaynia replied, a tiny smirk on her face. He'd missed her age by five years, and her thirtieth birthday was still fresh enough in her mind for her to derive a certain satisfaction at his misjudgment. She'd spent her entire twenty-ninth year dreading the upcoming milestone—looking back on how much she hadn't accomplished and realizing that ahead of her stretched out more months—years—of penny-pinching and browbeating contractors into finishing their jobs on time. More than once, she'd raced to get her final check from her current job in the bank a day before the electric company turned off her power.

The health club had been her one extravagance. No, not an extravagance, she reminded herself. People expected a woman interior designer to look sharp—reflect the image they were paying her to style into their surroundings. She always managed the dues somehow, but her stomach churned every time she thought of peanut butter and celery sticks . . .

". . . don't you think?" she heard Shain say.

"Uh . . . sorry." Alaynia pulled her thoughts back to Louisiana. "I'm afraid my mind was wandering. What did you say?"

"I asked if you didn't think that was a better job for a woman than being an inventor, like Jake thought you were when I first told him about you. We always allow our women pretty much of a free rein to decorate, once a house is up—within what we can afford, anyway. Gives them something to occupy their time when they aren't busy with the children."

"And just how many children do you have, Mr. St. Clair?" Alaynia asked in a deceptively sweet voice.

"Since I'm not married, I'd have to answer that none," Shain said with a chuckle. "And I thought we'd been calling each other by our given names."

"Then I guess your sister . . . Jeannie, did you say her name was? Does Jeannie have children?"

"Jeannie's only fourteen. I haven't even begun looking for a husband for her yet, but in a couple years . . ."

"How old are you?" Alaynia demanded.

"Thirty-two." Shain shifted around to look at her again. "What's all this got to do with your being a decorator?"

"A *woman* designer," Alaynia gritted. "A proper job for an unmarried old maid, isn't that what you're implying?"

Shain's face creased in puzzlement, but before he could answer, Alaynia went on, "If you think all I do is pick out pretty curtains and furniture covers, you're mistaken, *Mister* St. Clair! I've got a degree in architecture, and I've washed more sawdust out of my hair than you'll probably ever see in your life! I restore old buildings to their former grandeur, and my business cards read, 'Architectural Restorationist.' I'm also not married because I *choose* not to be married! If and when I decide I'd like to share my life with a child—that I can afford to raise one—I'm perfectly capable of having one on my own, without a man intruding in my life!"

"That ought to be a hell of a trick," Shain scoffed. "You'll have to tell me sometime how women in the future procreate, without a man around to help accomplish the conception."

Alaynia lifted her chin to reply, but Shain turned back to

face the road. "Right now, we're coming into Chenaie, so remember who you're supposed to be. Jeannie's too smart for her own good at times, and we're gonna have to be on our toes to make sure she doesn't trip us up in our story."

Alaynia peered around his shoulder, dismissing her outrage at his chauvinistic attitude as new worries crowded her mind. Ahead of her, acre after acre of cleared fields stretched on both sides of the road. She recognized cotton plants in the rows closest to her, but beyond them were plants she hadn't seen before. Several mules pulled plows through the rows of plants, and behind each driver walked a man with a hoe, chopping at stray weeds.

"What do you grow here besides cotton?" she asked Shain.

"Planted some sugar cane a couple years ago," he told her. "But it's not making a profit yet."

The road curved just ahead, and as soon as they rode around the bend, Alaynia saw the plantation house at the end of a dirt lane lined with Spanish-moss-draped trees. She drew in an astonished breath, recalling the pictures the attorney had forwarded to her, which he'd written were taken after her great-aunt's death. This was definitely not the decrepit structure she'd anticipated.

The road beneath the tree-shaded lane wasn't weed-choked, and no tire tracks or hoof prints broke the evenly-distributed expanse of dirt. Closer to the front veranda, a smooth lawn lay in green splendor, and rose bushes riotous with blooms lined the entire front of the house. The drive curved in a circle in front of the house. Inside the circular area, neat flagstone paths wound between more plants, and here and there small, weathered statues were set on pedestals.

A spindle railing across the front porch shone bright

white, a perfect backdrop for the red, yellow, and white colors. On each side of the steps and both edges of the porch, huge columns supported an upper balcony. Windows sparkled with sunlight, and she couldn't see even an inch of peeling paint. Yet it was the same house—her architectural eye left no doubt of that.

"It's Chenaie," she breathed.

"Hell, yes, it's Chenaie," Shain said as he reined the horse to a halt in the wide sweep of drive in front of the veranda. Swinging his leg across the stallion's neck, he jumped to the ground and turned to reach up for Alaynia. "I told you that's where we were going, didn't I?"

Ignoring his outstretched arms, Alaynia continued staring at the plantation house. It stood there in the splendor she had visualized when she had superimposed her imagination over the recent pictures. Growing fear clawed at her with sharp tentacles. Out on the dirt road, it had been easier to contradict Shain and Jake's contention that she was a time traveler. Here at Chenaie—her Chenaie, which was already restored to the grandeur she'd thought she would have to bring it back to herself—she found irrefutable proof of their insistence. There was no other possible explanation, unless . . .

Gulping back her terror, Alaynia slipped a sideways look down at Shain.

"Are you going to get down?" he asked.

"Ghosts," she breathed. "You all have to be ghosts. I . . . I died when the car crashed, didn't I?"

"I assure you, Alaynia," Shain said with a chuckle, "everyone here at Chenaie is very much alive, including you. Well, almost everyone. And you saw that your car wasn't damaged—it just won't run."

Alaynia's eyes continued to widen in panic as he reached

83

up and lifted her from the horse. When she tried to struggle free, he held her even more tightly in his embrace, trying to calm her fear.

"Whoa, now," he said. "I thought you'd already figured out that you had nowhere else to run."

"Please," Alaynia responded with a whimper. "Please let me go home. I'm not ready to be dead yet."

"Hey." Shain pulled her closer and cupped her chin in one palm. "What brought that on? No one's gonna hurt you here at Chenaie. Look, I know we got off on the wrong foot, but I haven't given you any reason to be afraid of me, have I?"

Terror stricken, Alaynia stared into his brown eyes, searching for the spark of madness that would be her total undoing. Slowly she became aware of the tenderness she found there instead—the concern for her fear. His thumb gently stroked her cheek, and she fought the urge to rest her cheek on his broad shoulder, bury herself in the haven from the surrounding dementia she sensed he could give her.

Something in Shain sparked in response, and he slowly murmured, "I won't let anything hurt you, Alaynia. I'll take care of you. Don't be afraid."

"But I am afraid," she admitted with a little moan of despair. "Terribly afraid. What's happened to me?"

Desperately she clung to him, closing her eyes in denial, still fighting the knowledge of her unexplainable predicament. She felt his hand in her hair, his firm arm holding her close. Right then his body was the only thing standing between her and the nineteenth century she had tumbled into, and she urgently needed something to bolster her failing courage.

Shain stroked her hair, tangling his fingers in it. She trembled against him, the defiance she had faced him with earlier buried beneath her raging panic.

"Alaynia, honey." The endearment penetrated her cloud of terror as he laid his chin on her head. "Listen to me. I can't explain what's happened any more than you can. But I'll help you face it. I won't leave you to handle it on your own."

"You don't understand." Alaynia pulled back in his arms to study his face. "This can't be happening. You're . . . you're not real in my world. You're . . ." Drawing in a breath, she forced herself to continue, "You're dead. If you were alive in my time, you'd . . . you'd be over a hundred and sixty years old!"

Brown eyes crinkling in amusement, Shain lifted his hand from her hair and touched his face. "Nope, I'm still alive. I can feel myself." He touched her face next. "And you're real, too. Very, very real."

Hesitantly, Alaynia covered his hand with her own, then reached up to feel the side of his face with her other hand. The blue-black shadow of his beard rasped against her palm, and she traced the firm line of his chin with her fingertips. When her index finger brushed his lower lip, the softness contrasted with the semi-roughness of his face. He bent his head slowly, and she willingly lifted her mouth to meet his.

No ghost could have kissed her like that—sipping just a taste at first, feathering a faint brush of his tongue across her lips, then catching her mouth more fully with firmer pressure. No ghost could have such a solid chest and shoulders—a faintly sweat-slick neck beneath her touch. No figment of her imagination could have sent such an intense, unexpected spiral of desire curling through her veins—brought that little whimper of need from her and answered it with a moan of demand for more of his own.

Curling her fingers in his hair and her other arm around

his neck, Alaynia leaned against him and he tightened his embrace in return. His kiss deepened, drawing her further into the sensations flowing between them. When he lifted his head a long moment later, she languidly raised her eyelids to meet his desire-laden gaze.

"Maybe you are a witch," Shain whispered. "You've bewitched me from the first second I saw you getting out of that machine."

"Ahem!"

Alaynia jerked from Shain's arms, and a flush of embarrassment immediately replaced the heat of desire on her cheeks. A teenage girl stood barely five feet from them, her arms crossed over her chest and a slippered foot patting the ground beneath the hem of her white gown. Blue eyes under a mop of golden curls fixed Alaynia with a disdainful look, but Alaynia thought she detected a twinkle of mirth in the disdain. The girl's lips appeared to be struggling against a tendency to curve in laughter.

"Brother," she drawled sweetly to Shain, "am I to take this as a new lesson on how to greet our guests at Chenaie? The next time Billy Ben comes over, I'd sure like to impress him with knowing how to show hospitality in a modern way."

"You do and I'll haul you out to the woodshed," Shain threatened. "After I knock young Billy Ben on his ass, of course."

The girl threw back her head and laughed, then propped her hands on slim hips and cocked her head to one side. "You'd have to ask Lee's army for help in dragging me to that woodshed, brother dear. You don't have the heart to do it yourself."

"Well, I wouldn't be that lenient with Billy Ben, sister, dear," Shain warned in only a half-teasing tone. "I want you to meet Alaynia Mirabeau, Jeannie. Alaynia, this is my bratty little sister."

"Hello, Jeannie," Alaynia said, extending her hand.

Jeannie looked puzzled for a moment, then reached out to meet Alaynia's grasp. "Pleased, I'm sure," she murmured. "Do all women where you come from shake hands like men do?"

Realizing her mistake, Alaynia threw a pleading look for assistance at Shain.

"Alaynia's from Boston," Shain said, avoiding a direct response to Jeannie's question. "Has Jake already been by here?"

"He dropped off a strange-looking case and said he needed to borrow a mule," Jeannie confirmed with a shrug. "I asked him what he needed the mule for, but he was acting really strange, even for Jake. He said you'd explain when you got here."

"My . . . uh . . ." Alaynia quickly marshaled her thoughts. "The road we came here on was empty," she said to Shain, hoping he would get her meaning. "I didn't see my Uncle Jake."

"We came down a different fork," Shain explained. His admonishing glance told her that he realized she was asking the whereabouts of her car, but warned her to let him tell their prepared story himself. "I guess you didn't notice, since you were riding behind me."

"Jake's your uncle?" Jeannie asked. "Gee, I've known him almost all my life, but he never mentioned having a niece. And what on earth are you doing, making Alaynia ride over here to visit on your horse, Shain? Surely it wouldn't have been that much of an inconvenience for you to come back and get our buggy."

As Shain nonchalantly drawled the false tale of Alaynia's

background to his sister in a convincing manner, Alaynia bit her lower lip in anxiety. Her own feminine instincts told her that Jeannie was absorbing everything with a tinge of disbelief which, despite her young years, she managed to cover up—at least to Shain. Still, Alaynia had read enough about Southern customs in this century to realize that Jeannie was mulling over the discrepancies in Alaynia's arrival. A proper Southern lady, planning to stay for a while, would have arrived in a buggy piled with her trunks. Shain's words about Jeannie's sharpness replayed in her mind, but right now she could only go along with the charade.

She studied Jeannie's white, ground-length gown. The long sleeves came all the way down to her slender wrists, and the slightly scooped neck bared only a scant expanse of skin, covering even Jeannie's collarbones. Thank God she'd had Patti make her the nineteenth-century outfits, even though she'd had absolutely no concept of the use she would put the clothing to when she ordered it. But at least she hadn't arrived wearing something Jeannie would consider scandalous—or had to explain why she didn't have clothing of her own to the young girl.

Then, recalling Jeannie's slippered foot, Alaynia glanced down to make sure her running shoes were hidden beneath the hem of her own gown.

"I would think not," she became aware of Jeannie's saying, and concentrated on the young girl again. "Why, Alaynia couldn't possibly stay over there with Jake and Zeke. Didn't you write to your uncle first and tell him that you were coming, Alaynia?"

"Uh . . . I did, but when I didn't hear back from him, I just assumed it was all right to come visit," Alaynia said hurriedly.

"But what about your family in Boston?" Jeannie

prodded. "Surely they didn't let you go off on your own without being assured you'd have a place with a relative at the end of your trip?"

"Alaynia doesn't have any other family," Shain put in. "And you're forgetting your manners again, little sister. It's awfully darned hot out here, and it's not very polite to make our guest stand out here and endure your inquisition."

"Oh, I'm sorry," Jeannie apologized. "Let's go inside, Alaynia. I'll get you something cool to drink and then show you up to the Rose Room. It's right next to mine."

"No, you won't give her the Rose Room, Jeannie," Shain contradicted sternly. "You'd be popping in and out of it every chance you got. Show her to the Camellia Room, where she'll have some privacy."

"That room's right next to yours, Shain," Jeannie replied. "But then, you're never home, so I guess you won't be intruding."

Jeannie flounced around and headed for the porch steps, but Alaynia didn't follow at first. "Aren't you coming in?" she asked Shain.

"I need to go over to Jake's to get his agreement to go along with our story. Thank God he didn't let anything slip while he was here."

"Yes," Alaynia conceded worriedly. "Still, I don't think Jeannie believes us completely. And what am I going to do while you're gone? What if I screw up somehow and make her more suspicious? Shain . . ."

Shain placed his hands on her shoulders. "We don't have any choice, Alaynia. If you run into any problems, just allude to the differences in your backgrounds. Jeannie's only fourteen. You ought to be able to handle this."

"But there are other people I'll have to contend with, too. You said you had a cook, and other servants."

"Alaynia," Jeannie called from the porch. "Are you coming? You don't even have a bonnet on. You shouldn't stay out in the sun so long—you'll get freckles."

Ignoring Alaynia's pleading look, Shain gently squeezed her shoulders before he removed his hands. "I won't be gone long," he promised.

Alaynia waited until he mounted his stallion and started back down the driveway. Then she stiffened her shoulders, walked over, and climbed the veranda steps. Jeannie stood holding the door open, and just before Alaynia went through it, she turned and glanced down the driveway. Shain had pulled his horse to a halt, and he waved briefly at her when he caught her look. Despite the distance separating them, Alaynia thought she also saw him nod his head in reassurance.

Turning, she walked ahead of Jeannie into the huge manor house she had set out to find earlier in the day. Only she entered as a visitor, instead of as its owner, as she had anticipated.

Chapter 7

Francesca and Sylvia watched Alaynia disappear into the house, and Sylvia grumbled, "Now, you tell me, Frannie. How can you maintain an emotional distance over this? Alaynia's scared to death, and if she should fall in love with Shain, why, think what could happen! They could end up separated, with her beyond his reach in the future!"

"Good heavens, Sylvia. They've just met."

"Yeah, and there's already sparks flying between them. And you saw that kiss. It was so tender—so sweet. Shain didn't just kiss her to calm her—he kissed her because he's been wanting to do that since the second she stepped out of that car."

"Our assignment is to talk to Basil, Sylvia. Not to get involved in any relationship between Shain and Alaynia."

"Frannie, how are we gonna reason with this ghost fellow if we can't even find him?" Sylvia asked in exasperation. "I've never dealt with one of these human spirits before—a ghost who stayed on earth. He's evidently got a measure of power in his state of being. But, geez, how can he get away with being such a . . . a demon?"

"That's one of the things we'll have to figure out—why he's acting like this," Francesca explained, attempting to ignore Sylvia's first question. "Something's happened to change Basil. He's not a demon, Sylvia, but he's definitely acting differently than the loving grandfather that Shain remembers."

"But we have to find him and pin him down long enough to talk to, in order to figure out why, don't we?" Sylvia repeated.

"Of course we do," Francesca admitted grudgingly.

"And that's not gonna be easy, is it? We can't even see him if he doesn't want us to, can we? We've been looking all over this plantation for him."

"We'll just have to look again. Come on."

Francesca flew from Chenaie's roof and, after rolling her eyes briefly in irritation, Sylvia followed. First they flew into the sprawling barn and explored every nook and cranny of the enormous loft, with Francesca checking one end, where broken farm implements and open crates of worn-out harnesses and saddles were stored. Sylvia investigated the other side, searching among the bales of hay in neat piles, waiting to be cut open and forked down to the stalls lining the bottom story of the barn. She poked her head over one bale and let out a cry of delight.

"What?" Francesca said, immediately appearing at Sylvia's shoulder. "Did you find him?"

"No, but look. Oh, aren't they sweet?"

Sylvia propped her hip on a hay bale and reached down to stroke the tabby-striped cat's head. It purred loudly and half-closed its eyes. Four variegated-colored kittens suckled its breasts, their tiny paws pushing against the cat's stomach in relish as they filled their small tummies.

"Wonder how I missed seeing these before?" Sylvia mused. "I'm sure I looked behind this hay a while ago."

Francesca tenderly ran her finger along the back of a butterscotch kitten. "Maybe the mother got disturbed in her previous nest and moved them here," she said. "Cats do that—all mothers are protective of their babies, until they're ready to bring them out into the world and show them off."

"Thanks, Frannie." When Francesca looked at her in mystery, Sylvia continued, "I thought you might be thinking I hadn't searched seriously for Basil up here, since I didn't find the kittens the first time."

"Why, of course you searched diligently, Sylvia. You're very dedicated."

Allowing herself a tiny glow at Francesca's praise, Sylvia glanced back at the kittens. "The mother's not afraid of us, so she won't be disturbed and have to move her babies again. Isn't it nice that animals can see us, Frannie?"

"Very," Francesca agreed. "It can get lonely when you're on assignment, and animals are extremely good company. One of my angels told me that some nursing homes on earth are allowing their patients to have pets now. They help keep elderly people's spirits up."

"Hum," Sylvia mused. "Maybe we're going about this search the wrong way."

"I'm open to any idea you might have."

"Well, the animals can see this Basil guy, too. What if he has a special pet here? We might be able to find him by watching the animals."

"Let's try," Francesca agreed.

They flew from the loft and hovered for a few seconds in the open area of the barn, watching the horses in the nearest stalls. A pair of matched grays stood in adjoining stalls close to the door, both drowsing in the heat. Their stalls were well tended, with clean straw on the floor and full water buckets hanging beside feed troughs stuffed with hay.

"Must be their buggy horses," Francesca said. "Someone is probably planning on going visiting later, or else I imagine these horses would be out in the pasture, getting some fresh air."

"Uh-huh," Sylvia agreed. "Let's check the rest of the barn."

They flew on down the aisle, peering into each stall as they went. The remaining stalls were empty, though each was in as pristine condition as the one containing the grays. At the back of the barn, they found Shain's buggy between two farm wagons. Sylvia stared at the buggy in puzzlement.

"It looks sort of worn out, doesn't it, Frannie? I thought buggies back in this time were sort of a status symbol for their owners—you know, the way cars are in future times."

"It is faded in places on the outside," Francesca acknowledged. "But it looks like the seats have been recently recovered."

Sylvia lifted a finger, and the buggy top slowly began moving backward with a squeak of rusty hinges. Reversing the direction of her waving finger, Sylvia shook her head as the buggy top settled back into place.

"Needs some oil or grease," she said. "Or some of that WD-40 stuff that comes in those spray cans."

A yellow and blue spray can appeared in the air, but Francesca reached out and swiped it away from the buggy hinge. "Sylvia! You aren't supposed to do things like that!"

"Aw, Frannie, no one would know. Just a little squirt on each hinge?"

Francesca contemplated the rusty hinges and faded paint on the buggy for a moment. Finally, giving an agreeable shrug, she pointed the can's nozzle outward.

"Wait a second, Frannie," Sylvia said. "Here."

A small, hollow piece of red plastic appeared. Sylvia grabbed it and fit it into the nozzle on the end of the can. "There. I've seen women use this stuff on their office chairs when they start squeaking. I guess this little piece aims the goop inside, into the spots that rub together and squeak."

"Goop?" Francesca asked with a raised eyebrow.

"Goop, oil—I've never been interested in just exactly what's inside the can, but I've seen it work. You spray, while I wiggle the buggy top."

Francesca complied, and Sylvia waved her finger back and forth while the other angel poked the plastic straw into the hinge and sprayed. When that hinge stopped squeaking, they flew over the buggy and performed the same maintenance on the other side. Smiling at her companion in satisfaction, Francesca stepped back and flicked her wrist. The can sailed into the air but, instead of disappearing as Francesca had intended, it landed on the floor with a plop.

Francesca stared at it for a second, then laughed. "I forgot. You made it materialize, Sylvia, so you have to make it vanish."

Sylvia nonchalantly blinked her eyes once, and the WD-40 can disappeared. She raised and lowered the buggy top once more, nodding her head in pleasure when it moved smoothly and silently on its hinges.

"Okay, Frannie, that's done. Where do you want to look next?"

"Wherever else there are animals, I suppose. The pastures?"

Sylvia flew out through the back barn door, and the two angels glided over the empty corral and on out over the pastures beyond. Closest to the barn were a few cows, two with calves. The adjacent pasture held a lone bull. Cross-fenced in various sections, they found a few more horses—mares with colts in one, several geldings in another. All of the animals appeared to be interested only in grazing.

They flew back over the barn and investigated the pens on the other side. One held older pigs, with a sow and piglets occupying their own private section. Past that stood a faded, gray chicken coop, with dozens of hens pecking away inside the wire fence.

"I don't think Basil would have a hog or chicken for a pet," Francesca mused.

Sylvia giggled, then snapped her fingers. "A dog! I saw a kennel over there. Come on, Frannie."

They glided away from the chicken coop and hovered above the kennel. Two of the redbone hounds glanced up at them, but the other three just lay in the shade, tongues lolling out in pants. Safely ensconced in a separate section, a half-dozen puppies gamboled with each other, while the mother watched tolerantly from the doghouse door.

"I saw a dog running free earlier," Sylvia said. "Wonder where it's at?"

"Over there on the back porch of the house," Francesca said with a nod. "See? Right next to the dogtrot, which goes out to the kitchen."

"Kitchen? Frannie, isn't the kitchen in the house?"

"No. In these times it's so hot down South that people build their kitchens separate from the house," Francesca explained. "Food's prepared out there and carried inside at mealtime. Look through the roof at the interior. See? One whole wall of that building is a fireplace."

"I've never been on earth in this time period, remember? All I know is what I learned from the human spirits I talked to. Guess I'm used to the places I saw during the time I spent with Jacki—the ones with air-conditioning. Well, anyway, that dog doesn't look like it's paying any attention to anything except its afternoon nap. It's some sort of mixed breed, not a hound, like in the kennels."

"Cute, though," Francesca said. "Black and white fur,

longer than it should be to be comfortable in this heat, though."

"The only other animals left that I've seen are the mules working the fields," Sylvia said, dismissing the dog from her thoughts. She never had cared much for those slobbering animals—cats were more her style. "I guess we're back to prowling around the other plantation buildings again."

Sighing in disappointment over her idea not panning out, Sylvia flew over the garden laid out behind the plantation kitchen, into a small white building with a pointed spire on top. Inside, she immediately paused and gazed reverently around her.

"Isn't this a darling little chapel?" she whispered when Francesca appeared beside her.

"Yes, and it's kept up beautifully," Francesca murmured in reply. "Basil had it built, you know. The workers constructed it at the same time as the plantation house."

"Frannie, do you know the whole history of this Basil's family?"

"No," Francesca admitted. "Just the parts I was allowed to see when I got a quick rundown from the Archangel who gave us the assignment of talking Basil into leaving this plane of existence. Of course, we're to keep an eye on Alaynia, also."

"Alaynia wouldn't be in such a dangerous situation, if this Basil guy hadn't misused his powers and tricked her into driving through that time warp! Why don't we just lead Alaynia back through it?"

"Because we don't know what Alaynia's destiny is," Francesca said in exasperation. "That will be her choice now, and we have to keep ourselves completely out of that. And I wish you'd not always preface his name with 'this' or 'that guy.' Sylvia, Basil was a kind and loving husband at one time, and you already know that Shain thought the world of his grandfather."

"What sort of *master* was he?" Sylvia muttered.

"Master?"

Sylvia slanted a look at Francesca. "This *Basil guy* built that plantation house and everything else here, including this chapel, with slave labor, didn't he? How do you expect me to feel about him, Frannie? Men like him worked slaves to death, so they could live in all this finery!"

"Oh, dear. You're not supposed to judge, dear. Is that why you didn't want to go with me earlier, when I checked out the cabins where Shain's workers live?"

"I figured that would be wasted time," Sylvia snapped. "The plantation *master* wouldn't be hanging around his former slave cabins."

Francesca took a firm hold on Sylvia's arm. "Then it's time you did go look at those cabins, Sylvia. Right now."

She pulled a resisting Sylvia back through the chapel door and up into the air. They bypassed the smokehouse and blacksmith forge, only cursorily examining both for a sign of Basil. An instant later, Sylvia saw the cabins previously used to house the slaves on the plantation, laid out along two intersecting dirt roads. Huge trees lined the roadways, and each cabin had its own semi-private square lot. Every one was freshly whitewashed, and most had a small, well-tended garden behind the cabin.

The front yards were not bare dirt, as Sylvia admitted to herself that she'd anticipated from some of the stories she'd heard from human spirits of living conditions in the Old South. Neatly-clipped grass covered the spaces, except in some of the shadier spots, where pink-flowered moss grew. Flowers bloomed everywhere, along the paths from the road to the porches and lining the house fronts.

On one porch she saw two elderly black men sitting in rocking chairs, drinking from tall glasses and murmuring to each other. Behind several of the cabins, elderly women hoed weeds or picked produce from the gardens. Her eyes widened when she realized the women were black and also white.

Noting Sylvia's amazement, Francesca explained, "Chenaie runs on the sharecropping system, and both black and white families hire on with Shain. Each family of workers gets their own cabin on an acre of land to live in, and a share of the cotton or other crops for their own at harvest time. The gardens are theirs, too, and they can preserve what they raise for their own use or sell any extra in St. Francisville."

"Sounds like communism," Sylvia muttered.

"Oh, for pity sakes," Francesca said, close to losing her patience. "It's not the same at all. About half of these cabins and plots of land are actually owned by the workers—the families can buy them from Shain if they like. And see those two men on the porch?"

"Yes."

"They came to Chenaie under Basil."

"You mean he *bought* them and brought them here."

"Sylvia, I didn't realize you felt like this. Why, you actually sound prejudiced."

"I didn't know how deeply I felt myself," Sylvia admitted with a sigh, "until we came here. I admired Dr. King and his message of peaceful revolution, but look what that got him. I know we aren't supposed to judge people. And we're definitely not supposed to judge the overall plan, because it's not something we're allowed to know."

"Even as angels, we grow and learn," Francesca reminded her. "Our place in the scheme of things is being especially close to humans. Our experiences with them expand our own knowledge."

"Maybe I should go on back, and you can find someone else to work with you on this assignment," Sylvia said with a sigh. "I'm not sure I'm up to handling this one."

Francesca picked up Sylvia's hands in her own and squeezed them gently. "Give it a little more time. Please? Let me show you something else."

"Okay," Sylvia agreed begrudgingly. "As long as you try to understand, even if I'm not sure myself why I'm having these feelings. Maybe it's part of my own spiritual growth. None of us gives a second thought to the color of a human's skin. But ever since we got here, I haven't been able to forget what I saw when I started paying closer attention to that horrible slavery issue down here on earth."

"Chenaie's a little pocket of hope for those coming days, Sylvia. Let me show you."

More in comfort than concern that Sylvia wouldn't follow, Francesca kept one of the other angel's hands in her own as she led the way over the tree tops. In another clearing, they hovered above a sprawling, cheerful yellow building, which also had a spire on top. But in a yard scattered with swings and slides, teeter-totters, and even a maypole hung with hand swings, over two dozen black and white children shrieked and played.

A black man and two white women presided over the gathering, strolling among the children. They stopped now and then to offer a word of encouragement in a game of Red Rover Come Over, or intervene in a tiff over whose turn it was to push—whose to swing. One small black child took a tumble from a teeter-totter, and a woman lifted her skirts and hurried over to pick the child up.

"That's the school down there," Francesca said after a

while. "And the adults you see are all teachers. School's over for today, but they keep the children busy for a while after their lessons. Most of the men workers on Chenaie, and even some of their wives, work in the fields, but the women quit earlier than the men. In a few minutes, the teachers will deliver the children home to their mothers."

Confirming Francesca's words, the man walked over and clanged a bell to call the children to attention. The small girls and boys slowly and reluctantly left their games and formed two lines. The two oldest boys reentered the building with the man, while the women led the rest of the children toward the cabins.

"The man and the boys will clean up and rearrange the seats for church on Sunday," Francesca explained. "He's also the minister."

"Aw, come on, Frannie. With only those few children on the plantation, maybe I can see them going to school together. But you're not gonna make me believe that those white families go to church under a black minister in these days!"

"No, things haven't gone that far yet in this time, even on Chenaie," Francesca admitted, trying to ignore Sylvia's knowing smirk. "The other families go into St. Francisville on Sunday, as Shain and his sister do. But the point I was trying to make is that all the children on Chenaie have an opportunity for an education. What they make of it is up to their families. There will be some black leaders come out of those children below, or at least their children or grandchildren."

"I'd say that's the least they deserve," Sylvia said as she slowly waved her wings and started away from the schoolhouse. "After the way their parents were brought here in chains!"

"Nobody asked your opinion, girlie," a voice snarled. "*I* built Chenaie and my blood runs Chenaie!"

Sylvia whirled to face Basil boldly. "I told you to quit calling me those sexist names!"

"Since you didn't bother to introduce yourself earlier, like a proper lady would have, what the devil do you expect me to call you?" Basil asked with a snort.

"Y-you sure weren't a gentleman," Sylvia sputtered, her indignation and courage dissipating in the face of Basil's hauteur. Good grief, what was there about this ghost that frightened her? After all, he was only a man—or used to be, anyway.

"Will you two please behave yourselves?" Francesca said as she floated around Sylvia's shoulder.

To Sylvia's amazement, Basil grinned at Francesca and took her outstretched hand. Carrying her fingers to his mouth, he kissed them and said, "Hello again, Miss Francesca. You're looking lovely. Please accept my apology for the little fracas earlier, but you caught me at a bad moment."

"Obviously," Francesca replied. "Allow me to properly introduce my friend, Sylvia. She's already aware that you're Shain's grandfather."

"Sylvia," Basil said with a nod.

Sylvia's eyes narrowed at what she considered Basil's deliberate slight at addressing her without using a preliminary Miss, as he had with Francesca. "Basil," she ground out in return. "Or should I call you *Massa* Basil?"

Francesca groaned under her breath, but Basil only shrugged. "My Negroes called me Master while I ran Chenaie. Feel free to use whichever you wish."

"Listen here, buster . . ."

"Buster is not acceptable," Basil interrupted. "Insolence I do not tolerate."

"Sylvia . . ." Francesca began, but Sylvia overrode her.

"Were I a human black, I suppose I could get sentenced to a whipping for insolence. Is that what you mean?"

"I never whipped my female Negroes," Basil denied. "And rarely did I have to order a male punished. However, stealing was an offense punishable by the whip."

Francesca firmly stepped between the two of them and directed her words to the ghost. "Basil, we need to talk. You've committed a great breach of your powers by bringing Alaynia to this time period. It could be dangerous for her here. You need to come with us now."

"I've made up my mind to stay right here at Chenaie, and you're not going to change it, Francesca. So you might as well go on home."

"Can't we at least discuss why you thought it necessary to bring Alaynia here, Basil, and why you've made the choice you have?" Francesca asked. "Tell us where we can find you later, after you've thought about this for a while, and we'll talk some more."

"It's been delightful," Basil said in a polite tone, "but I really must take my leave now." He gave a brief bow and disappeared.

"Basil!" Francesca called, but received no response. Shaking her head, she sighed deeply and turned to Sylvia. "How in the world are we supposed to reason with him, if he won't stay around long enough to talk?"

"Huh," Sylvia said. "Even the few minutes he does stay are more than enough for me. He acts like he's some sort of king or something. Look at all this, Frannie." Dashiki skirt tangling and braids bouncing, Sylvia waved her hands and spun around. "He's got his own little city here—his own little kingdom filled with people to do his bidding! When he was alive, all he ever had to do was snap his fingers and open his mouth. He could order everything from a mint julep on a silver tray to his horse saddled and delivered to the front steps, so he didn't have to get his boots dusty walking to the barn!"

"Someone had to be in charge, to get all this built and keep it running smoothly, Sylvia."

"Yeah, so Massa Basil could be comfortable! Frannie, he's used to ordering people around—playing with their lives at his own whim. What makes you think he'll obey us, when we've chosen to use female corporeal bodies because those fit our own personal traits as the angels we are? He'll just think of us as two women, who were sent here to tell him to change what he's decided he wants done. Granted, we're from a different plane, but he sure doesn't appear to care about that. Maybe we should go back and tell them to send someone who prefers a male corporeal body—a big, strong, ornery male body—one ornerier than he is."

Francesca gasped in horror. "Oh, we can't, Sylvia! I've never failed in an assignment yet, and I'll be diddly darned if I'll go back and admit that I think someone else might be able to handle this assignment better than I can!"

"It appears to me that this man's getting the best of us," Sylvia grumbled. "And I don't like it one bit!"

"Harrumph," Francesca responded with a sniff of disdain. "I agree with at least one point you've tried to make before, and that's that women—human or angel—are just as capable as men and can handle anything men can. There's not a thing inferior about our brains."

Sylvia laid an index finger beside her mouth and half-closed her eyes in contemplation. "Then maybe we should put our superior brains together and see what we can do to outsmart that old rascal, girlfriend. Didn't he say something the first time we met about bringing Alaynia back here so she wouldn't disturb the peace on Chenaie in the future?"

"Yes, he did. Alaynia had it in mind to restore Chenaie and turn it into a bed and breakfast. I suppose Basil didn't want a lot of strangers trooping in and out of his plantation. And besides, Alaynia isn't descended from the St. Clairs. Her relationship to her Great-Aunt Tilda was through the remarriage of one of Tilda's nephews."

Sylvia flew over to a nearby cloud and sat down, crossing her legs and patting the space beside her. "Sit, Frannie. Thinking's hard work, and we might as well get comfortable."

As soon as Francesca joined her, Sylvia propped her elbows on her knees and cupped her chin. "Okay. Now, tell me what you do know about this assignment. How did Alaynia end up with Chenaie? She's an orphan, and if she was Tilda's only living heir—even by marriage—why didn't Tilda contact her earlier, while she was still alive?"

"Tilda was rather . . . ummm, eccentric," Francesca replied. "She didn't even bother to worry about who would take over Chenaie, until she was faced with having to go into the nursing home when she could no longer care for herself."

"So then she . . . what? Hired a detective to find out if she had any relatives left?"

"Exactly. And when the detective found Alaynia, Tilda, still being independent enough not to want Alaynia to feel obligated to visit her at this late date, just had the detective make periodic reports to her. Knowing that her great-niece had made a career of restoring old houses, Tilda was satisfied that Alaynia would care for Chenaie well."

"That was a double whammy for old Basil, though, huh? A woman, and not even his blood, taking over Chenaie— letting strangers have the run of it. I guess he'd rather see it empty and run down, so he could haunt in peace."

"He's not really haunting, Sylvia. Basil's stubborn, and he's kept his traits in this state of being. Like a lot of human men, he resents change. He would be perfectly happy living with us, if he'd just give it a chance. But he prefers to have his afterlife here—at Chenaie."

"Don't you think there might be a little more to it than that, Frannie? There's gotta be something else holding him here."

"If we can find out what that is," Francesca mused, "maybe we can reason with him a little better."

"Frannie, reasoning with a man's not the way to go. We've gotta dig into our bag of feminine wiles and make him think whatever we want him to do has been his idea all along!"

Chapter 8

Alaynia scooted onto the padded window seat in the room Jeannie had led her to earlier that afternoon and curled her arms around her knees. A night breeze feathered through the open window, and she laid her head back against the side of the deep window frame.

The Camellia Room, as Shain had called it, was at the back of the house, and she could gaze out over Chenaie's rose garden. A half-moon hung low, barely visible in the upper branches of a magnificent live oak on the far edge of the garden. Beyond the oak, she could see the graveyard, with smaller headstones neatly aligned on each side of one towering tombstone.

Graveyards had always fascinated her. She loved walking through the peaceful grounds, making up pretend stories about the various families in different plots. Whenever possible, she researched the history of the house she had been commissioned to restore—got to know the past family members as well as possible. At times, she would be lucky enough to even visit the graves of the people who had made the house come alive in the actual time period she aspired to attain in her restoration. Not really considering herself psychic, she still felt a stir of sensitivity whenever she studied the tombstones where the birth and death dates coincided with her restoration period.

Filling the house with imaginary people always brought out her best talents. She could visualize the former mistress of the house lovingly running a finger along a polished banister as she descended a winding stairway, or flicking a speck of dust from a table with a lace-edged handkerchief pulled from her sleeve. Sometimes, wandering through a flea market, she would be drawn to a piece of furniture others had passed over as beneath their notice. Mentally stripping away the layers of paint and dirt, she could see the perfect little table on which the mistress could set her silver tea service—or perhaps just the right stand to fill an empty corner and hold a prized vase. Her greatest find had been a mother-of-pearl inlaid sewing box from the early 1800s. That she couldn't bear to part with, and she had placed it in storage with the rest of her apartment furnishings.

She'd always loved prowling through the past—until now. Now she was living in it. The antiques were real, with only a linseed-oiled cloth needed to bring out their sheen. Without having to turn around, she could visualize the cherry wood armoire where she had hung her clothing—the huge, four poster bed with a canopy and netting that could be draped around the bed to keep the mosquitoes and other insects away at night. There was even a stepstool to use when climbing onto the high mattress.

The fireplace on the wall to her right would hold a fire on a chilly evening, but for now someone had placed the bronze coal bucket inside the hearth and filled it with decorative magnolia leaves. A stuffed armchair sat on either side of the fireplace. She'd sat on one of them earlier, but it had seemed rather small for her five-foot-six body. Somewhere she had read that the height of women in the nineteenth century averaged only four-foot-six.

She had politely refused Jeannie's offer of a tour of the manor house before supper. One thing to her advantage was the Southern acceptance of women's need to rest their supposedly-delicate constitutions after an arduous journey. Claiming fatigue, she had even managed to avoid the evening meal, although Jeannie had carried up a tray for her.

She had to have some time to think. But even privacy to sort through her experience that day hadn't brought any order to the turmoil in her mind. Acknowledgment of her fate at somehow being at Chenaie during its time of glory was coming, though slowly. She just wasn't quite ready to investigate the stately rooms and face the final confirmation.

She'd never fit in here. Jeannie had sent up a house servant to help her unpack, but she had firmly refused any assistance. How on earth would she explain the zippers in the gowns—the wickedly indecent underwear she loved to buy from Victoria's Secret? She had, however, accepted the servant's offer to carry up water for a bath. After the tub behind a dressing screen had been filled, she'd had to resolutely insist that she could handle her undressing and bathing herself. Shaking her head, the young black servant had finally left the room.

The dressing screen's height had seemed to confirm the smaller statures of women in this time period. It had a foot or so of glass on the upper portion, and when Alaynia stood straight after she undressed, anyone happening to be on the other side could have seen her breasts.

She turned to stare at the far wall, which contained a connecting door to the next room. From her earlier conversation with Jeannie, Alaynia recalled that the other room belonged to Shain. She could hear him moving around in it now, and a second later, a tap sounded on the door. She slid from the window seat and walked over to open the door. Shain had evidently recently bathed. His black hair was still damp, his face freshly shaven. She caught a hint of a spicy scent—either some sort of aftershave or masculine soap. At once she found her eyes on his full mouth and realized his kiss had hovered near the forefront of her mind all evening.

Murmuring a greeting, she quickly dropped her gaze. He wore a dressing gown over a nightshirt, and her lips curved into a smile when she studied the hem of the garment beneath his robe.

"Something funny?" Shain asked.

"It's just that men in my time wear pajamas to bed instead of gowns," Alaynia explained.

"Pajamas?"

"They're a loose-fitting set of pants and shirt. I've never seen a man in a nightgown."

"They're nightshirts, not gowns. And, for your information, I'm only wearing it for modesty's sake while I visit with you. I frankly prefer to sleep without any encumbrance."

Alaynia flushed slightly as she pictured his nude body between a set of sheets. She had a fairly good idea of his physique—she'd been in his arms, traced his broad shoulders with her hands, and even felt his growing desire when she backed into him that afternoon. She had to admit that he would be a magnificent specimen to wake up next to on a sleepy Sunday morning.

"Sorry, didn't mean to embarrass you," Shain said in anything but an apologetic tone. "I just wanted to check and see how your evening went—if you needed anything."

"What I need is something you obviously can't provide," Alaynia said as she turned and walked back across the room, away from his disturbingly-near presence. "To get back to my own time. And I have no idea how to go about that."

Shain followed and joined her when she sat on the window seat. Taking one of her hands in his own, he said, "Maybe Jake can come up with an idea. He's pretty fanatical when he sets his mind to things."

"In the meantime, what am I going to do?" Alaynia said in a muted wail. "This is awful. I've left my entire life behind—my apartment, my bank account, such as it was. But at least I had a good credit rating, and I could've financed Chenaie's restoration until I had it operating. Now all I have are the clothes I brought with me and a car that won't work!"

She leaned against Shain's shoulder and he slipped his free hand around her back. She wasn't going to cry again—crying never solved anything. But she desperately needed someone to share her turmoil, and she could let down her guard with Shain. With everyone else at Chenaie, she had to watch her words, her actions, and even hide her clothing from them. How long would it be before someone tripped her up?

Shain soothingly stroked her back and laid his cheek against her hair. "I understand," he murmured. "And I'm sorry I couldn't stay with you this afternoon. But, like I said earlier, I've got a plantation to run. My people depend on me. It's been rough for everyone in Louisiana since the war. The damned Yankees in Louisiana took a page from Sherman's book, when he ravaged Georgia from Atlanta to Savannah."

Alaynia could feel his tenseness as Shain gripped a tress of her hair, then relaxed his hold. "Sherman's idea of war was published in some of the papers the Yankees had taken over down here. He wanted everyone to know that all war is hell, and that included the civilians. He knew that not only destroying the rail lines, but also the homes—leaving the men's wives and children homeless—would break whatever resistance spirit the South had left. Other commanders followed suit, and they made sure a lot of our state would take years to rebuild. The carpetbaggers and politicians finished the job."

Alaynia lifted her head and studied his troubled face. His brown eyes were shadowed, and he stared across the room instead of returning her gaze. His hand continued to stroke her back, yet somehow she sensed his thoughts were far away.

Wanting to return some of the comfort he had given her, she said, "Chenaie will stay in your family for quite a while, Shain. I can at least tell you that. Aunt Tilda's last name on the deed is St. Clair. She's listed as a *femme sole,* though, which I understand means she wasn't married."

Shain dropped his arm from around her and abruptly rose to his feet. "Look," he said as he scowled down, "I don't think it's such a good idea for you to tell me what's going to happen in the future. It's not natural for me to know those things. And Chenaie's got enough weird stories going around about it, without you letting slip something that might fuel the gossip mill of those crazy voodoo practitioners."

Stifling a gasp, Alaynia gazed at him, her eyes wide with fear. "What . . . what do you mean by that?"

"Aw, shit," Shain muttered. Kneeling before her, he picked up both her hands. "I don't mean to scare you. After what you experienced, you're already frightened enough. But Alaynia, just in the brief time since you got here, I can tell that customs and beliefs are very different where you came from."

"You can say that again," Alaynia gritted, trying to ignore the way her hands seemed to fit just precisely so in his.

"I've got one advantage, though. I've read about the past, so I'm a little more familiar with your customs than you are with mine. But I don't recall anything weird about Chenaie in the research I did."

Shain raised one hand and tangled his index finger in a gold-brown curl, which had fallen over her shoulder. "You have incredible hair. In fact, you're a dangerously striking woman, Alaynia Mirabeau. Has anyone ever told you that?"

When Alaynia remained silent, Shain glanced at her with a narrowed gaze. "Is there someone back there that you left behind? Someone you're in love with—a fiancé? Husband?"

"N-no," Alaynia stuttered. She turned away and curled up again on the window seat. "Besides, what difference would that make? Maybe there would have been—in my future. But here, I don't even have a future. I don't have anything!"

Shain scooted her legs aside and sat down again. But the instant he began to speak, Alaynia's intake of fearful breath cut him off. She lifted a shaky hand and pointed out the window. "What's that?"

Shain followed her gaze and shook his head. "I don't see anything."

"There. In the graveyard. Can't you see it? It . . . it looks like . . . oh, my God. It looks like something floating around out there."

"Swamp gas," Shain said, though his tone told her he still couldn't see what had caught her attention. "It flickers on and off at times. I guess that's what started some of the stories about Chenaie."

"What stories?"

"It's late, Alaynia. You need to get some sleep."

Shain rose, but Alaynia quickly grabbed his hand before he could move away. "What stories?" she repeated. When

Shain stared past her out the window, she continued, "Your allusion to something weird at Chenaie and then clamming up is definitely not a bedtime story guaranteed to give me a good night's rest. Besides, I'm too wound up to sleep."

"Wound up?" Shain's lips quirked slightly. "I thought that was something we did to clocks."

"Oh!" Alaynia dropped his hand and slipped from the window seat. Flouncing out into the middle of the room, she turned to face him, arms crossed beneath her breasts. "Tell me something, Mr. St. Clair . . ."

"Shain," he murmured in protest.

"Don't interrupt me," she demanded, stamping her bare foot on the patterned carpet. "I seem to recall that people in 1875 knew each other a lot longer than one day before they took the liberty of using first names!"

"And a lot longer than that before they kiss," Shain said in an agreeable tone, moving toward her in that lazy walk she was beginning to recognize. "The most two people who aren't betrothed are allowed to do is touch fingertips as they dance . . . or a man can kiss the back of his lady's gloved hand when they meet. But we've already bypassed that by a long ways, haven't we?"

"I . . ."

He raised his hand and tenderly stroked her cheek with a fingertip, and Alaynia tightened her arms around herself for a second. A shiver of pleasure ran over her body and her eyelids began to close. Slowly her grasp loosened as her arms strained to move around his neck with a will all their own and her toes curled into the carpet.

"I think I like the customs where you come from better," Shain whispered as he bent his head. "If you feel like touching me or holding my hand, you do. If I feel like kissing you, you let me."

His breath already mingling with her own, Alaynia jerked away. She stumbled as her body protested the quick change in posture, and grabbed a bedpost to steady herself.

"You—you're wrong about that," she managed on an indrawn breath. "We don't . . . men and women don't . . . just kiss whomever they want."

"Oh?" Shain inquired. "Then there still has to be some sort of attraction for people to want to kiss each other?"

"Yes . . . no! I mean . . ."

He chuckled, and Alaynia whirled, her shoulder bumping his too-near chest. She instinctively pushed him away and walked farther into the room, where she glared at him from a safer distance. "You're changing the subject. We were talking about Chenaie."

Shain shrugged amiably and sat on the side of the bed. "You already know my grandfather built Chenaie. Zeke told me stories, since he grew up here. Grandfather and my grandmother, Laureen, lived in the kitchen area while the original main house was built. It had five lower rooms, and four bedrooms above. After my father married, they built on another section, where we are now—a parlor and study below, and a new master bedroom and the bedroom you're using. Didn't Jeannie give you a tour?"

"No," Alaynia replied. "I . . ." Drawing in a shaky breath, she admitted, "I couldn't face it just yet. It's too much to take in right now. This morning I left a hotel in Baton Rouge in 2005, and tonight I'm at Chenaie back in 1875."

Alaynia covered her face briefly with her hands, but dropped them quickly when she sensed Shain start to stand. "Don't," she said. "Just stay over there."

"Why? You're upset, and I can't comfort you from over here."

"Upset? Hell, yes, I'm upset!" Alaynia's voice rose a notch. "Put yourself in my place. How would you feel if you'd suddenly been transported into my time?"

She stalked over to the bell pull Jeannie had pointed out earlier and thrust her hand toward it. "See this? You use this to summon your servants when you need something. Well, a house this large back in Boston might have an intercom system. You'd just push a button to talk to someone in another part of the house. Or pick up the phone."

"I remember you using that 'phone' word before."

Ignoring him, Alaynia pointed at one of the kerosene lamps in a wall sconce. "You've probably got a servant that just goes around lighting lamps in the evening. Well, we've got electricity. You just walk into a room and push a button on the wall, and you've got light in the entire room. And we've got separate rooms just for bathing. All you have to do is turn the knobs on the tub for hot and cold water. It took that little black girl four trips to carry up my bath water this evening!"

"Black girl? Oh, you mean Netta? She's Negro."

"African-American," Alaynia corrected. "In my time, the different races are proud of their heritage. Indians are Native Americans!"

Shain stifled a yawn and got to his feet. "This is all very interesting, but we can talk about it later. Come on." He held out a coaxing hand. "Let me help you into bed."

"I can put myself to bed when I'm ready. I told you I wasn't sleepy."

Shain walked over to her and, before she could stop him, swept her into his arms. "Well, I'm dog tired," he said as he carried her protesting body toward the bed. "And I won't be able to sleep myself, if I know you're over here pacing the floor."

He laid her down on the bed, where the servant had already turned back a satin comforter. But when he reached for the ties on her robe, she grabbed his hands.

"I can do that!"

With a sigh, Shain turned his back and walked toward a lamp. "I'll extinguish the lights."

He lowered the wicks on the wall lamps, leaving the one on her beside table until last. Behind him, he heard the rustle of Alaynia's movements and could imagine the silken dressing gown sliding from her shoulders. The bed creaked slightly and the satin comforter whispered in the silence.

Satin and silk—like the skin on this woman who had dropped into his life. He rubbed his tingling palm against his dressing gown, where it rasped unpleasantly in contradiction to her skin. He hadn't been able to forget her for even a second all afternoon—the feel of her, the taste of her kiss. The way she unconsciously touched him to make a point, met his gaze without the shy demureness most women affected in his presence. The white-hot desire that swept through him when he held her—visions of the two of them entangled in the throes of a passion he somehow sensed would far outweigh anything he had experienced previously.

Through the open window he could see pinpoint stars spread over the night sky. Here and there they flickered with an almost roguish light. Alaynia's blue eyes held that same sparkle at times, but usually in indignation at his misunderstanding of something she said—or defiance of his orders.

He heard her settle more deeply into the bed and turned away from the window. One bare arm lay outside the pink comforter, and the other palm was tucked beneath her cheek on the pillow. As usual, she met his gaze directly, though her eyelids drooped in weariness. The lamp on the bedside table sputtered, almost flickering out, but he could see the dark circles beginning under her eyes.

"You're as tired as I am," he murmured as he crossed the room, his footsteps muted on the carpet. "Get some rest, and we'll talk in the morning."

He bent to the lamp and doused the flame completely. Almost total darkness descended on the room, and he heard her frightened gasp. "Hey," he said, sitting down on the bed. "You're not afraid of the dark, are you?"

"N-not usually," Alaynia whispered. "But tonight it seems so black."

"I'll stay with you until you drop off."

"No. No, you said you were exhausted. Go on to bed. I'll be all right."

Instead of complying, Shain settled more comfortably on the mattress.

"Do you always do exactly what you want, instead of what you're asked to do?" Alaynia murmured.

"Then you admit that you're aware of me wanting to stay here with you?"

"Aware of you?" she replied. "Oh, yes, I'm very aware of you, Mr. St. Clair."

"Shain," he corrected.

"Shain," she agreed, closing her eyes as he stroked her hair.

Chapter 9

The next morning, Alaynia woke fully alert and aware, yet she deliberately kept her eyes shut, testing her senses. Sometime during the night, she had thrown the comforter back, and she could feel the humidity in the room even through the sheet. Strain though she might, she couldn't hear the muted purr of an air-conditioning fan in her hotel room. Instead, bird twitters sounded faintly, then a raucous rooster's crow.

Sighing and clamping her eyelids tighter, she shook her head against the pillow. It hadn't been a dream—there sure as heck weren't any roosters outside the hotel in Baton Rouge.

Suddenly she heard another sound. Her eyes flew open and she twisted her head. Shain lay beside her, lips slightly parted and his breath feathering against her bare shoulder. In the murky, pre-dawn light, she could make out the dark shadow of his beard already growing again on his face and the long lashes surrounding his deep brown eyes. Her movement evidently disturbed him, and the lashes twitched against his cheeks.

Stilling herself in order not to wake him fully, Alaynia studied his face. The sun wrinkles around his eyes weren't quite as deep this morning, and jet-black curls tousled over his forehead. She caught a glimpse of his even, white teeth between his lips—full lips that pouted just a little in his relaxed state.

He must have removed his dressing gown before he lay down, since only the nightshirt covered his broad shoulders, and tight whorls of hair showed in the open vee down the front. Her finger twitched, beckoned to twine fingernails in the kinky curls. He lay outside the comforter, his nightshirt twisted high on his legs, baring brawny, muscled thighs.

She was right—he was a magnificent specimen to wake up next to in the morning.

Not that she had any other experience to which to compare this morning. In college, there had been Ted, the bedroom-eyed hunk to whom she had finally relinquished her virginity. Despite his powerful physique, lovemaking with Ted had been soft and carefree, just like Ted wanted his life to be. They'd drifted through their relationship without promises, each aware of their separate goals. They'd parted at graduation without tears or recriminations, Ted to see what was over the next mountain and Alaynia to strive for the sense of accomplishment her orphaned childhood had never given her.

Alaynia allowed her thoughts to touch on John Franklin, her one other intimate relationship, grimacing in distaste at her remembered naiveté. She'd read all the warnings in the women's magazines: Be suspicious if he never wants you to call him at work or home—never takes you to meet his friends—dines with you in out-of-the-way places.

John had had it down pat. How tenderly he had explained that he cherished their time together so much he couldn't bear to share her with anyone else. His real estate business flourished on weekends, when families had time to look at prospective houses, and her weekends were sometimes jam-packed as she searched estate sales and antique shops for furniture. Tuesdays and Thursdays were their nights, though he always left long before morning.

The mind games he had played with her about their sex life were what had almost destroyed her confidence in herself as a woman. A sigh and a pat on her hip after his passion was spent, which seemed to her to indicate his disappointment in their lovemaking. A quick rising from the bed, while she lay there, holding back tears and promising herself that the next time she would be more of a woman for him.

Young—she'd been so damned young, believing his murmured false attempts at comfort.

Alaynia hadn't made the connection at first, when she attended yet another estate sale. While she studied an ornate fireplace set that would be perfect in her current project, she'd heard one of the children next door call out a greeting to Mrs. Franklin, the stylishly-dressed woman making change from a wooden cash box. The child's mother walked over to chat with Mrs. Franklin for a moment, and Alaynia had unconsciously listened to the murmured conversation, until the words penetrated.

The two women were obviously friends, and the sympathy Alaynia heard in the neighbor's voice had seemed entirely appropriate toward someone who had just lost a family member. But the bitter tones in the other woman's voice had finally caught Alaynia's attention.

No, her husband, John, hadn't been much help in getting the estate sale organized. She'd thought that maybe he'd be a little contrite about not being with her when she needed him so badly—when her father had a stroke and died within hours. She thanked the neighbor again for coming, and no, she'd never found out where John had been that Thursday night.

Not at the real estate sales office, that's for sure. And he hadn't been showing a house, because the other salesperson checked the sign-out sheet they always kept. John must think her blind to not realize that his late nights always fell on Tuesdays and Thursdays. She'd even thought about hiring a detective, but with her father's death, she didn't have the energy right now to confront John with his deception.

Alaynia had had the energy. She didn't ever remember being so furious. She had stormed into the real estate office a half-hour later and slammed John's office door behind her. She got every hateful, venomous word out of her system, grateful to see him almost shrink inside his suit while she spat at him. Then, sick at heart at being so easily deceived, she'd left, swearing off men for all eternity.

Until now.

"Bull crap," Alaynia answered that thought aloud. If ever there were a man for her to keep her distance from, it was the one lying a scant six inches away. More than just the difference in their backgrounds separated her from him—over a hundred years in time was a gap that could never be bridged.

The wrinkles at the corner of Shain's eyes deepened into a frown and he muttered in a voice raspy with sleep, "I like that. I haven't even been out to the barn yet this morning. How can I smell like manure?"

Giggling, Alaynia sat up and pulled the sheet around her neck. "What are you doing in my bed? I don't recall inviting you to sleep with me."

Shain yawned hugely and reached up to tousle his hair even more wildly. "You didn't. But you were restless, and I thought I'd just lie down for a minute, until you were more sound asleep. You don't act too embarrassed at finding me here." He squinted an eye at her. "Are you used to waking up with a man in your bed?"

"This is the first time it's ever happened," Alaynia said in honest denial. "And, though I appreciate your concern for me, don't you think your servants are going to gossip when they find your bed still made up?"

"Probably," Shain admitted. "But there's time yet. It's early, and my household knows I don't like breakfast served until later—after I've been awake for a while." He sat up and studied her. "How are you this morning? Still scared?"

"To death. I need you to tell me how to get over to Jake's today. Maybe if I talk to him, I can figure out . . ."

Shain abruptly rose from the bed. "I don't have time to take you today. I'm behind around here after yesterday, and you're not to go wandering around without an escort. You—"

"Now you just wait a minute," Alaynia interrupted. "I'm not about to idle around here until you find time to *escort* me somewhere! I'm used to taking care of myself. All you have to do is lend me a horse and tell me how to get to Jake's house. If you think I need a keeper, you're sadly mistaken."

"A keeper? Hell, you need a guardian. How we act in private is our own business, but remember that you're a guest in my house. You can't flaunt convention and ride all over the country alone. It's not a proper influence on Jeannie, and my neighbors' tongues would start wagging. I don't need a scandal."

Alaynia threw the sheet aside and scrambled out of bed to face him. "A scandal?" Pointing a finger at his chest, she said, "You rode after me, when I would have been perfectly happy going on into St. Francisville and trying to find out from there what had happened to me. I didn't ask to be brought here and treated like an embarrassment. If you think I'm going to sit around here and do . . . needlepoint, or whatever your Southern women do to fill their days, you're sadly mistaken, buster. I've got a life to get back to, and come hell or high water, I'm going to find out how to get back to it!"

Shain leaned over her, forcing Alaynia against the bed. "Until you do," he gritted, "you'll behave like a proper Southern lady and obey me. There are reasons why we don't allow our women to travel without an escort. Even Jeannie's got sense enough to take her maid and one of the grooms with her, when she calls on someone."

Alaynia thrust her face toward his. "I'm not a teenaged girl—and I'm not going to let some man order me around. You can stick your *obey* word where the sun doesn't shine. That redneck viewpoint went out of fashion when Archie Bunker disappeared from television!"

Struggling to keep his eyes from her bare shoulders, where the two tiny straps of her gown had slid off to rest on her upper arms, Shain took a step back. Big mistake, because now he had an unobstructed view of her breasts beneath the thin, silken material of her gown. The darker pebbles of her nipples pointed at him provocatively, and the ice-blue material exactly matched the fury spitting from her eyes. The gown barely reached the top of her thighs, and an expanse of tanned legs tapered endlessly toward the floor.

He started to ask her who the hell Archie Bunker was, but his usual morning erection returned full force. He swung his back to her. "Get some goddamn clothes on!"

"Where's my robe?" Alaynia said at the same instant.

Behind him, Shain heard her scurry to the foot of the bed, where she'd left her robe lying across the footrest. He reached down and grabbed his own dressing robe from the floor, wadding it in his hand and striding over to jerk the door between their rooms open. When she half-turned to face him, hurriedly cinching the ties and opening her mouth to continue their argument, he glowered her into silence.

"You may not be used to obeying a man," he growled, "but you'll learn real fast that I give the orders here at Chenaie. If I want to, I can have you taken to one of the attic rooms and locked up until I have time to deal with you."

"You wouldn't dare!" Alaynia gasped.

"Try me," he snarled as he closed the door.

But once the tumblers clicked into place, effectively separating him from the other room, Shain leaned against the door and shook his head. Hell, if she had any sense, Alaynia would know that he couldn't follow through on his threat. Word would spread like wildfire across the parish that he had Jake's supposed niece locked up in his attic. Probably everyone within fifty miles already knew about her presence at Chenaie.

Today the story he had cooked up, with Jake's agreement, appeared full of holes. Every family in West Feliciana knew the background of every other family. Somehow, even the backgrounds of the new Yankee arrivals quickly became common knowledge. As Jeannie had pointed out yesterday, Jake had never mentioned a niece, and even though his shack and barn weren't a place that invited visitors, Jake knew practically everyone in the parish. Word was that Jake was a bachelor, with no family ties. A niece popping up out of nowhere was no doubt going to cause gossip and conjecture.

Damn, he'd have to find some time to ride over there today and see if Jake himself had thought of any other problems with their story. And he supposed there wasn't any reason Alaynia shouldn't go with him—if only so Jake could question her and try to confirm whether her time travel story held water.

The other possibility—that she was making up this wild story to cover up her connections to Fitzroy—didn't really appear feasible today. But if he ever did find any proof of that, he'd send her fanny packing without worrying about what happened to her.

Shain jerked the door open again. Alaynia sat on the window seat, still dressed in her robe. She didn't turn toward him, but her shoulders stiffened.

"Do you have a riding habit?" he said gruffly. "I don't think any of Jeannie's are big enough for you."

"I have one. Patti made that for me, too." Still gazing out the window, she continued, "Does that mean I can leave my room today?"

"Look—" Shain cut off his words when a knock sounded on Alaynia's door.

"Miss Mirabeau," someone called. "Are you awake?"

"Jeannie," Shain warned in a low voice. "Don't let her see what you're wearing under that robe."

Alaynia shot him a combative look and called sweetly, "Come on in, Jeannie. I'm up."

Shain barely managed to close his door before Jeannie burst into the room.

Chapter 10

"I always have chocolate and buns when I first get up," Jeannie said in the open doorway. "I thought if you were awake, you might want to join me. We never have breakfast until later, and by then I'm usually starved."

"That sounds wonderful," Alaynia admitted with a smile. "Only I'd prefer coffee, if it's available."

Jeannie turned to give her breakfast order to someone in the hallway, and Alaynia noticed the young girl was already dressed. She wore a light-pink gown, floor-length, of course, with capped sleeves on her slender upper arms. When she turned back into the room, Alaynia could see the same demure neckline above her young breasts, this one with a scalloped edging. Jeannie crossed the room toward the window seat, her golden curls bouncing on her back with the vibrancy of her movements.

"Oh!" Jeannie stopped abruptly. "I'm sorry. You're not dressed yet. I guess I shouldn't have bothered you. But . . . I thought I heard Shain's voice in here a minute ago."

"He was just checking on how I'd spent the night," Alaynia half-lied. "And please don't think you're bothering me. In fact, since you seem so full of energy this morning, how about that tour after a bit?"

"I always wake up full of energy," Jeannie said with a laugh. "Shain, now, he's the reason we wait a couple hours for breakfast. You can't even talk to him when he first wakes up."

Alaynia silently agreed with Jeannie on that point. *At least, not talk rationally to the man,* she qualified.

"And we'll have plenty of time for me to show you the house before our regular breakfast," Jeannie continued, bouncing on over to where Alaynia sat. "Do you want me to help you get dressed? I'm really sorry that we don't have a servant available so you can have your own maid, but . . . well, most everyone is short of help these days. Shain says it's because not enough people want to work for a living, but I know it's because we can't really afford anyone else. We just have Sara, our cook, and Tessa, our housekeeper. Tessa's daughter, Netta—she's the one who brought up your bathwater last night—she helps Tessa out now and then on the heavy cleaning days.

"Oh!" Jeannie clapped a palm over her mouth, her blue eyes dancing mischievously above her fingers. Slowly dropping her hand, she said, "Shain says I babble too much, and that's one reason he has to have breakfast later—so he's awake enough to listen to my chatter."

Still, adoration for her brother shone from Jeannie's eyes. Indeed, Shain's name punctuated everything she said. Never having had any siblings of her own, Alaynia could only imagine the relationship between this so very different brother and sister. The orphanage didn't exactly foster close relationships, since children came and went with frequency, and for some reason she had never formed a close friendship with another woman after she left to be on her own.

"I think your chatter is very refreshing in the morning," she said. "And to tell the truth, I'm not used to having anyone assist me in dressing and bathing."

"Didn't you have very many servants, either?" Jeannie asked.

"No, no I didn't," Alaynia replied, aware that she didn't dare explain anything further to Jeannie. "And I better get dressed, or our drinks will be cold by the time I get down to the dining room."

"We won't eat downstairs until Shain's ready," Jeannie explained. "Just come on over to my room." She turned and started for the door. "It's on the other side of the stairwell and two doors down on the right."

She closed the door behind her with an energetic thud, and Alaynia slid from the window seat, shaking her head. The room was awfully silent without Jeannie's presence, and—she glanced at the bed, where the extra pillow still held the indentation of Shain's head—she already missed him, too, despite the fact that their talk had deteriorated into another test of wills.

Suddenly recalling the scene in the graveyard the previous night, Alaynia turned and stared back out the window. Early morning mist hovered above the ground, foretelling another humid, Southern day. Yet there was no definition to the mist this morning—only a layer of rising moisture, which dissipated the farther it got above the ground.

She could see the hazy outlines of the headstones, and suddenly a shaft of sunlight broke through the trees, outlining the one, towering tombstone. Frowning in concentration, she knelt on the window seat cushion and steadied herself on the windowsill as she studied the array of headstones. She'd passed several churches on her journey from Baton Rouge the previous morning, noting their sites so she could return and explore at some later date. Even in those church graveyards, she had noticed a few of the above-ground tombs she'd heard about in the Southernmost part of Louisiana. It had surprised her that some families followed that custom this far north of New Orleans.

Her research indicated that above-ground tombs were a necessity in the below-sea-level town of New Orleans. She'd also planned to visit that historical city during her restoration of Chenaie, to get a proper feel for the background of the state and the early lifestyles of its people.

The shaft of sunlight brightened, outlining the towering tombstone in radiance. A strange fear stole over Alaynia, but she couldn't seem to tear her gaze away. Her muscles wouldn't respond to her mind's command for her body to move from the window seat, and the unexplainable fright heightened when her body wouldn't react. The only things not paralyzed were her hammering heart and her thoughts, which raced frenziedly, wondering if she could be having a heart attack or stroke.

Suddenly the brilliance around the tombstone disappeared, leaving behind only a peaceful mistiness in the graveyard. Alaynia wrenched her hands from the windowsill and stumbled backwards. Staring down at her arms, she saw them covered with goose bumps, despite the warmth in the room. The feeling spread over her body, almost as though she had walked through a nest of spider webs.

A hallway door slammed, and Alaynia shook the shock away, quickly telling herself it was only her frazzled nerves that had caused the experience. She glanced down at her arms, where the skin was now smooth and unmarred. Her heart still raced, but she took a few calming breaths and walked toward the armoire—away from the window. Her body responded perfectly.

She had to hurry and dress before Jeannie came looking for her again. It wouldn't do for the young girl to find her in mid-dress, without the cumbersome, old-fashioned underclothing beneath her gown. Hopefully, Jeannie's training in manners included not entering another's room without knocking first, as she had done a few minutes ago. Right now, though, the young girl's chattering presence would have been welcome in the eerily silent room.

A faint hint of floral perfume reached her when she opened the armoire door and, as she removed her riding habit, she made a mental note to ask Jeannie what sort of sachet they used in the freestanding closet. The Southern flowers were all new to her, but she would enjoy drying them and making her own blends.

If she ever had her own closets and drawers to place them in again. Drawing in another breath for courage, she began dressing for her tour of the plantation manor house, which she could no longer call her own.

Basil sat on the tombstone, frowning at the window on Laureen's old room. His wife had only used it to store her clothing, since she had slept in his bed during their lives. The pull he had felt when he saw Alaynia leaning out the window had surprised him. He'd become used to his loneliness, which began after Laureen's death and continued for the nineteen years he remained among the living. It was even his constant companion in his present state.

No matter how much he practiced his powers, he hadn't been able to penetrate the time barrier to the past, where he could again live with Laureen. For some reason, that area of time remained closed to him. He could only protect her gravesite, even though he felt the same emptiness there.

Come to think of it, Alaynia might be of some use, since he'd brought her back here to safeguard what he considered the future of Chenaie. None of his relatives had bothered keeping up the family history Basil had meticulously penned in his life, and he'd always meant to expand on it more than just birth and death dates. However, after Laureen's death, he hadn't been able to bring himself to make the effort.

The chit seemed interested in history—old families and old records. Might as well give her a suitable task for a female with which to occupy her time. Keeping a wary eye out for those two annoying angels, who seemed determined to interfere with his plans, he flew from the tombstone and into the window of the Camellia Room, then zipped on into his old bedroom.

Shain eyed Alaynia's blue riding habit with distaste again, as the groom led two horses from the barn. She had realized the moment she entered the dining room, where Shain waited for them an hour ago, that the habit wasn't proper attire for breakfast, though Jeannie hadn't mentioned it while they had their coffee and chocolate. However, she'd seen no reason to change clothing twice, when she knew she'd be riding soon after the morning meal.

But Shain's words denigrated more than the riding habit being improper breakfast attire—he obviously didn't care for its fit on her, either.

"That damned skirt's split like pants," he muttered as the groom came closer. "Before you wear it again, have Tessa fashion it into a proper skirt, and make it long enough to cover your boots."

Alaynia immediately bristled. "I ordered this habit made to be comfortable. Skirts weren't meant to be worn on horseback."

"All you've gotta do is drape them along the side of your saddle," Shain growled. "The horses women ride are trained to ignore the flutter."

The groom handed the reins of the two horses to Shain

and walked back toward the barn. Alaynia's anger diffused as she studied the charming little chestnut mare. The mare nudged her with a white-striped nose, and Alaynia cooed softly to the animal and stroked its muzzle. "Is this one for me to ride?"

"I take it she suits you then?" Shain asked in a softer voice.

"Oh, yes. She's gorgeous. Most of the riding I've done has been on farm horses, or a horse from a rental stable."

"I'm sure you can handle Ginger. She's a lady's mount. Let me help you up."

Alaynia moved around to the side of the horse and halted abruptly. "What the heck's that?" she asked, pointing to the sidesaddle with the wickedly high pommel on the front.

"What? The saddle? I thought you were used to riding. Surely you didn't ride bareback."

"I sure as heck didn't ride on a contraption like that." Alaynia tossed the ponytail she had swept her hair up into that morning back over her shoulder. "I told you, I ride astride. That's another reason my skirt is made in what's known as culottes. I saw one of those sidesaddles in a museum once—down under the arch in St. Louis. I thought then that it looked about as comfortable as riding on a Brahma bull's back with my leg around the hump."

She pointed at the saddle Shain had on his black horse. "The stables where I rode in Boston used English saddles on the horses, like that one. I'll wait until you change that other monstrosity out for one like it."

"Southern ladies—"

"Wait up!" Jeannie called as she raced toward the barn, now wearing her own riding habit. She had the skirt hiked up almost to her knees, and Shain glared at her when she forgot to drop the material from her hands as she stopped beside them.

Discerning the meaning of the scowl on Shain's face, Jeannie quickly let the skirt fall into place. "I figured you were going riding," she said in a voice breathless from her run. "Weren't you going to invite me along? You knew I didn't have any other plans for today, Shain. And it's been so boring around here lately. Where are we going?"

"*We* aren't—"

"Of course we'd love to have you ride with us," Alaynia interrupted. "In fact, you can ride Ginger. Shain was just going to have a different horse saddled for me." She shot him another one of those combative looks he seemed to bring out in her. "You see, I'm really more used to riding on an English saddle—like the one on Shain's horse. We were just talking about how much more comfortable I'd be on one of those."

Jeannie giggled impishly. "One of our neighbors, Miz Thibideau, rode her hunter over this spring using a man's saddle. She even went on the boar hunt with the men. Ever since then, I've been asking Shain to let me learn to ride astride. Why, my friend Bessie and I discussed how much more comfortable it looked, and Bessie told me the other day that she'd snuck out and tried it while her parents were off visiting, and it was more comfortable. She said her groom almost had heart failure, though, and—"

"Jeannie, you're prattling again," Shain interrupted in a resigned voice. "Don't you have lessons you need to get ready for, when your tutor comes tomorrow?"

"I've finished my lessons, Shain. You asked me that yesterday evening, remember? Now, can I go riding with you? Please?"

"I suppose," he replied hesitantly, evidently unable to

muster the fortitude to disperse the excitement in his little sister's face. "But we're riding over to Jake's, and I've got some private business to discuss with him. You're not to go poking around all over the place like you usually do, being a distraction."

"I won't. I promise," Jeannie said solemnly. But as Shain strode away to order another horse saddled, Jeannie's blue eyes sparkled at Alaynia. "It's always so much fun over at Jake's. You should see all the things he's always coming up with—his inventions. Oh, but I guess you know about them, since he's your uncle."

Aware of one invention that Jeannie had to be kept from seeing at Jake's—her car—Alaynia shrugged in feigned disinterest. "I really don't know that much about Uncle Jake's life. I didn't even realize he wouldn't have a place for me to stay when I decided to visit, remember?"

"That's right," Jeannie agreed. "Golly, I can't imagine traveling all that way to see someone, without knowing for sure what sort of place I'd have to stay when I got there. I've only been away from Chenaie for a week once, at my other friend Sissy's house after her family moved to Baton Rouge. And Shain took me there himself and came back for me."

"Well, I'm a little older than you," Alaynia said wryly. "And I don't have to ask anyone for permission to go where I want."

Thankfully, Shain came back with another horse before Jeannie could voice the further questions Alaynia saw growing in the young girl's eyes. The bay mare he led was also a fine horse, with a coat that gleamed in the sunlight, and an English saddle set on its back. Alaynia smiled sweetly into Shain's set face when he offered his cupped hands to help her mount.

A moment later, the three of them rode around the plantation house and headed down the front drive. Alaynia studied the fields with more interest this time as they passed. On one side of the road were mostly women and older children, dragging tote sacks while they picked the fluffy cotton balls from the dry-looking plants. Beyond them, teams of mules pulled plows, already turning the soil again.

"We plant two cotton crops a year," Shain explained when he noticed her interest. "Usually, we have a long enough growing season to harvest both crops."

"And that's your sugar cane back there beyond your cotton, on this other side of the road?"

"Yeah, not that it's doing real well yet. But I'm still studying the best way to raise it here."

"There's one thing I don't understand," Alaynia mused. "Most all of the plantation houses I read about—well, I sort of got the impression that the fields were always in the back of the house. Yours are on the land leading up to Chenaie."

"The land I own behind Chenaie is forest land," Shain said. "You find that a lot in this end of the state. And forest land's not rich enough to grow our crops, even if you clear it."

"Have you ever thought about selling some of the timber from your other land?" Alaynia stiffened in her saddle at the thunderous look that came over Shain's face. "I . . . well, I'm sorry. But with all the rebuilding in the South, I'd think lumber—"

"No one's stripping Chenaie land, like they've begun doing to the cypress forests south of us," he snarled. "Don't ever bring that up to me again!"

Alaynia clamped her mouth shut. Sparring with him over his ordering her around was one thing, but she'd never seen this deadly glint in Shain's eyes at those other times. Though the sun was already beating down, she stifled a shiver and kept her silence as they rode on toward Jake's.

She paid more attention to the forks in the road they took today, and a scant half-hour later, they rode into a clearing. She recognized the elderly black man who sat in a rocking chair on the porch of a ramshackle cabin as the man who had been driving the wagon yesterday. As soon as he saw them, he rose and hurried toward a huge barn beside the house.

Shain led the way to the hitching rail in front of the cabin and dismounted. He assisted Jeannie from the saddle, then glared at Alaynia, who had swung down on her own.

"I told Jeannie earlier that I didn't have any servants back in Boston," Alaynia said with a shrug in response to his scowl. "I'm used to getting off my horse by myself."

"Down here," Shain growled in a low voice as Jeannie moved away from them, "a lady waits for a gentleman to help her dismount."

"And does a gentleman sleep in a lady's bed uninvited?" Alaynia asked in an innocent voice.

Shain's eyes softened from walnut to a lighter hue, and his lips formed a half-smile. "Does that mean I might be invited sometime?"

Unable to resist his teasing, which she enjoyed a whole lot more than when they gritted threats at each other, Alaynia cocked an eyebrow and flicked a loose thread from his shirt sleeve. "I'm not supposed to tell you what the future holds, remember?"

"Witch," Shain breathed.

"No, no, Miz Jeannie!"

Alaynia and Shain turned toward the sound of Zeke's voice to see him leading Jeannie back toward where they stood. "Mister Jake, he's busy, Miz Jeannie," Zeke explained as they walked. "You know how he gets when he's a workin' on somthin' real important. Wouldn't do to bother him right now."

"Then I guess we'll have to go on home," Jeannie said. "Shain wanted to talk to Jake, but if he's busy . . ."

"Mister Jake probably won't mind if Massa Shain wants to talk to him," Zeke replied. He suddenly glanced at Alaynia and shuffled back a few steps, a mixture of apprehension and awe on his face. "Uh . . . say, Miz Jeannie," he quickly said, "that there old cow done went and had her calf. You come on with me, and I'll show it to you."

Jeannie reluctantly followed Zeke, and Shain watched them walk away with a frown of annoyance on his face. "Zeke's gonna blow this whole thing, if we don't watch out. I'll have to have a talk with him, too, before we leave."

Alaynia slowly nodded her head in agreement, but said, "This is horrible. He's afraid of me, and it makes me feel terrible. I've never had that effect on anyone before."

Tucking her hand in his arm, Shain patted her fingers comfortingly and led her toward the barn. "Take it easy, now. Zeke just doesn't understand what's happened. For that matter, neither do any of the rest of us, including you. Zeke wouldn't intentionally do anything to hurt you."

"*Intentionally?*" Alaynia said with a gasp. "You mean, he might do something unintentionally?"

"I hope not," Shain said in a grim voice. "Look, don't worry about it. I'll talk to him."

"Please do," Alaynia whispered as they entered the shadowed recesses of the barn. She sensed a movement beside her and stared into two huge, blinking yellow eyes. After an initial start of anxiety, she laughed softly when she recognized a barn owl sitting on a shelf.

"Look," she said, tugging on Shain's arm. "Isn't he cute?"

"Yeah, but don't bother Jake's owls," Shain warned. "Some of them bite."

"I let them stay around to keep the mice out of here," Jake explained as he walked over to them, wiping his hands on an already greasy rag. "Can't abide cats—they're such snotty creatures. Morning, Shain, Miss Mirabeau. Sorry to disappoint you, but I don't know any more about that car than I did yesterday."

"I think you're both going to have to understand something," Alaynia said. "That car's not what brought me here. Why, if that could happen, people would be traveling through time all over the place. In 2005, everybody over the age of sixteen owns a car."

"Really?" Jake said reverently. "Bet the man who owns the patent on those things is as rich as Midas."

"I have no idea how patents work," Alaynia said with a shrug. "But there's dozens of companies all over the world that make cars—everything from little compacts smaller than my rental car to huge limousines and buses that can carry dozens of people. I couldn't begin to tell you how many different types of gasoline-powered vehicles there are in my time."

Excitement dancing in his eyes, Jake took Alaynia's arm. "Well, little lady, why don't you tell me all about the ones you can remember?" He walked her toward a bench along one side of the barn, near where another wall separated his workshop area from the rest of the open space. He dusted off the bench with the rag in his hand, but Shain spoke before Alaynia could sit down.

"Sorry, Jake, but we don't have time for that today. We've got some other things to talk about."

"How do you expect me to help Miss Mirabeau out, if we don't spend some time together?" Jake said in an exasperated voice.

"Tell you what," Shain replied. "You can come over to Chenaie tomorrow morning and pick Alaynia up. No one will think it strange if she spends a day now and then with her uncle."

"Well, they diddly darn well better not!" Jake said huffily. "She's my niece, after all. Those nosy busybodies in the parish can just wag their tongues about somebody else!"

Alaynia frowned a little at what she considered Jake's overreaction. Why, he almost sounded like he believed she really was related to him. Her puzzlement turned to anxiety when Jake sat down abruptly on the bench and wiped his face with the dirty rag.

"Are you all right?" she asked.

"Fine, fine," he said, waving away her concern. "But Shain's got a point there. From now on, I want you to call me Uncle Jake, and I'll call you Alaynia. And you wear your best bib and tucker tomorrow, because we're going into St. Francisville for lunch. Why, we'll even do some shopping while we're there."

He looked at Alaynia's riding habit. "My niece ought to have lots of pretty dresses to wear, so I can show her off."

"Oh, I couldn't accept—"

"You don't have to do that, Jake," Shain interrupted in an irritated voice.

"Think I can't afford it, don't you?" Jake asked with a sly look at Shain. He chuckled wryly under his breath and stood. "Everybody thinks I'm not only crazy, but poor on top of that."

Sympathy for the wild-haired little man who had extended her nothing but acceptance since she arrived filled

Alaynia, and she touched his arm. "I'd be delighted to have lunch with you tomorrow, Uncle Jake. But you really don't have to buy me anything else."

"It'll break my old heart if you turn me down." Jake sniffed sadly. "Just break my poor heart."

Alaynia caught the hint of sham in Jake's attempt at emotional blackmail, and laughter bubbled in her chest. How many times had she yearned for a father to tease her— take her somewhere—buy her a pretty dress instead of the drab skirts and blouses she wore at the home? Jake sniffed again and slipped a sideways look at Alaynia, and she burst into unrestrained laughter. A second later, Jake joined her.

Her laughter finally abated a little, but Alaynia's eyes continued to twinkle. "Well, I'd be just as pleased as punch to have you squire me around town and buy me whatever my little old heart desires, Uncle Jake," she said in a drawl, imitating Jeannie's musical Southern cadence. She pursed her lips into a mock simper. "Why, I do declare. This morning I looked in my closet and I just didn't have a thing to wear except this old rag."

Jake guffawed and rubbed his hands together in glee. "Be my pleasure, my dear niece. Now, you be ready bright and early, so we can have the whole day together."

"Yes, Uncle," Alaynia agreed demurely.

Shain snorted in disgust and strode out of the barn. Beyond the door, he uncurled his clenched fists and wiped his hands on his trouser legs. Hell, he'd been about ready to shake that old codger silly when he offered to buy clothing for Alaynia. More rational now that he had a little distance separating him from their easiness with each other, he realized all Jake had been doing was putting Alaynia at ease— being her friend.

Making her laugh. He heard another trill of Alaynia's delighted laughter and slowly swiveled back toward the barn door. He hadn't heard her laugh like that since they'd met. At times her voice held a teasing lilt, but never that joyous freedom. How the hell could Jake bring that out in her, when Shain hadn't been able to?

Jealous? The word flashed through Shain's mind and he quickly dismissed it. He'd known Alaynia less than a day. *And already kissed her,* his mind reminded him.

"Yeah," he whispered to himself. "And I'd be willing to bet this year's crop that old Crazy Jake never gets a kiss from her like that."

Whistling a jaunty tune, he stuck his hands in his pockets and sauntered back into the barn.

Chapter 11

A man sat on a horse at one of the forks in the road on the way back to Chenaie. He looked somewhat familiar at first, until Alaynia decided he reminded her of Shain, only with longer hair. Jeannie's constant chatter ceased the moment she saw the man, and she whooped with delight and urged her mare forward. The man dismounted, and when Jeannie pulled her Ginger to a halt, he took her from the saddle and whirled her around once before he set her down.

One distinct difference between this other man and Shain that Alaynia noticed as the man swung Jeannie around was the low-slung holster and pistol on his hip. Shain had carried a pistol with him to the stables that morning and handed it to the groom. She assumed it must now be in the black stallion's saddlebags, but she had no doubt that Shain, too, had a weapon within easy reach.

"Cole!" Jeannie said around her giggles of pleasure. "Shain said you came by yesterday. Why didn't you come say hello to me?"

"Had things to do, little one," Cole said.

"I wish you'd stop calling me little. I'm fourteen, almost fifteen, and you and Shain still treat me like a child."

"Well, honey," Cole drawled. He pushed a disreputable gray hat back from his forehead. "Reckon you and me ought to start makin' them weddin' plans then. Don't want me no bride that's elderly and haggard—got wrinkles around her eyes."

"Sorry," Jeannie said with a smirk. "You're much too old for me, Cole. Why, by the time I got wrinkles, you'd be walking with a cane and all your teeth would've fallen out. I do like a man with a pretty smile."

Cole flashed Jeannie a gorgeous smile as Alaynia and Shain halted their horses beside the two of them. Shain dismounted and grasped Cole's extended palm. "Hope you're staying for supper today. Jeannie's not about to let you leave this time without having a sparring match or two with you."

"Be pleased to accept," Cole replied. "Looks to me like I'll have the pleasure of two pretty ladies' company this evenin'. Man would be a fool to turn down that opportunity."

He grinned appreciatively at Alaynia, and she smiled in reply. *A young Don Johnson in the flesh.* Cole's rugged good looks were only intensified by the two or three days' growth of beard, and that gorgeous smile should melt any woman's resistance. But for some reason, she compared Cole's smile to Shain's, with Cole's coming up just a little bit lacking.

"Alaynia Mirabeau, Cole Dubose," Shain said somewhat grudgingly. When Cole glanced away from her after bowing his head slightly in recognition of the introduction, Alaynia saw Shain shoot him a warning glare.

"Private property, huh?" Cole said in a low tone and with a conspiratorial wink. "Gotcha, friend."

Shain nodded, confirming Cole's false assumption, and Alaynia grimaced in irritation. Rather than voice her displeasure aloud in front of Jeannie, she settled for a glare at Shain, to let him know they would discuss that subject further. In privacy. He responded with a negligent shrug, but at least attempted to turn the conversation. "What are you doing back so soon anyway, Cole?"

"We'll talk later this evening," Cole replied. "After supper."

Suddenly Shain's stallion reared and jerked the reins from his grasp. An enraged javelina burst onto the roadway, snorting and snarling, and Jeannie screamed in fright. Alaynia's mare tossed its head in panic, neighing shrilly, and she fought for control as the other riderless horses scattered in terror. Cole grabbed Jeannie and pushed her behind him as he pulled his pistol in the same movement. Shain leapt toward Alaynia as she grabbed desperately at the mare's mane when it arched its back and plunged in fright. Trying to avoid the slashing hooves, Shain reached for the mare's bridle at the same instant a shot rang out and the mare reacted to the noise with added frenzy.

Alaynia landed with a sickening thump in the ditch beside the road. Shain reached her in a split second. Ignoring Cole's admonition not to move her, he gathered her against his chest as she opened her eyes and stared at him in astonishment.

"God, Alaynia," he growled, his voice reflecting his worry and his hand stroking her hair. "You could've been killed. Talk to me. Where are you hurt?"

"I . . . I . . ." She drew in a gasp of air and stared past Shain into Cole's face. "Did you shoot at me?"

Shain pulled her closer, leaned his forehead against hers, and hid Cole from her view. "He shot that damned javelina." He shuddered slightly and studied her face. "And that damned mare went even crazier at the noise of the shot. We've got to get you back to Chenaie and send for the doctor."

His face looked so ravaged that Alaynia reached up to stroke his cheek. "Really, I don't think I'm hurt that bad. If you'll just let me try to get up . . ."

145

"Damn it, you lie still," he ordered.

Over Shain's shoulder, Alaynia noticed Cole smile at Jeannie and indicate with a motion of his head for her to follow him. "We'll gather up the horses. I think your friend Alaynia's going to be all right."

"It'll take my brother a while to accept that," Jeannie said in a conspiratorial whisper, which Shain didn't appear to hear as he ran his hands over Alaynia's arms. But Jeannie glanced over her shoulder at Alaynia, a worried frown on her face as Cole led her away. "I was scared to death when that mare bucked her off, Cole. Are you sure she's all right?"

"If she's not, Shain will make it all better," Cole promised with a quiet laugh. "She'll probably have a few sore spots, but she's conscious and talkin' rationally. The ditch was filled with sand, so it cushioned her fall some."

They walked on down the road after the horses, out of earshot, and Alaynia pushed against Shain's chest one more time. "Really," she repeated. "How can I tell if I'm hurt, if you won't let me up?"

"You can just move your arms and legs while you lie right there. Tell me if they give you any problems."

With a sigh, Alaynia flexed first one leg, then the other. Shain allowed her to sit up a little, and she bent her arms at the elbows. "Feels fine. A little sore. But I'll probably feel worse tomorrow, when the stiffness sets in and I try to get out of bed."

"I'll let Jake know that you won't be able to go with him."

"You will not!" Alaynia eluded his grasp and scrambled to her feet. "See? I'm perfectly fine. I . . . oh, ouch!" She grabbed her hip.

"Sit back down," Shain ordered. "I'll catch Black and

ride to Chenaie—bring the buggy back. And I'll have someone fetch Tana to the manor house, so she'll be waiting for us."

"Tana?" Alaynia ignored his demand for her to sit and continued to rub her aching hip.

"She's a healer," Shain explained in a short tone. "Damn it, are you going to sit back down?"

"No." Alaynia smiled into his frustration. "And there's no need for you to go get a buggy. As soon as you catch my mare, I'll ride back."

"You need to be looked at."

"All I need is a soothing bath in some herbed water, or maybe some BenGay," Alaynia said in attempted exasperation, but the concern on his face melted her irritation almost at once. Her gaze caught his, and a thread of warmth circled between them, soothing her aching muscles much more effectively than any medicinal balm. She yearned toward him, and her body instinctively swayed in answer to her thoughts. He caught her tenderly, his arms sliding down her back and around her waist.

"Who's Ben Gay?" he murmured, and she giggled in reply.

"*It's* a kind of a liniment made from wintergreen—for sore muscles." She caught her breath as he bent his head.

He nuzzled her nose with his and whispered, "If that's what you need, I'll get it for you somewhere. And maybe I could help you rub it in—sort of massage away your aches."

"M-maybe you could," she stammered around the desire filling her veins with a completely different type of warmth. Her hands inched up his chest, aiming for the silky-damp curls around his neck. Her fingers reached their goal, and she twined them into his hair.

Shain sipped a tiny kiss and settled his hands on the

mounds of her hips, gently stroking the area she had been rubbing a moment ago. "Does it still hurt?"

"Huh-uh. Not a bit."

He opened his mouth slightly and covered hers again, slowly moving his head back and forth, caressing her lips with his own. "When that horse threw you, it scared ten years off my life, darling. How in hell have I come to care so much about you in this short time?"

His words sent a thrill of something much deeper than mere physical want through her. "And why does your caring matter so much to me?" she whispered in reply.

His arms tightened, pulling her against his length. Nothing she had ever experienced before had prepared her for the soul-shattering wave of passion that overwhelmed her. His mouth took hers almost ruthlessly, but Alaynia willingly accepted his plundering tongue, tightening her grasp in his hair and answering his growl of desire with a whimper of abject need.

The evidence of his need pressed against her stomach, an inch or two above where she wanted it to be. As though in answer to her urging, unspoken thoughts, Shain bent and cupped her hips, drawing her with him when he straightened. The ache in her core only intensified as he rocked her against him, and she threw back her head, offering him the delicate skin on her neck.

Shain drew in a ragged breath and slowly lowered her to the ground. In answer to her drugged look of hunger for more, he reluctantly shook his head. "Jeannie and Cole will be coming back in a minute," he growled in a voice laced with his own demand for a culmination of their bodies' raging desires. "Tonight. I'll come to you tonight."

"Promise?" She stroked his shoulders, then ran a finger-nail down through the vee in his open-necked shirt.

Twirling a swirl of hair around her nail, she tilted her chin up so she could gaze into his face. The wanting need there mirrored her own.

"I promise, sweet witch," Shain swore. "I promise—if you're sure it's what you want."

A stab of pain shot through her, and Alaynia stiffened. John had said almost those same words to her more than once.

Are you sure you want me to come back again? You seemed less than enthusiastic tonight, dear.

"How can you ask me that?" Alaynia asked Shain in a tiny, hurt voice. "I . . . didn't I show you how much you made me want you? Maybe I can't. Maybe I'm not enough woman for . . ."

"Who the hell told you that?" Shain snarled. He grabbed her shoulders and pushed her back a step. "Whoever said that is a goddamned liar!"

Doubts crowding her mind, Alaynia tore her gaze away. More than anything else, John's sly innuendoes had kept their affair going. His indifference made her endeavor to learn how to respond more properly to a man as she strove to find the heaven in his embrace the books had promised her.

Shain dragged her forward, grinding his erection against her stomach again. She gasped and curled her fingers into his shirt, her legs trembling as the white-hot need surged through her with renewed force. His deep growl of wanting echoed in her ear, and she could only cling desperately to him, responding with a throaty moan.

"I've never been this hard in my life," Shain whispered. "And part of it's because of how you're responding to me."

She met Shain's gaze with a directness that came from her heart. "Then I guess I've just never found the right man to respond to before."

149

"I take it that means I won't be your first?"

When Alaynia shook her head, she expected to see a look of betrayal on Shain's face. Instead, he cocked an inquiring, raven brow.

"The . . . the third," Alaynia explained, ducking her head.

Shain tilted her chin back up and said, "No. The best. You've got my promise on that. And something tells me that making love to you is going to be what I've always dreamed of finding all my life, Alaynia, my beautiful witch. I'm not a virgin, either, sweetheart." He chuckled when her lips twitched in a wry grin. "But I've never felt as hot for a woman as I do when I'm around you. And it's more than just wanting to roll in the hay with you. I'm almost afraid that I'll never be the same after I make love with you— never be able to look at another woman with even a hint of desire."

Alaynia gasped and pulled from his arms. "No! Oh, no, Shain. Then you have to stay away tonight. Don't come to my room. I'll . . . I'll lock the door."

"What the hell do you mean?"

"I . . . Shain, I'll be gone as soon as I can find the way back to my own time. You . . . you've got your life ahead of you here in this time. You'll get married to a woman here— one you can share a future with—have children with." Overcoming the stab of almost disastrous hurt that pierced her, Alaynia pleaded, "We have to stop this attraction between us right now, before it goes any further. We've only known each other for a day. It shouldn't be that hard."

Shain's eyes softened and he gently ran a finger down her cheek. "Hard? It's already hard, darling." When Alaynia blushed furiously at his double entendre, he continued in an amazed whisper, "You really have never felt this wild desire that's between us for any other man, have you, sweetheart? I really am going to be the first man to possess you completely—not only your body, but your soul."

Alaynia could only stare helplessly back at him. Someone shouted Shain's name, and he turned slightly. Cole and Jeannie walked toward them, leading three of the horses.

"Oh, lord, honey," Shain murmured, pulling her around in front of him. "Stay there for a second, while I think about a cold swim."

Smothering her giggles, Alaynia glanced down at her dress bodice and tried to nonchalantly smooth it back into place. There was nothing she could do about her pebbled nipples for the moment, and she raised her hands, smoothing at her hair, effectively hiding the puckers on the front of her dress. Hopefully, Cole and Jeannie would think her disarray resulted from her fall.

"You'll have to find that black bastard of yours yourself," Cole called to Shain as he and Jeannie approached. "We've been looking all over for him, and he's nowhere in sight."

Shain's ragged breathing slowed behind Alaynia, and a second later, a shrill whistle split the air, followed immediately by an answering neigh. Black appeared down the road behind the other horses and, trotting past them, came to a halt beside Shain. "Here he is," Shain said needlessly.

Cole shook his head wordlessly.

Jeannie thrust the reins of her horse into Cole's hand and stifled a horrified gasp. "Oh, no!" She started toward the other side of the road, but Cole grabbed her arm.

"Leave it alone," he said with a nod at the javelina, which lay in a pool of blood a few yards away. "I'll come back and bury it later."

Jeannie shook off his arm and pointed at the wild pig. "She's got babies somewhere. Look, you can see where they've been nursing. That's why she attacked us. We can't leave those babies alone to starve to death."

"Jeannie . . ." Shain began.

"She's right," Alaynia interrupted him. "The pig was only protecting her young. We have to find them."

"Javelinas are wild animals," Shain tried to explain. "They can't be domesticated."

"I'll take care of them," Jeannie pleaded. "When they get old enough, we'll turn them loose. Please, Shain."

Shain and Cole exchanged a resigned look, and Shain picked up Black's reins and tied the horse before he could wander off again. "Go help Jeannie tie the other horses," he told Alaynia over his shoulder. "They probably aren't afraid of baby javelinas as much as they are grown ones, but no sense taking any chances."

As Alaynia hurried toward Jeannie, Shain joined Cole at the edge of the underbrush. The men waded through the briar-laden growth, following a faint path left by the javelina sow. Almost at once, they heard squeals and came out on a creek bank, where six small, gray piglets wallowed on the muddy shore.

"Hell, they can't be over a week or two old," Cole said.

Shain, though, was studying the mud-encrusted piglets with an eye toward how he could carry them without ruining his shirt. He walked over and picked one up, holding it out in front of him. The piglet squealed in terror at the unaccustomed handling and wriggled free of his grasp. When it plopped back into the mud, its littermates joined its frantic clamor. Shain shook his hands to free them of the clinging mud. "Maybe we could tell them we couldn't find them."

152

"Shain!" Jeannie's faint voice came through the trees. "Did you find them? I can hear them squealing!"

Shain laughed, then reached down to grab another piglet. Slippery with mud, it, too, squeezed from his grasp. He lunged after it, and his boots sank in the gluey mud, throwing him off balance. He staggered a step or two and caught an overhanging tree branch a second before he toppled into the creek. Cole stood on the bank and guffawed, and Shain reached down for a handful of mud. It landed on Cole's shoulder, spattering against his face.

"Hey!" Cole yelled, wiping at his chin.

"The next one's going to land in your big mouth, if you don't get down here and help me catch these damned piglets," Shain said in mock anger. "You're the one who shot their mama. I'm designating you stepdaddy."

Cole grinned as he rolled up his shirt sleeves. "Well, friend, I don't guess a litter of pigs will tie me down as much as bein' a real daddy would. I'd rather face a javelina any day than some old fart with a shotgun."

"You've escaped that by the skin of your teeth before," Shain said with a chuckle. "Remember that Maxwell gal?"

Cole rubbed at a clinging piece of mud on his cheek. "I'd've done right by her, if things had turned out different. Only thing was, I wasn't real darned sure about it bein' mine when she told me. Turned out she delivered a little less than six months after I'd first had anything to do with her. The cutest little blond-haired, blue-eyed tyke you'd ever seen—and me and her both havin' black hair."

"Yeah, I know the story, and that blond-haired tyke's the same age as Jeannie right now. But I get your point. Now you get your ass down here and help catch these little runts, or I'm gonna sneak off back through the woods to Chenaie and let you go out there and explain to Alaynia and Jeannie why you don't have these damned pigs with you."

Cole slid down the creek bank, where the piglets were re-forming into a squirming bundle of tiny, grunting bodies, seeking comfort from each other in the face of the danger they suspected. Since his boots were already wet, Shain waded out into the creek and approached from that side, while Cole cautiously crept up from his position. Shain grabbed the nearest piglet, clutching it firmly this time. It squealed and wiggled frantically, but he dunked it into the creek water to wash off the clinging mud, then tucked it under one arm.

Cole snatched the tiniest piglet, and just as he tried to take a step out into the water, its remaining littermates scrambled in a mad dash between his legs. Caught off guard when his foot almost came down on one piglet, Cole wavered for a second, then sat down in the mud.

"Aw, shit," he muttered before he looked down at the little body in his arms. "Well, at least I kept hold of you."

"Oink," came his answer.

Chuckling with laughter, Cole got to his feet and strode out into the creek, where he sat down again. Holding the piglet between his legs, he cupped water in his hands to wash it off. Shain shook his head at them both and carried his squealing pig up the creek bank, starting back toward the road.

"I'll be back and help you catch the rest soon as I hand this little bugger over to the ladies." He glanced down at the flat nose and huge eyes staring up into his face. "Let's just see how they like trying to hold onto one of you squirming critters."

"Oink."

Chapter 12

When the groom hurried from the stable as the riders approached, Alaynia willingly handed the tiny piglet to him. Plucking the damp material on her bodice away from her skin, she waited on her mare while Shain instructed the groom to take the animals to a brood sow, which had recently birthed a smaller than normal litter. Jeannie happily tucked a piglet under each arm and helped the groom and Cole carry them away.

"Do you think the sow will accept strange babies?" Alaynia asked in a worried voice.

"We'll have to see," Shain replied. "If not, I guess we'll have to bottle feed them for a few days, until we can get them eating some watered-down mash. It won't be the first time we've had to hand-raise orphaned animals at Chenaie. And Jeannie's in her glory when she finds an animal to take care of."

Alaynia nodded absently, her gaze taking in the freshly whitewashed barn with the connected stable area, then swinging around to look at the expanse of lawn between the barn and manor house. The attorney had also sent her pictures of the rear of the house, but the grounds had been weed-choked and the barn a dilapidated structure sadly in need of repair.

The detached kitchen area had seemed the perfect place for her to use for her own quarters, and she'd been thankful when the attorney said Miss Tilda had updated the house with central air and heat ten years previously. Chenaie lacked that modern convenience now, but the large windows throughout the house opened, allowing cool breezes to filter in. The live oak trees scattered around the grounds were already mature enough to provide an abundance of shade, though they had grown even larger in the photographs she had.

Seeming to glean the direction of her thoughts, Shain said, "Is it so very different later on?"

Not wanting to wound him with how sadly neglected Chenaie would become in the future, Alaynia only shrugged. "I seem to recall a gazebo on the list of buildings."

Before replying, Shain held his arms up to her and she slid from the mare with the assistance of his strong grasp. His hands remained around her waist, and he pulled her a step closer. "I guess I need to let you in on a secret." He bent his head to share his confidence with only her.

"What would that be?" she asked around the catch of breath his nearness almost always caused.

He lowered his head further, to whisper in her ear, "Southern men always assist their ladies off their horses because that's another accepted way they can get their hands on them."

She giggled and swatted at his shoulder, twisting free. "Well, I'll wait patiently for your assistance in dismounting from now on, so I won't embarrass you by making people think you lack manners. But you've had your hands on me quite enough already today."

"More than my hands," Shain said with a chuckle. "And not enough, by any means. Remember, too, that the day's not over yet."

Alaynia scrutinized him fondly for a few seconds, but

when he reached for her again, she quickly stepped back. "You were going to tell me about the gazebo," she reminded him.

Shain cocked his head to one side and returned her gaze. "A white dress, with lots of lace," he said with a nod. "Don't let Jake buy you a white dress, because that's going to be my present to you. It'll be perfect for you to wear in the evening out at the gazebo."

"And the gazebo is where?"

Shain sighed in resignation and pointed in the general direction of the graveyard. From this lower level, the tombstones were hidden by a hedge on the edge of the rose garden, but the site remained fixed permanently in Alaynia's mind.

"There's a small pond back there," Shain said. "It was formed when Grandfather's slaves dug up the clay soil to make bricks for the chimneys and kitchen ovens. The chapel's also over there, a ways to the right of the gazebo. I'll have to show them both to you—after I get you that white dress."

Instead of responding to his teasing, Alaynia frowned a little. "I don't remember a chapel on the list of buildings."

"It's fairly small—only large enough to seat the family members. The gazebo's about three times as large itself. One of these days, when I get the time, I'll take you all over Chenaie—show you how the plantation runs, and let you meet some of our workers' families. Right now . . ." He took Alaynia's arm and started toward the back veranda. "Don't think I've forgotten about having Tana check you over. I want you to go on up to your room and rest while you wait for her."

"Darn it, Shain. I told you I was all right."

"We'll let Tana pass judgment on that. Well, what do you know?"

Shain paused, and Alaynia followed his gaze to the back veranda, where a tall, beautiful black woman stood up from one of the cane rockers.

"How that woman always knows when someone at Chenaie needs her, I'll never understand," Shain said with a shake of his head. "Come on. I think you'll like Tana."

Tana walked along the veranda in a graceful stride to meet them as Shain and Alaynia climbed the back steps. Up closer, Alaynia found her even more striking. A muted burgundy-colored gown encased her slender body, and she wore a matching turban. Her sculptured face reminded Alaynia of pictures she had seen of Cleopatra, lounging in a boat as her servants poled her down the Nile.

But Tana's brown eyes were anything but lazy, as Cleopatra's had always been pictured. She studied Alaynia with an inquisitive, probing gleam. "So," she murmured. "You have come from far away."

"Uh . . . yes, Boston," Alaynia replied.

"Not even farther than that?" Tana asked.

"Lord, Tana," Shain put in. "You could at least let me introduce you, before you go asking Alaynia for her life history."

Tana smiled at Shain. She was nearly as tall as he was, and Alaynia felt almost petite next to the two of them. When Shain made the introductions, Tana surprised her by holding out her hand for Alaynia to grasp. Instead of shaking her hand, though, Tana turned it over, palm up, and studied it briefly. Then, with a nod, she relinquished her hold.

"Tana's not only a healer," Shain explained in the face of Alaynia's mystified look, "she reads palms. Tana, I'm glad you're here, although I can't figure out how you knew I'd be sending someone after you. Alaynia took a spill from

158

her horse, and I'd like you to make sure she doesn't have any injuries she's not telling me about."

"I will do as you wish," Tana said in her quiet voice. "I have some ointment that will help heal bruises. Come," she said to Alaynia. "We will go to your room, so I may examine you."

"Alaynia's room is the Camellia Room," Shain called after them as they started walking away.

Alaynia glanced at Tana in surprise, when the woman drew in a startled breath and faltered a step, but Tana immediately walked onward and opened a door, revealing a steep stairwell. Picking up a small satchel from beside the chair she'd been sitting on, she motioned for Alaynia to ascend the stairwell.

"This leads to the bedrooms, also," she explained as they climbed the stairs. "I have come before, when someone at Chenaie was injured or ill."

At the top of the stairs, Alaynia preceded Tana down the hallway to her room. Inside the Camellia Room, she turned to see Tana hesitating at the door. "Come on in," she insisted.

Warily glancing around the room, Tana entered and set her satchel on the end of the bed. "You will need to undress," she told Alaynia.

Resigned to being examined by Tana, and frankly admitting to herself that there were a few aches and pains that would benefit from a soothing ointment, Alaynia picked up her robe from the back of a chair. Carrying it with her, she stepped behind the dressing screen, which also hid the bathtub, now empty. "I'll just be a minute."

When she reemerged, Tana stood by the window seat, arms crossed beneath her breasts as she stared out the open window.

"Chenaie's gardens are lovely, aren't they?" Alaynia said in an attempt to get Tana's attention.

Tana turned slowly. "You have the awareness. I saw it in your hand. What you have is even stronger than my own, though you have not worked to nourish it."

"A . . . an awareness of what?" Alaynia stammered, immediately recalling her fear that morning when she had felt herself caught in some power emanating from the graveyard.

"The spirits," Tana replied. "I think you have already experienced them. There is more than one at Chenaie, but one, he is very unhappy here, though he will not leave."

Alaynia's mouth dried instantly, and she unsteadily walked over to sit down on the bed. "I . . . Shain said you were a healer, not a psychic."

"That word I do not know, but my mother, and her mother before her, they could touch the other world. They only did it with respect, though, as I do. And as you must."

"I've got no intention of trying to speak to any spirits that might be haunting Chenaie, Tana. Please, let's don't talk about this, because it's scaring me. I don't intend to stay at Chenaie for long. I'll be leaving soon."

"It is a long journey back to where you have come from."

"It didn't take me very darned long to get here," Alaynia said before she could stop herself. Then she clamped a hand over her mouth and stared at Tana with a horrified look. Dropping her hand, she said, "You know. Don't you?"

"Not all of it." Tana quickly crossed the room and sat down beside Alaynia. "Sometimes I see things, even when I do not want to, but even then, there are riddles in the visions. I saw a woman who looked as you do, floating through the air. My mind told me that she would need me and that I should come when she arrived. I do not think your fall from your horse was the need the vision spoke of."

"Rubbish." Alaynia shook her head in denial. "Damn it, Tana, I've never been psychically sensitive. And I've never been to the South before," she added truthfully. "Everything's different down here—the weather, the customs, the people. My nerves are just a little frazzled from trying to get accustomed to things I'm not used to. That's all it is."

Tana nodded solemnly and stood to reach for her satchel. "The time may not be right yet," she said as she opened her bag and probed among the contents. "Time in the visions has no meaning. Sometimes it becomes clear the next day—sometimes months later." She handed Alaynia a bundle of herbs, but kept the small tin. "Use those in your bath water for two days. And if you will show me your aches, this ointment will soothe them."

A few minutes later, Alaynia rose from the bed as Tana washed her hands in the wash basin on the stand beside the dressing screen. She'd recognized the scent of eucalyptus in the ointment Tana rubbed on her body, and sniffed the herbs she still held in her hand, identifying the same odor there. Her skin tingled in her hip and back area, where Tana had smoothed the ointment over her skin in soothing strokes, and the warmth was already melting away the pain from her fall.

She smiled to herself as she recalled Shain's words that afternoon about helping massage away her aches. She hadn't changed her mind one bit about denying him access to her bed that night—it would just be too darned complicated for her to get any further involved with Chenaie's master in this time period. Unlike some women she knew, who considered an overnight lay with a man just a scratch for the itch of sexual desire, she preferred an emotional commitment with the physical one.

Neither her relationship with Ted nor John had been undertaken lightly. She and Ted had just drifted into different spheres as they matured, and parted with tender promises to get in touch some day. Of course, they never had. Her fury at John's deception had left her thinking at first that she'd broken off that relationship in a clean rift. But he'd left a lingering malaise in his wake.

Something told her that a commitment to Shain would be a complete, soul-shattering dedication, which she could never forget or put behind her. No matter how much she wanted it—and she truthfully admitted to herself that she'd never wanted anything more—she had to keep her head on straight. She'd always had only herself to depend upon and, for the most part, made mature decisions about her life. When she hadn't, she'd accepted the consequences and plunged forward again.

But she couldn't quell the thought that at least once in her life, she deserved to have a mad, irrational, passion-filled fling. The hell with being logical. The hell with the future—wherever it was now, with her living in the past. Shain St. Clair would definitely be worth the risk.

"Only a man can bring that look to a woman's eyes," Tana said in her soft voice.

Alaynia had almost forgotten the other woman's presence, and she was a little disconcerted at how easily Tana read her thoughts—and how close she came to the realities. When she caught Tana's gaze, she quirked her lips and shrugged. Instead of being irritated, she already felt a closeness to this woman that defied description.

"Maybe so," she admitted. She sniffed the eucalyptus leaves again, then laid them on the bedside table. "I appreciate your treatment. The eucalyptus is working already on my aches. I'll crumble some of the leaves in my bath this evening."

"You know of the uses for the plants?" Tana inquired.

"Some," Alaynia said. "I've always been interested in them. Mostly, though, I just make sachets from dried flowers or grow herbs to cook with."

"That is another of the ways to know those like ourselves," Tana said. "They have a closeness with the things that grow."

"Tana, please. I don't want to talk about this."

"The time will come when you need to," Tana said in an acquiescent voice. "When you do, you can come to me."

"I don't even know where you live, Tana."

"You will find me." Tana smiled enigmatically, then walked over to the fireplace mantle and picked something up. "You are interested in Chenaie's past?"

Alaynia frowned as she crossed the room to where Tana stood. "What's that? I don't remember it being there before."

Tana's eyes widened, and she placed the book back on the mantle. "I must go now." She started for the door, picking up her satchel from the bed as she passed. "I would like to see Cole before I leave."

"Wait!" Alaynia cried.

Tana turned in the doorway. "I must go," she repeated. "But remember, I am your friend. If you need me, I will know."

She disappeared and Alaynia couldn't even hear her footsteps in the hallway. Remembering Tana's gliding, regal walk, she recalled that she hadn't heard the other woman's footsteps while they walked down the hallway, either—only the sounds of her own boot steps on the wooden floor.

Frustrated at Tana's departure after the healer had filled

her mind with a host of more unanswered questions, Alaynia swung back to the fireplace. A large Bible lay on the mantle, beside a package of letters tied with a piece of string. They darned sure hadn't been there earlier, because she would have definitely noticed them.

She picked up the Bible and blew at a layer of dust. Opening the front cover, she squinted at the elaborate handwriting until she made out the details of names with birth and death dates on the pages. She closed it and laid it back down. Nothing unusual there. She'd run across dozens of family Bibles in her restoration work. Even in her own time, many families kept up that tradition, and the Bibles were valuable in tracing a family's genealogy, a popular pastime. She'd give the Bible to Shain at the first opportunity.

The letters, also, she decided. Maybe whichever servant had cleaned her room had run across them and thought they belonged to her.

Suddenly an unexplainable urge to read the letters overtook Alaynia. She even reached out and picked up the letters, and started to untie the string. Then she noticed the goose bumps on her arms and threw the letters back onto the mantle. Whirling, she stared around the room, her heart beating frantically.

Nothing out of the ordinary met her gaze, but she would almost swear that Tana hadn't closed the bedroom door behind her. It was closed now, though she hadn't heard the tumblers click into place. She gritted her teeth to calm herself and hurried over to the armoire to grab the first dress her fingers touched. Behind the dressing screen, she pulled off her robe. In less than thirty seconds flat, she ran from the room, carrying a pair of slippers that she didn't pause to put on until she reached the top of the front stairwell, which led down into the main part of the manor house.

Just before she started down the stairwell, she glanced back along the hallway. The door to her room—which she knew damned well she'd left open this time—slowly closed on its hinges.

Chapter 13

This was stupid—pacing back and forth in front of the fireplace, glancing at the door connecting her room to Shain's every few seconds and then back at the window, from which she could see the graveyard. Alaynia ceased her frustrated strides and sat on the edge of the bed. After the evening meal, Shain had caught her alone for a moment and told her of his plans to meet with his overseer, but assured her that he would try to wind up his business with the man early. Before she could inform him of her change of mind about their plans, he had strode out of the house.

The connecting door had no lock—not even a keyhole for an old-fashioned skeleton key. She supposed the plantation master's wife would never think of denying her husband access to her bed. And she didn't know herself if she could follow through on her decision, if the two of them were again alone in the room. The window could be closed and locked with a latch and hook, but nothing that flimsy would keep out what Alaynia could only sense—and what she felt Tana's actions had confirmed, that there was something utterly strange about her room.

She set her lips in determination and rose from the bed. A far better idea would be for her to wait for Shain downstairs. She jerked the hallway door open, and the young black girl outside it drew back, almost stumbling over a water bucket at her feet.

"Oh! I . . . I brought water, Miz Mirabeau. For your bath."

"Thank you, Netta," Alaynia said. "I didn't mean to startle you. Just pour the water in the tub. But first, tell me if Shain's come back in. I need to speak to him."

"He be in the study, Miz Mirabeau. Come in just now."

Netta picked up the water bucket, and Alaynia saw another pail sitting by the wall. Frowning in annoyance as she recalled the steep stairwell Netta had to climb to get to the upper story of the house, she grabbed the other bucket herself and started back into the room. That slender girl must have arms of steel to carry two of these heavy buckets upstairs at once.

Netta emerged from behind the dressing screen and hurried over to try to take the bucket Alaynia carried. "Oh, no'm. Be too heavy for you."

"Netta, I can . . ."

Netta tugged on the bucket and Alaynia relinquished it before their struggle caused the water to slosh onto the floor. Shaking her head, Alaynia turned back to the bedroom door.

"Miz Mirabeau?" When Alaynia glanced around, Netta said, "Thank you. But it be my job."

Alaynia smiled and nodded, but her smile left her face as she walked down the hallway. The people at Chenaie all had their duties—their jobs—but there wasn't one darned thing she could do to make herself useful. The afternoon had dragged after they got back from Jake's. Shain had already left the house by the time she came downstairs after Tana's ministrations. Jeannie must have spent the rest of the day with the piglets, and no one appeared to think that Alaynia might want something to occupy her time. When she made the mistake of wandering into the kitchen and offering to help slice vegetables, the cook had been so scandalized that she quickly departed. She wasn't used to this inactivity . . .

She paused at the top of the front stairwell. Down that other hallway, in the original portion of the house, were four more bedrooms, one of which was Jeannie's where she'd had her coffee that morning. She heard a strange sound from an open doorway at the end of the hall, and a second later a tiny animal scuttled toward her, Jeannie in hot pursuit.

For a split second, Alaynia was horrified at seeing Jeannie chasing what she thought was a large rat down the dim hallway, before she recognized one of the piglets. When the piglet came near, she scooped it up and held the squealing animal out to Jeannie.

"Oh, thanks, Alaynia," Jeannie said in a breathless voice. She cuddled it close and the piglet's squeals quieted. "If Tiny had gotten down the stairs and Shain had found him, my brother would've had a fit."

"I thought you said at supper that the sow was taking care of the new babies," Alaynia said.

"I didn't lie, truly I didn't, Alaynia," Jeannie insisted. "But when I went back out after we ate to check on them, Tiny was all by himself over in the corner of the pen. He's the littlest one—the runt—and it's too hard for him to fight through the others to eat. I'll take him back outside just as soon as he gets a little bigger."

"Tiny, huh?" Alaynia reached out and stroked a finger across the piglet's bristly head. "He'll grow fast with you personally taking care of him. I've heard that pigs make awfully good pets, Jeannie. You can even train them to use a litter box."

"A little box for what?" Jeannie asked.

"Not little—litter," Alaynia corrected with a chuckle.

"For when he has to use the bathroom."

Jeannie continued to stare at her with a mystified expression until Alaynia realized the young girl had probably never heard of a bathroom. "Like when you use the outhouse," she explained with a grimace of distaste at the thought of the little building between Chenaie's kitchen and barn. "Or the chamber pot."

Jeannie blushed prettily and ducked her head. "Shain says ladies never discuss things like that. But . . ." She slipped Alaynia a conspiratorial look. "After all, it is something everyone has to do. I've already had to clean up after Tiny twice. Do people really keep pigs for pets where you live?"

"Some of them," Alaynia admitted with a laugh. "I've always been too busy to look after an animal."

"How do you make one of those litter boxes?"

"It's just a box with some sand in it. Put Tiny back in your room and shut the door so he can't get out, and I'll show you how to make one. I'll bet we can find something out in the barn to use."

Alaynia waited at the stairwell while Jeannie carried Tiny back down the hallway and closed the door on him. When she returned, Jeannie said, "We better go down the back stairwell. Shain's sure to see us if we go through the front of the house, and he'll want to know where we're going." With a worried look on her face as they headed for the other stairwell, Jeannie continued, "It's not that I'm trying to be sneaky, Alaynia. But Shain can be so bossy sometimes, and I'm perfectly capable of taking care of one little pig. I'm going to be fifteen in two more weeks, but he still thinks that I need to ask his permission every time I even want to go riding. Why, Betty already has her own carriage, and she goes to St. Francisville at least once a week."

Rolling her eyes, Alaynia followed the chattering girl down the stairwell. On the back veranda, Jeannie took a lantern from a hook and lit it with the matches conveniently left in the drawer of a small table. Jeannie continued to enumerate the list of decisions she felt competent to make on her own in light of her advanced age as they walked toward the barn.

She doesn't know how lucky she is to have someone care what she does, Alaynia thought. At the orphanage, the rules were set in concrete—school during the day, homework in the evening, with maybe an hour allowed for an approved television program now and then. The sisters hadn't even permitted a television in the house until Alaynia was ten, when one of the wealthy patrons donated a set to them. And the nuns were far too busy caring for the physical and educational needs of their charges to spend much time befriending them. Still, Alaynia had realized in later years that she'd probably been better off in the orphanage with the sisters than bouncing around a slew of foster homes. Recalling her own rebellion at Shain's bossy attitude, she understood the caring interlaced with his commands—at least as far as Jeannie was concerned. She herself was perfectly capable of making her own decisions.

Jeannie seemed to know her way around the barn, and quickly found a small wooden box in the feed trough of one of the empty stalls.

"The groom puts grain in these for the horses," she explained to Alaynia. "The sides are small enough for Tiny to crawl over. There's probably a shovel in the tack room, and I think there's a pile of sand out by the old kiln, where they used to make bricks."

A moment later, Alaynia followed Jeannie around the side of the barn to a domed kiln, overgrown now with weeds. Jeannie handed her the lantern and set the wooden box down by a pile of sand. Taking the shovel from Alaynia, she dug into the sand and half-filled the box.

"That should do it." She stuck the shovel upright in the sand and reached down for the box. "I'll take the shovel back in the morning."

Alaynia sniffed the air, then laid her free hand on Jeannie's shoulder when the young girl started to walk away. "Wait a minute, Jeannie. Do you smell smoke?"

The lantern light outlined Jeannie's face as she lifted her head and smelled the air. She frowned, then nodded. "The groom was shoeing some horses today over at the black-smith shop," she said, "but he's supposed to put the fire out at night."

Alaynia set the lantern down and peered through the darkness. Her eyes adjusted to the dimmer light, and a stronger whiff of smoke reached her. She turned her head into the odor, toward the area of the plantation where Shain had told her earlier in the day that the gazebo and chapel were built.

"Jeannie, look. The moon's over there, but there's a light in the trees back that way. Jeannie, I think something's on fire."

"We have to get Shain!"

Jeannie dropped the box and ran. Alaynia grabbed the lantern and took off after her. They raced toward the manor house, with Alaynia cursing her long skirts and finally managing to gather them up in one hand and free her legs. As they passed the kitchen house, Jeannie pointed at a huge bell on the porch. "Ring it, Alaynia!" she shouted. "I'll get Shain!"

Alaynia veered toward the bell and set the lantern on the ground. She seized the rope hanging from the bell and pulled it frantically, over and over again. The loud clangs reverberated across the night and, almost at once, someone lit a lantern inside the kitchen house. An instant later, she saw Shain running across the back veranda of the manor house, closely followed by Cole Dubose.

Alaynia released the bell pull, and Shain paused for only a second beside her as Cole sped on to the barn. "The workers will be coming," Shain informed her. "Send them out to the fire, and tell them to bring anything they can find to carry water in."

Alaynia nodded, but he was already gone. By then, men were streaming into the yard and Alaynia shouted at them, pointing in the direction Shain had taken. The kitchen house door opened and the cook ran out, her arms full of cooking pots and kettles. She ran out into the yard, where she started handing out the containers to the arriving men.

Jeannie skidded to a stop by Alaynia, a grim look on her young face and holding four of the chamber pots from the upstairs bedrooms by their handles. She thrust two of them at Alaynia, and started after the men. Alaynia barely managed to snatch Jeannie's arm before she got out of reach. "Jeannie, I don't think Shain would want you out there! It's going to be dangerous!"

"They'll have to form a bucket brigade from the pond," Jeannie insisted. "They're going to need every person they can get, because the chapel's farther away from the pond."

"The chapel?"

"Shain said he thought that's what it was when he saw the fire from the back veranda. But it can spread, Alaynia. Come on." Jerking her arm free, Jeannie tore off across the yard.

"Miz Jeannie be right." Alaynia turned to see the cook standing beside her. "The women, they be coming soon's they get the children took care of," the cook continued. "Keep a couple here to help fix some coffee and food, I will, and send the rest out to the pond."

Lifting her skirts again, Alaynia ran after Jeannie. By now, flames lit up the night sky and she could easily follow the path everyone else had taken. At the pond, she saw a wooden bridge built over the narrow end, with the gazebo on the other side. A hundred yards or so from the gazebo, flames engulfed a smaller structure.

Alaynia raced across the bridge and down the other shore, to where the men had already formed the bucket brigade. She tossed her chamber pots at the man at the head of the brigade and took a place in the line beside Jeannie. Particles of flying ash filled the air, and she choked and coughed as she tried to breathe. But she had little time to worry about how her lungs would be affected, as bucket after pail after kettle of water passed down the line.

Sweat poured down her body from both exertion and heat from the burning chapel. At one point, when a bucket was slow in coming, she glanced down the line and saw it stretching out for at least three dozen more people, some of them now women, as the cook had promised. She had no idea how the people nearer the burning structure could stand the heat. And the water didn't seem to be impacting the leaping flames one bit.

Shain's voice shouted above the noise of the burning chapel. Fear gripped her when she realized how close he was to the fire. He waved his arms, and the men and women in the brigade began falling back toward the pond. Suddenly the chapel collapsed with a loud whoosh, and sparks and pieces of burning timber shot upwards.

"Let it go!" Shain shouted. "Concentrate on keeping the

fire from spreading! We'll need shovels and some feed sacks!"

Several of the men raced toward the bridge to return to the barn, and Alaynia started toward Shain. But all at once Jeannie screamed, and Alaynia swiftly turned. A flame flickered up Jeannie's long skirt, and Jeannie beat at it hysterically.

Alaynia launched herself at Jeannie and tumbled them both to the ground. She gripped the screaming girl tightly and rolled toward the pond a few feet away. As soon as they landed in the shallow water, Alaynia sat up and pulled the shuddering girl against her. "Jeannie, it's all right. The fire on your dress is out. Please, calm down now, so we can see if your legs are burned."

Jeannie buried her face on Alaynia's neck, then drew in a quavering breath. Shain splashed into the water beside them, and he immediately knelt to reach for Jeannie. "Jeannie! Good God, Jeannie, what are you doing out here?" he asked in a ravaged voice. "Let's get you back to the house."

Jeannie pulled away from Alaynia and flung herself against Shain's chest. He stood with her in his arms, gazing down at Alaynia. "Are you all right? Can you get up?"

"I'm fine." To prove her point, Alaynia rose beside him and stepped onto the shore. When Shain joined her, she examined Jeannie's legs, pulling away the burned skirt material and looking for any signs of blistering. She found one small red spot, but no sign of any other burns.

"Thank God you knew what to do," Shain murmured. "She could have died—or been scarred for life."

"I'm all right now," Jeannie insisted. "You need to help with the fire."

Shain reluctantly placed her back on her feet, but held

onto her arms. "I want you to go back to the house, Jeannie. Alaynia will take you. I can't be worried about you two and still do what's needed here."

"I will," Jeannie agreed.

"And put something on that burn on your leg. And rest."

Jeannie sniffed and nodded her head. Realizing the young girl was trying to maintain a posture of bravado in front of her brother, while still fighting the hysteria of nearly burning to death, Alaynia stepped forward and wrapped an arm around Jeannie's waist. "I'll take care of her, Shain."

Someone shouted for Shain, and he started to turn away. Just as quickly, he swung back and pulled both Alaynia and Jeannie into his arms for a brief hug. The flickering flames outlined his agonized face when he pushed them away. "Go on now, both of you," he growled. "Get somewhere safe."

He ran toward a group of men, who were shoveling dirt on the flames spreading through the grass and beating at them with wet feed sacks. Jeannie instantly began shaking with reaction, and Alaynia led her toward the bridge. Keeping an arm firmly around her, she walked across the bridge and down the path toward the manor house. By the time they reached the yard, Jeannie had stopped shaking somewhat. She looked up at Alaynia. "I'll go change clothes and come back to help the women in the kitchen."

"Shain said you should rest, honey. You've had a pretty bad scare."

"Not any worse than you did when your horse threw you," Jeannie said stoutly. "I can't just sit up in my room and do nothing. You'll help me make Shain understand that, won't you?"

"I'll try, Jeannie. But promise me that you'll at least rest for a few minutes—until you're feeling a little less shaky."

Jeannie nodded in agreement and lifted a trembling hand

to brush back a golden curl from her forehead. Her face was streaked and dirty, but she sniffled and straightened her shoulders. When Alaynia reached out to rub at a smear of ash on her cheek, Jeannie threw herself into Alaynia's arms once more. Alaynia held Jeannie close and soothed her, her own eyes tearing in sympathy as Jeannie's slight figure nestled against her and her arms clung tightly. A fierce stab of love for the young girl raced through Alaynia, and she laid her head against Jeannie's. How quickly her young life could have changed if Alaynia hadn't reacted to the sudden crisis. The flames had spread with amazing speed across the yards of skirt material and could have caught on Alaynia's clothing, also, but she hadn't given an instant's thought to any danger to herself.

Over Jeannie's head, she could see the burning chapel. Tongues of fire leaped high into the sky, glowing an evil orange and interspersed with thick, flying ash, and even pieces of wood borne on the gusts of rising air. It couldn't have been more than five minutes from the time she smelled the smoke until the bucket brigade formed in an attempt to save the structure, but it had already been too late. Jeannie's future could have been destroyed in only a few seconds—far less time than it had taken the fire to devastate the chapel.

Jeannie drew back and said, "I haven't thanked you, Alaynia. You saved my life."

Saying "you're welcome" seemed rather inane to Alaynia, and she bent to kiss Jeannie's forehead. "I'm just so glad you're all right, honey. Now, hadn't you better go change—and check on Tiny?"

"I guess," Jeannie agreed. "I'll take his litter box up with me."

Reluctantly, Jeannie stepped away from Alaynia. She swiped the heels of her hands against her cheeks, took a deep breath, and headed for the sand pile on the other side of the barn. Alaynia's arms suddenly felt empty, and she watched until Jeannie disappeared around a corner.

This must be how a mother feels when she's rescued her child from danger. Jeannie's bravery filled her with pride, and she experienced a surge of satisfaction at being there when Jeannie needed her—both when the flames threatened her young life and during the aftermath to help Jeannie gather her shattered emotions. Jeannie had trustingly clung to her, her shudders and trembling abating as Alaynia soothed her. She was rapidly growing to love the young girl, and her desire to return to her former life suffered a major rent when she realized she would have to settle for reading about Jeannie's later life in Louisiana census reports.

And—she turned her head and stared back at the site of the fire—she would also have to settle for only reading about Jeannie's brother in those same reports. The flames consuming the chapel had died somewhat, but she could hear shouts in the distance as the battle to keep the fire from spreading continued. She recognized one voice among the others—raised in stern command.

Suddenly she gulped and slowly shifted her gaze in the direction of the graveyard. When she returned to her own time—and to the Chenaie of the future—would she wander through that same graveyard? Touch the headstones with trembling fingers as she read the inscriptions? One of them would be Shain's tombstone.

Would there be another headstone beside it, inscribed with the name of the woman he married? That seemed a given, since in this time period he was the only male left to continue the St. Clair line. The ache of jealousy coursing through her left Alaynia trembling far worse than Jeannie had in her arms.

Chapter 14

Shain and Cole dismounted in front of the overseer's cabin the next morning as pink fingers of sunlight crept over the eastern horizon. They strode across the wooden porch, and Shain shoved the cabin door open without knocking. His overseer, Carrington, pushed his chair back from the table and rose so quickly the chair almost toppled. Wringing a tea towel in her hands, his wife swung around from the cook stove.

"Sit down, Carrington," Shain ordered. "We've got some talking to do."

Carrington slowly reseated himself, a look of wariness on his seamed face. He glanced at his small-statured wife, who immediately scurried over to one of the cabinets and removed two coffee mugs. When Shain and Cole sat, his wife set the cups in front of them and poured them full of steaming hot coffee.

"Thank you," Shain said instinctively before he turned his full attention on his plantation manager. "Damn it, Carrington! I want to know how the hell that fire could have happened!"

Shaking his graying head, Carrington slumped even deeper into his chair. "Mr. St. Clair, I been doing the best I can. I got two men watching the grounds at night, and that leaves us short in the fields 'cause those men gotta sleep sometime. I told you the other day when them mules foundered on spoiled feed that I didn't think it was an accident."

"I can tell you for damned sure that the chapel didn't burn by accident," Shain said in a grim voice. "We found a kerosene can in the woods nearby, and a broken lantern inside the front door."

"I didn't tell the men to patrol out that way," Carrington admitted. "Figured it was more important to watch the fields and house. You planning to put out some more guards, after what happened last night?"

He glanced inquiringly at Cole, and Shain belatedly introduced the two men, then shook his head in answer to Carrington's question. "I don't plan on turning Chenaie into an armed camp, but something's got to be done. Cole's going into St. Francisville this morning to report the fire to the parish sheriff. All we've got is evidence that it was set, though—nothing to tell us who did it."

Carrington glanced at his wife, who was standing over by the cook stove again, and the woman reluctantly nodded her head. Shain immediately sensed he wouldn't like whatever they had to tell him, yet he had to know everything— even rumors. Chenaie's future was his responsibility.

Shain leaned on the table and said, "Look, I know you two are closer to the workers here than I am and hear things I wouldn't. If you know something about this, I expect you to tell me."

"Well, it really ain't nothing I know for sure," Carrington replied. "Mr. St. Clair, I took this job 'cause I needed it and 'cause you offered to let part of my wages go to buy this place here for me and my wife. With a deal like that, I decided not to pay much attention to all them stories about Chenaie. And my job here's to manage the field crews and get the crops in—that's all."

As he waited for Carrington to continue, Shain picked up his coffee cup and took a sip. He didn't need to ask his manager what stories he'd heard—he knew them well enough himself.

People claimed his grandfather, Basil, still roamed Chenaie, even twenty-five years after the old man's death. Almost every worker's cabin had a French cross painted on the door to ward off evil spirits, and every time a flicker of swamp gas showed itself, the stories and rumors grew in new force. One tale even went that the Yankees had spared Chenaie because it was protected by a spiritual force.

Hell, even Tana admitted that the blue-coats had headed for Chenaie after they destroyed Cole's plantation, but turned southward with Chenaie already in sight. Shain had traced the army's still-visible path himself after he returned home and was at a loss to explain the abrupt change of direction.

"Uh . . ." Carrington cleared his throat. "I don't want you to think I'm speaking out of turn here, Mr. St. Clair, but . . ."

"Spit it out," Shain growled.

"Like I said, it wasn't me that heard. I was out in the fields all day yesterday. But Myra here . . ." Carrington shifted his head in his wife's direction. "She's at home all day—talks to the other women while they tend their gardens. And a couple of them saw that voodoo lady and her son at Chenaie yesterday afternoon."

"Tana's not a voodoo practitioner," Cole snarled, speaking for the first time since they'd entered the cabin. "She was here because Shain's guest, Miss Mirabeau, was thrown from her horse, and Shain wanted Tana to examine her. Tana's a healer—she's treated more than one of the workers here, and she's delivered almost every one of the babies born at Chenaie since she's been living here."

Recalling Cole's own joking words about Tana while

they gathered the piglets the day before, Shain shot him a wry look. Cole flushed slightly, but continued, "Tana and Little Jim don't bother anyone. And she always comes when someone needs her."

"Cole," Shain said. "Let Carrington go on."

Shrugging his shoulders, Carrington motioned Myra over to the table. She hesitantly took the only empty chair and clasped her hands on the surface. "It wasn't the woman they was talking about," she said in a trembling voice. "The boy . . . well, they say he's still a boy in his mind, but he's as big and heavy as you, Mr. St. Clair."

"Little Jim's never harmed anyone in his life!" Cole spat. "And Tana leaves him at home, unless she's free to keep an eye on him."

"He was here yesterday," Myra insisted. "Cammie, she gave him a watermelon from her patch, and some greens. Told him to give them to his mama to pay her for the medicine Cammie got last month for her stomach pains. And she said that when the boy left, she saw one of those voodoo dolls sticking out of his back pocket."

"I don't believe that!" Cole's fist thudded on the table. The coffee cups shook, and Myra sprang to her feet. She moved over behind her husband and gripped his shoulders.

"Looka here, Mr. Dubose," Carrington said, raising one arm to pat his wife's hand. "My Myra don't lie. She was just telling Mr. St. Clair what she'd heard—like he asked her to."

Cole scraped his chair back and stood. "I apologize, Miz Carrington," he muttered. "But I've known Tana all my life, and Little Jim since he was born twenty years ago. There's not a mean bone in Little Jim's body. Besides, it's a long step from seeing him with a voodoo doll that he could've picked up anywhere to accusing him of setting the chapel fire!"

"Calm down, Cole," Shain put in. "I don't think Carrington's accusing Little Jim of anything—at least not doing anything deliberately. Little Jim's mind is stuck at five years old, though, and a five-year-old doesn't always think before he does something. You and I were about that age when we started a fire over at your place with those firecrackers we filched."

Cole uttered a contemptuous sound, but instead of answering Shain, he walked over to the door and stared outside.

"I sort of agree with Mr. Dubose," Carrington said. "The things that've been going on here—like the fire—just don't jibe with what I've seen of that Tana woman's son. And I've noticed that you don't get many visitors from 'mong your neighbors here at Chenaie. Now, a body hears things, Mr. St. Clair. A lot of folks around here ain't too happy 'bout you not letting that timber company cross your land. And a company that powerful—well, appears to me they'd be kind of ashamed of letting one landowner stand in the way of what they wanted to do."

"And they'd do whatever it took to come out on top," Shain agreed, liking his overseer more by the moment. "I've thought of that, and it seems like a hell of a lot more plausible explanation for the *accidents* plaguing Chenaie than a poor kid whose mind isn't all there."

"There's still that voodoo doll," Myra said quietly. "Cammie's sure of what she saw."

"Voodoo's been a part of the South ever since they started bringing in slaves," Shain said as he pushed his coffee cup aside and rose. "The best way to counteract that black magic foolishness is by educating our people so they'll ignore it. And the same thing goes for the talk about spirits at Chenaie. I'm not about to even add substance to those rumors, because they're completely unfounded. And I'd appreciate it if my employees backed me up."

Shain held out his hand, and Carrington stood to shake it. "I enjoy my job, Mr. St. Clair," Carrington said. "You can count on me."

"Keep your ears open," Shain replied. "And you, too, Miz Carrington, if you will. I don't have to tell you that it's more than just my family's lives riding on Chenaie's crops being successful. We've got ten cabins filled with sharecropper families, plus another five families of people working the crops for the season."

"And if you can't pay your workers, they'll leave," Carrington added. "Won't be no job here for me, if I don't have any workers to manage."

"I hope it doesn't come to that. Carrington, you're aware that I fired the man who had your job before you. And I'll admit, after my experience with him and the problems we've kept having even under you, I wanted someone to blame. I'm glad we had this discussion, because I'm convinced now that you're doing your best under the circumstances, and I think the two of us will work well together. I want you to know that I'm more than satisfied with the job you're doing in the fields. You've even got that cane crop looking like it might be profitable this year. And the workers and their families appear happier than they were under the man I had before you."

"Thank you," Carrington said with a bob of his head.

"You can also tell the people that if the crops make enough profit this year, I'll try to get the plantation store open again. It'll have fair prices, too, not like the stores on some of the other plantations. We'll price things the same as they can buy stuff for in St. Francisville. As far as I'm concerned, the law that says the workers have to stay on the same land as long as they owe money at the plantation store is a way for the owners to underhandedly control their people."

Shain glanced around the small cabin at the freshly-mopped pine floor, neatly stacked dishes and supplies on the shelves behind the polished cook stove, and starched curtains hanging beside windows open to catch the morning breeze. His previous overseer had been married, also, but after one visit, Shain had refused to enter the filthy cabin again. Now the place sparkled with cleanliness, and he'd bet the bed in the adjoining bedroom was already neatly made up.

Against the wall to his left were a worn settee and arm-chair, the same ones the previous overseer had used. An attempt had been made to scrub the food stains from the arms of the furniture, but they were too deeply ingrained. Dark spots dotted the material, and the seat of the armchair sagged almost to the floor, making it an uncomfortable resting place for a tired man after a long day's labor.

"You've done a fine job with this place, Miz Carrington," Shain said. "You know, the attic over the kitchen house is filled with furniture that used to be in the manor house. Why don't you check with Jeannie and have her show it to you? Take what you'd like for your place, and see if any of the other workers can use any of it, after you choose."

"Oh," Myra said with a gasp. "It's probably much too nice for our cabins."

"Nonsense," Shain replied. "It's just sitting up there, gathering dust." He grinned at her and Myra blushed, the pretty color in her cheeks removing several years from her age. "Consider that an order, ma'am," he said in a mock-stern voice, laughing aloud when Myra teasingly curtsied and nodded her head.

In a graver voice, Shain continued, "We'll meet each evening from now on, Carrington. I'll see you in my study after supper. In the meantime, if there's anything I need to know before that, send someone to find me."

"I will, Mr. St. Clair. You can be sure of that." He glanced at his wife with a look of love on his face. "And thank you for making my Myra smile."

"You're completely welcome."

Shain walked to the door and clapped Cole on the shoulder as he passed. On the porch, he glanced through the open window to see Carrington slip an arm around his wife's waist. "Mr. St. Clair's a good man," Myra told her husband. "You were lucky to find a job here."

"Yeah," Carrington said with a lopsided grin at her. "Long as he doesn't ask me to mow that graveyard for him."

Myra stifled a small shiver. "Oh, I hope he doesn't ask you to do that."

"Long as he doesn't ask me to mow that graveyard for him," Basil mocked the overseer. "My grandson's got more sense of obligation than that. Family takes care of family resting places."

"Is that why you scare away anyone who even looks at the graveyard who's not family?" Francesca asked.

Basil whirled to face her and Sylvia. "I wish you two would mind your own business. Or pay attention to what you've been trained to do!"

"What's that supposed to mean?" Sylvia thrust her face forward, determined she wasn't going to back down from the ghost this time. "We're doing our job here."

"Not likely," Basil sneered. "You're guardian angels, aren't you? Well, where were you when you should've been guarding my chapel last night—when someone set fire to it?"

Sylvia opened her mouth in an indignant reply, but Francesca's wing brushed her nose as the other angel fluttered past her to place herself between Basil and her companion. Sneezing violently and rubbing at her tickling nose, she glared at Francesca's back.

"We protect people, not buildings, Basil," Francesca said, "as you'd know, had you followed the usual order of things and joined us in our world. But my and Sylvia's assignment is a little different this time than just watching over Alaynia. I'd tell you about it—if you'd stay around long enough for us to finish even one conversation."

Basil rolled his eyes and crossed his arms over his chest. Evidently he would finally give them a little more of his precious time. Sylvia kept her thoughts to herself and allowed Francesca to continue, since she was sure Basil would disappear in a blink if she voiced her exasperation at his condescending attitude.

"You've tampered with Alaynia's life—changed the order of things," Francesca said. "And you cordoned off that time warp, so she couldn't find it when she was searching for it right after she arrived. You're interfering with her choice of free will, Basil. Alaynia, alone, has the right to decide if she wants to stay here or go back."

"Back to what?" Basil snarled. "She's got more here than she ever had back there. She didn't have any family—no real friends. And I don't want Chenaie turned into one of those darned tourist attractions—a lot of strange people sleeping in Chenaie's bedrooms—wandering all over my grounds and trampling my grass and plants."

He waved an arm around him. "Have you been to Rosedown and Greenwood back in that future time?" When both Francesca and Sylvia shook their heads, he went on, "They bring busloads of people in and let them gawk. And at old Whiskey Dave Bradford's place, The Myrtles, they even let them sleep in the house—like that chit was gonna do with Chenaie."

"Ohhhhh!" Sylvia dodged Francesca's outstretched arm. "Since you've been visiting the *future,* you should know that calling women names like *chit* or *girl* can get you slapped with a lawsuit! It's called sexual harassment!"

Basil threw back his head and roared with laughter. When Francesca clapped a hand over her mouth in a fruitless attempt to contain her own giggles, Sylvia scowled at them both and planted her hands on her hips. Her wings fluttered in agitation, fanning the air around them into a brisk breeze.

"What's so darned funny?" she demanded.

"Oh, Sylvia," Francesca said around her giggles. "You can't . . . can't . . ." She broke off into unladylike guffaws and swiped at a tear of laughter trickling down her cheek.

"What she's trying to say," Basil said with a chortle, "is that you can't sue a ghost. 'Course you might give it a try— if you could find one of those shyster lawyers who's managed to make it into where you live."

A deep flush of embarrassment heated Sylvia's cheeks, and her lower lip trembled. Basil immediately stopped laughing and floated over to her.

"Aw, don't," he growled, laying a tentative hand on her shoulder. "I apologize. It's just that I've been alone for so long, I guess I've forgotten how to treat ladies."

Sylvia sniffed back a sob and shifted her delicate little

nose upward. "You always treat Frannie like a lady. It's just me that you always bicker with."

Basil brushed back one of Sylvia's cornrow braids and secured it behind her ear. "Well, I've sort of missed having a woman around to bicker with, too," he admitted in a gruff voice. "My wife, Laureen, she had spunk, like you do. You remind me of her a little bit."

"You mean because of the body I use? Your wife had black blood?"

A horrified look crawled over Basil's face, and he backed away. "No! Not at all! I mean, she was Creole and had their dusky skin and beautiful black hair. But she wasn't Negro!"

Sylvia glanced over at Francesca to see her companion's blue eyes dancing with twinkles of mirth. She pursed her face into a frown of concentration, then laid her index finger beside her mouth. "I see. It's the fact that your wife and I are both women and have a woman's character traits—traits men enjoy. Beneath our different-colored skins, that is."

Francesca chuckled and Basil quirked his lips drolly. "My Laureen would've said something like that," he replied. "She always could make me see when I was acting like an idiot. In the future, they say chauvinist, like you called me the first time we met."

"Idiot—chauvinist. They mean practically the same thing," Sylvia mused.

"Maybe we could start over." Basil reached out and took Sylvia's hand, carrying it to his lips to kiss the back of it. "Miss Sylvia," he drawled courteously, "I'm very pleased to meet you. And don't you look pretty today in that red gown. Has anyone told you that you have beautiful eyes? Why, I don't believe I've ever seen quite that shade of brown—such a deep chocolate. Those little sparkles in your eyes remind me of the wonderful, star-strewn sky over Chenaie at night."

"M-my goodness," Sylvia said in a flustered voice. "If all it takes to turn you from chauvinist to chivalrous is a little banter back and forth, I think I could come to like you very well, Mr. St. Clair."

"Basil, please," Basil murmured. "And I hope I haven't taken too much liberty by addressing you as Miss Sylvia. Such a delightful name, Sylvia."

"Well," Francesca said. "Now that you two have called a truce, maybe we can get down to business here. I have to be honest with you, Basil. You've interrupted our plans for a vacation, and we'd like to get this matter settled quickly. All you need to do is stop interfering with Alaynia's choices, and we'll leave you alone."

Basil rubbed at his chin, a look of speculation on his face. "Alone, huh? Why, Miss Francesca, Miss Sylvia and I were just discussing how charming I found the company of you two ladies. You wouldn't deprive me of your companionship so quickly, would you?"

"Basil, you'd have plenty of company, if you'd join us in our world." Francesca drew in an exasperated breath. "Of course, that's your decision. But first you've got to set Alaynia's life back in order."

"Let's discuss that for a minute."

Basil waved them over to a nearby cloud, which fashioned itself into two benches as they approached. Taking Sylvia's hand, he seated her, then bowed and offered his hand to Francesca. With a sigh of acquiescence, Francesca allowed him to seat her beside Sylvia. As soon as Basil sat down across from them, Francesca crossed her arms on her chest and stared at him.

"Let's look at the situation," Basil began. "Since Miss Mirabeau has already made the trip back here from the future, who's to say that wasn't the plan for her all along?"

"I don't understand," Francesca said. "You're the one who brought her back here. Are you trying to say that your interference in her life was what was supposed to happen to Alaynia?"

"Perhaps," Basil said with a nod. "My grandson is already very much taken with Miss Mirabeau. Perhaps her true future is with him."

"You sound like Sylvia," Francesca fumed. "I've tried to tell her over and over that we can't meddle in humans' emotional lives. It's just not done!"

"Now, Frannie," Sylvia put in. "If there is love developing between Alaynia and Shain, what right do we have to intervene in that? Huh? We might be thwarting Alaynia's true destiny."

"Oh, for pity sakes!" Francesca rose from the bench. "I told you what our assignment was, Sylvia. We were to come back here because Alaynia had zipped through time—against the natural order of things."

"Nature doesn't always follow an orderly progress," Sylvia insisted. "Haven't you studied evolution? The twists and turns in the past made people what they are today. And, yeah, you told me about our assignment, but—"

"Ladies, ladies," Basil soothed. "Let's don't get into a fuss here. Anyway, that's all beside the point right now. It took quite a bit of preparation on my part to manufacture the boost of power necessary to bring that ch . . . Miss Mirabeau here through time and cordon off that time warp. I don't have the necessary time now to make those preparations again. With Chenaie being threatened, I have to protect it. And, as I'm sure you're aware, I'm the only one who can undo what I've done."

"Well, since you've been to the future, haven't you . . . uh . . . *lived* through this period of Chenaie's history?" Sylvia asked logically. "Of course, Frannie and I were occupied elsewhere, but you've been here since you died, haven't you? So you should know what happens and if things will work out all right, without your having to stay here and watch over things."

"I can't remember," Basil admitted. "I guess when I tampered with time, I tampered with my memories, too."

"Someone else may have done that," Francesca explained.

Basil's mouth dropped and he glanced fearfully overhead. After a second, he said, "Well, I can remember why I brought her back here—my reasons for that. But now I don't know what's going to happen in this time period."

"That makes a sort of convoluted sense," Sylvia said. "Angels aren't allowed to look into the future, either. The overall plan isn't ours to see. I guess it has something to do with humans' right to their free will. The choices they make foster their own growth, and we can't disrupt that."

"Something else comes to mind as extremely sensible." Basil looked back and forth between the two angels. "Three heads would be better than one lonely old ghost's head in bringing whoever's causing trouble for Chenaie's people to justice. I really can't concentrate on anything else as long as the peace and quiet of Chenaie is in jeopardy."

"Once that's back on track, you'd have some uninterrupted time to set things right with Alaynia, then?" Francesca questioned.

"If you insist," Basil agreed. "At least, my powers of concentration will be free to focus on something else."

Francesca flipped her hand and a table appeared between the two benches. She sat back down beside Sylvia and grabbed a paper and pencil from the air.

"We'll get organized, then," she said. "Oh, I wish I had my computer here, but I guess this will have to do."

Chapter 15

Alaynia picked up a piece of buttered biscuit and tore off a small chunk. Instead of eating it, she dropped it on her breakfast plate among the barely-touched eggs and ham. Surreptitiously, she slipped a look at Shain, who sat drinking a cup of coffee at the head of the table on her left, his own untouched plate shoved aside.

He didn't look like he'd slept a wink. Dark circles purpled beneath his shadowed brown eyes, and though he'd obviously taken time to wash up somewhat, a smudge of ash streaked his forehead. The shirt he wore was clean, but unironed, as if he'd picked it up out of one of the laundry baskets, and the growth of beard on his face gave him a devilishly handsome look. But the set of his mouth corresponded with the worried, shady depths of his eyes.

On the other side of the table, Cole shoved his clean plate away and pushed his chair back. "I'm gonna find me a razor before I go into St. Francisville," he said to Shain. "And get one of your servants to press the extra shirt I've got in my saddlebags."

"Whatever you need," Shain agreed. "Jake will be here pretty soon."

"Oh," Alaynia said as Cole left the dining room. "I forgot all about going to St. Francisville with Jake. Maybe I should cancel that for today."

"Why?" Shain asked. "You might as well do something

pleasant with your day. There's nothing you can do around here."

"Nothing except maybe be here for you," Alaynia murmured. "Shain, talk to me. How did that fire start? Will you rebuild the chapel?"

"It's nothing for you to worry about." Shain's lips grew even grimmer. "You'll have an escort to town, since Cole's riding in to talk to the sheriff. I've also asked him to wait until you and Jake are done shopping and ride back with you."

"Then there is something funny going on. You didn't mention yesterday that I needed anyone besides Jake with me. And what's Cole going to tell the sheriff?"

"He's just going to report the fire."

"Buildings burn down all the time, Shain. The only time law officials get involved is when there's arson."

Shain got to his feet and stepped over behind her chair. With a sigh of displeasure, Alaynia rose, then turned to grab his arm as Shain started to stride away.

"You're avoiding telling me something. Is it because you don't trust me—or because I'm a female, who's too featherbrained to understand the problems a man has to deal with?"

Shain condescendingly patted her hand on his arm, and Alaynia's temper boiled. She gritted her teeth as he spoke, his words fueling her growing anger. "Just go into St. Francisville and find yourself some pretty dresses. If there's something you want that Jake overlooks, tell the shopkeeper to send the bill to me. Oh, and Jeannie's birthday's next week. We'll have a small dinner party for her, so you might look for a present for her, if you want. Here."

Shain dug in his pocket and pulled out a coin. When he held it out to her, Alaynia could barely see through the red mist in her eyes. She bit down hard on her inner cheek, forcing herself to calmly accept the coin and clench her fist around it. A second before her anger burst its bounds, Shain tenderly brushed her cheek with his index finger.

"Have a good time, sweetheart. Don't worry about the fire or anything else. I'll take care of things." He lowered his voice, though they were alone in the dining room. "And don't think I've forgotten what we had planned. There should have been a completely different kind of fire at Chenaie last night."

Alaynia's mind grabbed desperately at the trailing dregs of her anger, but they disappeared before she could capture them. Her legs trembled as Shain lowered his head, and her arms crept upward, finding their natural place around his neck. He kissed her softly at first, then gathered her into his embrace and tightened his arms, deepening the thrilling pressure of his lips.

A long moment later, he raised his head and pushed her gently away, but ran his palms up and down her bare arms. "I don't know what brought you here," he whispered, "or how long you'll stay. But don't believe for a minute that I don't appreciate your being here. You've got enough on your mind, though, and I told you that I'd take care of you. Now," he stepped back and released her, "enjoy yourself today."

"I'd rather you were taking me to town," Alaynia grumbled. "However, I understand that you've got things here to take care of. But you darned well better understand this, Shain. I'm not used to sitting around like some ornament on a knickknack stand. I need something more to do."

They both turned toward the open dining room window when the sounds of an arriving wagon and muted voices filtered into the room. "Sounds like Jake's here," Shain said.

"I'll have the buggy hitched up, so you don't have to ride in that decrepit wagon of his."

He started to leave the room, pausing at the doorway. "Alaynia?"

She stilled her hand, which had been unconsciously rising to caress the lingering feel of his lips on her mouth, and gazed questioningly at him.

"You can assist Jeannie in planning the dinner party, if you want something to do. That would be a help. And . . ." he continued in a growl just loud enough for her to hear, "you make an awfully pretty knickknack ornament." He disappeared out the door before she could say anything more.

"Damn you, Shain St. Clair," Alaynia murmured, but her mouth refused to alter from the huge smile spreading across it. The glow pervading her body tingled all the way to her fingertips, which finally traced a lingering path back and forth across her lips. With an ironic shrug of her shoulders, she chastised herself for so easily disintegrating beneath his touch—his kiss.

He was infuriating—he was gentle. He had a temper—he was so masculine. He made her feel so feminine.

Too feminine. For years she had competed with male restorationists, building her own reputation and letting her clients know that she could read a blueprint with the best of the men—clomp around in her work boots with steps just as loud as the men. In fact, many of her clients agreed that her ideas showed much more sensitivity in recreating the period modes than the recommendations offered by her male counterparts.

She could hammer a nail—trowel a brick—visualize the final result she sought in a room and make even the tiniest adjustment necessary to smooth the flow and bring it together. But her creative abilities were useless in dealing with the emotional aspects of falling in love.

And she was falling fast—on a downhill slide that no force on earth could neutralize. She hadn't had time to untangle the logistics of it, beyond coming to terms with the fact that she'd definitely entered a time warp when her car skidded down the highway. But she'd seen no trace of it afterwards. She'd have to find it again to return to her own time.

The pull to do that wasn't nearly as strong now as when she first arrived. Always Shain hovered in a corner of her thoughts. Chenaie was Shain—his plantation, his home. He superintended its people, its crops—walked its rooms—sat on the furniture—ate his meals at the dining room table. Chenaie would never be hers alone again, even if she did reverse the time warp's path.

Part of the problem, though, was that Chenaie was totally Shain's. He shared the shelter of the manor house with her, but completely maintained the management and concerns himself. How could she ever tolerate being pampered and cosseted, rather than sharing his life? She already desperately missed the satisfaction she got at the end of each day from knowing that she had filled the hours with accomplishments of her own.

But, damn, he pampered and cosseted so nicely . . .

"Mister Jake be a'waitin' for you, Miz Alaynia."

"Thank you, Netta," Alaynia replied to the young maid in the doorway. "By the way, have you seen Jeannie lately? I stopped by her room and had coffee with her, but she didn't come down for breakfast."

"She still be in her room," Netta answered. "Told me not to bother her 'til she told me it was all right to make up her bed."

Smiling secretly as she recalled the harness Jeannie had

been braiding for Tiny earlier, Alaynia realized that Jeannie wasn't taking any chances of the servants informing her brother of her new pet. Well, Shain would find out sooner or later, but she would let that be between brother and sister. She shoved the coin Shain had given her into a pocket of her dress and walked out of the manor house to greet Jake. Noticing his nice suit and his hair slicked back into a semblance of order, she grinned delightedly at him.

"Why, Jake, don't you look handsome today."

He shot her a shy smile and offered his hand to assist her into the buggy. "You didn't think I'd squire my ravishing niece around in town wearing my work clothes, did you?" he asked as he helped her climb up to the seat. "That wouldn't be proper at all, and I do know how to be a proper gentleman when it's called for."

"Well, sir," Alaynia drawled in a simper, "I'm just gonna be so proud to have such a fine escort."

Jake smiled with pleasure and took his place beside her. Jauntily, he lifted the long driver's whip and tapped the buggy horse into motion. As they passed the edge of the manor house, Cole threw down a cigarette he'd been smoking and ground it beneath his boot before he strode from the veranda and mounted his horse. He fell in behind them, far enough back not to invite conversation.

"Zeke took the wagon on back after Shain told us we could use the buggy," Jake said to Alaynia as they drove away from Chenaie. "We'll probably pass him in a second. I'll have to do something to thank Shain for the use of his buggy. It's a much more appropriate conveyance for me to transport my darling niece on her shopping trip. And the horse is a pleasure to handle, not like that addlepated mule Zeke thinks so much of."

"It's . . . uh . . . very nice," Alaynia managed, forcing

herself not to grab the seat to hold herself steady as the wheels encountered a pothole and the seat bounced up and down. The springs beneath them screeched in protest, but Jake didn't seem to notice. With a sigh, she thought of how comfortable traveling in her car had been.

The wagon appeared up ahead. Jake kept their horse at a steady trot as they passed, and she waved at Zeke. The elderly man's eyes widened, and he grabbed at a small pouch hanging around his neck, barely bobbing his head in answer.

Jake snorted in disgust. "Superstitious fool," he muttered.

"Jake, why does Zeke seem so afraid of me? And what was that around his neck? I don't remember seeing it yesterday."

"Probably some voodoo nonsense," Jake said. "And don't you worry yourself about Zeke. I've tried and tried to tell him that he's a fool for believing—" Jake abruptly shut his mouth, then immediately began speaking on a different subject. "Say, have you given any thought to what sort of shopping you want to do? I'm afraid there's not a whole lot of choice in St. Francisville, but if you stay around long enough, maybe we can go down to Baton Rouge—or even New Orleans."

"Jake, I've already had enough of a man telling me not to worry my pretty little female head over something he doesn't think I should let bother me for one day! You backtrack right now and finish what you were saying about Zeke. Why is he afraid of me?"

"Alaynia . . ." Jake released a sigh of compliance when she glared at him in determination. "It's just superstition," he began. "But I'm sure you know how superstition can influence a person's life. Why, my granny wouldn't even leave the house for a week if a black cat crossed her path. And one day, when a bird got inside the house, she fainted and took to her bed for a month. She was sure someone close to her was going to die. I do believe she was a little disappointed when that didn't happen."

"Jake!"

"All right. All right."

Before he could continue, Cole urged his horse up to Jake's side of the buggy, a dangerous glint in his brown eyes. "Jake, what the hell's goin' on with Zeke? Since when did he take to wearin' a *gris gris* pouch? When I passed him, he was makin' an evil eye sign."

Jake sighed and pulled the horse back into a walk. For a moment, he chewed at the side of his cheek, glancing back and forth from Alaynia to Cole. Alaynia sensed immediately that Zeke's fear of her stemmed from her mode of arrival in their time period, and that Jake was trying to think of some explanation which wouldn't reveal too much to Cole.

Cole's gaze centered on her and she quickly shifted her eyes away. When she still seemed to feel Cole's burning stare, she slipped her hand into her dress pocket to finger the coin Shain had given her. Somehow it comforted her—something that had so recently been close to his body.

Jake attempted a nonchalant shrug. "Zeke doesn't answer to me, Cole. He's my friend—not my hired help."

"Then you better presume a little on that friendship and tell him what sort of trouble he can get into practicin' that voodoo nonsense in our parish," Cole said in a grim voice. "Shain's got enough problems on Chenaie right now. All he needs is someone spreadin' that bullshit around."

"Watch your language, Dubose," Jake interrupted. "My niece is a lady!"

" 'Pologize, Alaynia," Cole said. "Where'd Zeke get that *gris gris,* Jake?"

"I really don't know," Jake admitted. "I tried to talk to him about it, but he clammed up."

Cole nodded to himself and reined his horse to the back of the buggy again. For a second, Alaynia wondered why he would choose to ride behind them in the dust stirred up by the horse's hooves and buggy's wheels, but Jake seemed to read her thoughts.

"Cole's a solitary person," he said. "Been that way since I've known him—when I came here just before the war ended. A Yankee general ordered his plantation destroyed, and the troops killed his family when they tried to protect the manor house."

"I've read history books about General Sherman's march to the sea over in Georgia," Alaynia told him. "Sherman's purpose was supposed to be to destroy the South's rail lines and bridges, but he burned all those lovely houses, too. And the other night, Shain talked some about what had happened in Louisiana."

"It was as much emotional warfare as anything else," Jake explained. "Sherman wanted to bring the South completely to its knees. The people down here already pretty well knew the war was lost—their agricultural society couldn't compete against the industrial strength of the North. That bastard Sherman pounded home to them that they weren't just losing all their men in battles—the families and homes were now part of the spoils of war."

"How did Chenaie escape destruction? Cole's plantation must be nearby, since he and Shain appear to be friends who go back a long ways. Wouldn't Chenaie have been in the troops' path?"

"You'll have to ask Shain about that," Jake said in a grim

voice with a hint of evasiveness in it. "Yankee troops came
through Alexandria, north of us, too. They destroyed everything except Kent House, which they left standing for some
reason. Maybe it was just to remind the people what they
used to have before the devastation."

"Jake, you're hiding something from me again. Does it
have to do with Zeke's *gris gris* bag? And what do I have to
do with that?"

Jake pursed his lips in thought and stared out over the
buggy horse's broad back. Stifling her impatience, Alaynia
allowed him a moment's silence to think. There were
strange happenings at Chenaie that she herself had experienced—not the least of which was her own mode of arrival
at the beautiful plantation. She glanced down the road
ahead of her. They'd already passed beyond the place where
she had submitted to Shain and mounted the black horse to
ride back to Chenaie. She still saw no sign of any break in
the underbrush lining the road, and the rutted dirt path
crawled onward ahead of them. It was every bit as hot today
as two days ago, although the buggy top gave them a little
shade, yet she saw no heat waves on the landscape.

Jake cleared his throat. "You have to remember, Alaynia,
that Louisiana's people have always been a superstitious lot.
There's all kinds of stories, and some of them I'm sure
came from the integration of the very different cultures that
settled the state. They brought their own stories with them,
but not many of them had ever seen country like ours—land
that's below sea level, swamps, plains, and then hills farther
north. The people here are Spanish, French, Creole, and
Acadian, and more recently American and Negro. They
don't understand each other and probably never completely
will. And suspicion breeds fear and distrust—and sometimes superstition."

"So Zeke's afraid of me because I'm different?"

"Yes, he doesn't understand you. And he's heard all his life about things like black magic and zombies—spells and incantations to protect people against other people."

"And Zeke won't be the only one thinking that about me, if people find out where I've come from," Alaynia mused. "That's what Shain meant when he said it could be dangerous for me here."

Jake dropped one hand from the reins and reached over to pat her arm. "Now don't you worry about Zeke causing you any problems like that. He'll keep his mouth shut. I told him they'd cart him off and lock him up, if he spouted off about how you got here. Think he was a senile old man."

"Oh, that's mean, Jake. He'll never like me now!"

Jake frowned. "Guess I didn't think of that."

They rode on down the road for a few minutes before Jake's troubled face brightened. "I know," he said. "Fear and distrust come about because people don't know each other well—like I was just saying. Now, if you and Zeke got to know each other better, maybe you could get to be friends."

"I don't know how that can happen," Alaynia grumbled. "Shain won't let me step one foot off Chenaie without someone shadowing me. To get to know Zeke, I'd have to be allowed to visit your place now and then."

"What were you planning to do with Chenaie in the future?" Jake asked. "You had the deed to it with you when you arrived."

Jake frowned and nodded as Alaynia explained to him how she had come to inherit Chenaie. As she told him of her background and education—how she loved her restoration work—his excitement seemed to mount. Finally, he rubbed his hands together gleefully, while keeping his grip on the reins.

"That's it, then," he said with a chortle. "And Shain can't say one thing against it, because he's been after me for years about that."

"And just what is *that?*" Alaynia asked with a lift of her eyebrows.

"Why, my cabin, of course. Shain's always sending someone over from Chenaie to fix it up, and I'll have to admit it gets sort of chilly when we have a cold spell. At my age, I ought to have a proper house to live in, don't you think, Alaynia?"

"You want me to supervise the repair work on your cabin?"

"Nope. I want you to supervise the building of the new house I want—complete with some pretty white columns on the front veranda and a nice garden to wander through, when I'm thinking about some problem with my inventions."

Alaynia's exhilaration grew as he continued, "And inside I want nice furniture and drapes—pictures on the walls. Do you think you could do something about that washtub we have to bathe in, too? I do despise having to risk chilblains when I take my Saturday night bath in the cold part of the year."

"Do you really mean it, Jake?"

"Uncle Jake," he reminded her. "And I sure as shooting do mean it. We can get started on what you'll need today. There's shops in town where you can order the stuff you'll have to have shipped in. And . . ." He gave her a stern look. "Don't you make the same mistake Shain has before—that just because I don't live real fancy means I can't afford to. Always wanted me an elegant house, but just never had the time to spend getting it done, because I'd rather work on my inventions."

"Do you think Zeke will like having a nice house to live in?" Alaynia asked worriedly. "Or will he resent me making changes?"

Jake chuckled mirthfully. "You just make that cabin over into a kitchen house for Zeke, and he'll be as happy as a pig eating slops. He loves to do his cooking, Zeke does. That'll be something the two of you can work on together. He can tell you what he'd like to have, and you can fix it up for him."

For the rest of the short ride into town, Alaynia discussed the details of the manor house she could already visualize in her mind with Jake. There would be problems, of course. She was used to having readily available lumber, Sheetrock, and trim—and plumbing and electrical supplies. Somehow she would have to ignore the modern conveniences unattainable in this time, yet still make a comfortable house for Jake. She glowed with his faith in her, determined that she would outdo even his expectations. She could continue her search for the time warp, also, but in the meantime, she would have something productive to fill the other hours of the day.

As they reached the edge of the town, she studied the houses they passed, disappointed at their plainness. Ahead of them, they gave way to the shops lining what must be the main street. The shops were small, also, wooden buildings stretching down either side of a dirt street. Cole rode up beside them and took his leave as soon as he and Jake set a time to meet for the ride back to Chenaie.

Jake clucked to the buggy horse, and it trotted down the main street. "What's wrong?" he asked Alaynia after a second.

"Nothing," Alaynia denied at first, then relented when Jake glowered at her. "Well, I expected a little more, I guess. I thought I might examine some of the houses here to get a few ideas about what you want built. But everything we passed coming into town was, well . . ."

"The houses you want to see are at the other end of town—with the Mississippi River past them," Jake said. " 'Course, they aren't as huge as some of the outlying plantation manor houses, but then, I don't want something as large as Chenaie or Greenwood. We get time, I'll drive by Greenwood or Rosedown on the way back—or we'll visit them another day, so you can see their grandeur, which is what I'd like to have on a much smaller scale. And we can take a tour right now of the houses here in town before we leave the buggy at the stables, if you like."

"Please," Alaynia murmured.

Jake drove on down the street, and Alaynia avidly studied the people as they passed. Several women, some with small children, strolled the walkways, and she examined their clothing. Had she not known better, she would have thought she was visiting a recreation of an early Southern town, with the people in period dress. These women, though, wore clothing straight from their closets, and one little boy wore short pants—too young yet for the longer length of a young man.

Jake waved and spoke to a couple of women, and Alaynia suddenly realized that the people were staring at her, not acknowledging her tentative smiles. Oh, God, she hoped Zeke hadn't defied Jake and spread the story of how she had arrived. Gossip would already be spreading about her in this small town.

"It's not you," Jake said when he noticed Alaynia's trepidation and the way the townspeople shot her grim looks.

"It's the fact that you're staying at Chenaie. A lot of people here are sore at Shain right now."

"Why?" Alaynia asked.

"We'll talk about that later. Right now, there's a nice house coming up. Across from the church there."

Chapter 16

Several hours later, Alaynia trudged tiredly beside Jake as they left the cafe after a delayed lunch. Her mind whirled with all she had accomplished—and the hundreds of things left to do.

The shopkeepers had been eager to take Jake's orders, though she groused to Jake about having to stay in the background as the men discussed the financial and shipping arrangements. The carpenter had been extremely excited when Jake first approached him, assuring Jake that he could gather a crew and get started immediately, as soon as he got the plans in his hands. But when Jake introduced Alaynia and informed the man that she would be directing the construction, the carpenter's face fell. Still, Jake explained as they left the man's house, there was little enough building going on since the war, and she should have no problems with the man. If she did, there was another carpenter in town just as good.

The main problem Alaynia could see was having to draw up those plans on her own. She'd always contracted with a firm in Boston when making structural changes to one of the old houses, both because they had the computer software to expedite the job and because she wanted to be free to do the creative work, which she enjoyed much more. She hadn't designed a complete house since college, but she darned sure was going to design one now. Amazingly, she felt a thrill of anticipation at doing what she once considered the drudge work. But then, she had never been given the responsibility for building a house that would be her own creation.

Jake opened the door on a small shop and indicated for Alaynia to precede him inside. She glanced overhead, but couldn't read the sign from her position.

"It's Madame Chantal Boudreaux's place," Jake said. When she looked at him with a puzzled frown, he chuckled and continued, "I forgot. You're probably the only woman in West Feliciana Parish who doesn't know who Madame Chantal is. She's our resident *couturiere,* our dressmaker. Claims she's from France, but the rumor is she used to run a brothel in New Orleans. No one will say that to her face, though, since no woman in her right mind would attend an important social occasion in the parish in anything but one of her gowns."

"She must be expensive," Alaynia said.

"You're not supposed to be thinking about money today," Jake reminded her.

With a nod of compliance, Alaynia walked into the shop. No sense arguing with Jake about the cost of the clothing, since she could easily deduct that from her commission for designing and supervising the construction of the house. Lord, it felt good to have a job.

A tiny woman flew from behind a curtain separating the main shop from what was probably a workroom in the back. She pattered over to them on almost noiseless feet, her mouth pursed and brilliant turquoise eyes sparkling. The pile of obviously-dyed, carrot-colored curls atop her head wobbled precariously, and she reached up to pat it back into place as she approached, the wobbly bosom on her petite figure threatening to spill from her low-cut gown.

"Monsieur Jake," she simpered. "You have brought your

delightful niece for me to dress. Ohhhhh. I have heard of you already, Mademoiselle Alaynia. The women who are my clientele, such gossips they are. Several of them have already visited me today. But I knew they were making light of your beauty, because they have all been throwing their daughters at Monsieur Shain for years now. Come." She took Alaynia's arm. "Come over here where the light is better. I must feast my eyes on your wonderful skin."

Alaynia glanced helplessly at Jake, but he only grinned and walked over to a chair set against the wall. Madame Chantal tugged Alaynia toward the window with a surprisingly strong grip for such a small woman. Once Madame had Alaynia positioned to her satisfaction, she took Alaynia's chin and moved her head back and forth amid more murmured ohh's and ahh's.

An instant later, Madame grabbed a bolt of tangerine cloth from a pile, unrolled it, and draped it around Alaynia's neck.

"Ohhhhh. See?" she said with a glance at Jake. "Half of my customers have wanted dresses from this cloth, but I would not sell it to them. No, no, no, I would say. Their complexions would disgrace this, no matter what wondrous dress I fashioned for them. But look how it makes the roses bloom on your niece's cheeks—and her eyes glow with hidden lights. What do you think, Monsieur Jake?"

"I'm used to choosing my own clothing," Alaynia gritted. She'd had about enough of kowtowing to males for one day. "If you'll just show me to a mirror . . ."

Madame's heavily rouged face broke into a frown that deepened the wrinkles she tried to hide with a layer of powder, but Alaynia saw a calculating look settle in her eyes. The *couturiere*'s attitude did an about-face.

"Why, of course, Mademoiselle," she murmured. "And

with your striking beauty, I am sure you have had considerable experience in knowing what will bring out your best features. Not that there is much you cannot wear. Oh, my other customers will be so jealous when they see you. They will be fighting to get me to design them something that will make them as lovely as you. But I will have to tell them that it is impossible. First, I will say, they must give me something to work with, and their so-protected, milk-white skins leave much to be desired when choosing a color to wear."

Alaynia tried to stifle her laughter, but a smothered giggle escaped. Lordy, was Madame ever a saleswoman. She would bet Madame would assure each one of her other customers that, why, of course, she could make them every bit as beautiful as Mademoiselle Alaynia. When she stared into the mirror Madame Chantal led her to, she had to admit the woman had chosen well for her.

She had no desire to compete with the other women in the parish, though. Only one person's opinion of how she looked mattered, and she studied her reflection, trying to see herself through Shain's eyes. Madame adjusted the material, then scurried over to bring back a roll of silver lace, which she draped across what would be the neckline. The delicate lace appeared as frothy as a dew-sparkled spider web, and Alaynia smiled and nodded her head.

Jake sat complacently for a full two hours, while Madame intermittently draped Alaynia with various other materials from the bolts lining one wall of her shop and pointed out the designs she had in mind in the crisp, new *Peterson's* on a shelf. When Alaynia mentioned having recently perused a *Godey's*, Madame pooh-poohed that as old-fashioned and provincial. Alaynia managed to hide her wry smile this time. Madame would be horrified if she knew that everything she showed Alaynia was old-fashioned in her former world.

Madame kept up a spatter of gossip as she worked. Since Alaynia knew none of the people, she finally tuned her out. Only once did she pay attention, when Madame mentioned Cole Dubose's name. "Such a darkly handsome man, do you not think, Mademoiselle?" Madame Chantal asked. "He is in town today."

"Yes," Alaynia casually responded. "He rode in with my uncle and me." She adjusted a *paille de riz* bonnet on her head and smiled at the jaunty ostrich feather tucked into the cerise velvet band. Women had lost much when hats went out of style. She liked the perky set of the bonnet on her head and marveled at the intricate weaving in the rice straw.

"Oh, oh, oh," Madame said with a giggle and a sly glance. "Madame Escott was in this morning. We would like to see them meet, would we not?"

Although Alaynia failed to respond, Madame prattled on about Cole until the innuendos fell into place. It appeared Madame Escott, the former Annette Maxwell, had once thought herself engaged to Cole Dubose, and even had a fourteen-year-old daughter named Colette. My, the parish had been scandalized when the young Mademoiselle Maxwell had given birth with no sign of impeding matrimony. She had instead married Monsieur Escott two years later—a man who everyone knew had married Annette for not only her beauty, but the plantation she inherited on her parents' deaths.

Alaynia's attention abruptly shifted from Madame Chantal's gossip. She hadn't heard the door open, yet she knew before she turned around that Shain was in the shop. She turned as Shain sat down beside Jake, crossed his long legs at the ankles, and tucked his thumbs into his trouser pockets as he slouched in the chair. A brilliant smile crept over her mouth, and Shain gave her a languid wink, then a nod when she reached up to touch the bonnet on her head and lifted her brows inquiringly.

"I'll take this one," Alaynia told the *couturiere*. "And I believe that will be all for today."

"Not quite," Shain said as he rose and sauntered over to her. Though he directed his words to Madame Chantal, his eyes remained on Alaynia. "What do you have in white? Something light and airy."

"Ah, yes," Madame said excitedly, with a glance at Alaynia. "I see exactly what you mean, Monsieur St. Clair. I have it in the other room."

Madame scampered away, and Alaynia murmured, "I thought you were busy today."

"Would you believe me if I said I missed you?"

"I'd like to," Alaynia admitted, "but something tells me you changed your plans about coming into St. Francisville for some other reason."

He covered up the dark hint of fury in his brown eyes so quickly she could almost make herself believe she had imagined it. Instinctively, she reached out to touch his arm. "What is it, Shain? What's happened now?"

"We had a couple of wagons loaded with cotton, ready to bring in to the gin today," he said. "Like a fool, I had the men leave them out in the fields overnight, and someone took advantage of the fire last night to haul them down to the creek where we found those piglets yesterday—dumped them and rode their horses around over the cotton. It's not salvageable."

"Oh, my God! Do you have any idea who it was?"

"No way to know. They came back into St. Francisville

on the road. No way to pick their tracks out from among the others closer to town. I've reported it to the sheriff, and Cole went back out to take a look. I stayed behind to escort you home."

"Is it a terrible loss for you?"

"Not only me, but my workers. They had a share in that cotton."

"Then maybe we should forget the dress," Alaynia insisted.

"Not on your life," Shain growled. "I've had enough grief for a while. Don't deprive me of this small pleasure."

Madame Chantal reemerged from her workshop carrying a bolt of material. Propping it against the shelf on the side of the wall, she hurriedly leafed through her *Peterson's*, then waved Shain over and laid her finger on one of the pages. Shain turned back and studied Alaynia, but when she started forward to look at the *Peterson's*, he quickly closed the book and picked up the bolt of material to finger it.

"Exactly," he said to Madame Chantal. "We need it by next Friday, since we're having a small dinner party at Chenaie."

Something told Alaynia not to demand to see the dress he had chosen, as she had insisted on earlier when Madame had deferred to Jake. Shain's face, set a second ago in lines of barely-concealed misery, had softened when he glanced over at her. She could at least give him this—the pleasure he'd contended he would get from selecting her dress.

Instead, she browsed among the bonnets on the shelf, finally selecting one she considered appropriate for Jeannie. After Shain and Madame ended their discussion, she carried it over to Shain to ask his opinion.

"It's rather a mature style for my sister," Shain said, eyeing the array of peacock feathers in the blue velvet band.

"I'd think something with ribbons and flowers might be more appropriate."

"Shain, she's going to be fifteen, not five. Good grief, I saw a couple young women about Jeannie's age while we rode through town. Not one of them had ribbons dangling down their backs. Jeannie would be embarrassed to death, if I got her a bonnet like that."

"Mademoiselle is right," Madame Chantal put in. "And this bonnet will be perfect with the gown I made for your sister. It is so saucy—so perky. It bubbles with joy, as Mademoiselle Jeannie does."

"Guess I'm outnumbered."

Shain attempted a smile, but Alaynia sensed the resignation in his voice came more from the disasters he'd had to deal with in less than twenty-four hours than having his opinion overridden. His shoulders slumped tiredly as he left them to join Jake, while Madame placed the bonnet in a hatbox and Alaynia paid for it.

Before they left the shop, Jake carried two more things over to Madame Chantal, then handed them to Alaynia, his glance warning her not to argue about accepting them. With a murmur of thanks, she slipped the change remaining from her purchase of the bonnet into the pearl-studded drawstring bag and started to push the white parasol open.

"No!" Madame leapt forward and grabbed the parasol. "Oh, no, no, no! Do not raise the parasol inside, Mademoiselle. Such bad luck it will bring!"

Rolling her eyes heavenward, Alaynia said, "Madame, that's only a superstition."

Madame huffed out her bosom in indignation, then glanced over at the bolts of cloth waiting for her needle, a calculating gleam replacing her annoyance. Alaynia knew she had realized that it wouldn't do to antagonize such a profitable customer. Instead, Madame flew into a flurry of action, apparently forgetting she carried the parasol with her.

"Mademoiselle Jeannie's dress!" she gasped as she scurried toward the back room. "You mustn't forget it."

Only a second later, she came back with a box in her arms, which she handed to Shain. Grabbing the hatbox, she thrust it into Alaynia's hands and accompanied them to the door.

"I will have the white dress and at least two of the others ready by next Thursday, Mademoiselle," she said. "Shall I have them delivered, or would you prefer to come back and try them on, in case there are any alterations needed?"

Thinking of how busy she would be with Jake's house, Alaynia replied with a laugh, "You measured everything from my neck to my toes, Madame. I've no doubt everything will fit perfectly. Please have them delivered, if it's not too much bother."

"No bother at all," Madame assured her. She followed them out the door, and not until then did she suddenly seem to remember she carried the parasol. With a grand gesture, she opened the lacy, white sunshade and laid it on Alaynia's shoulder with a twirl.

"Perfect!" she exclaimed as she clapped her hands. "And it will go with the dress Monsieur Shain has chosen, too."

With a wave at the two men, Madame disappeared back into the shop and closed the door.

"Such a fuss over a silly superstition," Alaynia said to Shain, but he didn't return her amused look.

"It's part of what some people believe in," he warned. "Don't underestimate the importance of it to them."

Recalling the *gris gris* bag Zeke now wore, Alaynia glanced at Jake. Rather than enter the discussion, he took her arm and steered her down the street.

"I've got one more stop to make," Jake said. "Need to check my mail over at the post office window in the general store."

The store was only two buildings down, and Shain and Alaynia accompanied Jake inside. Jake wandered over to a sliding window beside the counter, as Alaynia avidly studied the array of goods lining the shelves. She started down one aisle with shelves of kitchen implements and reached for a stained coffee grinder just as she heard a grunt of recognition from Shain, who had followed her.

Gazing down the aisle, she saw a dark-haired woman about her own age in deep conversation with a pudgy man dressed in a gray suit. She slipped a glance at Shain, whose face was creased into a scowl. The woman must have spied them at that moment, because her slightly shrill voice called a greeting to Shain, and she walked toward them, her stout companion right behind her.

"This must be your houseguest," the woman said, upon reaching them. "Won't you introduce us, Shain? I'd thought to have to wait until next Friday to meet her."

"Alaynia Mirabeau, this is Annette Escott," Shain said in an even voice. "And Evan Fitzroy."

Alaynia remembered to only touch fingertips as Annette extended her hand, though she ardently studied the other woman who, according to parish gossip, had once been Cole Dubose's mistress. She had to admit to herself that the story interested her—maybe only because she knew so little about the lives of the people in this time period. Or maybe because the mysterious Cole appeared to be such a different person around Shain's sister.

Evan Fitzroy took her hand the moment Annette relinquished it, bowing over it to place a moist kiss on the back.

With an effort, Alaynia kept from brushing her hand against her skirt to wipe away the lingering feel of his pursed lips.

"Charmed, Miss Mirabeau," Fitzroy murmured. "It will be a delight to enjoy your company, also, next week."

"I don't recall extending you an invitation to our dinner party, Fitzroy," Shain growled.

"Oh, Shain," Annette said with a simper. "Mister Escott will be out of town on some dreadful business matter or the other. I truly hope you don't mind, but I've asked Evan to be my escort, since it simply wouldn't do for me to attend the affair alone. All the other neighbors will be there, and Colette does so want to come visit with Jeannie."

"Chenaie's hospitality is always open," Shain replied grudgingly.

"Perhaps we'll have a chance to discuss some bus—" Fitzroy began.

"This party is for my sister's birthday," Shain broke in bluntly. "I intend it as an evening of pleasure, not an atmosphere conducive to conducting business. We'll see you both then."

Without giving Alaynia a chance to even murmur a leave-taking, Shain placed his hand on her back and fairly shoved her down the aisle. She managed one apologetic glance over her shoulder at Annette, but the other woman didn't appear to notice, as her gaze remained fixed on Shain's back. Piercing darts of anger emanated from her darkened eyes, and when Fitzroy caught Alaynia's backward observation, he stepped in front of Annette to block Alaynia's view.

"What's going on?" she asked.

Instead of answering, Shain clenched his hand in the material on her dress back, and Alaynia flinched when the zipper teeth bit into her skin. He immediately dropped his arm.

"Sorry," he muttered. "You ready to go, Jake?"

Jake approached them with a roll of paper under his arms and a sheaf of mail in his hands. "Yes, I'm done. And I have something for you, Alaynia," he said, extending two pieces of paper toward her. "They just came back in the mail. Pick one." Alaynia raised her brows in inquiry, and Jake continued, "It's my tickets for the Louisiana lottery drawing in two weeks. We have to mail off to New Orleans for them."

"That damned lottery's as crooked as a dog's hind leg," Shain said. "It's just a way for the politicians to raise money to finance their campaigns."

"Heck, it's fun, Shain," Jake said. "My old heart gets all excited while I'm driving into town to check the numbers each month. Come on, Alaynia. Choose one."

Alaynia chose one of the tickets and stuck it in her drawstring bag as Jake tucked the other one in his shirt pocket. As they walked out the door, Jake handed her the roll of paper, which she took after a quick glimpse at Shain's face.

"I hope this is what you need to draw up the plans, Alaynia," Jake said, ending any hope Alaynia had of confronting Shain in privacy with the news of her recently-acquired job. "I'll pick you up again in the morning, so you can get started."

"Started on what?" Shain asked.

"Why, on my house, of course," Jake said, as though Shain had been privy all along to their discussion. "You've been after me for years to build myself a decent place, and now I've found the perfect person to design it for me. But there's a lot of preliminary work to do before we can break ground, isn't that what you said, Alaynia?"

"Quite a bit," Alaynia agreed, resolutely not meeting Shain's glower. "I'll want to measure the site and see if we need any fill for the foundation. Get a better idea of the size of house you want, before I start drawing up the plans."

"You're not gonna be spending your days with a bunch of damned men constructing a house," Shain said angrily. "There's carpenters Jake can hire, if he wants a house built!"

"I'll be damned if you're going to tell me what I can or can't do," Alaynia spat back. "I've already accepted this job, and we've begun ordering supplies!"

"You should've checked with me first. It's not a proper thing for you to be doing. Once Jake gets the house built, we can talk about your maybe assisting him in furnishing it."

Alaynia whirled on him and stuck her face right up in his. "*We* won't discuss one damned thing, Shain St. Clair! Do I have to repeat myself? I've already accepted this job and, come hell or high water, I'll see it through. I'm going to plan this house and see it constructed right from the fruit cellar all the way through to hanging the last curtain! If you don't want me staying at Chenaie while I do that, I'll move over to Jake's. He can fix me up a room in the cabin!"

"The hell you will!" Shain shouted.

"The hell I won't!" Alaynia yelled back.

Chapter 17

Long before Jake arrived the next morning, Alaynia and Jeannie put their heads together over their morning coffee and chocolate. While they talked, Tiny curled up in a basket Jeannie had found somewhere and padded with a blanket, snoring gently.

"I'm sure our carpenter can make you a table like you want," Jeannie said. "What did you call it—a drafting table?"

"Uh-huh," Alaynia replied. "I've got all my drawing supplies with me, and the table needs to have a smooth surface, which I can tilt and spread my paper out on. I'll place it in front of the window seat, so I'll have plenty of light during the day. I'll need a stool to sit on, too, like the one I saw in the kitchen the other day."

"Can I watch while you work?" Jeannie said eagerly. "Maybe help you out? I promise not to bother you."

"You wouldn't be a bother at all," Alaynia assured her. "But you might as well know that your brother's not a bit happy about me being in charge of building Jake's house. In fact, I thought I was going to have to move over to Jake's to be able to continue with this job. He might forbid you to have anything to do with it."

"Oh, pooh," Jeannie said. "Shain's so old-fashioned. That's why I never tell him when I help Jake out. Jake's taught me what all his tools are for, and I'm going to learn to drive his harvest machine when he gets it ready. Shain's always so busy he hardly ever asks me what I do over at Jake's, so I never bring it up. And Zeke lets me help feed the animals and gather eggs. He's taught me to make jambalaya, too, and cook over an outside fire. Our cook won't even let me fix my own chocolate. It's so boring being a woman, Alaynia. Men have much more fun."

Hiding her smile, Alaynia replied, "But you've got your dinner party to plan, don't you? And lessons?"

"My tutor only comes two hours a day, three times a week, and I can plan the party in the evenings. The invitations are already out, and all that's really left is to decide on the menu. The cook will take care of ordering the food she needs, and Netta will help serve. Please, Alaynia. It must be awfully exciting to plan an actual house and have it built. Why, it must be almost like having a child—knowing something will remain for years after you're dead and gone."

Amazed at Jeannie's astuteness, since that was exactly how she felt herself, Alaynia reluctantly nodded her head. "But," she said when Jeannie's eyes brightened, "you'll have to ask Shain for permission. It won't go easy on either of us, if he thinks we're hiding something from him."

"He'll never let me go over and watch the house actually being built," Jeannie said with a pout. "He'll say the men might slip and say a swear word within my hearing. Shoot, listening to Shain and Cole when they didn't know I was around is where I learned a lot of words that they don't think I know. 'Course I don't know what some of them mean."

Alaynia laughed gaily and drained her coffee cup. She would enjoy Jeannie's company, especially since Shain had avoided her after they arrived back at Chenaie yesterday afternoon. Beyond growling a disgruntled "no" when she asked if she should get her things together and move to

Jake's, he'd had nothing further to say to her. He hadn't put in an appearance at supper and, though she had lain awake well into the night, she never heard him enter his room. This morning his booted footsteps clumping down the hallway had been her alarm clock.

His not understanding how much designing and building Jake's house meant to her hurt deeply. Instead, he only seemed concerned for appearances—what his neighbors would think about a woman working among a bunch of construction men. Her pride in knowing she could accomplish the job due to her own past arduous work at educating herself had suffered a severe blow at his denigration of her hard-won experience. Never mind the fact Shain was a nineteenth-century man—unused to the freedom women enjoyed in her time. He should have been able to see how she yearned for his support in this job.

She and Jeannie walked out into the hallway and started down the stairwell in search of the carpenter. Tuning out Jeannie's ever-constant chatter, she continued her thoughts in her head. Shain wanted a woman in a white, frothy dress, which swirled in the wind and was appropriate with the gingerbread backdrop of the gazebo. She offered him a woman in work boots, with dirt sometimes under her fingernails. Shain wanted docile femininity—she had only her pride in the accomplishments she'd gained herself in a male-dominated career field.

Why couldn't he understand she'd left her entire world behind when she drove through that time warp? He offered her protection and a place to stay—she wanted her independence back, along with her self-respect, which was a part of her sense of achievement at the end of a job well done. She'd never risen above the thrill of a new phone call from a potential customer, who'd heard about her work from someone else. She knew only one way to handle a job once she'd taken it on—to throw her entire creative being into doing top-notch work.

She loved a long, luxurious soak in a bubble bath as well as the next woman and religiously had her hair styled at least once a month, though her hardhat matted her curls. Beneath her jeans and work shirt, she wore skimpy, frilly bras and bikini panties. She relished the impact she made when she transformed herself by wearing a wickedly dangerous cocktail dress to a party given by one of her customers to celebrate the completion of a renovation job, but that happened infrequently.

And she darned sure enjoyed rubbing elbows with a crew of men hired to turn her creations into reality, instead of innocuous lines on paper—men who had to explicitly follow her directions, if they wanted payment for their work.

As she and Jeannie walked across the backyard toward the stable, where Jeannie had informed her the carpenter would probably be repairing the roof, a vision of the white bolt of material Madame Chantal had carried from her back room swam in Alaynia's head. Her lips curved into a secret smile. She could be both—feminine, as well as a woman able to hold her own in a male world. The attention she had gleaned from males at the cocktail parties made her aware that, dressed in a sexy outfit, she garnered her share of masculine regard. It wasn't really fair, though, she tried to tell herself, to use her feminine charms to entice Shain. But the desire between them had already proven to be a white-hot longing. There had to be some compromise somewhere. Or else . . .

As Jeannie called to the carpenter to please climb down from the roof so they could speak to him, Alaynia thought, *Or else I guess I'd better start looking more seriously for that time warp, before these feelings I have for Shain make me want to stay here just to be near him.*

That wouldn't work at all, she realized with a deep sense of pain. How many times had she heard the saying that real love meant wanting true happiness for the person you loved? Shain deserved to find a woman who suited his needs for a wife. She could never be that woman—more than a century of time and attitudes separated them.

If she couldn't find the time warp, though, how could she spend the rest of her life as a bystander to Shain's life on Chenaie? Of course, Jake would probably offer her a home, but she couldn't bear to watch Shain marry another woman some day—raise their children at Chenaie. Better for her to read the details in the genealogy section of the future.

She would at least get the plans ready and the construction started. It could progress without her after that, and maybe she would be able to find her creation still standing near the Chenaie waiting back in the future for her.

Late that afternoon, Alaynia wandered into Jake's barn, swiping at her dripping face with a bandanna. Despite her exhaustion, she felt better than she had since arriving in this past time period. The cutoff blue jean shorts and work boots she'd dug out of her suitcase and brought over to Jake's with her were faded old friends, and the tails of the sleeveless men's work shirt flapped comfortingly around her hips as she walked.

She wouldn't be able to wear her shorts when the work crews began arriving, but Jake hadn't batted an eye after she changed in his workshop and joined him to measure the house site. Now she pulled the notebook filled with neat figures from beneath her arm and walked to the far end of the barn, where she could hear Jake pounding on something.

Jake glanced up, then laid his hammer aside and waved her over to the wooden table where he was working. "Got some figures for me?"

"Yes, I do." She opened the notebook and spread it on the table. Instead of immediately explaining the figures, though, she frowned and tried once more to discuss what she had pointed out to Jake earlier that day. "I really wish you'd reconsider the site you've chosen. I don't like the sounds coming from that logging operation on the hillside behind you."

"Shoot, Alaynia, they'll be done one of these days; then the noise will be gone. And we decided to set the house facing away from that hill. I'll make Escott an offer for that property back there, since it won't be worth much after the timber's gone. Then I can hire it replanted with pine. It'll make a nice view from my back veranda after that."

"You'll have to do that fairly quickly. In fact, it'd be best to start replanting behind the timber crew. From what I've read about the weather down here, your winters are mostly rainy. Do you have any idea how fast erosion can ruin a hillside stripped bare of timber?"

"I heard Escott left town on business this week," Jake said with a shrug. "I can't talk to him until he gets back. Maybe I can work something out with him. For now, why don't you show me what you've come up with?"

"Jake, it's not just the erosion. There's a wicked overhang halfway down that hillside that I don't like the looks of. It's been protected by the growth all around it so far, but they're timbering above it, and part of your barn's right in the path of that, should it ever let go."

"It's stood for hundreds of years, but I'll keep your

warning in mind. Now, the figures?"

Stifling her worry over what could happen to the hillside, given her knowledge of the mudslides in California in her time, Alaynia spent the next ten minutes going over her plans, with Jake nodding agreement. When she was finished, she tore out one page of the notebook and handed it to him, explaining that it was a duplicate schedule of the different stages of construction, along with the time frames for each.

"If I'm not here to finish your house, Jake, you'll have this to go by. And once I have the blueprints ready, I'll bring them over here and leave them."

"Then you're still determined to try to get back to your own era?"

"Yes," Alaynia replied quietly. "I think it's best."

Jake studied her craftily for a moment before he shrugged and looked over at her car, which sat in a corner, gleaming in the dimness. The tarp he usually kept it covered with lay in a rumpled heap on the floor.

"How much do you know about how that thing works?" he asked. "I mean, beyond what you've told me so far—putting gasoline in it to make the engine run."

"Not much more than that," Alaynia said with a sigh. "That black box in the front's a battery, and beneath those screw caps, in the holes, is something called battery acid. Here, I'll show you."

They walked over to the car, and Alaynia waited until Jake raised the hood, then pointed at the battery compartment.

"Those clamps on the side connect it somehow to the rest of the engine," she explained. "When I turn the key in the ignition switch on the steering wheel column, the energy from the battery ignites the spark plugs, and they ignite the gas. There's something called an electronic ignition that does all that."

"Then if that battery doesn't work, nothing else will either, huh?"

"Yeah. In my time, a mechanic could connect the battery to a charger that works off electricity and recharge it. Then it'll work for a while, until you can buy a replacement. But there's no electricity here to recharge it with."

"Everything I know about physics says that traveling through time is impossible," Jake mused. "But since you did it, perhaps the trip drained all the energy from this system. I don't think we have a hope at all of making this work again with what we've got available back in this period. And I really don't think this car has anything to do with how you got here."

Alaynia chuckled wryly, and Jake frowned questioningly at her.

"I was just thinking about a movie I saw once," Alaynia said. "There was a car named Christine, and it had a life of its own. That was a fantasy, though."

"A movie?"

Alaynia's explanation of movies led to a discussion of all the other things Jake would consider wondrous in her world, and another half-hour passed. She found herself surprised at how many of the concepts Jake was already familiar with, until she remembered the sheaf of mail he had picked up at the post office. Evidently, some of his friends were inventors, and they traded discussions and theories in their correspondence.

It wasn't too much of a jump from telegraphs to telephones, Jake told her as they talked. The same concept of sending sounds over wires ought to work with voices. And Ben Franklin had theorized about electricity years and years ago. Harnessing that power could lead to all kinds of labor-saving devices.

"It's not too hard to imagine, either," Jake said, "that once people have more freedom from work, they'd want some sort of entertainment to fill their leisure hours. That they'd be willing to pay for things like your television and movies."

During their discussion, something kept niggling at Alaynia's mind, and she listened with half an ear as Jake expounded on the theory of how changing forms of matter released energy, which could be turned to man's use. Boiled water changed to steam particles, which could power boats. Burning gas released heat, which in turn caused chemical changes in the metal or other materials heated over the flames.

"Jake," Alaynia finally interrupted him, "you said something earlier that I don't understand."

"What's that?"

"You said that time travel's impossible. Yet, here I am, in a dimension that's not supposed to exist—with people who have been long dead in my time. If it's impossible, how did it happen to me?"

Jake screwed up his face and chewed his bottom lip for a long moment. Shrugging his shoulders, he avoided Alaynia's gaze and murmured, "I just said that it's against everything I know about physics—as in rational, explainable theories. You mentioned other dimensions, and some people do believe those exist. One of those is a totally unexplainable dimension, but almost every culture has made a stab at setting forth a rational theory on it. Everything has to be taken on faith, though, because no one alive can tell us what it's like in reality."

Alaynia's breath caught in her throat. She could feel the

blood drain from her face, and a cold chill ran up her spine. Her entire body froze into immobility, though her mind raced frantically. It couldn't be—it had to be. Disjointed thoughts burst into her consciousness one after the other, quickly denied as inconceivable and just as quickly surfacing to be scrutinized once again. Black spots danced on the edge of her vision, but her paralyzed muscles refused to relax so she could draw in a breath.

Jake grabbed her arms and shook her. "Alaynia! Snap out of it, Alaynia! You're going to faint!"

When she failed to respond, Jake slapped her smartly on the cheek. She flinched, then stared at the little man, gasping in a breath of air. Jake tenderly took her arm and led her over to the table, where her trembling legs collapsed beneath her. She grabbed the table top, until Jake hurriedly shoved a stool beneath her bottom and pushed her onto it.

"I'm sorry," Jake murmured over and over again. "Alaynia, I'm sorry. Speak to me. I'm so sorry I had to hit you. I wish I hadn't done that, but you weren't even breathing. Forgive me. Please."

Alaynia buried her face in her hands, and shook her head back and forth. A low moan of misery escaped her throat. "No," she whimpered. "It can't be that some sort of spiritual intervention led me into that time warp. I don't believe in things like that!"

Suddenly Jake pulled her hands away from her face and gripped her chin in his fingers, forcing her tear-filled eyes to meet his gaze. "All right, that's enough," he demanded. "What happened to the Alaynia who arrived here full of piss and vinegar? The woman I was proud to accept as my niece? The woman who's got Shain St. Clair wrapped around her little finger, when every female of marriageable age in this parish has been trying to get him to propose for years?"

"Shain," Alaynia whispered in a tortured voice. "Jake, he'll never accept this. He's alluded to the stories about Chenaie at times, but he thinks they're crap. They're not, Jake. I've felt something at Chenaie myself."

Jake pulled another stool closer and sat down, taking her hands in his and squeezing them comfortingly. "Maybe you better tell me what's been happening to you over there. I can't promise that I'll believe you either—after all, science has been my life for over sixty years—but at least I'll listen with an open mind. You have to understand, Alaynia, that stories like those told about Chenaie frighten some people."

"Shain's never been afraid of anything in his life," Alaynia scoffed.

"Yes. Yes, he has, my dear. Any man who's been in battle and seen death all around him's been terrified—questioned why he came through unscathed while his friends fell all around him. In the back of his mind, he's known that in the next clash he could be one of the bodies buried in a mass grave his loved ones will never find. Men don't tell their women about those fears, Alaynia. They only talk about them to other men, and then only to men they trust—men who know the talk about the glory of battle is meaningless and that a man's ideals falter awfully quickly in the face of all that carnage."

"Oh, Jake."

Jake continued as though she hadn't spoken. "They wonder, too, whether there really is an afterlife. Death is so final and unexplainable. One instant, there's a vital person, full of life and emotions. Then just a shell that it looks like the same person, but the essential part that made the person who he was—the life—is gone."

Studying Jake's wrinkled face, Alaynia realized, given his age, he'd probably begun wondering seriously about his

231

own mortality and state of being after he died. She slipped a hand free and brushed at his frazzled hair. Jake focused his gaze, which had turned inward with his thoughts, and chuckled deprecatingly.

"Listen to me," he said. "Here I am off on one of my tangents. Guess I'm getting senile."

"I need you, Jake," she said selfishly. "You've accepted me wholly, and I don't think I could have gotten through this so far without you. Please take care of yourself."

"Well," he mused, his pale eyes beginning to twinkle. "You've given me something to look forward to each day, niece. Now let's get back on track here, and you tell me what's been happening to you at Chenaie."

"I better change clothes while we talk." Alaynia rose unsteadily to her feet. Gritting her teeth and forcing an outward display of calmness her knotted stomach muscles belied, she walked over to where she'd hung her dress on a hook on the wall earlier that day. Jake agreeably stepped around the wall, giving her privacy.

Spoken aloud, as Jake replied with a word of acknowledgment now and then from the other side of the wall, her experiences at Chenaie seemed ridiculous. A fascination for the graveyard—and a few seconds of immobility, which could have come from her shattered nerves. The dusty letters and Bible, which she might not have noticed earlier for the same reason. One thing she couldn't explain was Tana's vision of her arrival, and the healer's uneasiness in the Camellia Room—the same uneasiness that overtook Alaynia at times.

Already sweltering in the yards of dress material, Alaynia joined Jake on the other side of the wall. "Jake," she insisted, "one conclusion you've come to is definitely right. That the car had nothing to do with me coming here. What happened was that I drove it through a time warp—a hole in time. And for me to get back, I'm going to have to find that hole again. It has to still be there. It was huge enough to swallow the car."

"But you've been looking for it?"

Alaynia nodded abruptly. "Every time I leave Chenaie, I watch for anything strange. But I'll never find it in all the underbrush along the roads and Spanish moss hanging from the trees, unless I can force myself to leave the roadbed and search on foot. And I've got sense enough not to do that alone."

They strolled toward the entrance to the barn. "For me to figure this out, you're going to have to tell me some of the stories about Chenaie. No one else will. We'll have to see if any of them fit in with what's happened to me."

"Tomorrow we'll . . . uh . . ."

The buggy was pulled up beside the barn door, and Shain leaned against one of the wheels, his long legs crossed negligently and heels of his hands propped on the iron wheel rim behind him. His stance stretched his white shirt tightly across his shoulders, and it gaped open in a vee down his neck. His brown eyes centered instantly on her, though the rest of his rugged face remained motionlessly stern.

Alaynia's stomach knotted again and she faltered a step. Then, lifting her chin a notch, she walked toward him as though pulled irresolutely by a silken thread. "Jake would've brought me back," she murmured. "You didn't have to take time away from your duties at Chenaie."

"Yes I did," Shain growled in a low voice, his eyes scanning her avidly. "I was making a bumbling idiot out of myself, because I couldn't keep my mind on my work. After I let Black wander down a row of cotton seeds one of the workers had just planted, Cole and Carrington ran me off."

He uncrossed his legs and straightened, reaching for her arms. "I went back to the manor house and tried to do some paperwork, but Jeannie came into the study and asked if I minded her spending time with you. After I gave her permission—well, after she wheedled permission out of me with those expressive blue eyes and threats to pout for days—I realized how much time had passed since I'd had any time with you myself."

"It was only yesterday afternoon," Alaynia said.

"Twenty-four hours that seemed like twenty-four years," Shain admitted. "And twenty-two of those years drug by last night. Jeannie went off to work on her lessons, so she could get that out of the way before you came home. And that damned house echoed with emptiness."

A brilliant smile crawled over Alaynia's face. Only Jake's presence kept her from flinging herself into Shain's embrace and wrapping her arms around his neck.

"Guess you've got a ride back to Chenaie," Jake said with a chuckle. "I'll see you tomorrow, niece."

Jake sauntered away as Shain and Alaynia both murmured a distracted goodbye. After climbing the rickety porch steps, he turned and watched the buggy withdraw down the lane. As soon as it disappeared, he determinedly pushed the cabin door open and called for Zeke.

The elderly black man stood up from his seat in a cane chair beside a wobbly table. "She be gone, Mister Jake?" he asked.

"She'll be back tomorrow," Jake said in a firm voice. "And you need to tell her what you want done for a kitchen house, instead of pretending you're too busy in your garden. I walked over that garden while you were out fetching the cow a while ago, and you'll have to start chopping down plants if you want anything to use your hoe on tomorrow."

"Got's to water it tomorrow. Ain't been no rain and my punkin plants needs water, you want any of that there punkin pie come fall. Sweet taters, they's about ready to dig, too."

Sighing in resignation, Jake sat down and motioned for Zeke to take his seat again. Zeke complied grudgingly, and picked up a bowl of peas he'd been shelling.

"Zeke, listen to me," Jake began. "I've got a feeling that you know a heck of a lot more than even I do about how Alaynia got here. You never told me why you decided to leave Chenaie and come over here to live with me. And I never pushed you, because I've been darned happy at the food you cook up—as well as the company and friendship."

Zeke nodded warily, his fingers continuing to break open pods and brush the peas into his bowl. "You never said it out loud, but I knows you 'preciate my cookin'."

"And your friendship," Jake repeated. "In fact, I probably owe you whatever life I have left in this old body, my friend. If not for you, I'd have laid there and died that day Stubborn knocked me senseless."

"Man goes when it's his time," Zeke said with a shrug of his massive shoulders. "Weren't your time that day."

Jake leaned his elbows on the table and sat quietly, studying Zeke's downcast face and the obstinate set to his lips. The silence in the room lengthened, broken only by the sounds of the pods ripping open and the peas dropping into the ceramic bowl. After a long moment, Zeke's hands hesitated, and he slowly raised his head and pushed the bowl aside.

"Massa Basil, him and me was good friends, too," he

whispered into the stillness. "Had us lots of talks. Thought that man was gonna go crazy when Missy Laureen died."

Zeke clasped his hands in front of him and laid his arms on the tabletop, gripping his fingers together tightly. "Him and Massa Christopher—Massa Shain's papa—they just never did hit it off like a man and his son ought to. Tried to talk to him about that once, 'cause it 'peared like there was so dern much love a'tween him and Missy Laureen, there ought to be some there for Massa Christopher. But Massa Christopher, he didn't seem to want to be close to either one a them. Heard Missy Laureen say one day the boy reminded her of her own papa—cold, and unfeelin' like."

"If Basil had all that love in him to give to Laureen," Jake mused, "Christopher must have been a big disappointment, being so standoffish. And I can imagine Shain didn't have an easy time, growing up with such a cold father."

"Didn't," Zeke agreed. "Sorta think that's why Massa Shain ain't never fell in love a'fore—seein' his own mama and papa always bein' so proper all the time—hearin' them call each other Mister and Missus. Probably didn't think bein' married to a woman was all that important. Massa Basil, he was seventy-two when Massa Shain was born, and he spent lots of time with the boy a'fore he died when Massa Shain was only six. Massa Shain might not realize it himself, but I think he remembers them years, and he's got a lot of his grampa in him. His feelin's run deep. Just wish he'd've found someone besides that Miss 'Laynia when he fell for his woman like his grampa did."

Zeke slowly lifted his eyes to Jake's. "He's gonna be just like his grampa—only ever gonna be one woman holdin' his heart. And time don't matter when a man loves a woman like that. Massa Basil, he ain't never been able to let go of Missy Laureen."

"Are you trying to tell me that Basil's spirit's haunting Chenaie?" Jake asked in amazement. "That's why you couldn't stay there any longer—because you could still feel Basil there?"

"Didn't just feel him—he be there. Saw him a few times, and scared the bejeebers out of me. Finally couldn't take it no longer, and I was out for a walk one day when I ran 'cross your place. You was eatin' them cold beans out of a can, and a man ought to have him a proper meal now and then."

Jake furrowed his brow in concentration. "You've only been with me a little over nine years, Zeke. I came here a couple years before the war broke out—after it got too crowded down by Lafayette. Basil had already been dead . . . what? Eight years? Why'd it take you all that time before you decided to leave?"

"Didn't nothin' happen 'til Tana, she come there to stay, after the Yankees burnt Mister Cole's house down. Missus Catherine, Massa Shain's mama, she'd already got word that Massa Christopher was dead. She was wore out, tryin' to take care of Missy Jeannie, who was 'bout two then. All the other black folks had took off—left us on our own. Tana, she run over ahead of them soldiers. Missus Catherine was already down with the yeller fever, and Missy Jeannie startin' to get sick, too. We nursed them, but we lost Missus Catherine. Pulled Missy Jeannie through, tho'."

Zeke shoved his chair back and stood. Sweat beaded his brow, and his hands clenched into fists by his sides. He stared wildly around the cabin, but Jake could tell his thoughts were turned inward, his eyes seeing beyond the confines of the wooden walls. He started to rise and go to Zeke, changing his mind at once when the other man spoke again in a voice filled with confused awe.

"Lookin' back on it, that's when it must've happened. I heard Tana shoutin' outside, and left Missus Catherine tossin' and turnin' on the settee in the parlor, carried Missy Jeannie with me. I'd had to keep Missy Catherine downstairs when she took sick. It would of been too much work—goin' up and down them stairs all day to nurse her—and I weren't in the best of shape myself, not havin' a whole lot to eat them days."

Zeke took a deep breath, then fell silent. After a moment, Jake prodded, "Zeke, what happened next?"

Opening his eyes with a start, Zeke appeared surprised to find himself not alone. Jake realized with a stab of compassion that it took everything in Zeke to continue.

"Tana said she didn't remember it later. But I seen it happen. She was runnin' across the backyard toward me, and she went down in a heap like she'd run up 'gainst a brick wall. Weren't a cloud in the sky, but it got black as midnight. Kept tryin' to tell myself it was them Yankee guns I heard, that rumblin' noise, but Tana said later they was already marchin' behind her. They'd finished all their shootin' over at Mister Cole's place—left everyone dead 'cept Tana. I thought she was dead at first when she fell— like maybe she'd made it that far after bein' shot herself."

Zeke shivered violently. "But then that darkness fell and that rumblin' started. I could barely see Tana layin' there— like a heap of rags, she looked. Couldn't make my legs move to go to her, and Missy Jeannie, she started screamin' to high heaven. Then there was a flash so bright it hurt my eyes and I shut them real quick. Missy Jeannie, she grabbed me 'round the neck and hushed right up. I must've stood there for at least a half a minute, and when I finally looked the next time, Tana was runnin' toward me again and it was light out."

Zeke carefully lowered himself into his chair once more. "Them Yankee soldiers never showed up at Chenaie," he said, his gaze riveted on Jake's face. "Went out the day we buried Missus Catherine by myself, to try to see which way they'd gone instead. There was a yeller fever flag nailed up on one of the trees 'bout where they'd changed directions and went south. Tana, she'd come through the woods, and I never nailed that flag up there. I left it hanging, but a week later, it was gone."

"You think Basil's spirit returned to Chenaie through Tana, who's able to contact the spirit world herself," Jake said quietly. "Basil nailed the flag up to protect his plantation and his granddaughter. And he's stayed at Chenaie to protect it and be close to Laureen's grave."

Zeke nodded his head ever so slowly up and down. "Think he stayed there after he died, but weren't a strong 'nuf spirit at first to be seen. Then when Tana come—a witch woman who talks to the other side—he come through her and got stronger. And he must've thought Miss 'Laynia was gonna do somethin' he didn't like with Chenaie, so he brought her back here instead."

Chapter 18

The moment he was out of sight of Jake's cabin, Shain guided the buggy to the side of the road and wrapped the reins around the brake handle. He pulled Alaynia to him roughly and kissed her until she sagged weakly against his chest and whimpered with longing. He traced her slender back with his palms, then forced one hand between their bodies to cup her breast. The nipple hardened against his thumb, and a moan of desire tore from his throat, sliding past his tongue to lose itself in the depths of Alaynia's welcoming mouth.

Wrenching his lips free with a gasp for air, he took her hand and guided it between his legs. "Feel what you do to me?" he asked harshly.

Alaynia smiled and gently rubbed her fingertips along his swollen need, and he closed his eyes in almost-pain. Suddenly her fingers slipped the top button on his fly loose. Before he could do more than open his eyes, the second button followed, and she closed her hand around him, stroking with a firm grip.

He jerked her hand away and trapped it between them as he pushed her back onto the buggy seat. "I don't have much control left," he muttered. "Unless you want your skirts tossed right here on this seat, you better concentrate on some other part of me."

"Ummm." She licked his chin, then ran her tongue around her lips. "You wanted me to touch you there."

Pinning her on the seat, Shain quickly scooped her skirt aside and ran a hand up her thigh. "I thought I could handle it," he growled, "but I was wrong. I forgot how quickly you change from an angel to a witch when you touch me. Let's see how it makes you feel when I touch you there, witch angel."

He delved his stroking fingers beneath her panties, and Alaynia immediately lost her last shred of control. Tugging her bodice down with his other hand, he slipped her breast free of the low-cut bra, captured her surging nipple and sucked greedily. She arched against him, a wordless moan keening from her throat.

With a wretched groan of loss, Shain sat up abruptly and swept her against him, crushing her and burying his face in her hair. His heart thundered in his chest, the frantic beat matching the cadence of her gasping breaths.

"No," he whispered harshly. "Not here. Not like a pair of animals in heat."

He cupped her face in his palms, staring down into her shimmering blue eyes with their desire-laden gaze. "I can't stand it when I think I've made you angry at me," he muttered. "And when I get a chance to have you alone again after we've fought, it's like nothing will make up for it except making love to you until I've wiped away all the angry words."

"It's my fault, too," Alaynia replied, sliding her arms around his waist. "I've been so mixed up—so scared."

Shain dropped his hands from her face and ran them up and down her arms. "I know. I promised to take care of you—to try to understand how you felt. And all I've done is attempt to force you to mind me like the child Jeannie used to be. I should've made time to be with you—or kept you with me."

241

Alaynia took a steadying breath. "I'm not scared of *being* here at Chenaie in 1875 any longer. I'll just have to make the best of it, until . . ."

"Until you can figure out how to go home," Shain finished for her in a flat voice.

"You really don't understand, do you?" Alaynia said with a wistful smile. "What I'm scared of now is what will happen if I don't go back."

"Don't?"

"Uh-huh. Going back to my own time now would devastate me, because it would separate me from you for all eternity. But staying here might be a fate just as horrible. I'm falling in love with you, Shain St. Clair."

"I didn't dare hope." Shain slowly lowered his head. "I didn't dare hope that you might love me in return, the way I'm coming to love you. I'm falling so damned fast—so hard."

Alaynia cherished the surge of awe and pleasure skittering over her body as she stared deep into his soft brown eyes, reading the truth of his words in their depths. That he had come for her, admitted their argument had disturbed him so deeply, and now confessed to the same feelings she had for him, filled her with a sense of ecstasy far beyond the physical comfort of being in his arms again. This man from across time was everything to her—everything she could have ever wished for herself.

It humbled her to think she was woman enough to captivate a man like this, one who cared so deeply when he unleashed the power of his emotions. For these few, precious moments, she would deny all the obstacles—wrap the treasure he offered her in a package to store in a special corner of her mind. Should the day come when she only had her memories . . .

Cutting off her thoughts, Shain kissed her tenderly, with a longing she would remember across any span of time—with a yearning she answered with her own craving to belong to no one except him. Desire still lingered, but it melded with their shared admissions of love to form a wondrous mixture of feelings so complete, Alaynia couldn't imagine anything more powerful on earth.

Shain sipped a final kiss from her lips, nibbled a path across her cheek, and gently nipped her earlobe. "Tonight," he confided. "Tonight we're going to make love. Nothing is going to stop that from happening. I don't know how much time we'll have together, but from now on there's not going to be a minute of it wasted."

"Tonight," Alaynia agreed.

Keeping one arm firmly around her to hold her close, Shain unwrapped the reins and snapped them on the horse's rump. Alaynia snuggled against him as he drove, reveling in the feel of his hardened body contrasting with her softness, and sighing in delight each time he bent to drop a kiss on her nose or lips. When they came to the spot where Cole had shot the javelina, she sat up with a worried frown on her face.

"Shain, isn't that where the raiders dumped your cotton? Over there on the creek bank, where you found the baby pigs?"

"Yes, but don't worry about it . . ." Shain began.

"Damn it, Shain!" Alaynia grabbed the reins and pulled the horse to a stop. After wrapping the straps around the brake shaft, she crossed her arms over her chest and scooted back away from him, glaring with disbelief. "How can you keep saying that?"

"What?" he questioned in return. "For you not to worry? What good will it do for both of us to be upset? You've got enough on your mind right now. Besides finding yourself in a completely different world, you've taken on a pretty damned big job."

"It's called sharing, Shain. That's part of a relationship. There're going to be days when I'll be ready to tear my hair out over this project for Jake. I know, because I've had days like that before on projects not half this large. I'd like to think I could talk to you about it—ask your advice—maybe just get some frustration off my chest. How can I do that if I know you're worrying privately about your own problems? That you won't talk to me about them?"

"I've always had to do it on my own," Shain said. "My father made it clear that women weren't to be bothered with a man's difficulties."

"Your father probably never met a woman who could build a house, now did he?"

"Nor one he ever wanted to share his very soul with," Shain said in a voice that caressed her with warmth.

Alaynia melted toward him, but Shain shook his head and leapt from the buggy. Before she could protest, he reached across the seat and swung her down beside him. Arm around her waist, he started toward the edge of the road. "I'll show you where we found the cotton."

Alaynia tried to plant her feet, but her thin slippers gave her no traction. She stumbled forward a step, shaking her head vigorously. "Uh . . . Shain . . . wait. No. I . . ."

Shain paused and looked down at her. "What's wrong? Don't you want to share this with me? I'll tell you what we found while we walk."

"There's . . . Shain, aren't there snakes in there?"

"Come to think of it," he said in a musing voice, rasping a hand across his chin, "Cole and I did see a water moccasin in the creek that day. Probably was after one of the piglets—it had a mouth big enough to swallow one. But it's probably gone off to find another meal by now."

Suddenly a nearby bush rustled intensely, and Alaynia screamed. Whirling, she scrambled back into the buggy, ripping her skirt hem on a splintered piece of wood. Shrinking back against the far side of the buggy, she frantically called to Shain, "Get out of there! Come on!"

Shain cocked his thumbs in his waistband and stared at her with a puzzled look. "Aw, honey, what kind of man would you think I was if I ran off scared of a little sound like that? Besides, it can't be a snake. Made too much noise for that. Snakes, even big ones, they travel pretty silently."

Alaynia's fright diminished, and she glared at him suspiciously. The bush rustled again, and a sorrel horse she recognized as the one Cole Dubose rode stuck its head out from the underbrush, reaching for a clump of grass on the roadside. "You knew Cole was waiting here, didn't you?" she demanded.

"He wanted to look the area over one more time," Shain admitted. "See if we missed anything yesterday."

"Oh," Alaynia said in a small voice. "Well, I guess something as large as a horse wandering around in that brush would scare off any snakes. Help me down again, will you, darling?"

Chuckling under his breath, Shain held his arms up. Bracing herself on the floorboards, Alaynia shoved him backwards. Shain sprawled in the dirt, and with a quick flick of her wrist, she unwrapped the reins and snapped them smartly.

"You and Cole can have time alone to discuss men's concerns while he gives you a ride back to Chenaie!" she called over her shoulder as the horse broke into a trot.

"Damn it, Alaynia! Get back here!"

She glanced behind to see him scrambling to his feet in the dust the buggy left. All at once, she broke into laughter and pulled on the reins, slowing the horse to a stop. It tossed its head and craned its neck to look around at her, wrinkling its upper lip. She giggled again, then guided the horse in a circle. Keeping it at a sedate walk, she fixed an innocent look on her face and headed toward Shain.

Instead of the scowl she expected, Shain greeted her with a wide grin as he brushed at his rear. "Where'd you learn to drive a buggy?" he asked. "Thought you drove things like that car in your time."

"One of my clients used to love dressing up in old clothes and driving in the Fourth of July parade in Boston. I thought it might be fun to know how to drive a horse, as well as ride."

A gleam of jealousy flickered in Shain's eyes. "So he taught you, huh?"

"*She* and I wore the same size," Alaynia replied with a smirk. "And *she* loaned me a different outfit each July, so she'd have company in the parade. Her father raised harness horses, and she'd been driving them in races all her life. She won quite a few, too."

"Good God," Shain muttered. "Women house builders and women harness race drivers. And you said the day I met you that women in your time don't even need a man to have a child. Tell me, witch angel, is there anything a woman needs a man for at all in your time?"

"For love," Alaynia said solemnly. "Nothing will ever replace the love a man and woman have for each other."

When Shain lifted his arms this time, she slid down willingly into his embrace. Parting her lips in invitation, she wrapped her arms around his neck and returned his kiss. After he raised his head, she laid her cheek on his shoulder and sighed with contentment. "We've still got a lot of things to talk about and work out, Shain."

"Yeah. We'll start tonight."

"Tonight . . ."

"Excuse me," Cole said so near Alaynia's ear that she jumped. "But I'd like to show Shain something a little earlier than tonight."

He flashed her that devastating smile when she turned on him, but it had absolutely no effect on Alaynia. "Your damned horse makes more noise than you do," she told him with a glare. "Maybe you ought to spend some time teaching it how to sneak up on people."

"Don't see how you can call it sneakin'," Cole said with a shrug. "Not when I've been standin' over there ever since the two of you stopped here ten minutes ago, waitin' for Shain to notice me."

Alaynia blushed, and Cole immediately looked contrite. " 'Pologize, Miss Alaynia," he said with an abashed shrug. "If it wasn't important, I would've waited to talk to Shain later. Wouldn't blame him a bit if he kicked my rear end for botherin' him when he had someone as pretty as you willin' to kiss that ugly mug of his."

Shain pulled Alaynia in front of him and wrapped his arms around her waist, crossing his hands over hers and pulling her tightly against him. "Jealous?" he inquired.

"Hell, yes," Cole responded with a wink at Alaynia. "You got yourself a woman who's not only the prettiest thing to show up in this parish in twenty years, but she don't take no guff from you when you try to scare her skirts off. And she can handle a buggy right well. Be a comfort to you in your old age, when you get all crippled up and can't drive yourself around."

At ease with their bantering, Alaynia joined their

laughter. She looked up at Shain's face, relaxed now in the camaraderie flowing between him and Cole, and he returned her gaze with a quiet look of love. Then it hit her how long Cole had said he'd been watching them—the entire ten minutes they'd been there. And he'd obviously heard every word they said. Trepidation filled her mind, and Shain frowned in concern.

"What's wrong, honey?"

"He heard us talking," she murmured, with a quick glance at Cole, who averted his eyes and pretended to be totally interested in a mockingbird in a nearby treetop. "Remember what we were saying?"

"Darling, tonight's our business, not Cole's. He . . ."

"No," Alaynia insisted. "About . . ." She lowered her voice even more. "About *my* time."

Cole stepped closer and touched Alaynia's shoulder. "Look, Alaynia, don't be upset. Maybe Shain hasn't told you, but Tana and I've been friends all my life. There's not much we keep from each other. She and Little Jim are all I have left from my life before the war—along with my friendship with Shain and Jeannie, of course."

"She told you then?" Alaynia asked.

"Yes. At least, as much as she understands herself from the vision she had. She seems to think you've come here from another time—for some reason or purpose that's not clear yet. And, yeah, I heard what you and Shain were sayin'. It pretty much confirms what Tana thinks."

"Did Tana mention her vision to you at Chenaie the other day?" Shain asked Alaynia. "You didn't say anything to me."

"She alluded to a lot more than just her vision, Shain," Alaynia replied. "And you haven't exactly been available for me to talk to—at least, about the things you're willing to discuss with me."

Shain's face closed up and Alaynia quickly twisted in his arms, reaching up to stroke his cheek. "Please. I'm sorry. You've had so much on your mind—the fire, as well as the other problems at Chenaie. My presence has only complicated things for you."

"Your presence has been the best damned thing that's happened to Chenaie since I was born there thirty-two years ago," Shain growled, his face softening and a slight smile on his lips.

Cole stuck his hands in his back pockets and began whistling a tune, rocking back and forth on his heels while Alaynia flushed with pleasure. No one had ever treated her as tenderly as Shain—holding her, touching her, and speaking to her with such deep tones of love in his voice, unconcerned with who overheard.

Still ignoring Cole, Shain tipped her face up and kissed her gently. "From now on," he said, "I want you to come to me whenever you need to talk about anything at all, no matter how petty you think the problem is."

For a moment, she considered telling him what she and Jake had been discussing—the possibility of spiritual intervention in her time trip—but she couldn't bring herself to shatter the mood between them. She already knew how he felt about any talk of spirits at Chenaie—how he refused to acknowledge the rumors he'd alluded to before. Besides, Cole was still listening to every word. There would be time for that discussion later.

"Hmm." She flicked her skirt hem. "I seem to have a tear in my skirt. What should I do about it, darling?"

"Order you a new dress, sweetheart."

Alaynia laughed and shook her head. "You do make decisions easily, don't you?"

"At your service, sweetheart."

Cole cleared his throat. "You two lovebirds have the rest of the day to chat. Think I might talk you out of at least a few minutes of 'darlin's' time right now, Alaynia?"

"If you must," Alaynia said with a mock sigh. "Sometimes business does have to come before pleasure."

"I promise I'll make short business of this," Cole said with a teasing wink. "Won't cut into your pleasure time too much."

Flushing once again, Alaynia ducked her head, and laughter rumbled in Shain's chest. Lordy, it was going to take some getting used to—this unabashed jesting. She might have to dust off her own comeback skills. She was definitely on the losing end with these two men. But Shain's arms, still locked tight around her, told her he felt no lack in her, at least not right now.

"Guess you'll have to wait in the buggy, Alaynia," Cole said after a second. "We need to go over to the creek for me to show Shain what I found."

Alaynia stared at the underbrush, then stiffened her shoulders. "I'll go."

"What about ssssss?" Shain hissed.

"Why, darling," she drawled, batting her eyes at him. "What snake in its right mind would bother me with two big strong men protecting me?"

"One big strong man's enough to protect a woman," Shain said with a laugh, sweeping her up into his arms. "Lead on, Cole."

"Me?" Cole took a step back, his eyes wide in feigned panic. "Why me? You're the big, strong protector. You go first. You just said there's snakes in there."

"I did, didn't I?" Shain mused. "Maybe we should let Alaynia go first then. She's not as large as us, but she's still bigger than a snake—big enough to scare them off."

Alaynia giggled and tightened her arms around his neck. "Not me!"

With a grunt of teasing scorn, Shain walked toward the underbrush with her in his arms. A few yards down the path, he murmured, "Guess men are good for a few things, huh?"

"I can think of one or two," she replied, nuzzling her nose against his neck. "Give me some time, and I might come up with some more."

"Well, I'm still interested in this procreation without a man's help."

"Yeah, me, too," Cole said from behind them.

Alaynia glanced over Shain's shoulder into Cole's teasing eyes. "I'll tell you both about it—some day."

All too soon, they came out onto the creek bank, and Shain set Alaynia down. She stared in dismay at the piles and piles of ruined cotton. As Shain had said, the raiders had dumped the cotton bolls on the muddy banks and into the creek. Most of the cotton was trampled into the mud, and the rest of it lay in water-logged clumps, with the creek water running over it sluggishly.

"It's horrible," she said.

"Yeah," Shain said in a grim voice. "When I get my hands on whoever did this, they'll wish they'd never seen a cotton boll in their life."

Cole walked over to an area of the bank and knelt down. When he rose, he handed half a horseshoe to Shain.

"This is what I found," he said. "And I didn't run across the other half of it anywhere on the trail to town. Someone was cruel enough to force his horse to carry him all that way with a hell of a sore foot. And he must've been smart enough to ride in front of whoever else was with him—so his prints would be wiped out."

Shain studied the half of horseshoe briefly, then gave it back to Cole. "You planning on checking with the blacksmith?"

"Tomorrow," Cole said with a nod. "And I'll turn this over to the sheriff."

"It won't hold up in court," Alaynia put in.

When Cole and Shain glanced at her in surprise, she shrugged and said, "I like to watch shows with court trials on TV. *CSI*'s pretty good at teaching a person to pick up clues, too."

The men continued to stare at her in mystification. "What don't you understand?" she asked. "Court trials or clues?"

"TV," they both answered.

"Oh. Well, I'll let Jake explain that to you, since he understands it better even than I do. But what I meant about the horseshoe is that you'd still have to prove that actual horse and rider were here on the night of the raid. The owner might claim he'd been riding around here some other time."

"If he had that shoe repaired the day after this raid," Shain said logically, "it'd be pretty damned good evidence in my book."

"Circumstantial," Alaynia said. "He can say someone borrowed his horse without his knowledge—that he found him like that in his own stable the next day."

"I think I'm losing my jealousy," Cole told Shain. "Don't know as I could handle life with a woman smarter than me."

"She's right, though," Shain replied. "So I guess we'll have to get a bigger pile of circumstantial evidence, or catch that bastard in the act."

"Yeah," Basil mused from his seat on the tree limb.

"Yeah, what?" Sylvia asked. "Yeah, you agree Alaynia's right?"

"That, too," Basil conceded, disregarding Sylvia's satis-fied smirk at his admission of Alaynia's feminine mental tal-ents. "But what I meant is, whoever's sabotaging Chenaie won't stop now. With the three of us, we can keep watch better—catch him or his hired hoodlums when they come around again."

"Too bad we don't have Frannie's computer here," Sylvia said.

"Computer?"

"It's an electronic piece of equipment Frannie uses to keep track of all of her angels when we're at home," Sylvia explained. "We could program in our suspects and have it keep watch on them."

"It'd have to handle a lot of people," Basil grumbled. "Any one of Chenaie's neighbors could be behind this. They all want that timber company's money in their hands as fast as they can get it."

"Frannie's computer can handle anything we put in it. But who's got the biggest motive? You've been watching what's been going on down there for a lot longer than Frannie and me."

"Fitzroy and the timber company," Basil spat. "I've known it's him all along, but like Alaynia says, we've got to have something that will stand up in court. He's been smart enough to make friends with the people who need his money so bad—keep them stirred up and ticked off because Shain won't let the company cross Chenaie land."

"That's the way he protects himself, I guess, by making it look like it could be any of dozens of people retaliating against Shain."

"Right," Basil said. "Say, wasn't Francesca supposed to join us?"

"She had to make a trip home. Violet—that's who took

over for Frannie when we left supposedly on a vacation—wanted to talk to her about something. She'll be back soon."

"What's it like there?" Basil asked quietly.

"Wonderful," Sylvia replied unhesitatingly. "It can be peaceful and quiet, or you can get involved, like Frannie and I do. It can be whatever you choose it to be."

"Well, I sure wouldn't want to sit around. I'd want something to do."

"That can be arranged." Sylvia quickly decided to take advantage of the interest Basil expressed in life beyond the plane on which he now existed and expand on what he could expect. She wouldn't tell him much, she reminded herself, recalling the plan she and Frannie had decided upon. They would tantalize him, but allow him to think he had total control of his decision.

Which he really did, she mused as she fell silent and watched his contemplating face. There was also that other question she and Frannie needed answered, and maybe he would consider responding to her inquiry now, given their improved relationship.

"Why do you want to spend your existence here, Basil?" she asked.

His face immediately closed up. "Chenaie has always been everything I wanted."

Sylvia sighed in consternation. Frannie's rationalization about a human male's resistance to change was evidently true.

They watched Shain and Alaynia start back toward the buggy, with Cole trailing along behind. After the buggy headed down the road toward Chenaie again, Basil rose and glided after it. Sylvia followed him on silent wings, not speaking again until they reached the graveyard near the manor house, where Basil drifted down beside the tomb-stone towering above the smaller monuments.

"You wife's buried there, isn't she?" Sylvia asked in a respectful voice.

"Yes, my Laureen. She loved Chenaie, just like I did. I used to tell her sometimes that I thought she'd only married me for Chenaie. 'Course she joked back at me, saying I'd only courted her to have a mistress for Chenaie."

"It must have been a lot of responsibility for a woman—running a place this complicated."

"She got tired sometimes," Basil admitted. "But so did I. We were each other's strength, though."

"How did she die?" Sylvia asked.

For a second, she thought he wouldn't answer her. Then he spoke in a voice gruff with clogged grief. "It was so stupid. And it was my fault. I never could deny her anything, and she saw that darn stallion Thibedeaux had for sale—thought it would be a perfect stud for Chenaie. I had to leave on a business trip to New Orleans the same day Thibedeaux delivered that son of a gun. I never thought she'd try to ride him. The fall broke her neck."

"Oh, dear."

"They sent me a couple wires, but they didn't catch up to me until I got off the steamboat in New Orleans and went to meet with my factor there. They couldn't keep her until I got back—they had to go ahead and bury her. I never saw her again."

Sylvia maintained a considerate hush as Basil flicked a live oak leaf from the top of the tombstone. For a second, he studied the flowers in an urn placed at the front of the large stone, which were wilting in the heat. He blinked his eyes, and a fresh bouquet replaced the bedraggled one.

She was beginning to understand Basil a little better. At

first, she'd thought he wanted to hang around Chenaie because it fed his ego to survey the results of his lifetime of work—built with the labor of people he'd bought. But perhaps his reasons for the opulence were more to have what he considered a proper place for his wife to live.

And he definitely carried a load of guilt over Laureen's death. She knew quite a bit about guilt. At times, the human spirits under her care had lamented how they had lived their lives. Part of her job had been to counsel them and remind them of all the good things they had achieved. One way she had helped them overcome their regret was to quickly integrate them into their new plane of existence, which now included friends and family from their previous lives.

An idea began forming in her mind, and she could hardly wait for Frannie to return so they could discuss it.

Chapter 19

Alaynia prepared for the night as carefully as though it were her wedding night. After lavishly scenting the water with floral bath salts, she bathed in the tub and shampooed her hair, rinsing it with a pail of water she'd kept back for that purpose. Blessing her hair's natural waviness, she combed it free of snarls and roughed it up with her fingers, allowing it to dry on its own. She sprayed a mist from the only bottle of perfume she'd brought with her and walked through it, wanting the fragrance on her entire body.

Slipping into the nightgown she had packed in Boston—the shortie with the spaghetti straps—she covered it with her floor-length robe. When she received her commission from Jake, a couple more nightgowns were on her list of needed items.

A smile of anticipation tilting her lips, she turned the rose comforter back on the bed, smoothing and tugging until it lay in a neat triangle, exposing the snow-white sheets. She fluffed up the pillows and propped them against the headboard. This was right—so right. She wanted Shain—wanted to make love with him and feel him a part of her. The intensity of her feelings—her love—mocked anything she experienced before. She had not one inkling of doubt that their night together might be a mistake, or that their commitment to each other was wrong. Whatever else happened—however much time they had together—at least she would always have her memories of this night with Shain.

Briefly the thought crossed her mind that, should she eventually return to her own world, she might go pregnant. She could support a child—she would dearly love having Shain's child. But it was unlikely for her to become pregnant at this time of month, with her menstrual cycle due in another four days and her always being regular.

She'd tried birth control pills with John, at his insistence. However, after only a month, her gynecologist had taken her off them, citing what the doctor considered a tendency toward blood clots due to the hormones. Not wanting the invasion of any other artificial deterrent to conception in her body, she carefully studied and practiced the rhythm method, much to John's disgruntlement at times.

She had decided to take no precautions with Shain. If she became pregnant, if she had enough time and opportunities to conceive a child with Shain, she would welcome it.

With nothing left to do until Shain joined her, she walked over to the drafting table, which the carpenter had already finished under Jeannie's direction. Turning the wick up on the kerosene light in the wall sconce, she adjusted the tabletop for the best illumination. Beside her case of drawing pens lay the stack of letters. Darn it, she knew she'd left them on the mantle. She glanced at the fireplace and saw the Bible in the same place, but the cover open. Swiveling, she stared through the open window at the graveyard.

It was peacefully serene, with no sign of mist hovering over the large tombstone, and she didn't feel frightened this time. Her usually pragmatic mind had come to her rescue, telling her this was something she had to deal with. But instead, frustration built. She'd tried to bury her conversation with Jake in her subconscious and concentrate on the coming night with Shain, but she remembered every word of the discussion. Too many things pointed to the one conclusion she and Jake had reached—she had traveled through time on the basis of some spiritual intervention.

The lack of any other explanation topped the list of reasons, but she still had no idea why it had happened to *her*. Tana had experienced a vision of her arrival. She, herself, had felt something—someone?—the first morning she woke in the Camellia Room. The letters and Bible weren't in the room prior to the time she and Tana entered after her fall from the horse, and Zeke was scared to death of her.

Reluctantly, she picked up the letters and untied the string once again. Flipping through them, she read the faded addresses—some to Basil St. Clair of Chenaie Plantation, St. Francisville, and others to someone named Laureen Loreauville, Alexandria, Rapides Parish. The last two were addressed to Laureen St. Clair of Chenaie, and one of them was unopened.

She carried the letters with her and walked over to the fireplace. On the inside of the Bible, she studied the names more carefully. Basil's parents were listed as being from Boston, which didn't surprise her too much. The attorney had sent her a copy of the initial report the detective had made to Great-Aunt Tilda, confirming her distant connection to the St. Clair family by the marriage of one of her now-deceased relatives into the line.

She traced across from Basil's name and read that of Laureen Loreauville, of Rapides Parish, and the date of their marriage—September 9th, 1809. They had only one child, Christopher, born in 1812. Christopher married Catherine Amite of East Baton Rouge Parish in 1842. The lineage history continued with notes of Shain's and Jeannie's birth dates, in 1843 and 1860, respectively, and ended with a note in a different, more feminine hand of

Christopher St. Clair's death in 1863, annotated as killed in battle that year in the War Between the States.

She desperately wanted to discuss all this with Shain, but despite his declaration of love for her, she felt their relationship was still too tenuous to be put to the test of that strain. Yet she realized she was doing the same thing she accused him of that afternoon—not sharing with him a disquietude over something troubling her. Why on earth had she been selected to look into Chenaie's past, as the appearance of the letters and Bible seemed to indicate? Even more puzzling—why had she been transported into this time period? What effect would her arrival have on future events—both here and back in her own time?

Surely, her disappearance had caused the attorney to start an investigation. They would find nothing, though, except her unmade bed in the hotel room. Assured by the hotel management of being able to return and find another room if she needed it, since they were infrequently booked up in the July off-season, she had repacked before she checked out. The attorney had promised to have the utilities at the manor house reconnected and the house cleaned before she met him, yet he had mentioned some problem with the hot water heater. Hopefully, the plumber should have had a new one installed before she reached the house, but one could never tell.

Her car and all her belongings had been transported, along with her, through the time barrier. Her apartment lease had been up for renewal, and she had made up her mind as soon as she received the attorney's notice of her inheritance to reside at Chenaie. Cleaning out the apartment hadn't taken long—she donated her worn furniture and other things she didn't want to the Salvation Army and rented a small storage shed for what she decided to keep—

mostly books and a couple of antiques she'd found and restored, which she couldn't bear to part with, as well as her stereo, television, and DVD player. She'd paid the rental fee for a six-month period, and when she didn't return, the contents would be auctioned off after a while.

She had to talk to Shain about this—overcome her reluctance to bring up a subject she knew he found distasteful. Or perhaps it might behoove her to discuss it first with Tana and gather more information to uphold her and Jake's conclusion. The healer had offered her friendship, seeming quite confident Alaynia would eventually need to accept it.

The connecting door opened, and Alaynia turned from the fireplace. Shain's face wore a brooding look she at first mistook as worry over either the catastrophes at Chenaie or a new problem. She glided toward him, bare feet whispering on the carpet, and he hesitantly held out his arms.

She immediately sensed the reason for his concern. Why, he was anxious about what was about to happen between them. *How sweet.* She curved her arms around his neck and tilted her face up for his kiss.

Shain's words confirmed Alaynia's thoughts. "I want this night to be right for both of us," he murmured. "I want us to remember it for the rest of our lives—whether we're together or apart."

"You'll always be a part of me, Shain. Whether I'm with you or not."

He kissed her tenderly at first, but the ever-present desire between them quickly flared into deep longing. One large palm cupped the back of her head, fingers tangling in the dark brown curls as he tasted inside her mouth. His other hand smoothed a path to her waist and tugged at the belt on her robe, slipping it free from her careless tie.

Nudging the robe apart, he slowly inched toward her

straining breast, caressing her through the silky gown and sending waves of pleasure cascading over her body. His thumb stroked the underside of her breast, the path of the swirls creeping ever closer to her puckered nipple. When he finally brushed it, Alaynia tightened her arms around his neck to keep from wilting beneath the onslaught of desire, and moaned deep in her throat.

Shain answered her in kind and swept her up to carry her over to the bed. Instead of laying her down, he allowed her to slide down his length and feel the evidence of his own need. Arching her hips, Alaynia rocked against him, teasing and tantalizing him until the rhythms of their gasping breaths matched the cadence of their movements.

"Witch," Shain growled, sliding her robe from her shoulders. "Beautiful witch—my angel."

The robe pooled at her feet, and Alaynia untied the belt of Shain's dressing gown with trembling fingers. Still locked against him, she slid it from his wide shoulders and kneaded the corded muscles bared to her seeking fingers. It caught between them for a second, but Shain splayed his hands on her hips and pushed her away far enough for the dressing gown to slip to the floor. Capturing her close again, he kissed her deeply as he inched the short gown upward.

Her tongue played willingly with his until he broke the kiss and kissed a path to her ear, then down her neck, tarrying at the spot that brought a whimper of longing from her. Raising his head, he stared down into her face as he pulled the gown on upward, tugging gently until she lifted her hands from his shoulders and allowed him to remove it completely.

"I love you, Alaynia," he whispered. "I want to see all of you."

Stepping back, he studied her as she proudly posed for

him and swept his eyes slowly, inch by inch, down her body. Her breasts swelled even more when his gaze touched them, the nipples clenching with need. She perused of him in return, starting with the cap of black hair tousled by her fingers into tempting disarray and almost losing herself in the deep, desire-laden depths of his sleepy eyes. His partially-open mouth beckoned with promises of pleasure, and the corded neck set on shoulders wide and sweeping. The dark spots of his own nipples crinkled amid the swirls of kinky hair, which narrowed down his chest toward his waist.

He was magnificent. She could sense his gaze traveling lower on her body, and the moistness between her legs responded. She had touched him in the buggy earlier that day, but now her eyes could see the blatant evidence of how much he wanted her. He surged as her gaze touched him there, and his hands clenched beside his muscular thighs.

"Will I do, my love?" she asked with in an impish tone, wandering her gaze back up his body and fixing it on his face.

"Perfectly," Shain responded. "You're beautiful, Alaynia. No man could ever want more than you."

He cupped her breasts and flicked his thumbs back and forth across the nipples. Her eyes drifted almost closed and her lips parted, and when he lowered his head to touch one nipple with his tongue, she gripped his shoulders and slowly wilted onto the bed. He followed her, catching her hips and moving her across the cool sheet to lie down beside her.

Alaynia held his head against her breast as she reached down between them and caught him in her hand. His moan of need at her touch was smothered against her breast, and she stroked his length, circling tantalizingly around the tip. Releasing her breast, he lifted himself over her, then gripped her arms and raised them above her head.

"I want this to last, lovely witch," he murmured. "I want you wild with wanting for me—as wild as I already am for you."

"I want you now, Shain," she insisted, arching up against him.

But he caught both her hands in one of his and lowered his head. His kisses and swirling tongue began covering her body, starting with her eyelids and moving down her cheeks, her neck. His other hand slicked down her side, his fingers gently kneading and caressing. When his mouth found her breast again, his fingers found their home between her legs. With an incoherent gasp meant to be his name, she clenched around his hand as he slipped his fingers into her and rubbed a thumb across her center of desire. Her body crescendoed into a thousand pieces in a shattering ecstasy such as she had never experienced.

His nudging for entrance brought her back to the reality of realizing her passion was far from quenched. Wrapping her legs around him, she offered herself willingly. Arms free now, she held onto the bulging biceps of his upper arms and opened her eyes. As he slipped inside her, Shain's face contorted into an agonized mask of pleasure. She gasped with the beginnings of a new fulfillment, forcing herself to keep her eyes open and watch him. His obvious ecstasy sent spirals of flames over her entire being. He moved tentatively at first, struggling to prolong their enjoyment. Her own sense of womanhood flared, the wonder of being able to give so much to him filling her with a joy she couldn't contain.

"So hot, so sweet. I love you so much."

"I love you, Shain," she gasped in a barely audible voice. "Be with me this time—oh, God, be with me in the wonderful feeling you give me!"

He responded by burying his face in her neck and quickly carrying them both into a swirling sea of peaking desire. Both their bodies trembled and quaked, and Alaynia rode the wave of sensation even higher with the sense of Shain traveling with her into the ever more towering waves of pleasure. The shattering culmination lasted on and on, until her body reached a satiation so deep it exhausted her.

Vaguely aware of rumpled sheets and crushed pillows, silky, passion-slick skin contrasting with rough, masculine skin, Alaynia drifted toward sleep cuddled in Shain's arms. His throaty growl of her name left her no doubt she had satisfied him with her womanhood.

And she realized she loved him even more intensely now. He was her soul mate—the one man for all time who was the other part of her.

Chapter 20

Alaynia woke druggishly, savoring the immediate realization of Shain still holding her close, his even breathing feathering against her hair. He had evidently pulled the sheet up over them, since she had fallen asleep against the warmth of only Shain. Now a cool breeze filtered through the silent, inky room, chilling her back. She glanced over Shain's shoulder to the wall sconce, which she remembered had still been burning while they made love. It was dark, perhaps out of kerosene. A dim shaft of moonlight fell through the open window, but beneath the bed canopy, darkness surrounded them.

Cautiously, averse to disturbing Shain's peaceful sleep, she edged out of his arms and sat up. The comforter lay heaped at the bottom of the bed, and she stretched toward it. Her movement dislodged it, and it slipped over the footboard to the floor.

Shivering, Alaynia inched away from Shain and crawled over the footboard. Picking up the comforter, she carried it around the bed and spread it over Shain. He mumbled something unintelligible and shifted to his side, reaching out and drawing her pillow into his embrace. Cradling it against his chest, he relaxed once again into deep sleep.

"Huh," Alaynia whispered. "Let's see if you can tell the difference between me and that pillow after I get back in place."

She started toward the foot of the bed, so she could

crawl over it again instead of Shain, and her foot caught in her robe. She picked it up, deciding to put it on to counteract the chill, since her shortie gown was anything but warm even if she could have found it. As she tied the robe sash, her gaze fell on the open window.

Slowly, almost reluctantly, Alaynia walked to the window, her bare feet padding soundlessly across the carpeted floor. Warily she glanced out. Her hand instinctively clutched her throat when she saw the ghostly light hovering over the towering tombstone in the graveyard. The beckoning sense flowed between her and the light, but this time she was more prepared. Resisting the pull, she took two steps backward, assuring herself that her body responded to her own mind, not whatever force waited beyond the window.

"I don't know who you are," she whispered more mentally than through her moving lips, "but I'm tired of being afraid of you. I'm tired of you leaving signs around, confusing me, and stirring up more questions than answers. If you can communicate with me, do it. I've got some questions of my own for you."

The scene beyond the window remained unchanged, though Alaynia thought for just a second the ghostly light brightened briefly. Her temper flared just as fleetingly. Shoving aside the thought of returning to the safety of the bed and trying to analyze things in the morning, she determinedly headed for the bedroom door and left the room.

Alaynia had walked down the shadowy and dark hallway enough times to know just how long it was. Still, her heart thumped erratically as she gazed down the tunnel of blackness ahead of her. She was far too mature to be carrying a fear of the dark with her. She trailed her fingertips along the wall to guide herself. The hall floorboards groaned in one spot as she headed for the stairwell, and another protesting board creaked beneath her foot as she descended through the even deeper darkness of the steps toward the back veranda.

She shoved the door at the bottom of the stairwell open and stepped out. The roof overhead left the veranda, too, in almost total gloom, and she hurried down the steps and into the yard. There moonlight gave enough illumination to see a little better. She turned left toward the line of huge live oak trees separating the graveyard from view.

Spanish moss dangled in spiraling lengths from enormous, gnarled limbs, swaying silently in the night breeze and brushing the massive tree trunks in places. The scene, so peaceful and soothing in the daylight, took on a different, more unearthly beauty in the night. Pale white moonlight feathered mistily down through the tree leaves and branches, sheltering that area of the grounds in a protective haze. Somewhere on the veranda behind her, a cricket chirped, and the full-throated, deep voice of a bullfrog called out by the pond, the sounds an accompaniment to each other and a melodic backdrop for the mystery the night held.

Consciously willing herself to move, Alaynia strode resolutely across the dew-soaked grass. Counteracting emotions crowded her mind. One second, she felt a strong desire to confront whatever force had tampered with her life. The next she had to compel her leaden legs forward again, almost as though moving through the thigh-high resistance of water. One portion of her mind chastised her foolishness, telling her that she was not only unwise but absolutely stupid to be walking through the night at what must be after midnight to try to talk to a ghost. Another portion eagerly prodded her forward, tired of the upheaval of uncertainty.

Beyond the trees, a fence surrounded the small graveyard. Alaynia stubbornly headed for the gate, chin high with determination, and her gaze on the hovering light. As her hand touched the iron gate, the warring factions of her mind froze her into immobility once more. Her fingers clenched around the cold iron, and the tiny hairs on the back of her neck and her cheeks lifted amid the goose bumps cascading down her body, across her arms and stomach. Her mind went blank, her body a stone statue. There was a presence here—something she could perceive as distinctly as she could feel her own heart pounding in her chest.

The light shifted shape, forming into the semblance of a man's body. Unable to tear her gaze away, Alaynia watched features form on the face, the body become more visible, dressed in a gray coat and darker trousers. She could still see through the body, which drifted a few feet above the tombstone and hovered, watching her in return.

"Who are you?" Alaynia croaked.

A twig snapped behind her, and Alaynia whirled with a gasp. Shain stood a few feet away, and for a moment she thought the apparition had appeared there in full body. But Shain wore his night robe, and though his features were similar to those on the presence, she could discern the differences easily enough.

Quickly Alaynia turned her head back toward the graveyard. The presence was gone. Only spatters of moonlight shifted here and there through the tree leaves, bouncing around on the marble stones as the breeze set the branches trembling. She uttered a faint moan of distress, mixed with relief.

"Did you see him?" she asked Shain without turning to face him again. "Who was he?"

"Alaynia, what are you talking about? And what are you doing wandering around out here at this time of night?

Come back to bed and we'll talk there."

"No." Alaynia shook her head in denial and lifted the latch on the gate. It swung open with a rusty creak, and she avoided Shain's grasp when he reached out to stop her. "I want to know who's buried there. You can wait here, if you want, but I'm not going back inside until I figure out what's going on in my life!"

"Damn it," Shain said, following behind her. "My grandmother's grave doesn't have anything to do with you."

Stopping in front of the tombstone, Alaynia traced a fingertip over the lettering of Laureen St. Clair's name. "Your grandmother?" she murmured. "No, it wasn't her. He was a man."

"Who? Who the hell are you talking about?" Shain asked.

Alaynia recalled Shain's testiness every time their conversation approached the topic of the rumors about Chenaie. He adamantly refused to discuss them, and denied any possibility that there could be a smidgen of truth in the stories. But now he would have to listen to her. She had seen the proof with her own eyes.

Alaynia swung around to face him and took a deep breath. "I just saw a ghost here. I've felt him before, up in the Camellia Room. And there've been strange things happening that can't be explained. I need to talk to you about them."

"Bullshit!" Shain spat. "I've told you before that Chenaie's not haunted!"

"No, you never said that," Alaynia replied patiently. "You changed the course of conversation whenever that subject came up. Look." She laid a tentative hand on his tensed arm. "If you don't want to discuss it with me, I'll accept your decision. But, Shain, I'm going to follow up on this. Before a few minutes ago, all I had were feelings and confusion about how such a baffling thing as my traveling through time could have happened to me. But I saw him, Shain."

"You saw moonlight shining on the fog—or swamp gas. A person's eyes play tricks on him at night."

"Did you see anything like that?"

"No, but I was watching you. I wasn't paying attention to anything, except trying to catch up with you. I thought you might be sleepwalking."

"I'd never been more awake in my life. Every sense I have was alive when I came out here. I know what I saw— just not who it was. And I know what's been happening to me is real. There's no other explanation, Shain. And I have to get to the bottom of it."

Shain stared down at her, his lips grim and his eyes pooled into bourbon-colored, unforgiving depths. He evidently didn't believe a word she'd said. She sighed in defeat and turned back to the tombstone, knowing in her heart that puzzling out the riddle would begin here, in this peaceful place, amid Chenaie's previous inhabitants. She had traveled to another dimension—a dimension where, as impossible as it seemed, people long-dead still existed . . .

She touched the smooth marble, running her hand across the surface. It felt warm beneath her palm, as though the sun rather than the moon shone on it. Glancing down, she saw a vase of dew-kissed, fresh flowers sitting on the stone ledge. Their scent drifted up to her, similar to the aroma lingering in her room from time to time.

She asked Shain, "Who leaves the flowers for her?"

When he didn't answer, she peered over her shoulder, expecting to find him gone, although she hadn't heard him leave. He stood in the same spot, glowering at a smaller headstone in the next row of the graveyard. In the dimness, Alaynia couldn't make out the name on it.

"Shain?" she asked softly. She stepped back from the tombstone and took one of his clenched hands in her own, prying at his fingers until she could slip hers between them. "Shain, talk to me. Don't shut me out."

After a moment, Shain muttered, "I sure as hell wouldn't like to believe that *he* was still around here. He hated Chenaie. When he left with his regiment, we never had even one letter from him. Zeke told me after I came home that the first word Mother heard was when a soldier brought word he'd been killed at the Battle of Missionary Ridge up in Tennessee. He's not even buried there. Zeke said Mother insisted on a headstone, though."

"Your father?" Alaynia asked.

"He planted the seed I grew from," Shain said with a shrug of dismissal. "And the ones for the other babies Mother lost just about every year, until she managed to carry Jeannie to term. But I knew from the time I was old enough to begin rationalizing things out that he intended to leave Chenaie just as soon as he felt I could take over and manage it. I spent most of my childhood learning how to be what my father felt a gentleman planter should be. And that was fine with me. Chenaie's all I ever wanted."

He looked down at Alaynia, a deep yearning in his velvety eyes. "Until I met you. Fell in love. Alaynia, why can't you let it be? You're here now, and Chenaie's complete with you here. I didn't even realize there was something missing until you came. Mother was mistress of Chenaie, but she was really just a figurehead. She managed to put in an appearance at the balls and other gatherings my father insisted on giving, if she wasn't recovering from a confinement. You've made Chenaie come alive—made the manor

272

house a place I want to come home to in the evenings, instead of just somewhere to do the bookwork and sleep at night."

"Jeannie . . ." Alaynia began.

"Jeannie's been begging me for over a year to let her go up to Boston to school when she's sixteen," Shain interrupted. "She's restless, like our father was. Oh, she loves Chenaie, but in a different way than I do. I'll let her go when it's time. She's got a fine mind, and I don't want her to grow to resent Chenaie."

"Like your father did," Alaynia said.

"Yes."

Reluctant to antagonize Shain, since the times he opened up to her were infrequent, Alaynia nevertheless felt her eyes drawn back to Laureen's tombstone. Shain's fingers clenched around hers when he caught the direction of her gaze, and he sighed in resignation. "You're not going to let it alone, are you?"

"I can't," Alaynia admitted. "Because it's not letting me alone. Or he's not."

"Damn it, Alaynia! There's no such thing as ghosts!"

Tilting her chin up defiantly, Alaynia faced his anger. "Then what the hell was it I saw here a few minutes ago? Or more on the point, *who* the hell was *he?* And who put the packet of letters belonging to your grandmother and grandfather in my room? Who's been leaving the Bible open on the fireplace mantle?"

"The servants . . ."

"Netta keeps that room spotless," Alaynia insisted, "and there was dust all over both the letters and Bible, as though no one had touched them in years." Shain's lips parted again to speak, but she rushed on, wanting him to understand everything, now that she had his attention. "How did

I get from 2005 to 1875? How? All right, I know I drove through a time warp, but what happened to it afterwards? It wasn't there when I looked for it. It was enormous, Shain— massive enough to swallow the entire car. It couldn't have just disappeared." Suddenly she gasped. "Unless . . . unless something with the power to do so kept me from seeing it again."

Shain snorted in derision. "Maybe you ought to talk to Tana about that. She's the one who's supposed to be in touch with the spirits!"

"I intend to." Shain's frown deepened at her words, but Alaynia continued, "I have to know, Shain. You can't imagine how I feel. Put yourself in my place. How would you handle it, if you were galloping along on that black horse of yours one day and all of a sudden you rode through a time warp before you could stop? You found yourself at Chenaie in the future—with everyone you knew caught somewhere in the past, where you'd never see them again?"

"If you were there with me, I'd manage."

"What if I wasn't? Or what if whatever . . . whoever led me into that time warp decides I've served my purpose— whatever that is—back here? I was caught off-guard that first time. Will I have to be vigilant for the rest of my life— at the whim of some spiritual being playing with my life again? How can we build a lasting relationship together, if we don't know how much time we'll have with each other?"

Shain pulled her roughly into his arms and bent his head close to hers. "Then you admit you want us to be together always."

"Oh, yes," Alaynia breathed. "I want it more than I've ever wanted anything in my life. I love you."

"Then marry me, Alaynia. Be my wife, now and forever."

The stab of exhilaration spread through Alaynia rapidly, washing through her senses and crowding out thoughts of anything else but Shain's proposal. Her lips parted in anticipation, and she returned his kiss, curling her arms around his neck and burying her fingers in his hair. Being in Shain's arms felt so right, so exactly right. Flashes of past loneliness briefly intruded. A vision of evenings in an apartment she had once thought cozy now centered on her in the extra bedroom which served as her at-home office, a half-eaten sandwich on her desk. The phone rang only when she had a call about her business—never with an invitation for a few hours of only fun. The men who called were interested in a pretty ornament on their arm for a social occasion to advance their own careers, and then a tug of war at her apartment door. None of them were as sensitive as the man who held her so tenderly now, kissing her with an aching need that told her how much he loved her.

Never had she felt more fulfilled—even at the peak of their culmination earlier that night. Never had she wanted anything more than to tear her mouth free and shout to the world that yes, she wanted to be Shain's wife.

And when he lifted his head, gazing down at her with a quirked eyebrow of inquiry, she threw all caution to the night wind and joyfully smiled up at him. "Yes," she said adamantly. "Yes, yes, yes, I'll marry you. When can we do it?"

Shain laughed eagerly and lifted her into his arms, swinging her around once before he set her down. "How about right now? We can ride into St. Francisville and wake up the minister."

Alaynia giggled and ducked her head shyly. "Don't you think we should at least get dressed first?"

"Do you mean you'd really do it?" Shain asked in awe. "Do you care that much for me?"

Alaynia looked up into his face and caressed his cheek. "How can you doubt how I feel?" she teased. "I've accepted your proposal in a graveyard, of all places." Shain gave a start and glanced around them, but Alaynia pulled his head back to hers. "And I can't think of a more appropriate place for us to pledge ourselves to each other, Shain. There's just one thing, though."

Shain closed her mouth with a tender kiss. The ever-close-to-the-surface passion flared, and he groaned, dragging her body against his, hungrily sweeping her mouth with his tongue. Her eager reciprocation thrust any doubts from his mind as he sought to fill her thoughts with only himself and their love for each other. He lifted his head and gazed down into her blue eyes, which were dimly sparkling with moonlight and flares of feeling.

"Are you sure there's only *one* condition attached to your love for me?" he murmured.

"Oh, Shain, it's not a condition. My love for you is absolute, without any qualifications. I want it all, though—all our lives spent together. I want to stay here at Chenaie with you, but I want to be certain that's possible and what my future's supposed to be. I want our children to know their father—and their mother, for that matter. I don't want to read about my family across a span of time and realize I can never touch you, or them, again."

Shain sighed and gazed over her head at the tombstones lining the graveyard. For years, he'd scathingly denied the possibility of anything supernatural at Chenaie—denounced any hint made by anyone brave enough to defy his ire and bring up the subject. Then a package of femininity perfectly suited to his arms and emotions dropped into his life on a dirt road one day, insisting she came from a time he himself had no hope of living into.

Looking back on it, he realized he had casually accepted the circumstances of Alaynia's arrival—too casually. Jake's explanation had been an easy out, especially when he had all the other problems at Chenaie to worry about. He hadn't bothered to rationalize any further than being all too grateful that the woman he hadn't even realized was missing from his life had finally appeared—no matter the mode of her manifestation.

"Shain?" Alaynia whispered.

Gazing back down at her, he said, "If you left me, I'd search this earth for you. But crossing time wouldn't be an option. That would be one barrier I could never span."

"Unless we knew how it was done—whether something actually played with my life and will now let me make my own decision as to whether I stay or not," Alaynia replied. "Please, Shain. I have to know."

Though it went against everything he had ever believed in, Shain reluctantly nodded his head in agreement. "All right. I won't interfere, unless I think you're getting into something dangerous. You have to let me know what's going on at all times, Alaynia. I don't believe in this nonsense, but I'm willing to try to keep an open mind. Especially since I don't want to ever lose you from my life, now that I've found you."

"I'll be careful," Alaynia promised solemnly.

"You better be," Shain said gruffly. "But I think you're going to have a problem finding time to talk to ghosts."

"Why's that?"

"Because you're already spending all day working over at Jake's. And I've got plans of my own for our nights—plans that no damned ghost is going to interfere with!"

He swept her up into his arms and started out of the

graveyard. She giggled and laid her head on his shoulder. When he nudged the gate open wider, it creaked with a rusty sound again, and Alaynia lifted her head to stare behind them. He paused a second and turned back to look himself. The tombstones stood in peaceful serenity, but then, what else could they do?

With a grunt of perplexity, he swung around and headed for the manor house. "How soon can you get dressed?" he asked.

"Dressed? You weren't kidding then? You really want to get married tonight?"

"Changed your mind?" Shain's voice growled with a deceptive softness.

"Nope," Alaynia said impishly. "But what about a license? And blood tests?"

"Blood tests?" Shain said in astonishment. "What the hell do you want my blood tested for?"

"Whoops," Alaynia said with a laugh. "I forgot that's not necessary in this time."

Shaking his head, Shain carried her up the veranda steps. At the steep stairwell, Alaynia shifted in his arms, evidently thinking he would put her down. Instead, he tightened his grasp and effortlessly climbed the shadowed stair treads.

"Shain, I can walk up here. Put me down."

"Haven't you ever heard of being carried over the threshold?"

"That's after we get married," Alaynia protested, but he was already at the top of the stairs, his breathing only slightly strained.

"Who's getting married?"

Shain allowed Alaynia to slide to the floor and peered toward Jeannie's shape, where she stood at the intersecting hallway to his left. In the dim light, her long white gown stood out eerily, almost unnerving him.

"What are you doing out of bed?" he asked sharply, in order to counteract his uneasiness and total derision at himself for his alarm. Damn this talk of spirits in the middle of the night.

"Who can sleep with people carrying on at all hours—walking up and down the stairs and hallways?" Jeannie replied with a shrug. She moved a step closer to them. "Are you two in your night clothes? What's going on?"

A scuffling sounded in the hallway behind Jeannie, and she turned with a gasp. Crouching down, she grabbed something into her arms, then rose and started toward her room. "I'll be back in a minute, and you then can answer my questions," she flung over her shoulder.

"Jeannie, get your butt back here right now!" Shain called. "What's that you're hiding from me?"

Jeannie hesitated, took one more step, then turned with a sigh. Eyes adjusted to the lack of light, Shain could see the front of her night robe bulging and quivering. A snuffling noise reached his ears, then a faint oink.

"Jeannie," he said in shock. "Have you got a pig in this house?"

With a resigned though steady gait, Jeannie came toward him, while beside him, Alaynia muffled a giggle when a piglet poked its nose from the front of Jeannie's robe. His mouth gaped, and he groaned in disbelief. The piglet oinked louder, leaving no doubt as to its species.

"I'm only keeping him in my room until he's strong enough to fight the other piglets for his food, Shain," Jeannie insisted. "Tiny's not making any trouble."

"Tiny," Shain said. "That animal isn't just a pig, Jeannie, it's a javelina. He'll be growing tusks before you know it!"

"Right now he's just a piglet," Jeannie fired back.

"Pigs are messy . . ." Shain began.

"Not Tiny," Jeannie denied. "He's cleaner even than a cat. Why, he even knows how to use the bathroom in his box."

"Use the . . . Jeannie, who's been teaching you things like that?"

Alaynia tried to surreptitiously slip away, but Shain barked her name and she halted. Retracing her steps, she passed him and slipped an arm around Jeannie's shoulders. "Shain, Tiny's been in the house since the day we found the piglets," she said, "and he hasn't caused any trouble yet— or any messes. When it's time, I'm sure Jeannie will put him in the pen outside."

"You knew about this?" Shain asked.

"Yes," Alaynia admitted. "The night we saw the chapel burning, we were out by the barn, fixing up a litter box that Tiny could use to go to the bathroom in."

Shain stared from Alaynia's face to his sister's, mentally groaning as he felt his status of unquestioned master of Chenaie slipping further away. He would never be a match for the feminine wiles Jeannie was developing, wherein she seemed to feel that not asking for permission for what she wanted to do was the best avenue to gain her own way. And Alaynia didn't bother to even ask. She just self-assuredly made her own plans, whether he was agreeable or not.

Amazingly, he found he really didn't give a damn. Whatever made the two most important women in his life happy—whether it be building a house or making a pet of a pig—gave him a contented feeling in return. Alaynia had, though, agreed to one of his own plans, and Jeannie's quizzical face as she stared at Shain in his night robe brought that thought to the forefront of his mind.

"Now that we've got that settled," Jeannie broke into the stretching silence, "who's getting married?" She prattled on before Shain could answer, "Since you and Alaynia are the only two here, I guess it's you two. I suppose you were just going to slip off and tell me about it later. Well, I like that. I sure plan to ask you to my wedding, brother. And I darn well intend to come to yours!"

Shaking his head in incredulity, Shain stared at the two women through the dimness. Jeannie was more a child-woman yet, but on the verge of blossoming into full woman-hood not only physically, but mentally. He'd helped her grow into this independent, assured person, confident enough of his love for her to stand up to him and speak her own feelings openly.

And Alaynia, his love and soul mate. He could never ask for a better woman than the woman he had fallen in love with to be an advisor for his sister, to help steer Jeannie through the years yet to come. If Jeannie matured into half the woman his Alaynia had become, the man his sister chose some day would be a truly lucky devil—as lucky as he was going to be to have Alaynia for his wife.

But he had to get that ring on Alaynia's finger first. Perhaps the holy vows they took would act to bind her to him forever—be a commitment even the spirits would shy away from tampering with. But he didn't believe in spirits, he reminded himself.

"Well, brother?" Jeannie demanded.

Stepping forward, he brushed a golden curl from Jeannie's face and gazed at her lovingly. "I wouldn't think of getting married without you there, Jeannie. It wouldn't be a proper ceremony without the two women I love the most there."

Jeannie threw one arm around Shain's neck and hugged

him delightedly. Pulling away, she said, "It won't take me a minute to get dressed!" She hugged Alaynia for good measure and scampered down the hallway.

"Uh . . . Jeannie," Shain said. When she paused, he asked, "Do you think you could leave the pig at home? Not that it would bother me that much, but the minister might think it strange."

Giggling impishly, Jeannie blew him a kiss. "Will do, brother, dear."

Alaynia slipped an arm around Shain's waist as they watched Jeannie disappear. "You've done a wonderful job with her, Shain. You can be proud of her."

"Not half as proud as I am of myself," Shain replied, nuzzling her hair.

Alaynia glanced up at him. "Oh? And where did that ego trip come from?"

"From winning you," Shain said softly, cupping her cheek and gently tracing her cheekbone with his thumb. "From having a woman like you say she loves me—purr in my arms and then climb with me to an ecstasy I never thought was possible."

Alaynia's eyes filled with tears, and he caught her to him. She wrapped her arms around his neck, and he kissed her with all the tenderness and love he could dredge up from the very bottom of his soul.

"But it's not ego, darling—it's humbleness," he finally murmured. "I'm in awe of the fact that you've agreed to marry me—share your life with me. I love you, Alaynia."

"Oh, God, Shain. I love you, too. And it's a forever love, my darling. I'll love you forever, no matter what that turns out to be."

Chapter 21

"I wish Frannie were here," Sylvia grumbled. "I've got a feeling she's not going to be real happy with this."

"About what? The wedding?" Basil settled on a tree limb as Shain's buggy pulled up in front of the small, white-washed house where the minister lived. A bare hint of rose tinted the eastern sky, and a light shone through a window. The noise of the buggy pulling to a stop brought a portly little man already dressed for the day to the front door.

"Well?" Basil prodded when Sylvia didn't answer. "What do you think Miss Francesca's going to be upset about? After all, I heard her say that angels aren't supposed to get involved in the emotional affairs of their assignments."

"If you think about it," Sylvia said finally, "that's just what you've done. If you hadn't led Alaynia through time, this wedding wouldn't be happening."

"That statement must be some female twist of logic," Basil said. "Maybe I created the physical situation, but my grandson and Alaynia fell in love on their own. I had nothing to do with that. My powers aren't used for things like that voodoo nonsense."

"Voodoo?" Sylvia gasped. "What in the world are you talking about?"

"Oh, you know. Some girl wants a man for her own. Let's say this girl's name is Peggy. And we'll call the man she wants Joe. But Joe, he wants a different girl, who we'll call Amy. Well, Peggy's determined to make Joe fall in love

with her instead of Amy, so Peggy visits one of those supposed voodoo priestesses—or maybe old Marie Laveau herself, if she lives in New Orleans. She gets one of those love
potions and tries to win Joe for herself. I guess the law of
averages says often enough that the Peggys will end up with
the Joes they want, and those stories get around and give
these priestesses their presumed powers. The Peggys the
spells don't work for are too ashamed to ever admit they
tried something like that, and they keep their mouths shut."

"I wasn't accusing you of voodoo!" Sylvia exclaimed.
"Why, how could you think such a thing?"

"Now, Miss Sylvia," Basil soothed. "That's not what I
meant at all—that you were accusing me of tampering with
their minds. I was just explaining that love between two
people isn't something anyone can make happen or not
happen. It either develops on its own, or never comes at all."

"Oh," Sylvia said in a mollified voice. "Well, that's sort
of what I've been trying to tell Frannie all along. But she
keeps saying there's a thin line between protecting someone
and matchmaking. Sometimes, though, you can see that
two people would be just perfect for one another—like that
truck driver was for my first assignment. Jacki had been
alone for so many years. She was pregnant with her
daughter when her husband got killed in a car wreck, and
she raised the kids on her own. Mac, the truck driver—he
was so lonely, too, because he'd always done long hauls and
never had time for a relationship."

"What made you think your Jacki would be able to build
a life with a man gone all the time driving a truck?"

"You see, that was just it," Sylvia said eagerly. "Mac
wasn't doing long haul anymore. He was already negoti-
ating for a business in the town where Jacki lived. He
wanted to settle down."

"So you just accidentally arranged for them to meet?"

"I had nothing to do with the tire on Jacki's Jeep blowing out," Sylvia said stoutly. "And Mac was gentleman enough to turn his truck around and help out a woman alone."

"How did he know she was alone?" Basil asked. "I've been to that time period—that's how I found out what Alaynia was going to do with Chenaie. And I'd think it fairly impossible for a man barreling down the highway in one of those big trucks to pass a car going in the opposite direction and see there was a pretty woman in it, driving alone. Especially with those smoky windows on those cars, like the one Alaynia drove back here in."

Sylvia giggled. "Mac didn't really see Jacki. Some truckers just have this ingrained sense of helpfulness when they notice another vehicle broken down on the side of the road."

"Not all of them. There must've been a little prod there—something that told this guy that he was needed."

"I'm sure that relationship is going to work out fine," Sylvia said firmly. "Oh! Oh, look, we're missing the wedding. Shain's already getting a ring out of his pocket to put on Alaynia's finger!"

"Then come on over here and sit down so we can watch the rest of it," Basil growled. "You can see through the wall of that house as well as I can, and we've got a perfect view from here."

Sylvia glided over and arranged her dashiki skirt beneath her. Folding her wings against her back, she leaned on the live oak trunk and sighed deeply. "Isn't Alaynia stunning? And her face is so full of love for Shain."

"That's what I've been trying to tell you and Miss Francesca. If you'll look at my grandson—who, by the way, is just as handsome as his bride is beautiful—you'll see how much he loves her. Now, what could be wrong with them getting married?"

"Nothing, I guess," Sylvia murmured. "It's just that . . ."

"If you're worried about me letting Alaynia find that time warp and giving her an opportunity to go back to her own time, set your mind at ease. I've got no intention of allowing Alaynia to disappear from Shain's life, now that he's found a woman he can love as much as I did my Laureen."

Sylvia shifted uncomfortably on the tree limb, but kept her eyes on the wedding in the parlor of the minister's house. The minister pronounced Shain and Alaynia man and wife, and Shain tilted Alaynia's chin up with his finger. Shain's tender kiss left Alaynia misty-eyed, and even Jeannie sniffed and pulled a handkerchief from her dress pocket. Love flowed between the bride and groom as they stood gazing at each other, wrapped in a world that contained only the two of them.

Suddenly Shain grabbed Alaynia and stepped behind her, wrapping his arms around her waist and looking at Jeannie and the minister's wife. "I want you both to meet Mrs. Alaynia St. Clair," he said. "My wife and the woman I love."

Jeannie rushed forward and threw her arms around Alaynia's neck, hugging her tightly and stretching on tiptoes to kiss her cheek. "Welcome to the family, Sister Alaynia," she said, then tugged Shain's head down and kissed his cheek. "Congratulations. I hope you'll both be very happy."

"Thanks, Jeannie," Shain replied. "I already am."

Sylvia caught Basil surreptitiously wiping beneath his eye when she turned to look at her companion.

"There. See?" he blustered. "My grandson's been lonely, just like your Jacki and Mac were. And Alaynia was, too, even though she buried herself in her work. What could be better than the two of them finding each other?"

Sylvia chewed her bottom lip as she glanced overhead, desperately wishing Frannie would appear. Her superior angel had assured her before she left that she had complete confidence in Sylvia being able to handle things while she was gone, despite Sylvia's shorter span of experience as a guardian angel. However, Sylvia felt completely out of her depth.

She and Basil were forming a friendship, along with some mutual respect. She didn't want to appear pompous about knowing more than Basil as to how lacking the powers he was so proud of actually were when compared to the overall scheme of things. They needed to work together to help Shain bring whoever was sabotaging Chenaie to justice. Yet he was waiting for some sort of explanation.

"Uh . . ." she began as, below them, Shain assisted Alaynia into the buggy, and Jeannie handed something to the minister's wife. Both of them tossed their hands toward the smiling couple, and a shower of rice fell on Shain and Alaynia. The minister joined his wife and Jeannie in peals of gay laughter.

Basil crossed his arms on his chest and smiled smugly as everyone murmured one last leave-taking and Shain handed Jeannie into the buggy. Climbing in after her, he settled between the two women, then lifted the reins. The buggy horse tossed its head and trotted off, just as the sun rose in a beautiful morning sky.

"Basil," Sylvia said in a tentative voice. "This might not be the best time to mention this. I mean, I realize your grandson just got married, and you're feeling pretty happy about it."

"That I am," Basil admitted. "Some folks think it's women who have the most feelings for their kids or

287

grandkids. Christopher and I never developed a close relationship, but in the little time I had on earth with Shain, I came to love him like it was an ache in me. I want him to have a good life, and Alaynia's just the woman to make him happy."

"If she stays with him," Sylvia murmured.

Basil swiveled toward her. "What do you mean? I told you that I've got no intention of sending her back to her own time."

Sylvia released a deep breath. She glanced overhead once again, sending another thought winging toward Francesca. Either the distance of time separating them was too great, or Francesca chose to ignore her, because the superior angel made no appearance. Avoiding Basil's gaze, Sylvia smoothed at her dashiki skirt.

"Sometimes it's not up to us, Basil," she said. "There's a higher order to things, and we've got absolutely no control over the events that take place. In a way, it's like it was when you were living. All you could do then was cope with the circumstances life handed you. You couldn't change things or twist them into what you wanted them to be."

She clenched her hands together and continued, "If Alaynia was supposed to have found that time warp and returned before this, you wouldn't have been able to keep it hidden from her. And, to tell the truth, your powers didn't bring Alaynia back here, Basil. You might have been the channel through which it happened, but meeting Shain was what was supposed to take place in Alaynia's life. What she did with the situation herself after that was her own choice."

Basil sat silently for several long moments. Sylvia slipped a brief glance at him from beneath her eyelashes, and he turned to stare down the road, although the buggy was no longer visible. Sylvia could see the meaning of her words sinking in and Basil's joy at his grandson's happiness fading into worry.

"What you're saying," he said at last, "is that even though Alaynia's here now, her destiny may not be to stay here. She might still be taken away from Shain sometime in the future."

"*May,*" Sylvia said. "We can't be sure. Staying here *may* be what's supposed to happen in Alaynia's life. Or it may not be. And I don't think I'd say that she would be *taken away* from Shain. It's just whatever her destiny is supposed to be."

When Basil only stared at her, silently demanding more information, Sylvia steeled herself to be truthful with him, despite knowing what she was going to say would hurt him deeply. "What's really out of place here—what you've done—is not give Alaynia access to the time warp again. You took away something very important to humans. Something given to them at their own creation."

"And what would that happen to be?"

"Her free will—her right to make her own choices."

"She says she wants to stay here now! She loves Shain."

"But she's still determined to find out what's happened to her. If you'd given her the choice at any time of going back or staying here, she'd be content in knowing that she'd chosen her own destiny. She'd be satisfied with her decision, and not worried about you interfering in her life again, even though she doesn't know it's you she's worried about. And Frannie and I could have been on vacation right now, instead of in this situation."

Basil gaped at her in astonishment. "You mean, I have to lead her back to that time warp? Allow her to decide whether to go back through it or not? That's easy enough, because I'm totally sure what choice she'll make. I'll just—"

"It's more complicated than that now. You've let all kinds of questions build up in Alaynia's mind. She's not going to be completely at ease until she knows every answer. Besides, you probably haven't recouped enough of your powers to remove the barricade to the time warp yet. And that's not something I can help you with, since you're the one who put it in place."

"How do we find out what I should do?"

"I don't know." Basil tossed her a furious look, and Sylvia held out her hands as she faced him. "I really don't," she stressed. "You have to remember, I'm fairly new to this guardian angel business and dealing with a human's free will. Like Frannie told me a few weeks ago, I've only been at this for a blink in time. The spirits I dealt with before were already on the next plane of existence, and you're the first spirit I've met who chose not to join us. I don't know if Frannie's ever run into a situation like this one before, or whether she might have some idea of what's permissible for us to do to correct your tampering. But I've got a firm feeling that we'd better be very, very careful, so things don't get even more complicated."

"So how can you find out?"

"I guess we'll just have to wait for Frannie."

"We need to know soon," Basil said sternly.

"I agree. But right now, we can't leave Chenaie. Something terrible might happen while we're gone, if that Fitzroy decides it's taking too long for him to gain control of Shain's timber rights. We'll have to wait for Frannie to get back."

"Can't you contact her now?"

"I tried a few minutes ago. She must be busy, or else she's decided I need to handle this on my own."

"You and I have plenty of time," Basil grumbled. "Eons and eons of time. But I'm not so sure about Shain and the situation at Chenaie. Come on. You need to see some things."

Basil floated into the air. A second later, Sylvia unfurled her wings and drifted after him. Instead of following the road below them, Basil veered in a different direction, motioning with one hand for Sylvia to accompany him.

They flew west, over St. Francisville, in the opposite direction of Chenaie. Below them, most of the houses were silent and dark. The town inhabitants never woke as early as their country friends, who had to use every available moment of daylight to assure themselves of bountiful crops at harvest. Here and there, Sylvia did see a few people walking toward the more spacious houses. From their mode of dress, they were probably servants on their way to a full day of caring for the town's more prosperous inhabitants.

When they reached the Mississippi River on the far edge of town, Basil pointed down at the muddy banks. Though the river was still wide and flowing smoothly, the water was several feet lower than it had been when she arrived. In answer to her questioning glance, Basil said, "There hasn't been any rain for months. Even the Grand Old Miss is showing signs of the drought. And look at this."

Basil blinked his eyes, and they both found themselves over the creek where Shain's cotton crop had been dumped. Only a small trickle of water flowed down the middle of the rock-strewn creek bed. The heaps of muddy cotton lay in dry piles, covered with baked mud.

"The pond at Chenaie's down, too," Basil said. "And the cisterns are so low, Shain's worried about the water. The wells on the plantation have never gone dry, but there's always a first time. They need rain."

"Shain's been bringing in the cotton crop, though," Sylvia pointed out.

"Yeah, but it's not as good a quality as it would have been, if he'd been able to wait a few weeks. And he's set his hopes on that cane crop making up the difference for getting less money on the cotton. Cane needs water, though—lots of it. He had Carrington raise the levy gate on the irrigation pond higher, but no one's sure if that will be enough water to assure a quality crop."

Next, Basil led her over Jake's house, and she glanced below to see Zeke carrying a bucket of feed out to Stubborn. Basil tilted a finger against his forehead in a salute and murmured, "Hello, old friend."

Zeke's steps faltered, and he craned his neck overhead. Stubborn reacted even more clearly to the invisible presences. With a bray of fear, he raced over to the small shelter at one end of the corral and disappeared inside. Zeke dropped the feed bucket, spilling grain around his feet and clutching at the *gris gris* bag around his neck.

Basil chuckled, and Sylvia frowned a chastisement at him. "Quit that, Basil. You're scaring the poor man, and he's not even sure what he's afraid of."

Basil shrugged. "All he feels is a little chill of goose bumps. And you'd think at his age, he'd know that voodoo nonsense is just that—nonsense." With a sigh, he continued, "I just miss him, that's all. He was a good friend."

"Well, you'll have to wait until he joins us to pick up your friendship again," Sylvia said sternly. "And while we're discussing things like that, I think you ought to be very careful about contacting Alaynia. I know what you did last night, while I was in town checking out Fitzroy's office."

"I want her to start writing Chenaie's history," Basil defended himself. "But she's too busy working on Jake's house."

"And falling in love, and getting married. Heavens, Basil, what do you expect? You led her into a life completely strange to her . . . good grief! Look at that mess below."

Basil hovered beside Sylvia as they stared at the ravaged hillside beneath them. "This is something else I wanted you to see," he said.

The hill rose steeply only a few yards behind Jake's barn. Smaller trees and brush covered the slope nearer the barn, but every living piece of greenery had been removed from a swathe above that area to the top of the hill and down the far side. Protruding rocks littered the barren, dry dirt. On a rutted road at the bottom of the far side of the hill, wagons filled with men holding saws and axes were approaching, ready for another day of timbering.

"It looks awful," Sylvia said. "As bad as the strip mining areas did before the environmentalists got enough power to force the mining companies to reclaim the areas they destroyed digging for coal."

"All anyone here's interested in right now is money in their pockets," Basil snarled. "They're not thinking about what this area will be like a few years from now, with nothing left to stop erosion. Jake's got the right idea—trying to buy this property from Escott and replant it, but this is just one little section. Eventually, the rest of the cutover land's going to be covered with underbrush and scrub timber."

"It's just awful," Sylvia repeated. "I can see how the drought's affecting Shain, but what does this have to do with Chenaie? Shain's determined not to let that company on his land."

Basil rubbed his chin. "Well, I'm not sure if it really has anything to do with Chenaie, but I've got a weird feeling about it. And this is something else I haven't been able to see the future about. I thought maybe you might be able to penetrate whatever's keeping me from seeing what's going to happen."

"I can't," Sylvia reminded him. "It's not within my powers."

"It doesn't make sense to me," Basil said in exasperation. "Why not?"

"I guess . . ." Sylvia paused, her face creasing into a frown of concentration. "Well, think of it. As a guardian angel, my job is to protect my assignment's body until I receive word that it's time for the body to die and the soul to join us. If I could always just jump into the future and see what was going to happen, there wouldn't be much for me to do. It's just not in the scheme of things, Basil. We have to accept that."

"Yeah, you're right," Basil admitted. "Like I told you and Francesca when you first came, I found out for myself that I couldn't go everywhere I want to. I thought maybe it was because I chose to stay down here, instead of ascending to a higher plane. All the ministers preach about how we have to accept the fact that people will never know the answers to why a lot of things happen while they're alive. Guess I assumed—like most of them do—that everything would be clear after we died."

"It doesn't work that way," Sylvia replied. "We better get on back to Chenaie. Frannie will look for us there when she comes back."

Basil nodded, and the two of them drifted toward the plantation on an air wave. Sylvia enjoyed the sensation of laziness, though it could be considered a frowned-upon trait. However, it was nice to float through the air without having to power herself with her wings. After all, she was supposed to be on vacation, and vacations were for lazing around and recouping energies.

They arrived at Chenaie the same time as Shain's buggy. Basil flew down to the swing sitting on the corner of the front veranda. He patted the seat beside him, and she joined him. Despite her worry over whether Francesca would approve of the wedding, she smiled delightedly as Shain lifted Alaynia from the buggy and swept her into his arms.

"Welcome to Chenaie, Mrs. St. Clair," Shain said.

He dropped a brief kiss on her mouth, and Alaynia sighed with contentment. Jeannie scrambled from the buggy on her own and skipped beside them as Shain carried Alaynia to the front steps.

"Oh," Jeannie said joyfully. "It's going to be so wonderful having you as a real part of Chenaie, Alaynia. Think of all the fun we can have together."

Shain paused on the veranda and gave Jeannie a mock frown. "Now, see here. You'll have plenty of time with Alaynia, but these first few days are mine. I expect when you get married, you'll want a honeymoon of your own."

"Most certainly," Jeannie said with a smirk. "How else will I get any time alone with my husband? Why, I've always got someone hovering over my shoulder, if a boy even looks my way. But you'll never get any privacy at Chenaie. Aren't you planning on taking Alaynia somewhere?"

Jeannie held the door open, and Shain carried Alaynia into the front foyer. "She's right about that," he growled under his breath for only Alaynia's ears. "The privacy part, anyway. There won't be any peace and quiet either, with my little sister's constant chatter."

Alaynia snuggled against him and remained mute. She didn't want to discuss Jeannie or even a honeymoon. All that mattered right now was the delicious knowledge that she was Shain's wife. Visions of the night just past in her bed with Shain filled her head, and warmth stole over her body. She stroked his chest with her free hand, and the muscles beneath her palm bunched in reaction to her caress. As he strode across the foyer, through the parlor and into the dining room, she nuzzled her nose against his neck. His quick intake of breath told her that he was having the same problems of maintaining a proper façade in front of Jeannie as she was.

His arms crushed her against him, and her nipples puckered in response to her longing to be alone with him. Giggling silently, she surreptitiously stuck out her tongue and licked the side of his neck. The slightly salty tang lingered in her mouth. Slipping one finger inside his shirt, she tangled her nail in the chest hair, twirling it into a curl.

"You better stop," Shain whispered in her ear. "Otherwise I'm going to carry you up to our room and keep you there the rest of the day and tonight. And the hell with what anyone thinks. In fact, I'm so damned hard with wanting you right now, I could toss your skirts here on the dining room table."

"You wouldn't!" Alaynia's eyes widened, and she pushed against his chest. In the depths of his brown eyes, she saw a matching flame for the desire she was desperately trying to keep banked in her body. A corner of her mind registered Jeannie's continuing chatter as the young girl lifted silver-plated lids to examine the food the cook had prepared for breakfast and laid out on the sideboard. The voice hummed undiscerningly until Jeannie said something about cold eggs and scampered out the rear door of the dining room to check with the cook in the kitchen house.

Shain slowly released her, and she slipped down his body while he kept his gaze on her face. She gasped and clenched her fingers in his shirt when his hardness slid along her thigh. As soon as her feet touched the floor, Shain cupped her hips. Pulling her to him, he nestled against her stomach and bent his head.

Alaynia helplessly returned his kiss. This was her husband now, the man she loved with her whole being. She had chosen this life—with all its inconveniences and unprogressive attitudes toward women, but she couldn't imagine ever wanting to leave. The time warp could remain hidden forever as far as she was concerned. Her life was now intertwined forever with Shain's.

She only had to make sure that darned warp and whoever . . . whatever . . . didn't meddle in her life again. Forever.

Chapter 22

Alaynia slit her eyelids a bare hint the next morning and found the master bedroom still dark. For a minute or two, she lay quietly, enjoying the sensation of Shain's muscular body pressed along hers, his arms wrapped around her and one hand cupping her breast. Soon a slow heat spread through her, and her breathing grew more shallow as flashes of the night they had shared crept into her mind.

How could she want him so soon again? She should be exhausted, since surely she hadn't slept more than an hour or two. Yet the bulges and planes of his body, even relaxed in sleep, made her yearn to feel them once again tightening and straining as he carried them both to a shattering fulfillment.

His breath feathered softly in her hair, but it would hiss inward if she ran her hand close to his hardness—or gasp as he called her name in need. The power she felt in his arms and broad chest as he hovered over her made her feel delicate and feminine, yet not the least afraid. Instead, she could allow her passion free rein with a complete knowledge of him glorying in her response, sharing her exhilaration, yet always cherishing her fragileness next to his strength. Her breasts budded as she recalled his uninhibited response when she had taken the initiative to explore his body as freely as he did hers.

She wiggled her hips slightly and, though she could tell by his still, even breathing that most of his body remained deep in sleep, one part of him reacted against her thigh.

With a smothered giggle, she bumped a little harder. To her disappointment, he released her and rolled onto his back, flinging one forearm across his eyes and settling back into sleep. His movements drew the sheet with him, leaving her uncovered in the chill morning air.

Alaynia scooted up. She really should let him sleep. He would probably need to be in the fields early today, trying to make up for the time he had spent with her yesterday. She should spend the day working on the plans for Jake's house. The tingling between her thighs, though, refused to be chased away by the early morning air.

She knew his body well enough now for her hand to instinctively find what it sought. Molding the sheet over him, she slowly cupped her fingers around him and moved her palm back and forth. He surged to complete fullness. Carefully she shifted to her knees, stopped stroking him and cupped her breast, then bent to run the nipple across his slack lips.

He grabbed her without warning and sucked her breast deeply into his mouth, then pulled her on top of him and held her in place, thrusting up against her. The mild tingle spasmed into racing desire. She bent her head and buried her face in his hair, her fingers clenching in his shoulders and her nails biting into his skin. "Shain!"

"Witch," he murmured as he moved his mouth to her other breast.

Her voice clogged in her throat as she lay helplessly on top of him. Her body spasmed, and she heard her whimpers of completion as though from far away. When she could think again, she raised herself and stared down at him, realizing that the darkness in the room had begun fading. The satisfied smirk on his face brought a sly smile from her in return.

She gripped his shoulders again and slowly moved upward, then back down. The fading throbs in her core ceased, and she tensed again. But she forced herself to remain in control this time.

Shain's eyelids drooped and he groaned under his breath as her movements continued. "Insatiable," he muttered. "You're an insatiable witch."

"Um-hum," Alaynia agreed as she lowered her head. "And you make me that way."

She licked the tip of her tongue around his lips, then slipped it inside his mouth to trace his teeth. All the while she kept her body moving, easing into a quickening tempo. When he greedily captured her mouth, she lifted her hips for a brief second and jerked the sheet from between them. With the same hand, she grasped him and held him in place, settling back down with him inside her in one easy thrust.

He broke the kiss with a deep moan, his head swinging back and forth on the pillow as he bucked upward in rhythm with her motions. His breath was hot now on her face, hissing between clenched teeth, and his muscles iron hard beneath her fingers. The ecstasy on his face fired her own need, and she closed her eyes, feeling only the sensations flowing between them as she settled into the final tempo.

He gasped her name and moaned his love. Alaynia fell against him, experiencing her second fulfillment of the morning—this time even more splendid, since Shain entered the spectacular world they created together with her.

A long moment later, Alaynia sat up with a shaky laugh and kissed Shain's closed eyes and full lips, murmuring, "Good morning, husband."

Shain flipped her over and captured her mouth in a

deep, probing kiss. When he finally lifted his head, he growled, "Good morning, witch angel, my wife. I'm going to enjoy having you wake me up like this every morning for the rest of my life."

"Maybe not *every* morning," Alaynia replied as she stroked the side of his face.

"Um. Why not?"

She crinkled her forehead into a frown, then slightly shrugged her shoulders. "You got me," she admitted. "Why not?"

Shain's face grew serious. "Are you happy, Alaynia? Do you feel like you've made the right decision?"

"Definitely yes, to both questions," she responded without hesitation. "My life's here with you now—with Chenaie in this time period. I never, ever want to leave. But I still intend to get to the bottom of how this happened to me."

When Shain frowned in annoyance, she explained, "I wish I could say that I could just forget everything, Shain, and walk with you into the future we have as man and wife. I wish it didn't bother me, and I could put it out of my mind. But last night you understood my need to find some answers. And I promise, I won't do anything dangerous. It's important to our future together, though. You realize that, don't you?"

Shain sighed and lay down beside her, gathering her against his side. With their new closeness, Alaynia sensed his reserve. They'd shared their bodies totally—no doubt about that—but she was hoping they had also begun building a bridge across some of the differences in their opinions. Still, Shain avoided her eyes by staring at the overhead canopy when she snuggled her head on his upper arm and looked into his face.

"Shain," she said. "We have to open up to each other now and discuss things. I want to be a part of your entire life, not just your bedmate."

He glanced down at her and quirked a raven eyebrow. "You mean, I can't even keep my mind private from you?"

"Do you want to?" she asked in an injured voice.

"Maybe sometimes," he admitted. When she thrust her lower lip into a pout, he continued, "I'm trying to be honest, honey. I've never had to share my thoughts with a woman I loved before. And never have any doubt that I love you totally, or . . ." He lowered his voice to a near whisper, "Maybe I didn't love you enough."

Alaynia jerked from his grasp and sat up, arms crossed beneath her breasts. "You better explain that one, buster!"

An embarrassed chuckle rumbled in Shain's chest. "See there? I'm already letting you into my private thoughts. I shouldn't have said that out loud."

"Now that you have . . ." Alaynia warned.

Shain scooted up and rested his back against the headboard. For a few seconds, he gazed at her before he reached down and grabbed the sheet, settling it around her shoulders and thrusting the ends into her hands. A flush climbed her cheeks as he drew the satin comforter over his lower body, then sat back again.

"Whenever you want us to talk things out," he said in a mock-stern voice, "I'd suggest we do it in a different state than naked. I have enough trouble keeping my hands off you when you've got your clothes on."

She shrugged the sheet from her shoulders and twisted the ends over her breasts. "There, I'm covered. Now, explain what you meant by saying maybe you didn't love me enough."

She glanced at him and almost lost her resolve. Shain's

eyes roamed over her face and across her exposed shoulders, centering on the breasts pushing out the sheet with a famished gaze she had thought satisfied moments earlier. Only the niggling hurt his words had given her kept her from flinging herself into his arms and demanding he make love to her once more. But she was determined to have her explanation, and she sat silently waiting for her answer.

He sighed in resignation. "We can't even go on a honeymoon," he said at last. "Even Jeannie mentioned that. There's just too much responsibility for me here at Chenaie right now. Maybe I should have waited until things were going smoother around here—when I had more time to spend with you."

She experienced a stab of understanding. "I'm just another responsibility, aren't I?"

"No!" he denied. She continued to stare steadily at him, but he returned her gaze with a level look. "You'll never be that. All right, there's a part of me that's scared as hell about having a wife. Chenaie's in trouble—and Chenaie's our heritage—yours now, too, and the children we'll have together."

He dropped his gaze for a second when Alaynia unconsciously placed a hand on her flat stomach. When he met her eyes again, he nodded briefly. "We'll have them, darling. We've rushed into this thing so fast, I guess we never discussed that. But one of these days, there'll be little independent bunches of femininity running around, keeping everyone at Chenaie on their toes."

"And little boys growing up with their father's handsome looks, getting ready to break every female heart in the state," Alaynia said with a gentle smile.

Shain held out his arms, and she curled close to his side but kept her head back far enough to see his face. "We did go into this pretty fast, didn't we? But I have no regrets. And I want us to share things—the troubles as well as the good times."

"The troubles will be easier to bear just because you're there with me, darling. One part of me wants to give you a life completely free from care. The rational part of my mind, though, knows there are rough times ahead. Hell, the rough times are going on right now. If this drought doesn't break, we'll probably lose the cane, and with what we lost of the cotton crop, we're gonna be hurting bad. But as long as I have you, we'll get through it."

"Shain," Alaynia said eagerly. "Jake's paying me to design his house and oversee the construction. I haven't got a handle yet on how much money's worth back here compared to . . ."

His muscles tensed, and his mouth thinned into a grim line. "That money's yours," he growled. "I'll handle Chenaie's finances."

"Oh!" Alaynia sighed in frustration, determined to proceed, even at the risk of marring their second full day of marriage with an argument. "Let me see now," she said contemplatively. "We're going to share, but the sharing has some boundary lines. What's yours is ours, but what's mine is mine. Does that mean when I have troubles, I have to bear them on my own, too?"

"Don't twist my words, Alaynia."

"Then listen to yourself, Shain. I'm proud of what I've learned to do over the years, and I love designing and decorating. How do you think it makes me feel, when you don't even want to talk about something I feel so much pride in?"

"It's not that I don't want to talk about it. Anytime you want to discuss it with me, I'll listen."

"Well, part of being good at what I do is being able to make money at it. And if you're going to act like that money's tainted somehow . . ."

"Then save it for our kids," Shain interrupted. "I'll make a decent enough living for us that you don't want for anything you really need."

He dropped a kiss on her mouth, stilling her before she could say anything else. "And," he said as he released her and sat up on the side of the bed, "speaking of making a living, I need to get out in the fields. I left things to Cole and Carrington yesterday, but there's some decisions only I can make. There's no sense in you getting up this early. Why don't you get a little more sleep?"

Alaynia glared at his broad back for a second. This discussion wasn't over yet by a long shot, she silently promised herself. For now, though, she'd accept the compromise he'd given her of saving the money for their children. That thought lifted her spirits, and she tucked her palm beneath her cheek as she settled down on one of the pillows. Today was the first of many mornings when she could watch how he started the day, and she wasn't going to let their near-spat spoil her enjoyment.

He crossed to the wash basin and dipped his cupped palms into the cold water, then splashed it on his face. She grimaced when he shivered and rubbed his damp hands across his tousled hair. One thing she would never get used to was not having warm water in the mornings, unless she rang the bell pull for someone to bring it to her. After drying his face on the hand towel beside the wash basin, Shain walked over to the huge armoire and pulled out some clothing for the day.

He turned to come back to the bed and saw her watching him. "Thought you were going to get some more sleep," he said as he sat down on the edge of the mattress to pull on his underdrawers and socks.

"I'd rather start the day with you," Alaynia murmured. "But my clothing is still in the other bedroom."

"I'd like you to move it in here, if you want." Alaynia frowned a question at him, and he shrugged. "My mother preferred to have her own bedroom," he said. "The Camellia Room was hers, and she kept all her things in it. But there's plenty of room for your things with mine. If not, we can move the other armoire in here."

"I'll help Netta move my clothes today," Alaynia told him with a contented smile. "I want to sleep with you at night."

"Good." He leaned over and kissed her, then finished dressing. Picking up a comb from a table beside the wash basin, he ran it through his hair as he asked, "What do you have planned for today?"

"Other than ensconcing myself in your bedroom?" Alaynia asked with a laugh.

"Other than that wonderful idea," he told her with a look that smoldered even across the room.

Alaynia caught her breath, then sat up on the side of the bed, forcing herself to look around the room for her nightgown in order to distract her thoughts. "Well, since I won't need the Camellia Room to sleep in, I thought I'd go ahead and turn it into more of a work room. I could use another table in there to spread plans out on and some shelves for my drawing supplies. I probably should ride over to Jake's today, too, to see how the clearing is coming."

"You won't go alone." Shain's words were more of a statement than a question.

"No," she agreed, covering up her feeling of restriction. "If it's all right with you, I know Jeannie would like to go.

And we'll take one of the men from the stable with us."

Shain nodded acquiescence. After crossing to give her one last, lingering kiss, which held the promise of more to come later on, he left. She scooted out of the high bed and grabbed her nightgown, pulling it on as she walked through the connecting door to the Camellia Room.

As she dressed, she studied the room, mentally rearranging it into her work room. There was plenty of room for the armoire in the master bedroom, and she could have the bed disassembled and moved somewhere else—perhaps stored in the attic. That would give her plenty of room for another table.

The fireplace was an added delight. If things went well with Jake's house, she could get other jobs. It would be extra cozy on chilly days with a fire flickering as she worked on the drafting table. She would line the mantle with pictures of Shain, Jeannie, and any new additions to her family.

Her lips thinned as she looked at the Bible and packet of letters on the mantle. No matter where she left them—and she clearly recalled leaving the letters on the drafting table the last time she handled them—they appeared in a different spot each time she entered the room. It was as though someone kept moving them to assure she paid attention to them. Brushing her hair, she walked over to the window and once again gazed at the graveyard. It held a wonderful memory now—the memory of Shain's proposal. Yet it still contained a mystery, or perhaps more than one. She could never rest easy until she had the answers.

After tying her hair back, she dropped the brush on the window seat and left the room. A few seconds later, she tapped lightly on Jeannie's bedroom door.

"Come in."

Jeannie glanced up in surprise when Alaynia walked in. "I thought you'd probably sleep late this morning," she said with a grin. "I intend to laze around for at least a month after I get married."

"Shain's already gone out to the fields. And I've gotten used to us having our morning coffee and chocolate together. It's way too long to wait for my caffeine until Shain's ready to have breakfast."

"I agree," Jeannie said. "Netta should be here in a minute, and I'll ask her to bring your coffee up."

When Alaynia came over to the small table in the room, Jeannie stood and hugged her tightly. "Oh," she said when she stepped back. "You don't know how glad I am that you're part of my family now. It's going to be so much fun having you for a sister. Whenever I thought about that brother of mine getting married, I didn't dare hope he'd find someone as wonderful as you—someone I could be friends with, too."

Alaynia cocked her head. "What sort of woman did you figure Shain would marry?"

"You know," Jeannie said with a vague wave of her hand. "Some simpering woman who only thought about dresses and needlepoint—those feminine things that all women are supposed to be interested in."

"Shain told me you wanted to go to school in Boston."

Jeannie nodded eagerly. "Has he said he's going to let me? I never could pin him down about that, but I don't intend to live my entire life in West Feliciana Parish, that's for sure. Be just a plantation mistress and keep the servants in order, plan parties, and go calling at specified hours."

"What *do* you want to do with your life, Jeannie?"

"There's so much, Alaynia. I love animals, and I want to have lots of them wherever I live, maybe horses. And it's so interesting watching Jake work on his inventions. What you do, building houses, is fascinating, although I don't think it's what I'd like to do for the rest of my life. I've written down a lot of things—I keep a diary." She ducked her head shyly. "I've never let anyone read it, but you could, if you want to."

"I'd love to," Alaynia replied, then contemplated Jeannie for a moment. "Are you interested in keeping track of your family history?"

"Uh-huh. I've also written down some of the stories I've heard about my family. I never knew any of them, you know, except Shain. But somehow writing down what I do know makes me feel more a part of them."

Netta knocked briefly at the door and came through with a tray. As soon as she saw Alaynia, she smiled. "Didn't think y'all would be here this mornin', Mistress. I be right back with you some coffee."

Alaynia thanked her and turned back to Jeannie as Netta left. "There's a Bible with the St. Clair family history in it that I found in the Camellia Room. And some letters written between your grandfather and grandmother. Have you ever seen them?"

"No," Jeannie said with a trace of awe. "Can we go look at them after a bit?"

"Of course. Now, what else do you have planned for today? I thought I'd go over to Jake's, and you can come if you like. Of course, Shain insisted we take someone with us. And then I'd like to go visit Tana, so we can go there from Jake's."

"Tana? Oh, Alaynia, you'll never get anyone from Chenaie to escort us to her house. Unless Shain can spare Cole."

"That's ridiculous. Why not?"

Jeannie twisted a linen napkin and stared at the tabletop. "Well . . . uh . . . she lives way back in the woods. She and Little Jim. In a small cabin, like those our sharecropper families have."

"So?" Alaynia asked with a shrug of irritation. "For goodness sakes, Jeannie, you don't think because Tana doesn't have a big, beautiful manor house like Chenaie that it's beneath you to visit her, do you? And who's Little Jim?"

Jeannie concentrated on the napkin. "Alaynia, it's not Tana's house. Why, I care for Tana almost like a mother. She and Zeke took care of me after my mother died. Tana escaped and hid Little Jim in a hollow log while she ran over to Chenaie to warn Zeke and my mother that the Yankees were rampaging and on their way here. I . . . I wrote down the story Zeke told me, but I really don't believe it. And Little Jim is Tana's son. He's . . . well, a little backward."

"But why wouldn't one of your employees do as you asked and take you there? You haven't explained that to me. Are they afraid of Tana's son?"

Netta pushed open the door and carried another tray over to the table. "Why, Missy Jeannie," she said. "Your chocolate be gettin' cold. Look. It's already got a scum on it. Want I should take it back and warm it again?"

"No, Netta," Jeannie murmured. "It's fine." She picked up a spoon and stirred the chocolate, then took a sip. "It's still warm. But thank you."

Netta set the silver coffee urn and a china cup in front of Alaynia. After she poured the cup full, she dug in her apron pocket and handed Alaynia a folded piece of paper. "Boy brought this here to the kitchen door, Mistress. Says I was to give it to you."

"Thank you," Alaynia replied. As Netta left the room,

she opened the note and scanned it. "Jeannie, this is from Tana. She's inviting me to lunch today."

"She always knows," Jeannie murmured. Alaynia lifted a quizzical eyebrow, and Jeannie sighed. "She somehow knew you wanted to see her. Alaynia, Tana's a healer. But you know that part of it, since she took care of you when your horse threw you. But . . ."

Jeannie chewed the side of her cheek, and Alaynia silently waited. She could have prodded her, demanded Jeannie answer the questions rambling through her mind from the tidbits of information she had dropped, but she loved Jeannie too much to be brusque with her.

After a long moment, Jeannie spoke. "Some stupid people call Tana a voodoo priestess, Alaynia." Alaynia smothered a gasp, and Jeannie faced her directly as she continued, "Tana's not. She uses the healing remedies of plants that her mother and grandmother and even great-grandmother passed down to her. But she does have a strange power that she admits to. All the females in her lineage have had it."

"Her vision of me," Alaynia murmured without thinking.

"Did she predict your arrival?" Jeannie exclaimed. "I haven't talked to her alone since you came."

Realizing she was treading on very dangerous ground, Alaynia sipped her coffee. Shain would blow a gasket if he found out she and Jeannie had been discussing the things he had adamantly informed her to keep private. He was loosening his reins on his baby sister ever so slightly, but he considered protecting her a top priority in his life. Besides, she and Shain hadn't worked everything out themselves yet.

He had more or less gone along with her insistence that she had to keep investigating all the strange happenings in her life until she had conclusive answers. But she had promised to keep him informed and not take any unnecessary chances. Bringing Jeannie into this was definitely a bad idea, even though his sister seemed to be a lot more aware than Shain imagined her to be.

From the corner of her eye, Alaynia caught a movement on Jeannie's bed and swung her head around. The comforter rippled and shivered, and suddenly Tiny poked his head out. Brown eyes gleaming and snout wrinkling, he oinked and scrambled to his feet, shaking the comforter from his back.

Jeannie giggled gaily. When Alaynia shook her head and glanced at her, Jeannie's blue eyes sparkled with laughter. "He wants his chocolate, too," Jeannie explained.

Glad of the distraction, Alaynia rose from her chair. "Well, we better give it to him, don't you think? Good heavens, Jeannie. Look how much he's grown in just a few short days."

Alaynia picked up Tiny, and the piglet snuffled his nose against her neck before she could grasp his head. She laughed and quickly shifted her hold on him. Grabbing a napkin, she wiped it across the dampness left by the piglet's nose.

"Bring him over here, Alaynia."

She turned to see Jeannie pouring the remainder of her chocolate into Tiny's feeding bowl. Carrying Tiny over, she sat him in front of the bowl, where he immediately slurped at the chocolate. A second later, he sat on his haunches, staring up at Jeannie and oinking. She shook a finger at him.

"No more until after breakfast. And remember, I told you we'd go for a walk today. In fact, maybe you can come to Jake's with us."

She glanced at Alaynia, and Alaynia smiled at her eager face. "I don't see why not. You've been leash-training him, and Shain's aware he's in the house now. But does he sleep in your bed every night, Jeannie?"

"No," Jeannie admitted with a chuckle. "He stays in his own bed at night, but he usually wakes up before me in the mornings. So he comes over and climbs my step stool up to my bed. Then he'll go back to sleep for a while."

Shaking her head, Alaynia walked over to the table and gathered the dishes onto the tray, while Jeannie put Tiny in his harness and attached the leash. The first morning she had carried the dishes down to the kitchen house, Netta had been very apologetic, wringing her hands and insisting she would have come and retrieved them if she or Jeannie had just pulled the bell rope. Now, she only gave Alaynia a grateful glance each morning, since it meant one less trip up that steep stairwell in her busy day.

Very obediently, Tiny pranced ahead of them down the hallway, and even climbed down the back stairwell on his own. Jeannie led him on out into the yard while Alaynia carried the tray to the kitchen house. She left the tray on a table inside the door, but picked up the note from Tana and slipped it into a pocket on her skirt. When she walked back outside, Shain sat on his huge, black horse, smiling indulgently at Jeannie, who was leading Tiny around the yard.

Shain immediately swung his gaze to her. "Morning once more, darling."

"Hi," she replied. "Aren't you back a little early for your breakfast?"

"Cole and Carrington ran me off again. Said being back out there in the fields when I should be spending time with you would look like I didn't love my wife. Have to admit, I didn't fight them too hard." He dismounted and led his horse toward her.

"Shain, I understand that you've got things you need to take care of . . ."

He dropped the horse's reins and climbed the two steps to her. Sweeping her into his arms, he kissed her senseless. When she finally drew back, he cupped her face with a callused palm and rubbed his thumb across her cheekbone. "I want no doubt in anyone's mind that I love you," he murmured. "Or in your mind, for that matter."

"Shain, I'm completely certain of your love. How could I not be, after the nights we've shared?"

She felt his response against her thigh and the heat of the blush flushed her cheeks. Digging her fingers into his back, she muffled a whimper of desire, her eyelids drifting shut. Oh, lord, what this man did to her—how alive and feminine he made her feel.

"Honey," Shain murmured close to her ear. "We've got an audience."

With a gasp, she drew back and whirled to face the kitchen door. The cook and Netta quickly ducked out of sight, but she could hear their muffled giggles. All at once, Netta stuck her head through the door and winked at Alaynia, then nodded her head quickly at Shain and disappeared.

"I do believe our servants approve of us," Shain said, turning her to face him. "Now, what shall today's plans be? Our plans, I should say."

Alaynia tilted her head and moued her mouth. Giving a nod as brief as Netta's, she replied, "I'm very glad to hear you asking me to be a part of our planning. As it so happens, I really feel I should at least briefly check on the workers at Jake's. I need the Camellia Room changes made, so I can work in there, also."

"Just leave instructions for Netta. She can have the stable hands do anything heavy, and the attic is full of furniture."

"Great. Oh, and I received this a while ago."

She pulled Tana's note from her pocket and handed it to him, carefully watching his face as Shain read it. To her relief, he nodded an acquiescence.

"There's a couple things I'd like to talk to Tana about myself," he said. "We'll have plenty of time to check over at Jake's, then ride out to Tana's. Was Jeannie planning to go along?"

"I'd like to go to Jake's," Jeannie said from behind Shain.

Alaynia glanced over Shain's shoulder at her, then down at her feet. Jeannie quickly flipped her skirt hem to cover her bare toes, sneaking a conspiratorial smile at Alaynia. So that's why she hadn't heard the young girl approach, though she would have thought Tiny's feet incapable of a silent advance. Then she saw the piglet out in the yard, touching noses with Shain's horse.

"You don't want to go to Tana's?" Shain asked.

"Uh . . . well, the invitation only came to Alaynia," Jeannie explained. "Although I'm sure Tana knows someone from Chenaie will accompany her. And I'd much rather stay here and read the Bible and letters."

"The ones Alaynia found in the Camellia Room?" A scowl began on Shain's face.

Suddenly the black horse snorted and the piglet squealed, and Alaynia smothered a giggle at the tableau in the yard. The horse stood with its neck stretched out, and the piglet with its head twisted over its shoulder, staring back at the horse from a few feet away. Tiny slowly reversed himself and cautiously sneaked toward the horse.

They touched noses again, and Tiny oinked. The horse snuffled some sort of reply, then lifted its head, and Tiny walked between the horse's front legs. He circled once, then plopped down between those deadly hooves and closed his eyes.

"God in Heaven," Shain said with a groan. "That's all I need—for those two to get attached to each other. We had a horse once that raised cain in its stall unless a certain hen was allowed to sleep in there with it at night. The hen even hatched a batch of eggs in the feed trough, and that gelding never stepped on a one of those chicks."

"I remember him," Jeannie said with a gay laugh. "Dusty, that dun gelding. Once the cook made the mistake of chasing Dusty's hen with the hatchet, wanting a chicken for her stew pot. The poor hen was cackling and running to beat the band, and Dusty jumped the corral fence. The hen flew onto his back, and Dusty stalked the cook all the way back to the kitchen house." She glanced at Alaynia with twinkling blue eyes. "You can bet your boots the cook never went after *that* hen again."

Alaynia joined in Jeannie's laughter, and Shain shook his head at them before he started toward his horse. Jeannie quickly followed and grabbed Tiny's leash, leading him back to the manor house as Shain headed for the stable. The black horse kept glancing back at the piglet, and Jeannie had to tug Tiny along, finally lifting him to carry.

Chapter 23

"Boo!"

Alaynia's mare half-reared, and Shain's stallion skittered sideways. Alaynia quickly controlled her mount and glared at the giant who had jumped into their path. The huge black man immediately hung his head and shuffled a toe in the dirt.

"I sorry, Mister Shain," he murmured.

Shain leaned on his saddle horn. "Little Jim, that was not a nice thing to do. I know you have better manners than that."

The giant lifted his shoulders around his neck, and his bottom lip protruded. "I sorry," he said again, glancing at Shain with tears pooled in his brown eyes.

"We accept your apology," Shain said, and Alaynia noticed him hide a smile. "Now, would you like to come over here and meet my new wife?"

Little Jim's face brightened and he straightened, nodding his head up and down. He slowly shuffled toward the horses as Shain introduced the two of them. "Little Jim, this is my wife, Alaynia."

"Miss 'Laynia," Little Jim said, holding out a huge hand. "It . . . uh . . ." He frowned, then smiled in remembrance. "It be nice to meet you, Miss 'Laynia."

"And I'm pleased to meet you, Little Jim." Alaynia tentatively clasped the massive hand, but Little Jim very carefully closed his hand around hers and gave it a small shake.

"You very pretty, Miss 'Laynia."

"Why, thank you, Little Jim," Alaynia replied as he dropped his hand, stepping back and glancing at Shain for approval.

"Very good, Little Jim," Shain said. "Now, I'll bet you could lead us back to your house. I wouldn't want to get lost along the way."

"I can!" Little Jim said excitedly. "I know the way, I do. I won't let you get lost. Mama's fixin' gumbo. Um, um, um. Mama makes the best gumbo."

"I agree," Shain said. "So lead the way. We don't want the gumbo to get cold."

Little Jim nodded eagerly and turned. His steps shuffled, but he waddled back and forth, hurrying along the path. Alaynia nudged her horse forward, and Shain fell in beside her again.

"He seems pleasant," Alaynia said. "Jeannie told me about him this morning—that he was mentally challenged."

"Haven't heard it called that, but yes, he's frozen in his mind at around five years old," Shain replied. "But he's never harmed another person or animal. He loves to catch fish, but Tana has to send him off on an errand or something in order to clean them. She said once she baked a coon and forgot to cut it up before she served it, so Jim wouldn't know what it was. He cried for two days and wouldn't eat any sort of meat from then on unless she cooked it in a stew, so he couldn't recognize it."

"A . . . coon? Tana doesn't by any chance put coon in her gumbo, does she?"

Shain glanced tolerantly at her. "No, it's probably got fish or crabs in it—maybe sausage. But you don't know what you're missing. A coon baked with bell peppers and apples is a mighty tasty dish."

"I believe I'll pass on that, thank you," Alaynia said with a grimace.

A moment later, they emerged into a clearing. A small log cabin sat amid hundreds of different plants, all blooming in riotous colors. White rocks lined the neat flower beds, and a crushed-shell-covered path led up to the porch. Beneath some of the huge trees, pink-blossomed moss grew in profusion. Baskets of plants hung from the porch eaves, and boxes filled with herbs were beneath sparkling windows. Off to the left was a small shed with a fence around it. A spotted cow stood placidly chewing its cud inside the enclosure.

A rabbit hopped over by another fence, which surrounded a neat garden patch. Instead of scurrying off, it sat up, ears alert and nose wiggling. Beyond the garden, a doe with a half-grown fawn watched them, and birds flitted from tree to tree, their songs a perfect music to accompany the peaceful scene.

"It's a beautiful place," Alaynia said. "And the animals seem to think the same thing."

"Yep," Shain agreed. "Little Jim likes to garden, so he helps Tana with the plants. And sometimes I think he can talk to the animals. They never seem afraid of him."

Little Jim hastened his pace and hurried up the steps. "Mama! Mama, our company's here!"

He opened the screen door and moved back. Tana emerged, her regal presence a contradiction to Little Jim's excitement. She walked to the edge of the porch and waited as they rode over to the hitching rail to dismount.

Alaynia allowed Shain to help her down. While he tied the horses, she approached Tana. "I got your invitation. I've been looking forward all morning to seeing you again."

Tana wore a gown of various hues, which rivaled the

beauty of the flowers surrounding the cabin. Her green turban complemented one of the shades in the dress, and today she had several golden bracelets on her arms, which jangled when she reached out a hand to welcome Alaynia.

"I have heard of your marriage, and I wish you and Shain happiness," she said. "You are right for each other."

Dropping all pretense, Alaynia clasped Tana's extended hand and said fervently, "I hope so. I want so much to be his wife forever. But I have to have some answers before I can be totally at peace with this situation."

"We will talk," Tana agreed. "But first, I will welcome you to my home. Come."

Shain joined them, and after nodding her head in greeting, Tana turned to open the screen door again. Little Jim shyly stepped forward and held out his arm. Realizing he wanted to escort her inside, Alaynia smiled and slipped her hand into the crook of his arm, leaving Shain to follow.

The interior of the cabin was as neat and beautiful as the yard. Multi-colored rag rugs were scattered on a pine floor, and lace-edged white curtains were drawn back from the windows. Plants had been placed around the room, and the furniture consisted of a sofa between matching cypress wood end tables, two arm chairs, and a rocking chair in front of a small fireplace. Though not a large area, the scheme and light from the windows gave it a spacious appearance.

Little Jim led her through a door at the rear of the room, into the kitchen area, which was almost as large as the other room. The wall on the right had two windows, and beneath them sat a table draped in a snow white cloth. A centerpiece of flowers from the yard decorated it, and the place settings were already laid out. Tana stood at the stove on the left, stirring a huge iron pot. The spicy odors in the rising steam intermingled with the smells of various herbs and other dried plants hanging from the ceiling.

Alaynia's stomach growled loudly, and Little Jim giggled. "You hungry, Miss 'Laynia?"

"Well, I must be," she told him. "Or my stomach's just reacting to those delicious aromas."

Bobbing his head, he led her to a chair at one end of the table and pulled it out. "Mama's cooking makes my stomach growl, too," he said conspiratorially as she sat down and he gently shoved the chair beneath her. "And just wait 'til you taste it!" He glanced up at Shain. "You sit here, Shain. By me. I got to help Mama serve."

Shain took his seat and reached under the table, grasping Alaynia's hand and giving it a squeeze. "Huh," he muttered. "Guess we're not feeding you well enough at Chenaie. I never heard your stomach grumble like that in anticipation of the meals served there."

"Why, sweetheart," she drawled. "I wasn't focusing on the food there. It was the company that kept my attention."

He smirked in masculine satisfaction at her comeback, and she kicked him under the table. Before they could continue their teasing repartee, Little Jim carefully carried a bowl of gumbo over and set it in front of Alaynia. She sniffed and had to force herself not to dive in immediately. Little Jim placed bowls at each setting, then added a basket of fresh-baked rolls, a dish of butter, and plates heaped with crispy salad greens. Finally, Little Jim and Tana sat down, and after a brief blessing, led by Little Jim, Tana began passing the rolls, butter, and dressing for the salad.

Conversation flowed innocuously during the meal. Alaynia voiced her admiration of the beautiful landscaping around the cabin, and Little Jim beamed. Tana gave Alaynia some pointers on caring for some of the plants in the house, and told her what herbs did well in certain Southern growing seasons. When Alaynia asked for her second bowl of gumbo, Little Jim jumped up to fulfill her request, while Tana listed the spices she used in her recipe.

"If you do not have *filè*," Tana said, "no sense making gumbo. It is just not the same."

Alaynia laughed gaily, and Shain frowned at her. "What's so funny?"

"I can just see me waltzing into the kitchen house at Chenaie and shaking my finger at the cook," Alaynia replied, "telling her to make sure she uses *filè* in the gumbo. Why, she'd probably chase me out of there with her broom."

"Yeah," Shain agreed with a chuckle. "Or pack her bags and say she was going to work for somebody else, who appreciated her."

"You can come here and eat gumbo whenever Mama makes it," Little Jim said seriously, placing the bowl in front of Alaynia without spilling a drop. "We like company, don't we, Mama?"

Alaynia caught the frown on Tana's face, but she quickly covered it up. "Yes, son," she said. "Alaynia and Shain are always welcome."

Nodding happily, he took his seat and they finished the meal. As soon as Little Jim realized everyone's bowl was empty, he jumped up and hurried to the stove, opening the oven and drawing out a pan.

"We got peach cobbler for dessert," he said as he set the pan on the countertop. "And real cream. I milk the cow for Mama, and work the churn when we make butter. But we kept the cream this time, for the cobbler."

Alaynia groaned under her breath, but she didn't have the heart to spoil Little Jim's excitement and tell him that she was way too full for dessert. However, instead of bringing the dessert dishes to the table, he placed them on a tray and turned as Tana rose to her feet.

"We can have our cobbler in the other room," Tana said. "My son will bring it in."

"Oh, but I should help you clear the table," Alaynia protested.

"No, no, Miss 'Laynia," Little Jim said, shaking his head. "My job. Mama cooks and I clean up."

Shain stood and stepped behind Alaynia's chair to pull it out, and the three of them filed into the living area, sitting in the various pieces of furniture. After Little Jim served them the cobbler and cups of steaming coffee, he went back into the kitchen.

"Isn't Little Jim having his dessert with us?" Alaynia asked.

"He will have his for a treat after he cleans up," Tana said with a tolerant smile. "He says it makes the work easier, knowing he has a sweet waiting."

"He's a fine boy," Alaynia said. "And he must be a lot of help to you."

"He is everything to me," Tana said. "He fills my days with joy." She glanced at Shain. "I know you will care for him well, if it ever becomes necessary."

"You've had my promise for years on that, Tana," Shain replied. "He'll always have a home at Chenaie, and my care, should he need it."

Alaynia set her coffee cup on the end table beside the settee and dipped her spoon into the cream-covered cobbler. After one bite, she sighed in pleasure. "This is delicious, Tana. I thought I was too stuffed to eat another bite, but I think I'm going to be able to finish every morsel of it."

"I am glad you are enjoying your meal," Tana replied.

"Zeke brought the peaches to me, but as always, he only left them on the porch. He did not stay to talk."

Alaynia frowned, the bite of cobbler in her mouth suddenly losing some of its delicious tang. She swallowed, then said, "Tana, I've been wondering about Zeke. I've been trying to make friends with him while I work on Jake's house. But he avoids me like he thinks I'm going to cast a spell on him or something. I've never had anyone afraid of me before. It's very awkward."

Shain slipped an arm around her shoulders in comfort as Tana said, "Cole has told me you are building a grand house for Jake. And it is the same with Zeke, when he is near me. He still remembers how we had to depend upon each other before Shain came home, but he cannot forget what happened the day Cole's home was burned, when I fled to Chenaie."

"Tana," Shain cut in forcefully. "I don't believe that damned story. You said yourself that you don't remember it happening either."

"Zeke has no reason to lie about it," Tana said mildly. "And the occurrences since then have borne him out . . ."

Shain surged to his feet, a glare forming on his face, although he appeared to be trying to be polite. "Tana, I know Alaynia wants to talk to you about some of these things, and I'm a guest in your house. But I think I'll go help Little Jim."

"Sit, Shain," Tana ordered. "You have avoided this long enough."

Instead of complying, Shain's glare deepened. "I'm not interested in discussing this."

"That's not what you told me earlier," Alaynia said. "You agreed that we had to get to the bottom of what's been going on. How I got here and—"

"Damn it, we're married now," Shain almost snarled. "You've made a commitment to me—to being my wife. I've gone along with you on your idea of helping Jake with his house. Even though it's an embarrassment, I've allowed—"

"Allowed?" Alaynia sprang to her feet, negligently setting the dish of cobbler on the side table. "Embarrassment? You listen here, Shain. You knew before you asked me to marry you that I wasn't the type of woman to ask your permission every time I needed to use that darn chamber pot under the bed. I've compromised just about enough with you. I've let you or someone else hover over me every time I step a foot outside the manor house. I've let you dictate to me what I have to wear. I've even discussed my wanting to investigate the experiences I've been having with you, but I did *not* ask your permission to do so. During our *discussion,* you appeared to be agreeable, and said you'd help."

"I said for you to be careful and not put yourself in danger. I said for you to keep me informed."

"You've just been humoring me, haven't you? You figured as soon as you got that ring on my finger, I'd turn into a docile, obey-my-husband type. When were you going to order me to find someone else to work on Jake's house, huh?"

Shain's guilty look fired her indignation into anger. "You were, weren't you? That's what you drew Jake off to the side to talk about this morning, wasn't it? You thought maybe between the two of you, you could talk me into letting the carpenter build the house alone. Then I could *decorate* it."

"When it comes time for the interior work—"

"Damn waiting for that! Damn sitting around twiddling my thumbs, until you come in out of the fields every day. I've told you how much my work means to me."

"Evidently, more than being a wife!" Shain snapped. He turned away from her and bowed briefly to Tana. "Tana, I'm sorry we disrupted your wonderful lunch. I hope you'll come to Jeannie's party this Friday and let me try to make it up to you. For now, I think we better leave and continue this . . ." He shot Alaynia a forbidding look. "This *discussion* in privacy."

Alaynia plopped down on the settee and crossed her arms. "I apologize, too, Tana," she said with a glance at the other woman, whom her anger had made her forget was in the room. "But, unless you're kicking me out, I'd like to stay and talk for a while."

"You are welcome until you wish to leave," Tana replied with a faint smile. "My son and I will escort you home whenever you wish."

"You're coming with me, Alaynia," Shain ordered.

She reached over and picked up her cobbler. "I'm staying to finish my dessert and visit with a friend. I'll be home after a while."

She flicked him a taunting glance and scooped up a spoonful of cobbler to dish into her mouth. He stood there for a few seconds, a towering package of suppressed, masculine rage, then swung on his boot heel and stormed out of the house. The cobbler turned to ashes in her mouth, and Alaynia set the dish aside once again, swallowing the tasteless mass as tears misted her eyes.

"It won't work," she choked out. "Oh, Tana, I'm sorry we made such a scene, and please forgive us. But, darn it, trying to change someone after you marry them is one of the most destructive things to any relationship. Can't he see that he married me for who I was—not who he wanted me to be?"

Tana rose and moved over to the settee. Sitting beside

Alaynia, she placed an arm around her shoulders and squeezed gently. "I did not have much time with Little Jim's father. We jumped the broom, which was the only ceremony two people who wanted to wed were allowed to have back then. After our son was born, and the master saw he was not right, he sold us. My husband was sent to a plantation in Georgia, and Cole's father bought my son and me. After he heard my story, Cole's father tried to find my husband. But James had already been shot, when he tried to run and come back for us."

"Oh, Tana." Alaynia swiped at her eyes and raised her head. "I'm so sorry. And here I am crying on your shoulder. You've had it much worse than I have."

"No," Tana denied with a shake of her head. "I have had friends, and I have my son. You have been alone until now."

"How do you know that? We haven't talked about my life."

"I do not know how—I just know. I know you are a strong woman, and that you have become what you are through your own doing."

"Then you think I'm right in standing up to Shain? Not letting him take away some of the important things in my life?"

"I do not give advice," Tana said with an enigmatic smile. "As I say, you are strong. Strong women make their own decisions—and their own compromises."

Alaynia sat silently for several moments, eyes on the open front door. She hadn't heard Shain ride away yet, but now she heard the squeak of saddle leather and immediately after, the sound of hoofbeats. They galloped away instead of walking, scattering the shells from the pathway. The shells showered the front porch, ticking against the wood as they fell. In her mind, she imagined a twenty-first-century man, flinging himself in his car and taking off after a fight with his woman, tires squealing.

And she was his woman, despite everything—despite his domineering attitude, which she had to somehow find a way to contradict. He had claimed her body and soul. She could never leave him. He would haunt her forever, here at the Chenaie of the past, or should she return, at the Chenaie of the future.

Why couldn't he understand? She had to make sure she would stay with him. There were so many unanswered questions. Would she be allowed to stay, or was her destiny back in the future? Would her staying here cause some twist in time, which might alter everyone's life for the worse? Did the force she sensed at Chenaie have something to do with her arrival—and her uneasiness at times, as well as her determination to have her questions answered? Was it all intertwined?

Pain stabbed her inner cheek as she unconsciously bit down on it, and she quickly slackened her jaw muscles. She briefly closed her eyes, then took a deep breath and opened them to face Tana.

"I want to know what's happened to me. And I want to know what you were alluding to—your own experience, which Shain didn't want you talking about. I w-want to kn-know . . ." She took another steadying breath to stabilize her faltering words. "I want to know who the spirit is at Chenaie. Why he keeps contacting me and what he wants of me."

Tana's deep brown eyes studied her intently for several long seconds. Finally she said, "I will tell you what I know—and what I believe. The two things are not the same. I think Zeke could tell us more, but he will not speak of it.

At first, he was very afraid. He would discuss what had happened then, perhaps in an effort to handle his fear by talking about it to someone. But when Shain returned, he ordered Zeke not to speak of it again. Shain does not lose his temper easily, but when it happens, it is better to get out of his sight until he calms."

"I've seen him come close to losing control," Alaynia murmured. "But never actually go over the edge. And he's sure had enough problems at Chenaie to make him ragged." A flash of doubt and worry filled her. "Oh, Tana, maybe this isn't the time for me to push on this. All I'm doing is adding to Shain's burdens. He's got so many things to worry about at Chenaie right now, and I should be helping him bear those worries, instead of adding to them."

She shifted on the settee, trying to sort through her thoughts as she spoke. "Not that I'm going to give up my work on Jake's house," she continued. "But maybe I could leave this other stuff until later—after things are working better at Chenaie."

"I believe you have come here today to speak of these things for the good of Chenaie," Tana replied. "Perhaps your being there is part of the whole picture. I . . ."

A clap of thunder split the air, followed immediately by a spattering of rain on the roof. Alaynia jumped to her feet, staring worriedly out the window. "It's raining. Shain will get soaked."

"Perhaps it will cool his temper," Tana said with a tolerant smile as Little Jim came into the room.

"Mama, I better put Shain and Miss 'Laynia's horses in the barn, 'for they get wet," he said, then stared around the room. "Where's Shain?"

"He has already left," Tana told him. "But, yes, put

Alaynia's horse in the barn. She will wait here until the rain has stopped."

Little Jim nodded, but his lower lip protruded. "Shain didn't even say 'bye," he murmured as he crossed to the door. "Mama says it's not polite to not say 'bye, when a person leaves."

Tana shook her head, then reached for Alaynia's arm and drew her back onto the settee. "Would you like some more coffee or something else to drink?"

"No, I'm fine. Tell me what you know—and also what you believe might be. Tana, there have been times when I've tried to tell myself this all has to be a dream—that this can't be happening to me. And I fell in love with Shain so darned fast, I felt like this *had* to be my destiny. But the truth is, just a week ago, I was driving down a back road in a Louisiana Parish in the year 2005, trying to find Chenaie. I saw what looked like a huge heat wave in front of me. I jammed on my brakes, but the car just slid right on down the road. The next thing I remember, I was on a dirt road and Shain was standing across the road, under a tree. Within a couple hours after that, I was finally at Chenaie, but it was Chenaie in 1875."

"You do not remember how you made this journey through time?" Tana questioned. "I ask this, because in my vision I saw you tumbling through the air. I did not sense any danger to you, just much confusion on your part."

"Confusion's a heck of an understatement," Alaynia replied with a half-hearted grin. "I've thought and thought about it, of course. There's got to be some thread of connection having to do with Chenaie, since Chenaie was where I was headed to begin with. You see, I was distantly related to the woman who owned Chenaie in the future. She was my Great-Aunt Tilda, but I'd never met her. She had traced me, however, and left her estate to me when she died. The estate consisted of Chenaie and a few thousand dollars—enough, I thought, to restore the manor house and open a B and B."

"B and B?" Tana asked with raised eyebrows.

"It's short for bed and breakfast," Alaynia explained. "Rather like . . . ummm . . . a hotel. Only there's not a complete staff and twenty-four-hour service, like in large hotels. The guests are welcome to stay the night and have breakfast the next morning, but then they're on their own to go sightseeing in the area."

"The house is opened to strangers, then," Tana murmured. "Always new people—who are curious, rather than a part of the house."

"Well, yes," Alaynia admitted. "But the alternative, unless you have plenty of money, which I didn't have, is to let the house go to ruin. Or find a historical society that will take on the maintenance of it. There's a big lack of funds for stuff like that back in my time, however."

Another clap of thunder sounded, then rolled away in diminishing waves. The sky opened up, and sheets of rain poured down the open sides of the front porch, giving a surreal appearance to the landscape beyond. The bright flowers took on a fuzziness when seen through the rain, reminding Alaynia of the mistiness of the cemetery at night and calling her attention back to the discussion she had planned to have with Tana.

She shifted again on the settee. "Tana, who is the spirit haunting Chenaie? Or, is there more than one?"

Chapter 24

For the next half hour, Alaynia sat enthralled with the story Tana related. She had always been fascinated with the history of the houses she restored—the past lives of the former occupants. But now she was hearing about the people of Chenaie—her Chenaie. They were also her own relatives—only by marriage, but nevertheless her family. She had been without family all her life.

Some of what she would tell her, Tana explained to Alaynia, she had heard from the slave grapevine, since they all loved to gossip about their owners. Some things she had learned later on from Zeke. To begin with, Alaynia had to understand the deep love between Shain's grandfather, Basil St. Clair, and his wife, Laureen, and their disappointment in their only son, Christopher. Chenaie had been a monument to their love, and they could not understand the cold distance Christopher always kept from both them and the land. They desperately wanted Christopher to care about Chenaie as much as they did, but finally began pinning their hopes on any children Christopher might father.

Alaynia's heart wrenched when she heard how Laureen had died and of Basil's horrible grief. But Shain's grandfather had proven strong, and continued to keep Chenaie a lovely and prospering plantation, in memory of his wife.

Within the bounds of society's strictures, Basil had made Chenaie as pleasant as he could for his slaves. He could not bring himself to flaunt the rules of conduct, since it would have meant his family would be ostracized—and family meant everything to Basil. Therefore, he never offered his slaves a chance to buy their freedom, as Tana had heard of one plantation owner down by New Orleans doing. But Basil did reward elderly slaves who had been in his service most of their lives with freedom when they were too old to work, and he allowed them to stay on at Chenaie. That had become a somewhat accepted practice of plantation owners just before the war. When his father died in 1849, Christopher continued the philosophy at Chenaie, although more from lack of interest than any feelings for the people of Chenaie.

"No matter how they were treated," Tana mused in a soft voice, "they were still not free people. When the war broke out, most left. They preferred the unknown and their freedom to life in bondage. On the day Basil returned to protect his Chenaie, there were only Miss Catherine, Miss Jeannie, and Zeke living there. Miss Jeannie was only two."

"Came back!" Alaynia said with a gasp. Though she had thought herself prepared for this, her heart thudded and she struggled for breath, much as she had in the barn with Jake that day. She finally licked her tongue around her lips, barely moistening them. Staring at Tana, she realized the woman was waiting for her to gain control before she continued speaking.

"Go—go ahead," she managed. "I'm assuming you mean he came back from the spirit world."

"No," Tana denied with a small smile. "He will always remain a part of the spirit world. He is, after all, a spirit, and he cannot be a man again."

Alaynia clenched her fists, determined to follow this through, although the hairs on her arms and the back of her neck rose as though a surge of static electricity had passed over them. She glanced down at her forearms and saw evidence that the sensation was actually physical, not just her mental imaginings. The tiny hairs stood at attention, rather than lying in place. Quickly running a palm down one arm, she smothered a gasp when the sensation increased for a split second, then disappeared.

A crash of lightning split the air, and finger-flickers of light cascaded into the room. Shadows danced around her and Tana, and suddenly Tana groaned and slumped back against the settee. Horrified, Alaynia instinctively reached for her, pulling the unconscious woman into her arms. Tana slouched almost bonelessly, and immediately a spreading sensation of spider webs crawling over her body filled Alaynia with terror. She had felt this before—at the window in the Camellia Room and in the graveyard.

She tightened her arms on Tana while she stared wildly around the room. The sensation crawled down her back, through her stomach, and prickled along her legs. Another spear of lightning crashed, and a dim blue light filled the room. Choking in fear, Alaynia let Tana fall against the back of the settee again and scrambled to her feet.

She backed away, brushing at her body. The sensation remained with her, intensifying to the point where she could almost feel the tiny legs scrambling over her body. The light in the room fuzzed the objects, then brightened them, as though someone had placed a revolving black light globe in the center of the ceiling. She hit the edge of the door and swung around desperately. But the door slammed shut. When she reached for the handle and jerked frantically, it refused to budge. Whirling again, she flattened her back against the door and stared wildly around the room.

The eerie light danced crazily, the cracks of thunder and lightning outside the cabin accompanying it. She screamed and covered her ears. Suddenly Tana sat up on the settee, and Alaynia surged toward her, only to stop as abruptly as though she'd run into the immovable door behind her. Tana's eyes were still closed, but she opened her mouth to speak.

"Sorry, girl. Can't help the display. I've only tried this once before." The voice came out in a slow, Southern drawl—definitely masculine—instead of Tana's melodious voice.

"My God!" Alaynia gasped. "Who are you?"

The light continued to dance eerily around the room on the edge of her vision, but she couldn't tear her eyes from Tana's almost motionless face.

"No time to explain," the voice said. "Just make your decision carefully. That's all I ask."

"Wh-what decision?" Alaynia choked out.

"The decision of your heart," it replied. "And tell Shain to be careful. I can't help. It's up to him."

"Basil, what are you doing?" a feminine voice screeched through the air, and a split second later the room was normal.

Alaynia's eyes widened in disbelief as Tana gazed curiously at her from the settee, as alert as though she hadn't been slumped unconscious an instant before. Alaynia scrutinized the room, but it appeared ordinary, only shadowed by the lack of light from the windows due to the cloud-covered sky. Outside, the storm was fading, though rain still pattered on the roof.

A knock sounded on the door, and Alaynia choked on a scream as she swung around to stare at it.

"Mama," Little Jim said from beyond the door. "Mama, the door's locked."

Repressed hysteria bubbled in Alaynia's throat as she

gaped at the iron latch, tipped into place above the door knob. She tried to force herself forward and lift it, but her legs refused to budge. A second later, Tana glided past her and opened the door.

"I didn't want to come in, Mama," Little Jim said. "Just wanted to tell you I was gonna check the garden and pick up any 'maters the rain knocked off the plants."

"Keep your slicker on, son," Tana admonished. "And hang it up back here on the porch before you come inside. Don't be dripping all over my clean floors."

"Yes, Mama."

Tana turned, leaving the door open. Clean, rain-scented air drifted into the room, but Alaynia continued to imagine she could smell the ozone-layered atmosphere of a few minutes earlier. And she was still frozen in place, unable to move.

Tana reached for her, and Alaynia collapsed in her arms. Shaking horribly, she allowed Tana to lead her over to the settee and shove her gently down. As soon as Tana released her, she covered her face and bent forward over her knees. Behind her closed eyelids, dots of light danced, reminding her all too strongly of the room as it had been when the voice spoke to her.

She started to jerk upright, but Tana smoothed a hand over her head and said, "Take a deep breath and relax, Alaynia. You can tell me what happened in a minute, when you are able."

Instead of obeying, Alaynia straightened and stared at Tana. "You know! You must know what happened."

"No." Tana shook her head and curled her fingers around the hand Alaynia reached out. "But something has. I can tell from the change in you. One moment you were sitting beside me—the next you were across the room and so frightened I could feel your fear."

"It wasn't like that," Alaynia said determinedly. "You were unconscious for a least a minute. Maybe longer. I couldn't tell you even now how long he was here. Then she came. She called him . . ." Alaynia took a deep breath. "She called him Basil. It was Shain's grandfather, Tana. He was speaking from inside you. I've no idea who the woman was—all I heard was her voice."

Tana nodded slowly, seeming undaunted by the fact that Alaynia had just told her a spirit had taken over her body. But a tiny shiver ran through the dark hand Alaynia held tightly in her own. "Tell me what happened," Tana said. "What did they say?"

Alaynia frowned in concentration, trying to overcome the memory of the terror she had suffered. She desperately needed to share the experience with Tana. Shain would never allow her to talk about it, although she was quickly realizing that the entire episode directly involved her relationship with Shain. And part of what she had heard had been for Shain.

"You fell unconscious," she told Tana, clinging tightly to the other woman's hand, although Tana hadn't tried to pull free. "There was an eerie light in the room, and I could feel something—like something was invading the space where we sat—invading you . . . and me. I've felt this before, only at Chenaie, and never this strong. It was like a chill, but it really wasn't cold, and it lasted a lot longer than the chills we all get sometimes. You know. When we say someone must have walked across our grave?"

Tana nodded, but Alaynia still felt her description was sorely lacking. She continued, "It . . . was like hundreds of spiders crawling over my body. And it kept spreading, until it was all over me. And intensifying, until I had no doubt that there was something actually here. Actually in this room with you and me." She searched Tana's face, but her gaze remained shuttered. "You spoke, but I knew it wasn't you. It wasn't your voice—it was a man's voice. He apologized for scaring me, then asked me to make my decision carefully. When I asked him what decision, he said the decision of my heart."

Seeing a flicker in Tana's eyes, she said, "He was talking about my feelings for Shain, wasn't he?"

"The words are always riddles, which we have to find the meaning of," Tana replied. "It could be, but I do not think he was referring to the argument you just had with Shain. He would not come through for something as slight as that."

"Slight? Tana, this problem between Shain and me is threatening our feelings for each other—our love."

"Perhaps," Tana agreed. "But perhaps there is a deeper decision for you to make, rather than just whether you wish to continue to assert your hard-won independence."

Tana's hand twitched in hers and Alaynia stared down. Her fingers were tightly clasped around Tana's, surely hurting the other woman. She quickly loosened her hold and flexed her hand, playing over in her mind once again the words she had heard in that masculine voice issuing from Tana's mouth.

"A decision," she murmured. "I thought I'd already made my decision, when I said yes to Shain's proposal— when we were married. But . . ." After a second, she continued, "But the moment I found out Shain was trying to mold me—that he had just been humoring me—I was ready to throw everything back in his face. Try to hurt him. Instead, I should have tried to work things out."

"Marriage is a commitment," Tana said. "A lifetime

commitment—not just for the good times, but for the hard ones, also."

Suddenly Alaynia gasped. "Tana, he said something else. He said to tell Shain to be careful—that he couldn't help him. I have to get back to Chenaie and tell Shain that his grandfather is trying to warn him about something."

At the doubtful look on Tana's face, her shoulders slumped. "But he won't believe me, will he? He's not going to believe a ghost spoke to me."

"You said there was a woman, also," Tana prodded.

"Just for a second. She called him Basil, and asked him what he thought he was doing. A second later, everything was back to normal. Everything except my pounding heart and scared-senseless brain, that is."

Silence lingered as she waited for Tana to speak. "Well," Alaynia demanded finally, "what's the meaning of all this?"

"I cannot tell you. No more than I can tell you why you are here—or if you will decide to leave. Even if you should stay or leave. What happened was not one of my visions—not a forewarning or a glimpse of what is to come. It was your own vision."

"It wasn't a vision. It happened. Basil was here, until the woman . . . whoever she was . . . interrupted."

"But they did not include me in the happening," Tana explained. "I was only the channel. I am your friend, Alaynia, but there is only so much I can do. I cannot explain to you what I do not understand myself."

"Oh, lord." Alaynia moaned and clasped her head. "This would be so much easier to handle, if only Shain would talk to me about it—share it with me. I can't shake the feeling that all this is leading up to something horrible. Maybe my presence here is causing these things to happen. It's not natural, you know, for a person to travel to a different plane of existence—to travel through time. Maybe my doing that has caused all kinds of havoc."

"And maybe it was meant to be." Tana shrugged. "Maybe there is a purpose for it. Who can know?"

"Basil would," Alaynia said decisively. "Damn it, I have to talk to him again."

Tana shivered delicately. "Alaynia, I do not think . . ."

"Thinking hasn't done a damned bit of good so far," Alaynia interrupted. She rose to pace the floor. "I've thought and thought and thought, until my brain's scrambled with thinking. It's time to take some action and get to the bottom of this. How can I concentrate on working out the problems in my relationship with Shain, if I don't even know for sure if I'll have a future with him? If Basil brought me here, he could just as easily send me back. I have to know if he has that power, or if my decision to stay here is stronger than his power to return me to my other life."

Tana nodded reluctantly, but Alaynia could see the fear on the black woman's face and pooled in the depths of her brown eyes.

"Don't worry, Tana," she reassured her. "I won't ask you to help me. I'll do this on my own."

Straightening her shoulders rigidly, Tana stood. "No! You must not! You must ask Shain to be with you, or I must be there. You do not understand. It could be dangerous."

"I'll be careful. Don't fret about it. Now, I really need to get back to Chenaie." She walked over to the door and looked out. "It's still raining. I thought after that storm, the rain would stop. Usually a violent storm like that passes over quickly."

"We have not had rain for a very long time," Tana said as she joined her and stared at the sky. "The clouds are thick. I think the drought has finally broken. Little Jim will be glad he does not have to carry water for the garden every day, but I hope we do not get all the delayed rain at one time."

"There was . . . uh . . . will be a horrible flood." When Tana glanced at her in alarm, Alaynia hastened to say, "Not now. I mean, well, I don't know what will happen now. But back in my time, it rained for weeks. The tributaries into the Mississippi flooded, and the Mississippi did, too. Levees broke, and land for miles on each side of the river was covered with water. I flew into St. Louis during that time, for a trade conference, and it was a horrible sight from the air."

"Flew?" Tana murmured.

"Oh, dear," Alaynia said with a laugh. "When we have some time, Tana, I'll tell you all about planes and even rocket ships. Right now, I'm more interested in how I'm going to get back to Chenaie without getting soaked."

"I have a rain slicker that my son has outgrown. I will get it for you, while my son gets the horses ready."

The rain continued the rest of the day and throughout the evening. Alaynia spent the time in her newly-refurbished work room, scaling out the plans for the landscaping around Jake's house. Jeannie eagerly joined her, with Tiny curling up beneath the work table while the young girl shared her limited knowledge of the different blooming periods of the plants Alaynia was thinking of using on the grounds. Throughout the long hours, however, Alaynia kept straining for the sound of Shain entering the house.

At one point, she swallowed her pride and asked Jeannie if she'd seen Shain. Jeannie only shrugged and said the last time she'd seen her brother, he'd been leaving with Alaynia to visit Tana. Perhaps he was checking the irrigation systems, Jeannie suggested, to see how the rain was affecting them.

He didn't show for supper, either, and Alaynia returned to her work after the lonely meal. Jeannie informed her that she wanted to re-read the letters Alaynia had given her that morning before she discussed them with Alaynia, and retired to her room. After realizing she had been staring at her plans for an enormously long period without the lines registering in her mind, Alaynia threw down her pencil and gazed out the window facing the graveyard.

The darkness beyond acted like a mirror, reflecting the interior of the room and her own shadowed body back at her. She gave a tiny start before she realized the figure in the glass was herself, then shook her head at her jittery nerves. Determined to overcome her trepidation, she walked over and sat on the window seat, curling her arms around her upraised knees as she peered through the window pane.

Though she could see past the reflection now, she still couldn't make out anything beyond the window, except sheets of silvery rain falling. The lantern light behind her glittered on the drops tracking down the pane and dropping from the sky, but it couldn't penetrate the ebony reaches of the night.

She tried to imagine the graveyard and huge trees, but only Shain's face came into full being in her mind. His thunderous brown eyes when he had ordered her to accompany him back to Chenaie. The grim set of his lips when she taunted him with her disobedience. His eyes softened with tenderness or deep mahogany with hungry passion. His lips approaching hers for a tender, soul-wrenching kiss.

She laid her head back against the wall behind her.

* * * * *

A crack of thunder woke her, and Alaynia sat up abruptly, then scrambled from the window seat. The room was lighter, but not from the flashes of lightning piercing the smoky sky outside. She'd spent the entire night on the window seat, and her cramped and knotted muscles attested to the unsuitableness of her bed.

Shain. Why hadn't he woken her to share their bed? He must be still boiling with anger at her.

She started across the room, almost tripping on the blanket at her feet. Funny, she didn't remember having that the previous night when she fell asleep. Stepping over it, she hurried over to the connecting door and opened it. The spread on the huge bed was turned back neatly, the sheets smooth and unwrinkled, obviously not having been slept on. At first a stab of anger flared in Alaynia, but she quickly gnawed her bottom lip in worry.

She crossed the master bedroom and hurried into the hallway. Maybe he'd stayed downstairs last night, in an attempt to make her come to him. She descended the front stairwell and searched the lower rooms in the manor house without success. The empty silence mocked her uneasy thoughts as she strode onto the back veranda, where she peered through the pouring rain. She could make out lights in the kitchen house windows. The cook was obviously already at work. Perhaps Shain was having a cup of coffee with her.

She grabbed the slicker Tana had loaned her from a nail beside the door. Shrugging into it, she walked to the edge of the veranda nearest the kitchen house, then pulled the slicker hood over her head and dashed for the other building. The cook glanced up when Alaynia pushed open the door, her face immediately creasing into a frown of annoyance at being disturbed in her domain.

"Uh . . . I was looking for Shain," Alaynia hastened to say.

"He is not here, Miz St. Clair." The cook stared pointedly at the water dripping from Alaynia's slicker onto her spotless floor.

Alaynia hurriedly backed out and closed the door. Standing beneath the overhang, she gazed toward the stable. Determinedly, she ran into the yard and, feet splashing water from the soggy ground, raced toward the stable. Another violent flash of lightning lit her way, accompanied by a ringing crash of thunder.

Inside the barn, she stared down the dark aisle between the stalls. Straw rustled beside the door, and she froze, thinking it might be a rat. A sleek, gray cat rose and stretched, then let out a loud meow. It walked over and sat down in front of her, gazing up.

"Sorry, kitty," Alaynia said. "You'll have to wait until the stable hands come to feed you." She bent down and ran a hand over the cat's head, then started down the dark aisle.

A moment later, she was satisfied that Shain's stallion wasn't in the barn. Returning to the barn door, she gazed out into the pouring rain. He darned sure wasn't riding around in that, was he? And, if not, he had to have taken shelter somewhere besides the manor house.

A lantern hung on a nail by the door, and she picked it up, searching with her other hand in the tray beneath it. Pulling out one of the matches, she struck it against the wall and lit the lantern. The little mare she usually rode was in one of those stalls, but she'd have to find the tack room before she could saddle her.

Chapter 25

As soon as she climbed into the saddle, Alaynia realized she
had no idea where to start searching. She knew the way to
Tana's house and had traveled to Jake's and also St.
Francisville, but Shain had yet to fulfill his promise to show
her around the plantation grounds. She walked the mare to
the barn door and stared out at the rain.

The night of the fire, she had seen the workers coming
down a trail running between the barn and the kitchen
house. She could see just a little better now—at least
enough to make out the trail. The mare stepped willingly
out into the downpour, and she reined her onto the trail.
Probably Shain was only childishly making her worry because of his anger at her, she told herself. But she couldn't
shake the feeling that he wouldn't resort to such infantile
tactics. No, despite his anger, he would confront her, rather
than cause her this much anxiety.

And there had been too many unusual happenings at
Chenaie. The fire that destroyed the chapel—the ruined
wagon of cotton. The sick mules Shain had mentioned in
passing at supper one evening. She'd been so embroiled in
her own thoughts and experiences, she had hardly discussed
with Shain whether he considered the mishaps truly accidents or an intentional infliction of harm to Chenaie.

The wagon of cotton couldn't have driven itself to the
stream and emptied itself, she realized as she emerged onto
a wider trail which ran between a row of neat, whitewashed

houses, where lights burned in the windows. She rode toward the first one, which was a little larger than the rest, and dismounted at a hitching rail. As soon as she crossed the porch and tapped on the door, a chubby woman with gray hair opened it.

"My word!" the woman said. "Come in. Why, you must be soaked. I'm Myra Carrington, and you must be Miz St. Clair."

Alaynia smiled and started to shrug out of her slicker, then froze when she glanced beyond Mrs. Carrington. Shain and Cole sat at a table, both with plates of food in front of them. They looked perfectly fine—and dry. Another man emerged from a doorway on the side of the room, hesitating when he saw her.

"Why, Miz St. Clair," he said. "Please, come on in."

Shain dropped the fork in his hand, starting to rise.

"Don't bother!" Alaynia told him. "I was just wondering where you'd spent the night. Now that I know you aren't lying out in the rain somewhere with your brains knocked out, I'll go on about my own business."

She whirled and strode from the porch, then flung herself onto the mare. As she headed back toward the manor house, she forced herself to remember the muddy trail could be dangerous for the mare to traverse and held her down to a trot. By the time she rode into the barn again, the stable hands were feeding the horses, and one of them hurried over to her as she slid from the mare.

"Miz St. Clair," he said with a gasp. "You shouldn't be out in this weather!"

"I'm not out any longer," she said grimly. Knowing he would care for her mare, she walked out of the barn and headed for the manor house. On the back veranda, she paused and shrugged out of the slicker, re-hanging it on the nail before she stared out through the rain. As soon as she realized she was watching to see if Shain had followed her—and comprehended that he'd had plenty of time to get there if he had—she snorted in disgust and angrily stalked into the house.

She found Jeannie in the dining room, and the young girl jumped to her feet as soon as Alaynia entered. "Alaynia! Oh, I've been so worried. I found your bed not slept in and couldn't find you anywhere in the house. You always have your coffee with me, and I couldn't imagine where you'd gone in this horrible storm."

"I was looking for your brother," Alaynia spat. "He didn't see fit to come home last night."

"Oh," Jeannie said in a nonchalant voice. "He probably stayed out at Cole's house."

"Cole's house?"

"Uh-huh. Cole's been staying in an empty house one worker's family used to use. That family moved on last summer, and Shain's used that house before, too, when he's had to stay out near the fields at times. It's close to the irrigation dams, in case they have to keep an eye on them."

"Doesn't he have men to do that for him?" Striding over to the sideboard, she poured herself some coffee. "And why wouldn't he at least let us know he was going to be out all night? He could have sent someone to tell us, if he was too busy to ride over here himself."

Jeannie's face puckered into a frown. "I don't know," she admitted. "He usually does that—send someone with a message, I mean. Maybe he just got busy and forgot."

"Forgot, hell," Alaynia said without thinking. "He meant to make me worry."

"Have you had a fight with Shain already?" Jeannie asked worriedly. "Oh, I hope it's not over something I've done. I've been trying so hard to stay out of your and Shain's way—so you can have some privacy. Maybe, since Shain can't get away to take you on a honeymoon trip, I could go stay with one of my friends for a while."

Regretting her outburst, Alaynia hurried to Jeannie's side. "Jeannie, no. It's not you at all. Why, with Shain out in the fields so much, I need someone to chat with now and then. And you can't leave. Your birthday party is Friday night, and all of the guests have sent acceptances."

"If this rain keeps up," Jeannie grumbled, "no one will be able to come anyway. They won't want to get all dressed up and have their finery ruined getting here."

"Surely the rain won't last until Friday. Let's look on the bright side. You said you wanted to make name tents for the table, so why don't I show you how to use my lettering template?"

It continued to rain while they worked on the lettering, and the dreary weather was an appropriate accompaniment to Alaynia's dismal thoughts. She tried to put on a cheerful face, not wanting to involve Jeannie in her problems with Shain, but at times she found herself looking out the window while Jeannie bent over her drafting table. They broke for lunch, and as Netta carried a tureen of soup into the dining room, she informed them that Shain would not be joining them. He had sent word his attention was needed out at the irrigation ditches.

Jeannie tossed her a relieved look, but tension knotted Alaynia's shoulder muscles. She barely touched her soup, and picked at the broiled fish Netta brought for the next course in disinterest. Only the thought of the cook's miffed feelings if she returned the entire plate to the kitchen un-touched coerced her into eating part of it.

She spent the rest of the afternoon alternately pacing

and staring out the rain-drenched windows. Jeannie curled up with a book, but when Alaynia chose one from a shelf in Shain's study and joined her in the parlor room, she soon closed her book in resignation at her lack of concentration.

After the evening meal, which she again forced herself to at least move around on her plate in order for it to look like she'd eaten a portion, Alaynia stood from the table to murmur a polite leave-taking to Jeannie. Before she could speak, she heard booted footsteps on the back veranda. She bit her lips in indecision and glanced at the dining room door. She ought to hurry on up to her room, and let Shain come and apologize to her. After all, he'd let her ride back to the stables in that darned storm this morning without a thought for her welfare. But Jeannie rose to her feet and quickly glided to the door.

"I'll let you and Shain have some time to talk," she said as she passed, making Alaynia realize she had utterly failed to hide her frustration and agitation from the young girl all day.

She heard Jeannie call a good night in the hallway, and Shain respond. Another voice also called to Jeannie, and Alaynia recognized Cole Dubose's rumbling masculine tone. She stood waiting for them, but their footsteps by-passed the dining room and went on down the hallway to Shain's study.

Thinning her lips in indignation, Alaynia went after them.

They'd left the study door open, and she halted in the hallway. Both men were slumped in chairs, with Shain behind the walnut desk and Cole leaning forward in an armchair at the side of the room, elbows on his knees and shaking his head. Their clothing was drenched and muddy, their appearance a far cry from when she had seen them that morning. Shain ran his hands over his face, palm rasping audibly on his new growth of beard. When he dropped his arms, Alaynia stifled a gasp at his haggard expression and the dark circles beneath his eyes.

"Well, we can probably forget about the damned cane," Shain said. "It needed water, but it's flooded beyond saving now. Guess I should have planted rice."

"Ah, you know you're too far north in the state for rice to thrive," Cole replied. Straightening in his chair, he spat, "It's that goddamned timbering. There's nothin' on the surrounding hills to stop the water when it rains like this now. Hell, it's only been raining a little over a day, and looks like it'll keep up for a week. Nobody tampered with that irrigation dam—it just wasn't built to handle a flooded creek like that."

"I should have realized something like this could happen," Shain said in a tortured voice.

"How?" Cole snapped. "How could you have realized the timbering on surroundin' land would affect you? It never crossed my mind, either, that the creeks on adjoining properties would fill and come ragin' across your land like damned rivers! We're just damned lucky we were able to fill enough sandbags to protect the workers' homes."

"They won't stay protected for long, if this keeps up. We've got to keep the men and older boys working in shifts, and we might have to call on the women to help, too. It'll depend on how fast that water rises."

Lightning flashed outside, and a crash of thunder shook the manor house. It barely faded into a rumble before another violent crash followed. Shain grabbed a crystal-cut decanter from a tray on the edge of his desk and poured two glasses nearly full of amber liquid. Handing one to Cole, he drank half of his glass before he spoke again.

"One of us is going to have to ride into St. Francisville and wake up the general store owner. Get some more bags for sand. I want to check on Alaynia first, and explain to her what's going on. I should have gone after her this morning, but the teacher came running, telling us he'd seen the irrigation threatening to give way when he passed it on his way to open the school house."

Guilt filling her, Alaynia stepped into the study. "You don't have to apologize, Shain." She crossed the room to stand by his side and ran her hand over his tousled hair. "I'm sorry I acted so foolish this morning. I should have waited for you to tell me what was going on. What can I do to help? Can I go after more bags for you?"

Shain pulled her into his arms and buried his face on her breasts. She heard Cole rise and leave the room, but she tightened her arms around Shain's neck and rocked him soothingly. "I'm sorry," she murmured. "Is it awfully bad?"

"Bad enough," he mumbled. Raising his head, he gently urged her onto his lap and cupped her face to smooth a thumb across her cheek. "I'm sorry I . . . ."

"No!" She placed her hand over his mouth. "Please. Don't say you're sorry. I should have tried harder to understand. I . . . ." She gasped when he drew her index finger into his mouth, teasing it with his tongue. With an effort, she pulled her hand free. "We . . . ah . . . you have things to do. And I want to help."

"You're giving me the best help you could right now," he murmured. "Just having you in my arms for a few minutes. I wish I had an hour of this, instead of this brief time. Alaynia, I tried all day to get a few minutes to come back to the house—see if you were all right. I did send Carrington to the stables, to make sure your horse was there and you'd gotten back in one piece."

She frowned in remembrance of the early morning trip, but quickly tried to cover up the nagging thought in her mind. Shain needed her support right now, not her badgering over something that probably had a logical explanation.

"What is it?" Shain asked.

"Nothing. Really," Alaynia assured him. "Why don't you finish your drink?"

She reached for the glass on the desk, but Shain caught her arm. "Alaynia, tell me what's bothering you. I don't need to be worried that you're keeping something from me, when I should be concentrating on what this storm's doing to my plantation."

"Since you put it that way," she grumbled. "It's just that when I saw you and Cole this morning at the Carringtons', neither of you looked like you'd been up all night in the rain."

"Who do you think put that blanket over you last night?" Shain asked. "I would have carried you to bed, but I was afraid I'd wake you. I came back an hour or so before dawn and got some dry clothes. Didn't want to wake anybody by spending too much time here, so I just took them to the Carringtons' and changed."

"Oh. I wish you had woke me, though. What can I do to help now?"

"This, for right now."

Shain kissed her, slowly, deeply and savoringly. Just as the kiss threatened to creep around the bend into passionate, he released her and laid his forehead against hers. "I need a lot more of you than that, but I've got to get back out there."

"Should I . . . ?"

Shain quickly kissed her again. "I know you want to help," he said when he broke the kiss, "but I'm going to ask you to do something I know is completely against what you've got in mind for yourself. Cole's probably already hitching up the wagon to go after the sandbags." She started to rise, but he held her in place.

"No, I don't want you to go with him. I'd like you to stay with the women." Alaynia stiffened, but he continued, "It's going to be just as important to keep food and hot coffee ready for the men all night. I know it's useless to ask you to stay here at the manor house, now that you know what's going on. But you could help Myra Carrington organize the women."

Studying Shain's gaunt face for a second, she couldn't bring herself to argue with him. "I'll do whatever's needed," she promised. *But,* her thoughts continued, *if it becomes necessary for you to call in the women to help with the sandbags, I'll be with them.* "I'll go change into some sturdier clothes."

Shain nodded and allowed her to stand. He followed her up to their room, enumerating the supplies she should ask the cook to gather up for her as they walked. She unselfconsciously changed her clothing in front of him, balling up her wrinkled gown and tossing it in a hamper when she saw it had been mud-stained from sitting on his lap. She dressed in her split skirt and riding boots, pausing once when she felt a flush cover her skin.

Turning, she saw Shain sitting on the bed, his eyes on her and lids at half-mast. The deep longing flaring between them was almost tangible in the room. She took a step toward him, but he held up a hand. "If I touch that satin skin of yours right now," he growled in a low voice, "I'll never get back out there."

"Well," she teased in an attempt to overcome her own need, "I'm not really partial to making love on muddy sheets."

Shain jumped to his feet and stared down at the bed. Laughing at his expression, Alaynia walked over and pulled the comforter over the stained sheets. "There. I'll change them myself when I get time."

Shain pulled her into his arms and kissed her. Reluctantly, he released her, and said, "I love you, Alaynia. I'd make love to you in a sea of mud, if that was the only place we had. But even there, I'd want more time to savor you than I have right now. When things get back on an even keel around here, I'm going to take you off somewhere on that honeymoon Jeannie suggested. I want you all to myself for at least a month, so you be thinking of where you'd like to go."

"I'll go anywhere," Alaynia murmured, "as long as you're with me." She tilted her face impishly at him. "Besides, with you around, I doubt if I'll see very much of the scenery anyway."

He growled under his breath, then nuzzled her neck. Her knees weakened, but before she had to cling to him for support, he pushed her gently away. "We better get going. But before we do, I'd like you to finish buttoning your blouse."

She glanced down, then giggled. Her blouse hung completely open, and the scanty black-lace bra revealed far too much of her breasts. Slipping a teasing look at Shain, she very slowly buttoned the blouse. As she finally reached to tuck the hem into her skirt, his pent-up breath whooshed over her face.

"You can bet your entire wardrobe of those tiny scraps of lace that I'm going to be thinking of how you look under that blouse every time I see you," Shain said with a groan, placing her hand on himself to reinforce his words. "I don't know how I can want you this badly, as tired as I am, but you can see that I do."

"No, I really can't," Alaynia said with a grin. "See, I mean. But I can feel—and remember." She dropped her hand and backed away. "And I'll be remembering that, while you're remembering my wardrobe of sexy underthings."

Several hours later, Alaynia was growing increasingly more worried over what she had been hearing from the workers who came in for coffee and food. Several of them were standing on Myra Carrington's porch, visible through the open door. She'd helped Myra hang several lanterns from the pitched roof, and she could clearly see the men's faces while they spoke.

"Must've been raining up north before it hit down here," one said. "Dubose said he checked out the river while he was in town. It's rising fast."

"Yeah, it's the runoff, as much as the rain," another replied. "And it's gettin' ahead of us. I figure even if this damned rain would stop right now, we'd have another day of rising water. Thing is, it ain't even the damned river botherin' us. It's the rainwater all around us, filling up them creeks with water that's tryin' to get to the Mississippi River."

"Well, we better get back out there." The man threw the dregs from his coffee cup over the porch rail and set the cup on a windowsill. "I heard Carrington and St. Clair talking about asking some of the women to come out and help us. Soon as they can get the kids gathered up in somebody's house, so the older girls can watch them."

Alaynia pulled off the apron Myra had loaned her and tossed it on the back of a chair. When she turned to the overseer's wife, the other woman nodded in understanding.

"The irrigation ditch with the broken dam is about two

hundred and fifty yards from here," Myra said. "Come on out onto the porch, and I'll show you which way to go. Then I'll see what I can do to help with the children. We'll split them up into a couple houses, since there are too many of them to all sleep in one house."

Alaynia followed Myra out the door and shrugged into the slicker she'd left out there. Taking the lantern Myra handed her, she walked to the edge of the porch, holding it high and waiting for Myra to indicate the direction she should take. But instead of pointing the way, Myra called to someone walking past her house. "Cammie! Are you going out to help the men?"

"Yes, ma'am." The black woman held her own lantern a little higher. "Mister Shain sent word he needs our help."

"Take Miz St. Clair with you," Myra said. "She's going, too."

"Yes, ma'am."

Alaynia hurried down the steps. The rain wasn't as vicious now, but it still fell steadily. After a brief nod of greeting, Cammie started off, and she trailed behind the other woman. The path led through the huge trees, with darkness beneath them. Shortly, however, she heard voices and spotted flickers of light ahead of them.

The scene on the bank of the irrigation ditch filled her with fear. A line of women and men stretched out from a muddy pit to her right, much as they had the night of the chapel fire. But this time they were passing bags of sand along the length of the line, rather than buckets and pails of water. Several men shoveled sand into more bags, jerking the drawstrings tight as soon as they had them filled and handing them to the nearest person to pass down the line.

The stack of bags along the ditch was already over four feet high, but at times water still gushed over the top.

Shouts would go up, urging attention to the place where the protective pile of bags threatened to give way. Eyes adjusted somewhat to the dark, Alaynia could see the water pouring through the broken wooden dam. A huge, splintered board gave way, swirling through the current and hitting the barrier of sandbags. It flipped high into the air, sailing over the heads of the workers and landing just beyond them, skidding along the ground.

Alaynia gasped in horror. If that board had hit anyone, the force of the water behind it would have caused it to pierce completely through the body.

She glanced around for Cammie and saw her already heading for the line of men and women. She took a step after her, then frowned as she again studied the area. A distant rumble of thunder told her another interval of violent wind and rain was on the way—probably even now deluging the area north of them with torrents. The barrier of sandbags, already shaky, would never withstand the additional onslaught of runoff.

Her eyes searched for Shain, but the men were unrecognizable, some wearing slickers as she did but all of them drenched and soaking. Suddenly something tugged at her mind, and she could almost swear her thoughts were forming words lured from her subconscious. She felt drawn toward the muddy pit. Instead of joining the line of men and women passing sandbags, she strode to the far edge of the pit and lifted her lantern in order to see into the darkness.

A flash of lightning aided her, and she could see the fields of cane, nearly covered in roiling currents of water. Her engineering mind calculated the layout of the fields, the irrigation ditch, and the cabins she had just left. Shain was sacrificing his cane by shoring up this side of the ditch, but saving the workers' cabins—at least for now. Should the barrier of sandbags break, the water would gush through the trees and inundate the cabins, which were on a slightly lower elevation.

Something whispered again in her mind, and Alaynia swung her lantern around. In the next flash of lightning, she saw what was needed. But she had to find Shain. The men would never listen to her. Slipping and sliding in her haste, she raced back around the pit. She nearly lost her balance on one especially rough stretch, and a shadow loomed, catching her before she fell. "Are you all right?"

She recognized Cole's voice, and Alaynia dug her fingers into the arm he held out to steady her. "Where's Shain? You're going about this the wrong way. You need to change the course of the water in that ditch."

"Whoa, Alaynia. Shain rode back to the manor house, to see if maybe there were some tools stored up in the barn loft. We need more shovels." Cole stared away from her, his face haggard in the lantern light. "What we really need, of course, is about a hundred more people to help out here."

"No, you don't," Alaynia insisted. "Come with me."

"Alaynia, I've got to—"

"Damn it, Cole! That sandbag levee's never going to hold. Look at it! The water's risen a couple inches just since I got here, and I've only been here about five minutes. But those men have already deepened that pit by filling those bags, and if you'll put them to working on the other end, I think you can divert enough water to make the levee hold. I don't know where the water you'd divert would go, though. I need you to come over here and tell me what you think."

When Cole continued to hesitate, Alaynia grabbed his hand and started back to the far side of the pit, pulling him with her. Thankfully, Cole followed, because he was way too large for her to force him, should he dig in his heels. She led him to her vantage point of a moment ago, and in the next flash of lightning, pointed to the creek bed she'd noticed before.

"Look," she said. "See how that's laid out in comparison to the irrigation ditch? It looks like this was the old creek bed, and the dam was built on it, then the ditch dug to divert the creek's path and irrigate the cane fields. But if the men would dig through that ditch wall, the water should flow back into its natural path. The sand pit is deep enough to handle the overflow, until the water recedes some."

Stifling her frustration, Alaynia watched Cole scrutinize the creek bed, then glance at the irrigation ditch. The creek bed was over fifty feet wide, but more important, it was at least fifteen feet deep. From what she could tell, the path led in a direction that would not only keep the water from flooding the workers' cabins, but also allow the water to drain from the cane fields. What she didn't know, not being familiar with the layout beyond them, was where the water would go once released from the ditch.

"It might work," Cole mused. "That creek used to run on back into the hills south of us. In fact, a mile or so from Chenaie, there's a larger creek that flows into this same gully. It goes all the way to the river, on down past St. Francisville. There's nothing in the way for the water to damage, even if it overflows those banks."

"Then, let's get busy."

"Shain should make this decision . . ." Cole began, just as a shout went up from over beside the ditch. They both swung around to see two people steadying a stack of sandbags, while several other people ran toward them with new bags to reinforce the pile.

Alaynia gasped. "We've got to hurry!"

"Where do you suggest the men dig?" Cole demanded.

Alaynia hastily explained her plan to Cole, and he strode back around the pit, yelling at the men. At first they didn't seem to comprehend, but Cole ordered half of them into place on the other side of the pit by the irrigation ditch. Directing the rest of the men to continue filling sandbags, he headed across the pit.

Alaynia followed him, then studied the barrier of sandbags. "Cole," she said above the rising wind. "We'll need to shift some of the sandbags around. That way, when the water starts diverting, we can make sure it moves in the right direction."

"Can you handle that?" Cole asked. "I'll keep an eye on these men, so they'll dig in the right place and not ruin the entire plan."

"If they'll listen to me," Alaynia said.

Raising his voice to be heard by everyone, Cole yelled, "Listen up! We're going to divert this water, and Miz St. Clair will show you what to do! Pay attention to what she says and follow her orders!"

Alaynia raced over to the line of men and women and immediately began guiding the placement of the new sandbags. She ordered part of them placed in an intersecting line, and some others as an additional reinforcement to the layer of bags where the water would rush into the pit. She had no idea of how much time passed, but it couldn't have been more than fifteen or twenty minutes. Without the attention to building the barrier higher now, water soon lapped over the top.

"It's fixin' to go!" Cole shouted. "Are you ready down there? Another six inches up here and it'll flow through on its own!"

Alaynia quickly took stock, then yelled to Cole, "Ready!

Get your men off there, because some of that wall where they're standing will collapse!"

Cole motioned the men away, and they scrambled back around the pit. He stayed, and in the next flash of lightning, Alaynia saw him shoveling.

"Get out of there, Cole!" she screamed. "The force of the water will take care of the rest of it!"

Another streak of lightning split the air, followed by a crash of thunder. Cole raced along the bank of the pit and the noise of earth giving way sounded even above the rumbling thunder. The sky opened up, and rain poured down as water rushed into the pit and the workers scurried back from the barrier of sandbags.

Somehow Alaynia sensed something else through the turmoil and whirled, wiping the rain from her eyes as Shain pulled his huge stallion to a halt beside her and leapt from the saddle.

"What the hell's going on here?" he snarled.

Ignoring his angry voice, she started to explain what she'd done. "We've diverted the water from the ditch," she said eagerly. "I think the cabins will be safe now, and . . ."

"You think?" Shain growled as Cole joined them. "What did you do?"

"She had us dig through the irrigation ditch wall and let the water run into that old creek bed," Cole said, slapping Shain on the shoulder. "Damn, and just in time, too. Look. The water's droppin' already."

"You risked the lives of my people on some plan you *thought* might work?" Shain asked in an enraged tone.

"Hell," Cole put in before Alaynia could voice her indignation over Shain's lack of respect for her engineering skills. "If that barrier had collapsed, we'd probably have lost every person here who can't swim—and some of those who could.

You got any idea of the force behind that water? It's roilin' down that old creek bed over there like rapids. Alaynia was right about the pit here holdin' some of the overflow, until the water leveled out."

Shain caught her glance briefly, then looked away. The pride in her accomplishment diminished as though eroded by the pouring rain. She looked at the workers, and the moment they saw they had her attention, a ringing cheer went up, followed by another. She tilted her chin and focused again on her sense of achievement as she waved at them. Dawn was approaching, and she could see the men and women around her better now, but the continuing rain would make it yet another dreary day.

"You need to get back to the house and out of those wet clothes," Shain said. "Come on. I'll take you on Black."

"You have to post some men here," Alaynia said. "To keep a watch on the sandbags and reinforce them if necessary."

"Damn it, Alaynia, I know what needs to be done next. Get on the horse."

Aware of the crowd watching her, Alaynia bit back the sharp retort her mind formed. She stalked over to the black stallion and mounted without waiting for Shain to assist her. Picking up the reins, she stared down at Shain. His strained, worried face tugged at her, but his thinned lips indicated his still-simmering annoyance—or was it dented masculine pride, or perhaps his chauvinism showing again? Whichever, her own ego had been battered by him, and she was not in a forgiving mood just yet.

"I'm perfectly capable of riding back to the house by myself," she said around her tight lips. "I'll send one of the stable hands back with your horse."

Without waiting for his concurrence, she reined the

stallion around and headed back for the cabins. Just inside the line of trees, she pulled the horse up and turned. Shain had already taken charge of the workers, motioning for some of them to head back to their homes and others to take up their duties at the ditch.

He walked over to the side of the pit and stood alone for a few seconds, evidently scrutinizing her handiwork. Her hope that he would finally realize her plan had been the solution to averting the danger to the cabins faded when Shain dropped his head, shaking it slowly and rubbing his hands across his face.

Chapter 26

As Madame Chantal had promised, the white dress arrived on Thursday morning. In fact, Madame delivered the dress herself, along with the tangerine dress, and one other dress more appropriate for everyday wear. The rain, which continued intermittently, didn't appear to bother Madame. She drove a garish buggy painted almost the same color as her orange hair right up to the front steps of Chenaie, and pulled the white horse to a stop with a flourish. Once in the manor house, she herded her two charges ahead of her to Jeannie's room. For the next hour, Madame flitted around both Alaynia and Jeannie, tucking here and smoothing there, until she was satisfied her creations would suitably impress her current and any potential customers.

Her tongue flew even faster than her hands, as she chatted about the gossip and rumors her customers had passed on to her—someone's daughter, who was hastily planning a marriage; someone else's son, who was driving his poor, widowed mother to distraction by his refusal to select an appropriate wife; another son, who had been seen with a female companion definitely not his betrothed.

Alaynia listened with half an ear, her mind more on the continuing rift between her and Shain than on the lovely handiwork of Madame Chantal. Her husband hadn't gone so far as to shun her bed, but he came in late, always well after the evening meal and after she had already crawled into the empty bed first. The thought crossed her mind once that he waited until he saw the light in their bedroom window, then delayed a while after she extinguished it before he entered the house. But she tried to tell herself that he was only consumed with the plantation's continuing problems.

She always stayed awake until he came in, and he always assured her things were under control. He even kissed her good night, but only one kiss. And her pride would not allow her to snuggle up to his broad back after he turned away from her and settled into an exhausted sleep.

"Oh, la, la, Mademoiselle Jeannie," Madame Chantal's voice broke into Alaynia's thoughts. "You will have the swains fighting for every dance tomorrow night. Is she not lovely, Madame St. Clair?"

"Yes," Alaynia agreed. "You're very beautiful, Jeannie. Here. Let's try your hair this way."

She worked with Jeannie's hair for a few minutes, threading the top of it into a French braid, then looping the glorious blond mass before letting it fall down her back. Tugging a few wisps of hair free, she curled them around Jeannie's piquant face and stepped back to let Jeannie look into the full-length mirror on the back of her bedroom door.

Jeannie gasped in awe, then bent forward in childish wonder. "Is that me?" she breathed. "I . . . I look like a *woman*."

Madame and Alaynia chuckled. "You are nearly a woman, honey," Alaynia said. "And you'll definitely be the belle of your own ball."

Madame Chantal began gathering up her sewing things, and Alaynia stepped behind Jeannie's dressing screen to change from the white dress into the everyday one. Carefully carrying the white dress over her arm, she left

Jeannie's room to hang the lovely creation in the master bedroom wardrobe, beside the tangerine dress. By the time she had returned to Jeannie's room, the young girl had also changed, and Madame was heading out the door.

"Please do not bother to show me out," Madame said with a negligent wave of her hand. "I must hurry back to town, as I have two more dresses to complete before to-morrow."

"Jeannie's been afraid people might not come, with the weather like this," Alaynia said.

"Oh, no one would miss it," Madame assured her. "The party is the talk of the town. There has not been a gathering at Chenaie for months and months. Everyone will be here."

"Thank you for doing such a wonderful job on the dresses, Madame. I guess we'll see you tomorrow night."

A tiny simper pursed Madame's lips and she nodded her head vigorously, almost toppling her orange hair from its high perch. "I must tell you, I was very surprised to receive an invitation, since I don't usually move within the circles of society," Madame said. "But I was so hoping it was not a mistake."

"Jeannie made out her guest list herself," Alaynia confirmed. "And we're looking forward to seeing you again."

With another vigorous bob of her head, Madame toddled down the hallway, her sewing bag clutched to her momentous chest. Alaynia watched her with a smile, but the smile faded as soon as Madame disappeared down the stairwell. Alaynia walked on into Jeannie's room again, finding the young girl bent over her writing desk, with Tiny curled at her feet.

"Madame didn't quite know what to think of Tiny, did she?" Alaynia asked to get Jeannie's attention.

Jeannie laughed and glanced up. "No. She didn't seem

to think a pig was an appropriate house pet."

"What are you doing now?"

"Finishing up my list of things to do," Jeannie told her. "The servants know what needs to be done, but they still expect us to tell them. Then they can show us in return that they already have everything well in hand."

"I guess I'll never learn all the ins and outs of running a household like this," Alaynia replied. "Indeed, I think I'll ride over to Jake's, if you don't need my help here."

"Got it under control," Jeannie reassured her. "You don't want me to go with you, do you?"

"No. I'll ask one of the stable hands to accompany me. You go ahead with what you're doing."

Jeannie bent back to her list, and Alaynia returned to the master bedroom to change once again. A few minutes later, she splashed across the sodden backyard toward the stable, wearing her riding skirt and boots and carrying the slicker, since the rain had let up for a while. But though she searched the interior of the barn, she didn't find anyone there.

Patting her foot in indecision, she stared at the stall where her little mare was standing. Shain never appeared for the noon meal these days, and she was sure Jeannie would assume she would stay at Jake's past the hour for the meal. She could get Jake to accompany her back.

Sylvia and Basil drifted overhead as Alaynia rode into the clearing around Jake's shack and barn. Bypassing the shack, she headed over to the barn and dismounted.

"Now, you shield your presence here from Zeke," Sylvia warned. "You've been pushing the bounds way too much lately."

"I knew that old creek bed was there," Basil argued.

"And if I hadn't shown Alaynia what was needed, Chenaie's cabins would have been flooded. Now even the cane might make at least a halfway decent crop. It needs at least some moisture to reach maturity."

"You came up with that idea of diverting the water in the irrigation ditch by tuning into Alaynia's mind—and her engineering education," Sylvia insisted. "But that's not what I'm talking about. If I hadn't found you when I did that day at Tana's cabin, you'd have probably given Alaynia a heart attack by appearing full-blown in front of her and sitting down to chat!"

Basil looked anything but contrite as they drifted through the barn roof and settled on one of the beams. Shaking her head in consternation, Sylvia sent a quick plea winging to Francesca to join them. It went unanswered yet again, and she frowned in vexation. Just what the heck was the superior angel up to? But she couldn't chance leaving for even a brief period to check it out. No telling what trouble Basil would get into, if she left him alone.

"I've been doing just fine and dandy here for all this time," Basil said, making Sylvia realize she hadn't protected her thoughts from him. "If you want to go look for your friend, feel free to take off."

"My assignment is to stay here. And here's where I'll stay, until I get permission to leave. Oh, darn. Look at Alaynia."

Below them, Alaynia buried her face on Jake's shoulder, and the wiry little man patted her uncertainly on the back. Sylvia immediately turned her attention downward, rather than upward.

Jake led Alaynia over to one of the stools and gently pushed her onto it. "I seem to remember this situation once before," he said in a soothing voice. "Now, you talk it out with Uncle Jake here. Tell me what's troubling you."

Alaynia straightened and backhanded the tears from her eyes. "Since the other night, I just can't get something Tana said out of my mind. She said perhaps I'd been brought here for a purpose, and I'm deathly afraid that my purpose has been accomplished. I also honestly don't think Shain would give a damn if I disappeared entirely from his life. I'm nothing but an embarrassment to him."

"Why?" Jake asked in astonishment. "Because you're still insisting on finishing the construction of my house?"

"Not just that." Alaynia went on to explain what had happened at the irrigation ditch, and Shain's withdrawal from her after that. "I think he's upset that I thought of the plan to divert the water," she finished. "It was an insult to his masculine pride that a woman—and his wife, at that—came up with it, instead of him."

"Maybe so," Jake agreed. "Have you talked to him about it?"

"When?" Alaynia asked with a sigh. "He claims he's busy. Oh, not in so many words, but he's out all day and falls asleep at night as soon as his head hits the pillow."

"So you feel your purpose here may have been to save Chenaie from that flood," Jake mused, "and now you'll be going back to your own time?"

Alaynia rose and paced back and forth. "I . . . something else happened at Tana's," she finally forced herself to say. She told Jake about the voices and her absolute conviction that at least one presence, perhaps two, had been in the room. "And I didn't think of the idea of how to divert the water all on my own. It was like something . . . someone . . . planted the thought in my head. I'm satisfied it was Shain's grandfather, Jake. From what I've learned about him, he'd go to any lengths to protect Chenaie, alive or dead. And now that I've done what he brought me here to do—save Chenaie from that flood—I've served my purpose."

Alaynia dropped back onto the stool, and Sylvia grabbed Basil as he started to fly from the beam. "No you don't!" she said. "Don't you dare go down there and appear to them!"

"But she's got it all wrong," Basil said. "I brought her back here to protect Chenaie in the future—to keep a bunch of strangers from taking over my manor house. Her being here and having the skills to avert danger to Chenaie in this period is an added bonus, I'll admit. And I've told you and told you that I've no intentions of sending her away from Shain."

"And I keep telling you that it's not your choice." Sylvia crossed her arms over her chest and glared at him. "It's Alaynia's choice. Your interfering in her free will won't be tolerated again. And you're supposed to be recouping your powers, so you can reopen that time warp and allow her to make her choice—so things will be set right. Instead, you're using your energies to cross out of your plane of existence and communicate with Alaynia—even try to appear to her!"

A flutter of nearby wings startled Sylvia, and a huge barn owl swooped past her. It flew out the barn door, and suddenly several of the other owls in the barn followed. Below them, she saw Jake gazing after the owls with a puzzled expression on his face.

"Those owls never fly in the daytime," Jake said. "I wonder . . ." Instantly his expression changed. "We've got to get out of here!"

Grabbing Alaynia's arm, Jake pulled her with him as he raced for the door. Sylvia heard the sound at that moment, and saw the look of horror on Basil's face as he realized what was happening. They exited through the roof and hovered high above the barn, watching the mud slide down the hillside behind them, picking up huge boulders as it went. Sylvia glanced down briefly to see Jake and Alaynia standing well beyond the barn, out of danger. Alaynia was holding the reins of her mare, which she had led away from the barn.

The mudslide rumbled on down the hill, as vicious as an avalanche and just as deadly. Within seconds, it hit the side of the barn. The structure held for a moment, creaking and groaning with the strain, while the mud built up higher against it. One huge boulder bounced against another one, flying into the air and landing with a thunderous crack against the wall. The structure trembled visibly, then began to collapse.

It folded on one end, as though kneeling in acknowledgment of the mudslide's superior force. Timbers cracked like shots from a gun, and the roof slid sideways, tilting down into the mud, which immediately buried it. A few more boulders piled on the mass, blocking the remainder of the slide.

For at least half a minute, the remainder of the barn stood against the onslaught. Then an interior beam split with a resounding, splintering crack, and the structure shivered in defeat. In a violent explosion, the roof caved in and the exterior walls disintegrated, tumbling down to cover the roof. Clouds of dust and flying pieces of wood were driven into the air by the force of the collapse, showering down on the tangled mass of the structure after they lost impetus.

The resulting silence after the cacophony of sound was so deadly it took Alaynia a moment to realize she hadn't been deafened by the explosion. She fearfully searched the mass for any sign of flames, trying to recall if Jake had had any lanterns burning when they were inside the barn. But she only saw the dust of years settling, and when a patter of rain fell on her head, she knew it would soon wash the air free of any lingering traces of that.

Jake moaned beside her. "My entire life's work," he said in a miserable voice. "Everything's gone, even your wonderful car."

"Jake, you've still got plenty of your work left. Your patents—your name among the other inventors. You . . ." Alaynia gasped as Jake grabbed at his chest and his eyes searched hers, terror and pain in their depths.

"I . . . Alaynia . . . it . . ."

His knees gave way and Alaynia grabbed him, struggling desperately to hold his inert weight. Sinking with him to the soaked ground, she stared around her, finally seeing Zeke in the shadowed recesses of the porch.

"Help me!" she screamed. "I think he's having a heart attack!"

Zeke ran from the porch, feet splashing in the water-logged ground. He hesitated only for a second when he reached them, his fear of Alaynia briefly crossing his face.

"Help him!" she insisted.

Zeke knelt in the mud and gathered Jake into his strong arms. Lifting him easily, he splashed back to the porch and inside the shack. Crossing to a battered settee in a corner of the room, he gently laid Jake down.

"Let me see him," Alaynia said.

Zeke moved aside and Alaynia knelt by Jake. Grabbing his wrist, she pressed her fingers against it, giving a sigh when she felt a very faint pulse. She studied his gray face, no-ticing his lips already turning cyanotic from lack of oxygen, as were the fingertips of the hand she held.

"A doctor." She gave Zeke a beseeching look. "He needs a doctor—quickly."

Huge, silent tears were rolling down Zeke's face, but he spoke in a distinct voice. "Miss Tana be closest."

"Take my mare, Zeke. And please, tell her to hurry. I've had CPR training, if I need it while you're gone."

Zeke hurried from the room, and a moment later, Alaynia heard hoofbeats as her mare raced from the clearing. Keeping a firm hold on Jake's hand, both in comfort should he rouse and to keep a check on his fluttering pulse, she bowed her head over his motionless figure.

"Please," she prayed. "If it's his time to go, please just let me tell him how much he's come to mean to me. And don't let him suffer. But if it's not his time, please let me know what to do to save his life."

Jake's wrist flexed beneath her fingers, and Alaynia's eyes flew open to search his face. It was still gray and lifeless, but she thought the blueness around his lips had faded somewhat. Beneath her fingers, the pulse steadied into a rhythmic beat, though it continued to be faint.

"What can we do to help her?" Basil whispered to Sylvia as they stood just inside the door of the shack. "Is Jake going to join us?"

"I don't know," Sylvia replied. "If it's his time, yes, he will. But we can't contact Alaynia. We can't interfere."

"I wish we could have interfered with that mudslide. That's what gave Jake this heart attack—seeing his life's work destroyed."

"If I'd had to intervene to protect either Alaynia or Jake, I would have," Sylvia replied. "My guardian duties only apply to humans, though, not natural disasters. I explained that to you after the chapel fire."

"Then what about Jake's heart attack?" Basil asked.

"I . . . Basil, I didn't have any warning of that. It's hard to define how an angel knows when her powers are needed and when she's to step aside and let events unfold. Since I had no forewarning of the heart attack, it was meant to happen."

Basil nodded slowly in understanding. "I guess you've seen lots of people pass over."

"Not that many," Sylvia denied. "My duties up until a few years ago consisted of working with already-departed spirits. But, yes, I've seen a few, though never one of my assignments, only those around them. I was there when Jacki's husband died, and her mother and father later on."

"Did all of them have the choice I had?"

"You mean, whether to pass on to the heavenly plane or stay in a dimension where they could still be close to earth?"

"Yes."

"Not really," Sylvia revealed. "Some spirits are ready and willing to go on to the next plane, and don't ask for that choice. In your situation, I assume you did."

Basil nodded agreement, then fell silent. They watched Alaynia continue her vigil over Jake, now and then smoothing the frazzled hair and whispering encouragement for him to hold on until Tana arrived. At one point, Alaynia stood and searched the room, then went into one of the bedrooms at the back of the shack. Reemerging with blankets, she lovingly laid them over Jake and tucked them around him.

Time passed slowly, but finally Sylvia and Basil heard the sound of galloping hoofbeats approaching. Moving out of the doorway, they glided off to the side of the porch.

"Remember," Sylvia admonished Basil. "Shield your presence from them. Both Zeke and Tana will sense you easily, and they need to concentrate on Jake."

"I will," Basil promised.

They glanced at the galloping horses entering the clearing to see not only Zeke and Tana, but also Shain on his huge, black stallion. Pulling their horses to sliding halts, they dismounted and raced into the cabin.

Alaynia rose to her feet, gratitude warring with the heartbreak in her eyes. Shain strode to the settee, his arms already reaching for her. "How is he?"

"Still alive," Alaynia murmured. She stepped out of Shain's grasp and moved away to allow Tana room to examine Jake. Shain followed her, his attention split between his concern over his old friend and Alaynia's bedraggled appearance. Her riding skirt was smeared with mud, as were her boots, and tear paths tracked through a layer of dirt on her face. Another tear snaked down her cheek, and she backhanded it with a negligent swipe.

Shain started to reach for her again, but Tana spoke. "Zeke, get some hot water. Alaynia, put some of these herbs in the water to seep." She handed Alaynia a bundle of herbs drawn from the black satchel of medications she carried, and Alaynia hurried beside Zeke to the stove in the rear of the room.

"Can I do anything, Tana?" Shain asked.

"Not until we see how the next few hours go," Tana said. "Then you may need to take him to Chenaie and watch over him. He cannot be left here alone, with only Zeke to care for him."

"Whatever needs to be done," Shain assured her. "Anything."

Tana turned back to Jake, and as Zeke and Alaynia approached again, Shain moved over to the door. When he realized he could offer no assistance, he stepped out onto the porch.

The rain had let up again, and he stared at the crumbled mass of timber, boards, roofing, mud, and boulders that had been Jake's barn. Clenching his fists at his side, he gazed past the pile of tangled refuse to the denuded hillside behind the barn, where a cliff side had given way to begin the mudslide.

God, what if Alaynia hadn't escaped the barn before it collapsed?

He'd found her mare gone when he rode Black into the stable after he decided to take a break from the vicious grind of the past few days and finally enjoy a hot meal at the manor house. He'd supervised what repairs could be made on the irrigation ditch dam, at least until the water receded a little more. On the far side of the cane field, he'd found a way to drain some more water off, channeling it into the creek bed. Maybe, just maybe, he could salvage some of the crop, if this rain would cease for a few days.

And it was time to have a talk with Alaynia—to see if they couldn't work out some sort of compromise in their relationship. Neither Cole nor Carrington had been a damned bit understanding about Shain's anger over Alaynia placing herself in danger at the irrigation ditch. What if that hare-brained plan of hers hadn't worked? Cole insisted he'd made the right decision in Shain's absence—to take a chance on Alaynia's strategy. Both Cole and the overseer were filled with admiration for Alaynia—but then, neither of them was in love with her. They didn't understand his vacillation between pride in her and his inadequacy at keeping her safe.

His physical tiredness and uneasiness about how to approach Alaynia to discuss the rift between them had allowed his temper to explode when he saw both the stable hands busy at work and realized Alaynia had left unescorted. The stable hands denied vehemently even seeing the mistress of Chenaie leave, but Shain knew at once she had gone over to Jake's—probably to check on the site of that damned house she was building.

He'd whirled Black out of the barn and met Tana and Zeke racing their horses down the road a half-mile from Jake's. Neither of them slowed when they spotted him, and he joined in their frantic gallop.

"A mudslide!" Zeke called to Shain as the horses pounded down the road. "The barn's caved in! And Mister Jake's dyin'!"

"Alaynia?" Shain shouted back.

"She got out in time—Mister Jake, too! But Mister Jake's heart give out afterwards!"

Pulling his mind back to the scene before him, Shain lifted a clenched fist and slammed it into one of the porch supports.

"Goddamn you, Fitzroy!" he growled. "And goddamn your company and all the money-hungry people it took advantage of. So far no one's been killed, but if Alaynia had been hurt, I'd have strangled you in front of the entire town!"

Hell, his thoughts continued, as he dropped his head and picked at a splinter of wood in one knuckle. Alaynia didn't need his protection—or his offer of vengeance on her behalf. She was more capable of taking care of herself than he was of caring for her. He loved her with his entire being and believed deeply in her love for him in return. But how long would her love last, if everything he touched continued to end in setbacks instead of growth?

"Shain." Alaynia's voice came from behind him, and he turned.

"Jake's rousing already. Tana believes we should take him to Chenaie. But their wagon was destroyed when the barn collapsed, so . . ."

"I'll go get a wagon from Chenaie," Shain assured her. "Is there anything else I can do?"

"I don't think so. I'll let Tana know you've gone after the wagon."

She went back into the shack, and Shain stepped from the porch. Picking up Black's reins, he vaulted into the saddle. Maybe he could at least get the wagon back here in one piece, without it falling apart on the way.

Chapter 27

"It doesn't feel right," Jeannie murmured as Alaynia worked on her hair the next evening. "Having a party while Jake is ill. I should be helping Tana and Netta care for him."

"What do you think Jake would want you to do?" Alaynia asked gently.

"Have the party," Jeannie admitted. "But I wanted Jake to be at it, too. And he's your uncle, Alaynia. I know how worried you are about him."

Tears filmed Alaynia's eyes, and she nodded without speaking. What could she tell Jeannie, anyway? The time might come when she felt comfortable informing Jeannie that she came from the future, but not yet. If she returned there, Shain would be the one to explain why they had invented a fraudulent relationship for her with Jake. Too, she didn't want to give Jeannie any false hope by assuring her Jake would attend her next birthday party. Tana had been far from encouraging as to Jake's chances of recovery. It would spoil Jeannie's party even further if she passed Tana's disheartening words on to the young girl, who cared so deeply for the elderly inventor.

"Netta's staying with Jake while Tana goes to check on Little Jim and get a little rest," she told Jeannie. "He won't be alone for even a moment. You've worked so hard for this party. Why, I'm totally amazed at how organized you are. You've even brought in some of the women workers to help the cook out and serve the guests. And it hasn't rained all day, so I'm sure everyone you invited will attend."

Giving a last pat to the perfectly-styled blond hair, Alaynia urged Jeannie around to face her and cupped her delicate chin. "Jake wouldn't want you to put your life on hold because he's ill, honey. I've gotten to know him very well, and he's a wonderful man. He hasn't regained consciousness, but we don't know for sure that he's not aware of what's going on around him. If he realizes today's the day of your party and it doesn't happen, it might be even worse on him."

"Sort of like all the relatives gathering when someone's getting ready to die," Jeannie muttered.

"Jeannie . . ." Alaynia hesitated, then went on. "Jeannie, Jake *is* very ill."

"I was out in the hall, and I heard Tana talking to you," Jeannie said quietly. "I know he might not make it. Jake told me once that he intended to live every day of his life just the way he wanted to, and to the fullest. And when he went on to the next life, he'd do the same thing there. He's not afraid of dying, Alaynia. We'll be the ones who'll miss him, but we'll just have to keep reminding ourselves that he's tinkering away to his heart's content, wherever he is. Who knows? He might even be able to travel through time and see how all those wonderful inventions he and his friends are working on are in use in the future."

"He'd love that," Alaynia agreed, amazed once again at Jeannie's maturity. Should she and Shain have a daughter, the little girl could have no better role model than her aunt.

But for her and Shain to have children—or even a life together—they had so many things to work out. Maybe tomorrow they would have some time to talk. She had spent the night spelling Tana with Jake's care, only managing to get an hour or so of sleep now and then on the cot they had placed in the bedroom where Jake lay unconscious. Right now, she needed to get ready to meet their guests herself.

"I'll be in the master bedroom if you need me, Jeannie."

"All right. I'm going to take Tiny out to the stables and leave him with Shain's horse. Some of the women guests may want to freshen up in my room, and I doubt they'd appreciate Tiny sniffing around their gowns while they did that."

Alaynia laughed with her and left the room, wondering if Shain had come in yet from the fields to get ready himself. Surely he wouldn't spoil Jeannie's party by not making an appearance. She had laid his evening clothes, which she'd found hanging in the other armoire in the room, on the bed earlier that day. When she entered the master bedroom, she saw they were gone. He had evidently slipped in and out without her knowledge, avoiding her once again.

Anger stirred, replacing the anxiety over their relationship which had plagued her the past few days. The hell with him! Recalling how she used to enjoy the looks of amazement at her transformation on the faces of the men at the cocktail parties she attended, she nodded her head in determination. She'd just see whether the men in the past responded as well to blatant sexiness as men in the future did.

She'd intended to wear the white dress—for Shain and in the hope they might slip away for a few minutes to the gazebo and talk. Surely he would remember what he'd said the day he chose the material, about how beautiful he would find her in that dress. But now she picked it up from the bed and re-hung it in her armoire. Netta had been her usual efficient self and pressed the tangerine dress, also. Stifling the recollection of how scandalously low the neckline had been when she tried the dress on yesterday, she laid it carefully on the bed and stepped behind the dressing screen to the tub of steaming water one of the house servants had readied for her.

After conscientiously scrubbing every inch of herself, she dried and slathered lotion over her body, then dug into the case of cosmetics she hadn't used since her arrival. She even had a bottle of Chanel No. 5 tucked into a side pocket of the case—a gift from a grateful client. She touched it to every pulse point before wrapping the towel around her and settling in front of the dressing table.

When she swept out of the master bedroom a half hour later, she had never felt more beautiful. Her hair wisped around her face, which she had made up so professionally no one would ever believe she wore cosmetics. Instead of restraining the rest of her hair, it tumbled down her back in a riotous mass of sexy curls. She had spurned wearing a bra, since the off-the-shoulder neckline called for a strapless one, which she didn't have with her. The silky material caressed her breasts, making the nipples stand out. She wore only one long petticoat, and her movements molded it and the dress skirt against her long legs.

She glided down the front stairwell just as someone knocked on the entrance door and Shain stepped out of his study into the hallway. Shain stopped as though poleaxed and satisfaction glowed within her. With a brilliant smile, she strolled over to him and slipped her arm in his. "Sounds like some of our guests have arrived, darling. We better greet them."

Instead, he swept her with him back into the study and slammed the door. "Let the servants answer the door," he growled just before he claimed her mouth with his own.

He kissed her deeply and ravenously, and she didn't give one damn whether he ruined all of her carefully-applied cosmetics or not. Wrapping her arms around his neck, she returned his kiss giddily, so glad to be in his arms once again she could think of nothing else. His hands roamed her body, leaving an inferno of sensations in their wake. When he cupped her hips and pulled her closer to him, she realized he was as stirred as she was. She rocked against him, and he broke the kiss to bury his face in her neck.

"God, Alaynia," he groaned. "We have to stop. But I don't know if I can. I've missed you so damned much."

His words dashed icy water on her emotions, and she pulled back. "It's been your own choice to miss me. I'm not the one who's been avoiding you."

"Avoiding you? Do you think that's what's been going on? Damn it, Alaynia, I haven't had a free minute these past few days!"

"I don't appreciate being cursed at," Alaynia responded coldly. "And it seems to me that we could have talked to each other at least briefly at night. Shared a little of each other's day."

Shain plunged his fingers through his midnight hair. His brown eyes were bleak with suppressed emotions when he looked at her again. She instinctively reached out for him, a horrible thought crossing her mind.

"Shain. You're not . . . I mean, I know how worried you've been. Sometimes it affects men in different ways. Whatever it is, we can talk it out."

Pushing her hand from his arm, he glared at her. "What the hell are you trying to say? You think I can't make love to you because I'm too damned upset over the problems I've been having at Chenaie? That they've made me . . . impotent?"

"No. Oh, no," Alaynia denied, lying through her teeth. "I . . ."

"Did I feel like I couldn't get it up a second ago?"

"You don't have to be crass about it, Shain."

He sneered contemptuously at her and walked over to open the door. "We've got guests to greet. Are you coming?"

"In . . . in a minute."

He stalked through the door and closed it behind him. Alaynia wrapped her arms around herself and dropped her head. How could she have insinuated such a thing to him? She knew how strong his masculine pride was. He'd been taught to cherish and protect women—to be the head of the family. And she had attacked his very masculinity.

She thought of the night by the irrigation ditch and Shain's agitation when he found her there. Had he been upset because she had taken command of the situation and found a way to safeguard the cabins when he had been on the verge of failure? Or had he been distressed because she could have been in danger, along with his workers?

Yet she couldn't accept being less than a partner to him, with all the game-playing she imagined it would entail. She lifted her head and caught sight of herself in a mirror on the wall. Her cheeks were flushed and her mouth kiss-swollen. Her breasts almost spilled from the low-cut gown. She snorted delicately in disgust at herself, then narrowed her eyes in contemplation.

Wasn't that just what she had done? Hadn't she played her own game with him? Hadn't she enhanced her very femininity in an attempt to lure him back into her arms? It had worked for a brief interlude, too. Was there anything wrong with that?

They were both strong, independent people, but they were still male and female. Their very masculinity and femininity brought them a wondrous joy together. Until lately, there had been no barriers between them in bed. They compromised by giving each other pleasure, which enhanced each other's delight. Why wouldn't the same compromising work in the rest of their life together? If she had to use her feminine wiles to get that message across to Shain, it couldn't demean her that much.

Could it?

Lifting her head to match the regal way the tangerine dress made her feel, she walked over to the mirror and checked her makeup. Her lipstick was gone, of course, but her lips looked fine without it. She tucked one strand of hair back in place, then went to find Shain.

The drawing room dividers had been removed for dancing later, and more guests had arrived. The floor-length windows lining the front veranda had been shoved open, allowing the evening breeze to filter in the room, and it carried the scent of perfumed women with it. She saw Jeannie with two young girls across the room, but Shain was standing right inside the doorway, where he could greet incoming guests and still talk to people circulating around the room.

She gave him a dazzling smile and walked up to him, circling his waist with one arm. "Hello again, darling," she murmured. "I forgot to tell you that you're looking awfully handsome this evening."

His lips tightened barely perceptively, but he replied, "And I forgot to tell you how beautiful you look. But I thought you had the white dress laid out to wear."

"I'm saving that one for a special time, when it's only the two of us." His dark eyes softened a little, and she felt him give a relieved sigh. "Now, shouldn't you introduce me to the guests I haven't met already?"

Several people were already approaching, and for the

next few minutes, she tried to keep their names straight in her mind. Suddenly, Shain stiffened. When she glanced at his face, he quickly smoothed a composed look over the thunder and nodded at someone behind her back.

"Fitzroy," he said curtly. "And Annette. You already know my wife, Alaynia. I thought you were bringing Colette with you, Annette."

"Oh," Annette said with a wave of her hand. "She ran across the veranda and went in through the front over there. See? She's already talking to Jeannie. I don't know where I fell down on teaching that daughter of mine her manners."

"There's refreshments on the sideboard," Alaynia said, watching Annette's eyes search the scattered guests. "Dinner will be served in a few minutes."

"Is . . . um . . . is everyone here?" Annette asked.

Jeannie rushed up to them at that moment. "Brother, dear, where's Cole? Oh, hello, Mrs. Escott. I apologize for my lack of manners, but Cole promised to be my escort for dinner, and he hasn't even shown up yet."

"What about Billy Ben?" Alaynia asked with a smile.

"He's such a youngster," Jeannie said haughtily. "And Cole promised."

"Cole should be here any minute, Jeannie," Shain assured her. "He's checking on one of the mares. Thinks she's about ready to foal."

"He better not come in with manure all over his evening boots," Jeannie said with a pout.

"Ah," Basil breathed longingly. "This brings back memories. Laureen and I had some wonderful parties here at Chenaie. And Jeannie reminds me so much of my Laureen at about that age. She was only sixteen when I first saw her."

"Basil." Sylvia nudged his arm as they sat half-way up the front stairwell. "Look. Where's she sneaking off to?"

"I don't know," he muttered as he watched Annette Escott slip down the hallway. "But she's definitely sneaking. See how she's glancing over her shoulder to make sure no one's following her? And there's Fitzroy, watching her from over in the corner. I don't like the feel of this, Sylvia."

They both floated from the steps and followed Annette. Basil glanced back once and saw Fitzroy leave the drawing room. He came down the hall behind them, his movements as furtive as Annette's.

Annette exited through the rear doorway and crossed the back veranda. She headed directly toward the stables, holding her evening gown up above her ankles to avoid the soaked grass. As she entered the stables, Basil saw Fitzroy pause on the back veranda to light a cigar, a crafty look on his face.

"We need to read what they're thinking . . ."

Sylvia interrupted him by pulling him with her into the stables. Several lanterns hung around, and Cole Dubose emerged from a stall and shut the stall door. Annette raced up to him and flung herself into his arms.

"Cole! Oh, darling, please. Just give me a few minutes to talk to you!"

Cole unwound her arms from his neck and pushed her away. "Annette, we haven't had anythin' to talk about for years. Go on back to the party."

"You don't know how wretched I've been," Annette said in a pleading voice. "All my husband cares about is that damned plantation I brought him when he married me. Cole, give me a chance."

"If you're tryin' to tell me you're sleepin' in a lonely

bed," Cole said, "you better remember how easily I've always seen through your lies. You and Fitzroy are the talk of St. Francisville."

"He's got business with my husband!" Annette stamped her foot and then tried to cling to him again.

Cole avoided her easily and started past her. "Yeah, and pigs fly."

Annette screeched in rage and flew after him. Tripping on her long skirt, she stumbled into his back and Cole swung around to catch her. Off balance himself, he couldn't stop them both from falling into a pile of hay. Her gown tore with a loud rip.

Instead of continuing to scream at him, Annette grabbed Cole's face and rained kisses on it. She wrapped her legs around him and tried to hold him to her, when he snorted in revulsion. Finally, Cole managed to untangle himself and stand.

"Damn it, Cole," Annette whined. "You didn't used to pull away from me."

Cole slowly ran a hand across his mouth, as though wiping away something repugnant, and turned. Annette scrambled up and lunged for the pitchfork stuck nearby. Hissing in fury, she went after him.

Sylvia tried desperately to focus on the pitchfork, but it continued its path as Annette swung it over her head, aimed at Cole. At the last instant, Cole seemed to sense something, but before he could turn, the heavy metal base crunched down on his head. He crumbled without even a groan.

Annette threw the pitchfork aside and clapped her hands over her mouth. Fitzroy stepped into the deadly silence of the barn and her eyes flew to him. Dropping his cigar, he ground it carefully under his boot.

"We wouldn't want to burn the barn down, now would we, Annette?" he said in a calm voice. "Or would you rather we destroy the evidence?"

"Evan." Annette stretched out her hands. "Evan, I . . . he accosted me. I held him off, but I lost my temper when I finally managed to get free of him. I . . . hit him."

"I can see that you hit him, but I don't believe a damned word about why you did it. I've been standing out there listening to you. Is he dead?"

"Evan! I didn't know you were there. It wasn't what it sounded like."

"Shut up, Annette. I know all about your . . . ah . . . shall we be polite and call them indiscretions? The men in the parish know you extremely well. And I'm also aware that your husband is in New Orleans visiting his mistress, not just on business. You're quite the actress, though, my dear, and extremely good between the sheets. We might still come to some sort of agreement about getting rid of that husband of yours and allowing you a modicum of freedom again, if you play your cards right here. Now, is Dubose dead?"

"I . . . don't know."

A squeal split the air, and Tiny wiggled through a loose board in the stall where he'd been staying with Black. Snuffling, he trotted toward Annette, but she grabbed her skirts and backed away. Tiny continued on to Cole and stopped by the fallen man's head, grunting and sniffing at Cole's ear. Cole never moved, but Fitzroy rushed forward and kicked Tiny viciously.

"Get the hell out of here, pig!" he snarled.

Tiny squealed in pain and disappeared back into the stall. Fitzroy stepped outside the door, then suddenly rushed back in to grab Annette and drag her to the doorway. "You listen to me, you whoring bitch," he snapped. "They'll hang you for murder unless you go along with me. And we can get St. Clair out of the way, too—or at least abolish any influence he has left over the people around here."

He grabbed Annette's dress and ripped it down the front. Then he slapped her, wrenching her head to the side. Her scream of pain, intermingled with outrage, drew the attention of Tana and Little Jim, who were walking toward the manor house.

"Oh, no," Sylvia breathed.

"Stop him!" Basil demanded. "Don't let this happen!"

"I can't stop it," Sylvia murmured. "The events will have to be played out on their own."

"Well, I'm sure as heck going to do something!" Basil flew at Fitzroy, but crashed into an invisible barrier. He picked himself up and started off again, but Sylvia laid a hand on his arm. "You can't interfere, Basil. You might as well give it up."

Basil glared at her, then struck the barrier with his fist. At least he could watch—and hear, both the words spoken and the unspoken thoughts.

"Scream again!" Fitzroy ordered Annette. "Loud." When she hesitated, he drew back his hand again. Annette screamed as though her dress were on fire.

Tana turned to Little Jim and pushed him away. "Run!" she cried. "Run, and do not go to the cabin! Go!"

"Mama?" Little Jim asked. "But why, Mama?"

"Go!"

Tana shoved him just as one of the doors on the back veranda opened and several guests ran out, drawn by Annette's scream. Little Jim lumbered off, but Fitzroy's roar split the air.

"Catch him! He tried to rape Mrs. Escott! And he killed Dubose when he tried to stop him!"

Little Jim whirled in confusion. "No!" he cried. "No, I didn't. Mama!"

Several of the men on the back veranda ran into the yard, and Little Jim turned and tried to flee once more. His clumsy legs only carried him a few feet before the men caught him. Little Jim struggled mightily, all the while calling for his mother, but the men wrestled him to the ground. When Tana tried to intervene, one of the men dragged her away.

Shain elbowed his way through the crowd, with Alaynia right behind him carrying a lantern she'd grabbed from the back veranda.

"What the hell's going on?" Shain demanded, as Alaynia held the lantern high.

Fitzroy shoved Annette into the lantern light, where she hung her head and bit her bottom lip. "That black bastard tried to rape Mrs. Escott," he said in a blunt voice. "I heard her first scream when I was out on the veranda having a cigar. Dubose must have heard her, too, because by the time I got to the barn, he was lying on the floor dead. What kind of man are you, St. Clair—sheltering a rapist on your plantation?"

The lantern shook in Alaynia's hand, and she turned a pleading look on Shain. "Shain, he must be lying."

But her voice was drowned in the outraged shouts from the men and women gathered around. Before Shain could stop them, they surged forward, and the men holding Little Jim dragged him to his feet and pulled him toward a large cypress tree. A man ran up with a rope.

"He's right," the man yelled. "I saw Dubose lying on the barn floor when I went in to find this rope. His head's caved in." He tossed the rope over a tree limb. "Let's hang the son of a bitch before he kills someone else or tries to lay a hand on another white woman!"

Tana screamed, then sobbed and begged for them to leave her son alone. Dropping the lantern, Alaynia flew to her side and slapped the man holding her. He lost his grip, but when Tana tried to go to Little Jim, two more men caught her. Suddenly Shain appeared beside Little Jim. He swung his fist at one of the men holding the frightened giant, and the man crumbled to the ground. Without hesitating, Shain rammed his fist into the stomach of another man, then landed a blow on the face of a third man, who didn't back off soon enough. The man's nose broke with an audible crack.

Shain faced the crowd as Little Jim sank to the ground sobbing. "Let go of her," he said in a deadly voice directed at the men holding Tana. They defied him for a second, then dropped their hold. Tana surged forward and knelt to wrap her arms around her son. Alaynia planted herself in front of the pair, her eyes defying anyone to come near them and her fingers knotted into fists at her side.

"Chenaie's my land," Shain continued, and the crowd quieted to hear him. "There'll be no lynching here. We'll let the authorities handle investigating what's happened."

"Don't listen to him!" Fitzroy shouldered his way forward, dragging Annette with him and turning to face the crowd, but staying well out of Shain's reach. "What kind of men are you? That bastard tried to rape a white woman—and he killed a white man! Are you going to let him get away with it? Tell them, Annette! Listen to her, people."

Annette stared frenziedly at the gathered people. Finally she glanced at Fitzroy and removed her hand from the shoulder of her dress. The material fell away, baring her chemise to everyone. She lifted one hand and pointed at Little Jim, then dropped her head.

The crowd surged forward only one step. Shain calmly leveled the pistol, which he'd retrieved from his study when he heard the initial scream, at Fitzroy. "You'll be the first one," he said in a lethal voice, continuing to the crowd at large. "Do you want me to kill your money machine here? I suppose the timber company will send another man, but it might take a while. Any of you waiting on payments from him?"

The crowd quieted once again, slipping sideways looks at each other. Shain kept his pistol leveled at Fitzroy, while he said, "I haven't had a chance to tell any of you this, but you need to go out to Jake's tomorrow when it's light and see what the timber company's disregard for our land has done. Without the trees for protection, the land eroded so badly in the rain that we had a mudslide, which destroyed Jake's barn. He and my wife were almost caught in it."

The crowd gasped, and here and there renewed, angry mutters began, now directed at Fitzroy. Many of them were fully aware of what erosion could do to their property. The land was their livelihood—their sustenance.

Shain raised his voice to keep their attention. "Jake's lying up in one of Chenaie's bedrooms right now, near death because the destruction of his barn and all his life's work brought on a heart attack. The reason Tana and Little Jim are here is for Tana to check on Jake—not for her son to . . ." He tossed Annette a sneer. "Not to attack a woman who's been known to need very little persuasion to spread her legs willingly."

Annette pulled her bodice up around her and glared at him, but Shain turned from her with a sneer of contempt. "And just the other night," he continued, "we found out that even Chenaie's lands are at risk from this eradication of the timber without regard to what will happen afterwards. The unchecked runoff nearly caused a flood here—and only my wife's quick thinking prevented it." He gave Alaynia a brief, loving smile. "Otherwise, a lot of people might have drowned—including some women and children."

The mutters in the crowd grew in force, with people glancing worriedly at each other. Shain again cut them off. "The party's over. Everyone get out of here, and we'll let the sheriff look into this tomorrow."

"You can't let him protect a murderer," Fitzroy blustered. "Get back here! There's only one of him. He won't shoot me—they'd hang him, too!"

Jeannie raced around the edge of the crowd and flung herself into Alaynia's arms. "Alaynia," she cried. "Cole's still alive. Please! We have to help him!"

Alaynia held the hysterical girl tight as Shain shoved the pistol into his frock coat pocket and faced the crowd weaponless. "There's a witness now. Is there any one of you who won't agree that we need to hear the whole story before we hang a man without giving him a chance to defend himself? Could any of you live with yourselves, if you found out you'd hung the wrong man?"

Two of the men broke away and walked over to Alaynia. "You need some help getting Dubose into the house, ma'am?" one said. Shain carefully watched the rest of the people mill around aimlessly as Alaynia and Jeannie hurried off with the men. Finally, Madame Chantal walked over to Tana, kneeling by her side and placing an arm around her shoulders.

"You helped me that time I was having those horrible stomach pains," she murmured. "Please. Let me help you now." With shameful looks on their faces, three other women approached the small group. They knelt beside Little Jim with no regard for their fine evening wear.

Shain started for the barn, while Basil glowered at Fitzroy and Annette, who were surreptitiously making their way around the side of the manor house to where the buggies were parked. Fitzroy shoved Annette into the buggy, then climbed in and picked up the whip.

"What do you think he'll do now?" Basil asked Sylvia.

"I don't know," Sylvia replied. "Probably, they'll let the authorities deal with him after they get a chance to talk to Cole. I can't bother with him right now. My place is here with Cole. I need to see if Tana will need my help as she nurses him. Look, she's getting control of herself. Madame Chantal's taking care of Little Jim, so Tana can see if she can do anything for Cole."

The men carried Cole toward the manor house on a makeshift litter, and Tana grabbed her bag and hurried after them. Madame Chantal's minute body looked incongruous beside the huge height of Little Jim, but she reached up and patted his face, her orange hair wobbling as she nodded her head and spoke reassuringly to him. "Your mama will be near, *petite*. Come. We will sit and wait for her in the rocking chair over there, and you can tell me all about yourself."

She slipped her arm through his and started to lead him to the back veranda, and one of the other women with them stifled a gasp. Little Jim glanced down, then reached to pick something up from the ground. Madame Chantal grabbed it from him, holding the voodoo doll distastefully at arm's length.

"What is this?" she asked.

"That man gave it to me," Little Jim replied. "The one who was so mean to me and said I hurt Mister Cole. I saw him in the woods one day, and he said it would bring me good luck. But I don't want it now. He's a bad man! He lies!"

"We'll get rid of it, dear," Madame Chantal soothed as she urged him across the yard.

"I'm going after Fitzroy," Basil growled. "He's not going to get away with this—or Annette, either."

"Basil." The ghost halted when he caught the concerned tone of Sylvia's voice. "I wish you'd go try to get Zeke to come over here," Sylvia continued. "Without frightening him, of course. I think Jake needs to say something to him."

"You mean . . . ?"

"Before morning, for sure," Sylvia said calmly.

Chapter 28

In the privacy of their bedroom, Alaynia clung to Shain. Being in his arms again was the most wonderful feeling in the world amidst the turmoil of the past hour, and she soaked in the comfort of his embrace and consoling words.

"I love you, darling," Shain murmured. "When all of this is over, I'm going to show you just how much I care. We'll work everything out."

"I was so proud of you," Alaynia said, pulling back in his arms to stroke his face. "No one could have handled that crowd so well. You were basically alone against all of them, and it could so easily have had a tragic result."

"Then maybe I've redeemed myself in your eyes?" Shain asked with a wry grin.

"What?" She stepped back to study his face, a glimmer of understanding commencing. "Is this what all this has been about? You thought because you haven't been able to prevent all these catastrophes happening lately, it made you less of a man in my eyes? Oh, Shain, nothing could have been further from the truth. Why didn't you talk to me about it? These things have been out of your control, and I've got a feeling that monster Fitzroy has been behind some of them."

Shain sank down on the bed and buried his face in his hands for a second, then ran his hands through his hair as he looked at her. "I've been totally responsible for Chenaie and its people ever since I returned from the war. It's my duty to see that everyone is taken care of—including my wife."

She held a hand out to him, but before she could speak, he went on, "The only thing was, my wife was perfectly capable of taking care of herself—in fact, more capable than I was. And if you weren't satisfied here, you could always return to your own time. As soon as you made contact with whatever brought you here, that is."

Alaynia stared into the tortured depths of his eyes, her heart shattering at the misery she saw there. She'd caused that misery, though inadvertently. How could she have known her determination to get to the bottom of the mystery of her arrival at the Chenaie of the past would cause him so much untold uneasiness—would affect their relationship so disastrously? Yet the facts remained—her trip through time and the firm belief she had of some spiritual intervention.

Choosing her words carefully, she said, "If I went back, my life would be empty, Shain, because the man I love with all my heart would be missing from my life."

"Then, why . . . ?"

She nudged his legs open and sat down on his knee to brush back a lock of midnight hair from his face. "I have to find out how I got here in order to assure myself that I can stay. I didn't want to accidentally slip back through the time warp somehow and be separated from you. I can't risk it. My life is here with you now, and I'd die of a broken heart without you."

"God, Alaynia, if I'd known that, I'd have put everything aside while I helped you out."

"Shhh, shhh, shhh." Alaynia touched his lips, then followed her fingers with a kiss. "Like you've said so many times before, you have responsibilities of your own, darling. But you're wrong about one thing—dead wrong. I'm not capable of taking care of myself. Ever since you appeared in my life . . . or I guess it was the other way around; I appeared in your life." She giggled quietly and tucked her head against his neck, swirling a fingernail in the dark hair at the open vee of his shirt. "Ever since that day, I've known how empty my life had been up until then. Without you in it, my life would return to the same emptiness, and I'd just be a robot moving through the days. That's not living, Shain. It's just existing. You've brought my life alive—something I wasn't able to do for myself."

"A robot?" Shain murmured.

"It's something Jake would really be interested in. I'll tell you about it some day." Alaynia quickly sat upright. "Shain, I need to go check on Jake and Cole. And Jeannie brought Tiny back in with her, so she could make sure he kept off his leg. He was limping awfully bad. I think that horrible man kicked him in the barn."

"Shhh, shhh, shhh." Shain repeated Alaynia's words, then kissed her to make his point. Reaching over to the bedside table, he turned the wick down in the only lantern left burning in the room, then tenderly laid Alaynia across the bed, settling beside her.

"I checked on everyone right after I sent you in here to rest for a while, darling. Jeannie's asleep, with Tiny curled up with her. She even gave that darned pig one of the pillows on her bed. Tana's with Cole, and she said he stirred a little, so she thinks he'll come out of it soon. When he does, I'm pretty sure he'll confirm what Tana told us—that Fitzroy and Annette instigated this whole mess tonight, then tried to blame it on Little Jim. They figured it would cause even more agitation between my neighbors and me. But when the sheriff finds out what's happened, you can bet Fitzroy will be, at the least, run out of the parish."

He sighed and tightened his hold on her. "And I think

we can save enough of Chenaie's crops to get by this year. Next year, they'll be even better, without someone sabotaging us."

"What about Annette?"

"That, too, will be up to Cole when he wakes up. But, knowing Cole, he'll probably just be satisfied with everyone knowing Annette's still spreading lies every time she opens her mouth."

"And Jake?"

"Zeke showed up a while ago, insisting that he wanted to sit with Jake." Though she could barely see him in the darkness, Alaynia sensed Shain shake his head. "Jake's lived a long life," he murmured. "Exactly the way he wanted to live it. Tana said his heart is weakening, rather than recovering."

Tears filled Alaynia's eyes, and she wrapped her arms around Shain, burying her face against him. He held her and rocked her for several long moments, then tenderly tipped her face up, covering her lips with his. The kiss was full of comfort and consolation—promise and anticipation. It deepened almost imperceptibly—almost questioningly— and a whimper of need escaped Alaynia's throat. Shain's palm feathered down her back, across her hips, and settled on her thigh, urging her closer to him. With a muffled cry of surrender, Alaynia complied with his entreaty.

Jake stirred on the bed, and Basil quickly stood from his seat on the window seat. Zeke immediately half-rose from his chair and swung his head toward the window, his eyes widening in fright as Sylvia murmured a caution to Basil. Apologizing in a quiet voice, the ghost used his powers to shield his presence while he watched Jake move a gnarled hand from beneath the blanket covering him.

"Zeke?" Jake whispered.

Zeke sat back down, extended his dark hand, and entwined it around Jake's pale one. "Mister Jake," he said in a choked voice. "You gonna be all right, Mister Jake. You soon be eatin' my good cookin' again."

Jake turned his head slightly, focusing on Zeke's ravaged face. "No, my friend. But I will be all right. I'm not afraid, Zeke. I want to see all the wonders Alaynia has told me about. And I don't want you to mourn for me."

"No, Mister Jake." Zeke hung his head. "Please."

"Listen to me, Zeke," Jake said in a slightly stronger voice. "There's something I need to say. You've been my friend through a lot since we met. Can you please be my friend through this, too?"

Zeke sniffed mightily, then rose from his chair and knelt by the bed. With his free hand, he smoothed back the wiry wisps of hair on Jake's head. "We always be friends, Mister Jake. If you ain't with me, we be friends in my rememberin' of you."

"Thank you, Zeke." Jake's breath caught in his throat, but he finally managed to draw it in once more. "My Will is with Carl Beauville, at the bank in Baton Rouge, Zeke. The land and cabin are yours now, and there's enough money to build the house, if you want—and enough to take care of you."

"I'll see it's built, with Miss 'Laynia's help," Zeke replied. "I gonna call it Jake's House."

Jake managed a smile. "Then you've gotten over your fear of Alaynia?"

"Yessuh. When I seen how much she care for you when you took sick, I knew she came to make your life happy while she could. She give you some powerful things to think on in that mind of yours."

"She did that," Jake agreed. "There's also some other

bequests in the Will, Zeke. One for our little friend, Jeannie. The rest is for a scholarship fund, to be used for bright young men or women who want to pursue the scientific field. Alaynia will help you manage it."

"Yessuh."

"And I didn't get a chance to tell Alaynia, but that lottery ticket I gave her was one of the winning ones. Make sure she cashes it in, because it's worth ten thousand dollars. Shain's gonna piss and holler at her, but Alaynia can handle him."

Zeke tried to speak again, but his voice choked in his throat and he only nodded.

"Well," another voice said, and Basil and Sylvia peered out the window. "I know you're concerned about what's happening here, but there's something else that needs your attention."

"Frannie!" Sylvia flew through the window to join the other angel. "Where have you been? Why haven't you answered me when I tried to contact you?"

"I've been busy, dear. We'll talk later. Look."

Basil joined them, and he and Sylvia gazed in the direction of Frannie's pointing finger. They mentally dissolved the roof of the manor house, and Basil growled deep in his chest when he saw Fitzroy slipping up the dark stairwell from the back veranda, a pistol in his hand.

Sylvia rapidly tuned into the man's thoughts. "He's coming to kill Cole!" she said with a gasp. "He doesn't want him to live to expose the scheme he and Annette Escott tried to pull off. We've got to stop him!"

"Wait," Frannie cautioned. "Look. Over there in Jeannie's room."

Tiny snorted once and woke, then scrambled down the steps on the side of Jeannie's bed. Limping only slightly, he crossed the floor, slipped out the half-open door, and raced down the hall, his nose wrinkling and faint oinks sounding. He skidded around the corner beside the top of the stairwell just as Fitzroy raised his foot for the top step. The pig barreled into the man without pause.

Fitzroy screamed in terror, dropped the pistol, and grabbed wildly for the banister. His fingers fell an inch short, and he wobbled precariously for one long second. Tiny scurried back as Fitzroy fell, his body tumbling out of control down the steep stairwell. At the bottom, he lay without moving.

"He's dead," Basil said with a nod. "He won't bother Chenaie again. Are we going to have to deal with his spirit now?"

"No," Frannie said in a grim voice. "He'll be whisked away by someone else, who will take care of what happens to him." A sudden, brief flash of light accompanied her words. When it faded, Fitzroy's body still lay at the foot of the stairwell, and Shain and Alaynia were running down the hallway.

Fingers of faint dawn light flowed through the open window in the Camellia Room as Alaynia entered it. She walked over to her drafting table and smoothed a hand across the landscape plans she'd been working on for Jake's house. Bowing her head, she offered up a silent plea for her friend's spirit.

She turned toward the door as Shain entered. "How's Jeannie?" she asked.

"Asleep again," Shain said. "She'll be all right. She said she and Jake had talked once about how he'd die a long time before she did, but he promised to always watch over her, if he could."

"Do you believe he can?" Alaynia asked quietly.

"I . . ." Shain hung his head for a second, then came toward her. "I've been doing a lot of thinking the last few hours. I think maybe he can. Just like my grandfather's probably been doing what he can to watch over Chenaie. All the stories seem to point to him. I have to believe it, don't I? After all, he's probably the one who brought you to me."

"Well, son," Basil said from the window, "it's about time you appreciated what I've done for you."

Alaynia stifled a scream and flung herself into Shain's arms, which closed reassuringly around her. She stared at the figure of the man she'd seen briefly in the graveyard as he floated through the window and stood before them, materializing into a somewhat firmer shape.

"Now, I don't have much time, so get your fear under control, Alaynia. It's not as though we haven't spoken before, you know."

Shain glanced inquiringly down at Alaynia, and she choked out, "At Tana's. He . . . he told me to make my decision carefully."

"If I remember right," Basil said with a wink, "I told you to make it with your heart. And I've been telling those two pesky angels that . . ."

"Angels?" Alaynia interrupted with a squeak. "The . . . other voice I heard at Tana's?"

Basil turned slightly and crooked a finger. "Come on, you two. Show yourselves, so Alaynia can tell you herself what she wants to do." He glanced back at Alaynia. "That's the only way they'll let me alone and allow me to go be with Laureen."

"Laureen?" Alaynia squeaked again.

"She was my grandmother," Shain whispered, falling silent again when Alaynia gave a start as two heads appeared just above the rim of the windowsill. The dark one propped her chin on her crossed arms, and their wings of snowy feathers rose from their shoulders, almost completely filling the window. They reclined in the air as easily as though lying on a bed. The blond angel wore white, but the black one wore a brilliant red gown, sparkling with jewel-like tints even in the dawn light.

Alaynia shoved against Shain so hard, he stumbled backwards a step. Another glance at his face told her that he wasn't quite as terrified as she, though she detected a paleness under his tanned skin. He kept his arms tightly around her. She stared back at the window and licked her lips with a sandpaper tongue. "Who . . . ?"

"I'm Sylvia," the dark face answered. "It was my voice you heard at Tana's. Annoyance isn't supposed to be an angel trait, but I forgot for a minute when I found Basil trying to appear to you. I didn't shield my voice from you when I spoke." She nodded at the golden-haired countenance beside her. "And this is Francesca."

Francesca spoke in a soft, consoling voice. "Please don't be frightened, Alaynia. We were sent here to work out the trouble our friend Basil instituted with his interfering ways."

"At least you called me your friend," Basil grumbled. "When you two first showed up here, I had my doubts if we'd ever be able to speak a civil word to each other."

Sylvia giggled, then lifted her head. Alaynia never saw her move, but the next instant, she stood in the room beside Basil. She recognized the gown the angel wore as a dashiki. Her bare, dusky feet poked out from beneath the hem, an endearing characteristic that alleviated Alaynia's awe a little—but not much. She only realized her nails were digging into Shain's forearm when he muffled a grunt of pain and pried at her fingers.

"You can't doubt Frannie's friendship," Sylvia told Basil. "Why, as soon as she helped Violet straighten out that computer mess, she searched all over until she found Laureen for you. You could have been with your wife all this time, if you'd just ascended on to the next plane."

"A computer?" Alaynia murmured. "In . . . in Heaven?"

Francesca joined the other two figures. "Oh, my, yes, my dear. I don't see how I got along without it all these years. But Violet—she's my replacement until Sylvia and I get back from our sabbatical . . ."

"If we ever get going on our sabbatical, girlfriend," Sylvia reminded her.

"Yes, well, that's our next priority. But like I was saying, Violet was playing with the icons. Now, I'm still not sure how she did this, but she swears that little mouse came to life. I told her that was impossible and she must have been playing instead of paying attention to her duties. But she had icons on top of icons on top of icons. Took me forever to get them sorted out. I . . . ."

"Frannie," Sylvia said in exasperation, and Alaynia snapped her wide-eyed gaze to the other angel, whose dusky toes tapped beneath her gown. "Aren't we bending the rules here, so Basil can do his thing and we can, hopefully, have everything back in the proper order?"

"His thing?" Francesca asked with a frown. "Oh, yes, you're right. Alaynia, the most important aspect of your mortalness is your free will. Our friend here tampered with that in your life, and he's truly sorry. Aren't you, Basil?"

Basil sighed, then squared his shoulders. "Well, no. I'd be lying, if I said I was sorry for what I did."

"Basil," Sylvia warned.

"I'm not," Basil insisted. "I think it's like we talked about once—perhaps Alaynia's destiny was for me to bring her back here. Look how happy she and Shain are. The two of them will fill Chenaie with little St. Clairs, like Laureen and I wanted to do."

"Excuse me," Alaynia said, gaining a little courage now that she was becoming more accustomed to the spiritual beings in the room. "You said you didn't have much time, and I have a couple questions to ask."

"Umm . . . well, I don't know if we'll have time for that, my dear," Francesca answered for all of them. "First, you have to make your choice. Basil?"

"My choice?" Alaynia asked the ghost. "Like you told me to do when you spoke to me at Tana's?"

"See?" Basil said with a haughty look at Francesca. "I've been trying to let her choose. Even though the two of you wouldn't believe me."

"Grandfather!" Shain's low-throbbed growl silenced the ghost, and even the angels floated a step back. Alaynia sighed in relief as Shain took control of the situation.

"Grandfather," he said again, "whatever choice you have to offer Alaynia, do it now. We've been up all night, and my wife is exhausted. The three of you may not need any rest in your states of being, but we do. And . . ." He slipped a purely masculine wink at his grandfather. "If you want Chenaie filled with great-grandchildren, you'll have to give us an opportunity to make them."

Alaynia blushed and reached over her shoulder to smack at him, but Shain grasped her hand and kissed her fingers. She started to turn in his arms, then stared around her in dread. She wasn't in the Camellia Room any longer. Instead, she stood on the dirt roadway, where she had found herself after she drove through the time warp. And she was totally alone.

Chapter 29

Alaynia stood frozen for a long moment, even her mind too paralyzed for her to think coherently. Finally, her eyes were burning so badly, she blinked. Very slowly, she gazed down at herself, noticing she still wore the robe she'd had on when she was in the Camellia Room.

But it was also the robe she'd packed when she left Boston. It couldn't have all been a dream—could it? She glanced across the road at the live oak tree where she'd first seen Shain. A few streaks of sunlight filtered through the leaves, dappling the ground beneath the tree. No one stood there to greet her.

"Shain?" she whispered, all the while knowing no one would answer. And when someone did, she gasped in fright and whirled to face the speaker.

"It be all right, Miss 'Laynia," Zeke soothed. "Maybe all the rest of them left you all on your own, but I be here for you."

"I—I—" Alaynia clenched her hands at her side and cleared her throat. "Were you in the Camellia Room a minute ago, too? Are . . . are you alive, or . . . ?"

"I be alive as I can be," Zeke assured her. "Don't know what brought me here, but had me this urge to come back to this place a while ago, just after Mister Jake passed on. Sorta thought I heard Tana's voice, but I ain't real sure. Still, I hitched old Stubborn back up and we come along."

"Thank God," Alaynia breathed, noticing the gray mule

and decrepit wagon a few yards behind Zeke. "I was standing here thinking I had totally imagined everything. But at least I know you were real."

"It all be real, Miss 'Laynia." Zeke nodded his wiry gray head in reassurance. "And you appeared this time, just like you did the last time—'cording to Massa Shain, anyway."

"I think one of the angels sent me here," Alaynia explained. "I'm supposed to make a choice, but I don't know what I'm supposed to choose between."

Zeke's eyes widened. "Uh . . . angels? Them beings with wings?"

"Oh, yes," Alaynia admitted. "Wings and robes and the whole shebang. Well, come to think of it, I didn't see any halos on their heads. And Zeke, one of them was black. Her name was Sylvia."

Suddenly a vibration ran under her feet, and Alaynia's head whipped around. Stubborn let out a frantic "hee haw," and Zeke quickly ran over to the mule to grab his bridle. As soon as she could force her feet to move, Alaynia raced toward Zeke, and he wrapped his free arm around her waist.

"Lordy, what is that?" Zeke asked in an awe-stricken voice.

Alaynia gazed at the shimmering wall of heat waves down the road. Immediately she understood. "It's the time warp," she told Zeke. "I'm being given the choice of going back to my own time, or staying here at Chenaie in the past."

She stepped away from Zeke, knowing she had to make it clear that her decision was totally her own. There wasn't one iota of doubt in her mind. She knew exactly what she wanted—who she wanted it with. Didn't she?

Something niggled her mind, and she paused to consider. She *did* want to stay with Shain, live her life at Chenaie, even with the lack of modern conveniences, the mentality of the society, the uphill track she faced in order to keep a part of herself whole and free. There would be problems, had been already. The past was supposedly a simpler time, less stressful, yet it had its own turmoil and disparity. Different people, good and bad. Different times, yet were they so different? The past had its own distinctive setting and character, but here, also, lay a future, as in any time, for all its inhabitants. A future that meant as much to its people as to people in any time period.

More importantly, here lay *her* future: the man she loved, friends she'd made, a world she'd already begun to carve out for herself. A future she could work hard to design, along with the man who made that future a hell of a lot more worthwhile than anything she had ever had in her old world.

The niggle firmed into two certainties. One side told her that her deepest desire—the desire to live into her future with Shain, the man she loved with her entire being—was the right choice. The other side told her that she had to make this choice wholeheartedly, of her own free will, with proper solemnity. She closed her eyes, took a deep breath, and formed her resolution and request with everything in her.

Raising her voice, she called, "You can close it back up again, Basil. I want to stay here. I want to stay with Shain— live the rest of my life with him and the children we'll have. And I'm making this choice of my own free will. Did you hear that, Sylvia and Francesca? And if anyone else is listening, you'll know that my decision is coming from my heart. I want to stay here!"

For a moment, nothing happened. Then the wall of heat

waves started shrinking. It dropped in height at first, but the sides also began closing in. Within moments, there was only a shimmering space about the size a human could walk through. That space steadied, as though to give her one last chance.

"Get rid of it, Basil," Alaynia said with an imperative wave of her hand. "I never want to see it again."

With a tiny, almost imperceptible pop, the shimmering space disappeared.

Alaynia sighed in satisfaction. "Now, Zeke," she said as she turned toward him and headed for the wagon. "How about giving me a ride back to Chenaie?"

"Yes, Miss 'Laynia," he agreed with a chuckle. "Be glad to do that."

Holding Stubborn's reins in one hand, he assisted her into the wagon before he climbed up and joined her. The mule started off willingly enough, and they headed down the road. Alaynia curbed her impatience at their slow progress, afraid if she asked Zeke to urge Stubborn to a faster gait, the animal would plop down and refuse to pull the wagon at all. But her arms ached to hold Shain, though a peacefulness filled her heart. Never again would she have to worry about being whisked through a time warp and being separated from the man she loved.

When they reached the long, curving driveway leading to the manor house, Alaynia leaned forward eagerly. As soon as the house came in sight, she saw Shain pacing back and forth on the front veranda. Her impatience erupted into full-blown craving and, without warning Zeke, she jumped from the slow-moving wagon, crying Shain's name.

He met her halfway, sweeping her into his arms and hugging her breathless. She willingly denied herself further breath as he kissed her senseless. When he finally raised his head, she sagged happily in his arms.

"You came back," Shain murmured.

"Did you doubt I would?" Alaynia asked with a slight frown.

"No," Shain replied, caressing her cheek. "If I had, I'd have ridden out after you and dragged you back, no matter what those darned spirits said. I'd have fought Heaven for you, and Hell if necessary."

"My masterful husband," Alaynia said with a smile, laying her head against his chest.

"Sure," Shain said wryly, his laughter rumbling beneath her ear. "I'm the boss around here, remember? And you know what my most important responsibility is?"

Alaynia drew back to gaze into his face. "What?"

"Making sure my witch angel always knows how much I love her."

"I love you, Shain," Alaynia said, his name muffled against his lips as he lowered his head and kissed her again. Without breaking the kiss, he bent and lifted her into his arms. He only took one step toward the veranda, however, before Stubborn's frenzied bray sounded.

"Now, what the hell?" Shain asked as he turned with her in his grasp.

They watched the mule break free from Zeke's hold on its bridle and tear back down the driveway, the wagon bouncing along behind him. Zeke plopped his hands on his hips, then shrugged. He started walking toward Alaynia and Shain, then halted, his gaze settling beyond them.

Shain turned again, and Alaynia saw the group on the veranda. Sylvia sat dangling her legs over a railing, with Francesca standing behind her. Basil stood on the top step, his arm around a woman Alaynia hadn't seen before, though she looked like an older version of Jeannie. Feet crunched on the shell-strewn driveway, and Alaynia glanced over Shain's shoulder as Zeke stopped behind them. The elderly man's reverent gaze was tinged with trepidation, and he made sure he stayed behind Shain.

"That's Missy Laureen," he whispered reverently.

"It sure is, my old friend," Basil called. "We just wanted to say goodbye—for now at least. And I wanted to let you know, Shain, that Laureen assured me we'd still keep an eye on things. If you've a mind to, Laureen would be a pretty name for our first great-granddaughter."

"You're a fine man, my grandson," Laureen said in a soft voice, which nevertheless carried to them. "Don't worry any more about rumors as to Chenaie having spirits floating around. Now that your grandfather and I have found each other again, I'll keep him much too busy to bother you, and the stories will fade out."

"Thank you, Grandmother," Shain called.

"And, Alaynia," Laureen said. "I couldn't ask for a better wife for my grandson. I wish you all the happiness in the world, my dear—and in the next one, too."

"Thank you," Alaynia replied.

"Say," a different voice said, drawing Alaynia's attention to the faintly-defined figure stepping out from behind one of the veranda support posts. "Are we going to stand around here chatting all day, or are you all going to take me to see this computer thing?"

"Mister Jake," Zeke said in a devout voice.

Jake turned and waved at them. "I'll see you some day down the road, my old friend, Zeke. You two, also, Shain and Alaynia. But right now, I'm sort of itching to get on with this new facet in my life—or, maybe I should say, my afterlife."

Francesca floated down the steps, growing in height and

her wings spreading wide, concealing the figures behind her. A brilliant glow surrounded her, and Alaynia realized they were leaving.

"Goodbye!" she called.

A faint chorus of responses answered her.

"Thank you! Thank you for bringing me here, Basil," she cried, but without so much as a flicker, the figures were gone. The veranda was peaceful in the early morning sunlight, with no sign the spiritual visitors had been there. For just a brief instant, she felt a wrench of loss, but a deep serenity quickly filled her and she settled against Shain's chest.

"Zeke," Shain said, tightening his arms around her. "Do you want to come in and have some breakfast?"

"No, suh, Massa Shain," Zeke replied. "Ain't quite ready to walk 'cross that there porch yet. And I figure that mule's a waitin' for me just down the road. Gonna go find him. 'For I leave, Mister Jake told me to remind Miss 'Laynia to check that there lottery ticket. And I sure would like it if you and Miss 'Laynia come over to supper tonight."

"We'll do . . ." Shain began. Alaynia pinched his arm, and Shain flinched, gazing down at her in question. However, he didn't need an explanation. "Uh . . . would you like to go over to Zeke's this evening, darling?" he asked with a quirked eyebrow.

"Sounds lovely to me, sweetheart," she replied.

Zeke nodded and trudged back down the driveway while Shain carried Alaynia toward the veranda. After climbing the steps, he avoided the doorway and walked over to the swing in a shadowed corner, where he sat and adjusted her on his lap. She tilted her head back, sure he was going to kiss her, but after a few seconds, she opened her eyes.

He was staring toward the graveyard in the distance, a

look of pure bewilderment on his face.

"What is it?" she asked. "You've been acting like you were perfectly comfortable with our visitors—your normal, take-charge mode. I do believe I would have fainted and missed all of it, if you hadn't been there for me."

"Then I'm sure as hell glad you couldn't read inside my mind," Shain growled. "Or feel my stomach trying to clench around those butterflies flying around in it. Do you realize we've just got through talking to two angels and a ghost? No, three ghosts."

"No, darling," Alaynia explained. "I believe your grandfather was the only ghost. Laureen and Jake were spirits. They're only called ghosts when they stay on the earthly plane and keep contact with us, instead of ascending to . . ."

"Alaynia," Shain interrupted. "Shut up so I can kiss you."

"Yes, darling," Alaynia agreed.

"Ah-ha," Shain murmured. "I think I've finally found a way to get you to do what I ask of you. Just offer to kiss you."

"Dream on, darling," Alaynia replied, tracing a finger down his cheek. "Don't you want a kiss in return? We need to make this a cooperative effort."

"Cooperative," Shain said, as though he had only discovered the word. "Similar to compromise, huh?"

"Right. I'll talk to Zeke this evening and see if he still wants the house built. If so, I fully intend to finish the job. But I'll wait until we get back from that honeymoon you promised me, if you want."

"Alaynia."

"What, Shain?"

"Shut up so I can kiss you and you can kiss me back."

"Yes, darling."

About the Author

Trana Mae Simmons lives in an historical town in East Texas, and she enjoys researching her historical romances as much as writing them. When not writing, she loves to travel and explore both off-the-beaten-path and tourist sites with her husband, Barney. Her Web site at http://home.swbell.net/ghostie/trana.htm lists her romance novels, and www.iseeghosts.com is the site for her mysteries.